SILENCE THE DEAD

For Karen,
For when deep sleep is essential!

SILENCE THE DEAD

Jack Fredrickson

severn House

This first world edition published 2014
in Great Britain and the USA by
SEVERN HOUSE PUBLISHERS LTD of
19 Cedar Road, Sutton, Surrey, England, SM2 5DA.
Trade paperback edition first published 2015 in Great
Britain and the USA by SEVERN HOUSE PUBLISHERS LTD.

Copyright © 2014 by Jack Fredrickson

British Library Cataloguing in Publication Data

Fredrickson, Jack author.
Silence the dead.
1. Murder–Investigation–Illinois–Fiction. 2. Cold
cases (Criminal investigation)–Fiction. 3. Detective and
mystery stories.
I. Title
813.6-dc23

ISBN-13: 978-0-7278-8435-0 (cased)
ISBN-13: 978-1-84751-543-8 (trade paper)
ISBN-13: 978-1-78010-589-5 (e-book)

Typeset by Palimpsest Book Production Ltd.,
Falkirk, Stirlingshire, Scotland.

As always, for always,

For Susan

ACKNOWLEDGMENTS

It is said that truth is sometimes best told through fiction.

Mary Jane Reed was born on November 15, 1930. She died on June 25, 26, 27, 28, or 29, 1948.

It was Ted Gregory's reporting in the *Chicago Tribune* that began, for me, a search for the sense in two long-forgotten unsolved murders, an aftermath that reverberates to this day, and one mayor's relentless quest for justice. Dare we let our nation's newspapers struggle, really?

It was Mayor Mike Arians's story, of course, and the courage, tenacity, and patience he took to chase it, learn it, tell it, challenge it and defend it that became the truth behind much, but not all, of the fiction. It was Marge Craig's story, and June Arians's story, as well.

Warren Reed gave me the trust to show the youngest child's perspective of a family traumatized by murder, conspiracy, incompetence, and indifference.

Patrick Riley, Mary Anne Bigane, and Joe Bigane read the draft and gave me the guidance to do better. Gaylord Villers corrected me about bullets, and Don Rowley set up a strange interview.

John Silbersack showed me where to fix what was wrong.

Kate Lyall-Grant gave me enthusiasm! Sara Porter gave me great edits.

And Susan gave me encouragement, love and care to help me make this, as with everything else in my life, worthy.

VISITATION

Betty Jo Dean lay as she had for over thirty years, shrouded in black vinyl, forever seventeen.

None of them – not the two gray-haired forensics people, the state's attorney or the cops or even the bastards who'd long kept their fists on the lids in the town – dared breathe. The only sound came from the exhaust fan in the ceiling. It thrummed irregularly, loud then soft, rough then smooth, like a bad heart about to burst. As though it, too, feared what Betty Jo Dean was about to reveal.

The doctor, a man of many such exhumations, bent over the stainless-steel table and unzipped the body bag.

He froze. His assistant gasped, and dropped her metal probe to clatter on the cold tile floor.

The mayor, disgraced and exiled to the back of the room, pushed through the wall of stunned cops and looked down.

She wore only panties and a bra. No one had bothered to dress her. Her skin was mottled and gray.

Except for the skull. It was polished and shiny and, unlike the rest of her, arrogantly devoid of flesh.

And it was loose, wedged at the top of the bag like a grotesque afterthought, a thing casually tossed in. Its jaw had opened wide, as if screaming in outrage.

The mayor had imagined all sorts of horrors, but not this. He spun in a fury to shout at the hating eyes of those he'd forced to pull her from the ground.

'*That's not her head.*'

BOOK I: HER STORY

ONE

Her hands were too sweaty. The knob slipped away and the door slammed back, echoing a thunderclap through the dark, deserted town.

She pressed back against the siding at the top of the stairs, clenching her fists to make her whole body stop shaking, and looked down. No surprise he wasn't on the sidewalk; he didn't like the light. He'd be somewhere else, invisible, making sure she walked straight home from the phone company.

For a flit of a moment, she wanted please to believe he'd come to his senses over the weekend. Lord, she wanted that, but she couldn't dare hope it.

She touched her cheek. Though it was three nights since Friday, the bruise still throbbed. That was OK. The pain would give her courage to be strong. That, and pretending she was in a movie, and what she feared wasn't really real.

She stepped out of the shadow and into the light, slow and unafraid, like Kathleen Turner in *Body Heat*. Kathleen was purposeful. She'd had courage, even if it was for devilish purposes. Kathleen got what she needed because she didn't let being afraid stop her.

She took out her compact, mindful of the imaginary camera, and took her time inspecting her cheek. She'd sweated like a waterfall inside her operator cubicle all through her shift, maybe from the heat, more likely from the fear. All night long, she'd trembled.

The powder was doing fine, covering the bruise. Likely Pauly wouldn't notice, though maybe his noticing wouldn't be such a bad thing.

She'd called him two hours earlier. It was nervousness, but she needed to be sure he'd show up.

'So, gorgeous, we're still on for tonight?' he said, right off.

Relief calmed her like cool water. 'Remember, I finish at ten,' she said, careful to talk low so the biddies in the next cubicles wouldn't hear.

'The Constellation, right?'

'Yes.' She'd chosen it because it was just across the highway and up Second Street, so close she could practically run to it. Then, somewhat theatrically, she whispered, 'You might want to cancel, though.'

'What?' He sounded real concerned.

'Things are a little unsettled for me right now,' she said mysteriously. She'd decided it was only fair to give him a little warning.

'Meaning what?' he naturally asked.

'Meaning I'm of interest to other men. One's important. He thinks he owns me. There might be trouble if you come to Grand Point tonight.'

'Old boyfriend?'

'Not hardly – at least about the boyfriend part.' Old was right on, though.

'An older man? Don't worry. I don't get afraid,' he said, in a most manly way.

'Because you were a Marine, right?'

'*Semper Fi.*'

She did not as yet speak foreign languages, having quit high school for bigger things two years before, but she assumed he'd just said something reassuring. Absolutely, Pauly was a wonderful man.

The biddy in the next cubicle had leaned back so she could eavesdrop better.

'See you at the Constellation.' She clicked off, relieved. Though this would be only their first real date, she was sure Pauly Pribilski was a confident man.

That was two hours ago. Now, alone in the light at the top of the outside stairs, the comfort she'd felt was gone. The Important was somewhere down below.

She moved to the edge of the stairs and hesitated again, knowing now she was exposed to the windows above the Red Wing shoe store across the street. Likely it was nerves that imagined them going black the instant she stepped outside. Doctor Romulous Farmont liked his perch above the shoe store for looking down on them all, but that time of evening he liked the darkness of the Hacienda better, sitting back against the wall with the rest of the Importants.

She shuddered, remembering her time above the Red Wing just a few weeks before. Crazy afraid, she'd gone to the doc because he was the only doctor in Grand Point and she'd had to know. He'd drugged her a little, to calm her, he said, but not so she couldn't feel his fingers, working. She'd wondered how much of that was necessary.

An understandable concern after a minor indiscretion, he'd said in his fancy words, without asking who'd done the deed. If anything still developed, he'd take care of it. He would, too, without saying anything to anyone. He took care of things, especially for other Importants.

There was no sense remembering that now. She took a deep breath and went down the stairs. Nothing would happen until she got to the highway and didn't turn for home.

Like always, the sidewalks were empty. The few cars parked at the curb belonged to the other phone operators. She hurried toward the corner, her footsteps clacking the cement loud enough for even the deaf to hear.

Too soon, she was out from the safe shadows of the storefronts. To her left, the highway ran dark to the bridge. The moon was full, glinting off the river like a thousand eyes, waiting. But there were only two eyes likely to be watching to make sure she headed straight home.

No, damn it, she said in her head. She was only seventeen. She was entitled to a proper date with a nice young man. She stepped off the curb.

Headlamps appeared sudden in the east, speeding across the bridge toward her.

She ran across the street before the lights could find her, and up into the trees on the courthouse lawn, their craggly old branches making welcoming long shadows to hide her. She ducked behind the biggest tree and stuck her head out enough to see.

The headlights grew larger as the car got closer.

Surely, it was him.

TWO

The Important had gone crazy dangerous the previous Friday night.

She'd been walking home from her four-hour shift at the phone company, thinking for the thousandth time about the gorgeous

young man she'd met the night before. Tall, broad shoulders, blond,
he'd appeared at the Pepsi machine in the break room like a god.
She'd quickly closed her *Photoplay* magazine, cover down, so he
wouldn't think she was shallow reading about movie stars, and gave
him a semi-interested smile.

It worked. He came over and sat down. She had only four minutes
left on her break, but he was real charming and they talked for ten,
about nothing and everything, until the supervisor found her and
waved a bony finger. By then, Pauly Pribilsky said he'd drive her
home after work.

And that's all it was. They talked in his car for maybe fifteen
minutes, then they had a kiss – the one she'd been thinking about
ever since.

Walking home the next night, Friday, she'd been too lost in hoping
Pauly would call over the weekend to pay any mind to anything
else. She'd just passed the usual ruckus in the Hacienda parking lot
when the Important had stepped out suddenly from the bushes to
block her way.

His face had been purple with anger, and something wet was
dribbling from the corner of his mouth. 'Got yourself a boyfriend?'
he'd said, all out of breath and sneery.

'He's just a boy from work—'

'I know who he is,' he'd said, interrupting rapid-fire, still breathing
heavy. 'Paulus Pribilski, Polish, lineman for the DeKalb-Peering.
Lives up in Rockford. Hot shot, fancy car, likes to gamble too much.'

Truly, the Important's eyes were everywhere.

'He's someone my own age!' she'd shouted, then instantly
regretted it, because his face had puffed up like a kid holding his
breath to not cry.

'Look,' she'd gone on, trying to be nice, 'all's you and I do is
sneak off, and things went too—'

'I know about you seeing Doc Farmont.'

There was no hope to it. She'd been major flattered when he, an
Important, had expressed an interest in her one night when she was
walking home, almost in this very spot. A man like him could be
exciting, and she was leaving Grand Point anyway, soon as she
saved up enough for beautician school in Chicago. He was married,
but that would add to the excitement. Except it didn't. All he wanted
was to sneak off.

Now she'd met Pauly Pribilsky and romance needed to blossom.

Still, she wanted to be kind. 'It can never be anything between us,' she'd said, trying to smile.

He'd slapped her hard across the face. 'That's for being unfaithful,' he'd said, hissing like an animal.

Her eyes had teared up so quick she hadn't seen the second one coming before it slapped the numbness where the first had hit. 'That's for dressing so provocative.'

She'd backed up but not fast enough.

He'd hit her a third time. 'And that's to remind you to walk straight home after work. No car rides from anybody.'

'Go to hell!' she'd screamed, and ran off.

It had taken her a block to realize that the Important wasn't chasing. He didn't need to. Grand Point was small and he was big. He could find her whenever he wanted.

She'd waited fifteen minutes in front of her house for her breathing to get regular. Going in, she'd told her mother she'd run smack into a tree because she'd not been paying attention to her walking. She couldn't tell the truth. Her parents were from the east side of the river – Pinktown people. They'd suffer if she weren't careful. Importants controlled everything in Grand Point.

Saturday morning had been bad. She'd not been able to figure out what to do. So she'd stayed in her room, icing the bruise that was now ripe as an eggplant.

And then Pauly had called at two, saying he'd been thinking about that one kiss ever since Thursday night. She'd said she had too, but the back of her mind had been screaming no way should she see the new young man. Then, talking, she'd got to remembering Kathleen Turner and *Body Heat* and living strong and purposeful, so she'd said yes to Pauly Pribilski. But that had been Saturday when there'd been hours and hours ahead for staying safe in her room. Now, come Monday night, she was out, hiding in the trees on the courthouse lawn, thinking she'd made a huge mistake.

The car got stopped by a red light at Second Street, its engine rumbling low. It was still too far away to recognize. She pressed back against the tree, waiting. When the engine got louder, starting up, she snuck another peek. The car was turning onto Second Street.

It was a cop cruiser, slowing at the sheriff's side of the courthouse. She couldn't see which deputy was at the wheel. Every one of them, young and old, had invented a reason to talk to her at one time or another. Most were harmless, except for the one that was particularly disgusting. The car pulled into the sheriff's parking lot and disappeared behind the side of the building.

She stepped out from the tree, toward the darker shadows of the building. The old courthouse had been strung with red, white and blue banners for the Fourth of July, but already they were drooping like old women's underwear. The ancient bricks had baked in that same exact spot for over a hundred hot summers, wilting everything around them. She supposed if they could talk, they'd surely rather scream, from the sameness of it all.

The town had gone back to quiet. No cars, no footsteps.

Across Second Street, the goofy stars on the Constellation's sign winked slowly on and off, like the eyes of an old lech, of which Grand Point had too many. Its door was propped open, spilling light like milk onto the sidewalk, but no music came out. No one went to the Constellation for a lively time. It was a daytime place for county lawyers to down quick ones before going back to their more interesting towns. Nighttime, the Constellation was a crypt. That's why she'd chosen it.

She ran across to the unlit store next to the Constellation. Catching her breath, she checked her reflection in the darkened glass. She'd borrowed her future sister-in-law's blouse because the tan polyester caught the auburn in her hair and the hazel in her eyes. Her mother said the blouse was too tight in the wrong places, but it was only just a little. She looked good. Not just Pinktown good, but good enough for anyplace this side of the river, too.

She walked into the bar.

THREE

P auly sat facing the door. He wore a nice gray shirt that looked tailor-made especially for his muscular physique, the big silver watch he'd worn on Thursday, and a pair of dark blue checked pants.

Otherwise, the Constellation was as pathetically empty as she'd hoped. Other than Pauly, there was no one there except for Dougie and two ancient couples smoking and drinking red drinks at a table in the back.

Pauly stood up, a real gentleman. 'Betty Jo,' he said. He pulled out a chair for her to sit down, another gentlemanly thing.

The chair he'd pulled out meant her back would be to the door. She sat there anyway, even though not being able to see the door made her uncomfortable.

Dougie came over, fast as a fly to a light bulb. 'Hi, Betty Jo.'

'Hi, Dougie,' she said, with just the right amount of un-enthusiasm.

Pauly ordered them both beers, and she prayed Dougie wouldn't choose that exact time to ask for ID, knowing as he did that she was only seventeen. But Dougie was cooperating, and left to get the beers.

'How's the phone company tonight?' Pauly asked.

'Quite hot.'

'All those old switches, all those old lines,' he said knowingly. 'Guess what I heard?'

Dougie chose that precise moment to bring over their longnecks.

'Hi, Betty Jo,' he said again, braying almost exactly like a mule. He took his time setting the bottles down. Surely he was destined to spend his whole life in Grand Point.

'Hi, Dougie,' she said, being polite to his saying hello for the second time in five minutes.

She turned her attention back, as any lady would, to the man she was with. 'What did you hear, Pauly?'

Pauly waited as Dougie was still standing there, awkward as something newborn, and unwise. When Dougie finally got the hint and walked off, Pauly said, 'I heard our little telephone company is kept in business by the biggest phone company, Illinois Bell.'

She looked away, like she was carefully considering what Pauly said. It didn't make sense, a big company like Bell being nice to a second-floor operation like DeKalb-Peering, but she'd not yet studied business.

Behind the bar, Dougie was shooting moony glances her way.

'I suppose that's possible,' she said.

'Competition, see? Politicians down at the capitol in Springfield say they like lots of phone companies slugging it out to keep prices reasonable, but it's baloney. Those politicians get big contributions from Bell to keep other big competition away. Tiny fish like

DeKalb-Peering keep things from looking like Bell controls the state.' He sat back knowledgably and took a sip of his beer.

It appeared slimy behavior was everywhere, not just in Grand Point, Peering County.

'Lived here long?' he asked.

'My whole life, though I'm fixing to change that.'

'Leaving?'

She opened her purse and brought out the little pocket notebook. The thin cardboard cover was all frayed, and the curly wire at the top was squished from banging around in her purse, but it showed she was mature enough to have big plans.

'Every night after work I write down the money that's going to the bank come payday. I only make three-fifteen an hour, but a dollar of that goes to the bank, no excuses. In only seventy-four more weeks, I'll have enough for beautician school in Chicago.'

She told him how she'd quit high school to work in Grand Point's one beauty parlor, but how, after six months, it had closed, leaving her to find only part-time work as a nighttime phone operator.

'Well, don't leave before we've gotten to know each other properly,' he said, flashing a fine smile.

'That's a most agreeable idea,' she said. In fact, she was now thinking the whole business of Chicago might be slipping into a distinct second place if things worked out between herself and this sexy man.

Pauly glanced over at Dougie. 'I tried getting your friend to cash my paycheck, but he won't do it.'

Being as there was no one there except the ancients, she called across the room: 'Dougie, cash this man's paycheck.'

One of the ancients, a woman, looked over. The men had already been giving her the secret eyeball, probably recalling younger days.

Dougie's face got red from her suddenly paying attention to it. 'Not enough in the drawer, Betty Jo.'

She shrugged a what-can-I-do smile over at Pauly. 'Big check?'

'I do all right, climbing poles. Listen, let's try that Mexican-looking place across the river.'

Her mouth went dry but she kept her face calm. 'The Hacienda's a dump.'

'I saw lots of cars in their parking lot. They're bound to have a full register.'

'It's full up with creeps.' She touched her sore cheek. He might as well know.

'What the hell happened?' He leaned forward with encouraging concern.

'A man in this town doesn't want me seeing anyone but him.'

'He hit you?'

'Yes.'

'And this bastard will be at the Hacienda?'

She quickly held up her hand. 'I just need to stay away from him until he regains his senses.'

'I'm in a little jam,' he said. 'You can wait in the car while I get my check cashed.'

He'd been a Marine. It would be OK. They drained their long-necks and went out.

'Damn, what is it with cops in this town?' he said as soon as they hit the sidewalk.

A sheriff's cruiser was double parked alongside Pauly's hot car. Yellow, with two manly black stripes running back from its nose, she'd thought Pauly's Buick perfectly matched his strong physique when he'd driven her home Thursday night.

An officer had his face pressed against Pauly's side window, trying to see in. She couldn't see who it was. She backed into a dark doorway as Pauly walked up to his car.

A second later she heard voices. Pauly's . . . and little Jimmy Bales's.

It was a relief. She stepped out to join Pauly. Looking across the Buick's waspy hood, she said, 'Jimmy Bales, what on earth are you doing?'

Jimmy Bales was no real cop. Only a year older than her, he'd been hired to drive a cruiser around town in the evenings, to radio in reports of drunks getting into their cars. A real deputy would then speed over, and if the drinker was a nobody, write him a hundred dollar ticket. Word was it wasn't about stopping drunk drivers so much as getting the county more cash. People were always getting drunk in Grand Point, being that there wasn't much else to do.

'Ad-ad-admiring the car is all,' Jimmy stammered, nervous. He was another of those destined to spend his whole life rotting in Grand Point.

'You been admiring too many things, Jimmy Bales,' she said, thinking she'd demonstrate her self-assurance to Pauly.

Jimmy Bales seemed to grow even smaller. They'd given him

too big a uniform, making him look like he was drowning inside it. At least they hadn't given him a gun; for sure, the recoil would knock him on his butt.

'Keep . . . keep . . . keeping an eye out, is all.'

'Nothing about that car needs to be eyeballed,' she said, feeling in control for the first time that evening. 'Nothing anywhere else, either.'

Even in the dim light, she could see his face flushing beet red. Two months earlier, she'd caught him looking up into her bedroom window from his bike. He was a young, lustful boy.

For a moment, Jimmy Bales stood frozen in his too-big uniform. He'd caught the reference. He said, 'You hadn't ought to talk to me that way, Betty Jo. Something bad could come of it.'

'Jimmy Bales? If you would be so kind as to move your vehicle?'

The frozen Jimmy Bales unfroze himself enough to get in his cruiser and drive away.

Pauly turned to look at her. 'It appears you don't take guff.'

Without meaning to, she touched her cheek. 'When I can help it.'

He opened the passenger door for her, went around and got in. 'I guess my car is real noticeable here,' he said.

'It's not so much the car; it's you.'

'What's that mean?'

'My Mr Important likes to keep tabs on people. He knows you gamble.'

'Sometimes, after working lines here I stay to have a beer and roll some dice, is all.'

'Mr Important's friend knew about you driving me home, too.'

'Sheriff's people watched me doing that, too? Damn.' The engine rumbled as he started it and pulled away from the curb.

'We've hardly got regular police, just one per shift to answer phone calls about missing dogs and such. Everything else goes to the sheriff's department. That's the way the Importants like it.'

He laughed. '"Importants?"'

'The men who run the town.'

They got to the bridge crossing the Royal River, leaving Grand Point proper. 'How old are you, anyway?' he asked.

'Old enough,' she said.

He laughed again.

FOUR

East across the bridge, on the Pinktown side, Al's Rustic Hacienda squatted alongside the river, low and brown like an African shelter she'd seen once in *National Geographic*. Years before, Al had painted the roof red to look like clay tiles, and smeared nubby white stucco on the outside, all to make the place look Mexican. It hadn't. The million little stucco bumps caught dust from the highway, turning the place the color of dirt. Al's Mud Hut would now be a more fitting name, no different than the bait shack it had surely once been.

Still, go figure, it was the most popular bar in Grand Point. All the Importants went there. Folks who lived east of the river said that was because the Importants felt no shame in misbehaving on the Pinktown side.

For her, that night, the Hacienda was the most dangerous bar in Grand Point. Just beyond the parking lot was where he'd caught her the past Friday night. It was where he'd almost certainly be tonight.

She slid down in her seat as Pauly swung into the parking lot. It was crammed, as usual, with cars and trucks and people sucking on longnecks.

'I'll wait here,' she said.

'The man who hit you?'

'Likely he's inside.'

'I can straighten that out.'

She doubted that, extremely. 'It's best to leave him be. I'm hoping he'll come to his senses.'

'I should have a drink first, instead of just charging in and asking the bartender to cash my check. Do you really want to be out here all alone?'

It was a consideration. Pauly's was a noticeable vehicle. She'd be seen, no matter how low she stayed on the seat.

'You'll be fine with me,' he said.

It was enough. She got out, and they walked into the Hacienda. Two middle-aged men, bankers in town, acted most desirous of making room for her, even though she was with a man. But it took almost ten minutes for McGarrity to find time to take their order.

'He always that slow?' Pauly asked after McGarrity shuffled away.

'We used to go out. I broke it off.' It wasn't quite true. McGarrity had ended it real sudden, two days after the Important first took notice of her. She'd suspected McGarrity had been talked to, but at the time it only made the Important's interest in her more exciting.

'He's still upset?'

'He's not the one.' She made a smile, sure she was being watched. Maybe it wouldn't hurt to be seen smiling and unafraid, like Kathleen Turner.

'But he's here?'

'I haven't looked under all the rocks yet,' she said, sounding now like Bette Davis.

He laughed big, and she tried, too. The evening was progressing marvelously, all things considered.

She took a casual look around. She knew the Hacienda well from her time with McGarrity. Like always, it was jammed full of what crawled in Grand Point. Two sheriff's cops, both in uniform and on duty, sat at their normal spot at one end of the bar. A couple of punks from two towns away sat at the other end. In between were the soggy usuals: a farmer who lived south of town but spent too much time driving too slow past the junior high school and who'd offered her a ride in seventh grade; the suffering, look-away wife of the sheriff's chief deputy with one of her barfly friends; the guy who kept the accounting books at the Materials Corporation and supposedly a thousand dirtier ones in his room above the theater.

The Importants – those that controlled the town – were never at the bar. They sat at the small round tables in the shadows against the back wall, vultures in a row.

Doc Farmont, whose hands she could still feel probing her insides, was there, of course. He was talking to somebody she couldn't see. Likely it was that slobbering bit of squirrel meat, Randy. The doc told folks that Randy came in only occasionally to help with non-medical stuff, but nobody believed there was anything occasional about it. During her last time in that rat's nest of small rooms above the Red Wing, she'd sensed Randy close by, scuttling softly, at the ready for any opportunity to see parts of a woman he'd never encounter on his own. They were a pair, Doc Farmont and Randy – Doc's fast fingers and Randy's fast eyes.

Horace Wiggins, the newspaper publisher, was two tables down, sucking on one of his stinking, plastic-ended Tiparillos. The paper's other employee, a bird-faced, chestless woman, was right beside him. McGarrity said that everybody in town knew what else she was taking in besides dictation.

The funeral director, Bud Wiley, was in the darkest corner. Ripping drunk and red-faced, ash hanging from his cigarette, he was jabbing his finger into the chest of his nephew, Luther. Rumor was that Bud Wiley enjoyed pictures of young boys and girls that he had to go to Chicago to buy. She shuddered, imagining the funeral director's shaking, sticky hands on her. Please God, let that man be dead before my time comes.

Luther, the pale-faced nephew, was growing to be just as repulsive. He'd taken a run at her once, in this very establishment. She suspected he used rouge to color his white cheeks, and he smelled of formaldehyde.

Unseen, but surely there, was Clamp Reems, the sheriff's chief deputy. He wouldn't be talking so much as sitting back, smoking a broke cigar stuffed in his corncob pipe, watching and listening and tucking it all away for future use.

Even Jimmy Bales, the runt in a grown cop's uniform, had wandered in to stand near the town's rulers, like he belonged.

The Importants, and those who hung onto them, were all there.

McGarrity set their gin bucks down hard, slopping the tops of their drinks onto the scarred bar.

Pauly made his move. 'Cash my check, will you?'

McGarrity laughed.

'Come on, it's a DeKalb-Peering check. They're solid, right here in Grand Point.'

She turned to look closer at Pauly's face. He was smiling but she heard desperation in his voice.

'Damn it,' Pauly said. 'It's a solid check.' For sure, he was desperate.

McGarrity moved down the bar, probably because he wanted nothing to do with anyone she was with.

Pauly checked his big silver watch. 'Quarter to midnight. I know another place.'

'What's with that check, anyway?'

'I need to pay a debt, is all. In cash.'

'Tonight?'

'There's a place south of here,' he said, not answering. 'They stay open until four.'

Leaving the Hacienda was fine with her. They set down their drinks, half-full.

The parking lot was alive with drunks. They hadn't gotten ten feet when a fat woman with sprayed-up orange hair stepped in front of her and threw up a huge arm jiggling with fat and cheap silver bracelets. 'Well, looka here,' the woman said, trashed. She was with a stick of a man half her size.

Pauly, already four steps ahead and mindful only of getting his check cashed, kept walking.

She didn't recognize the woman. Nor the stick man.

'Little tramp,' the fat woman said, loud enough to stop everyone's talking.

Loud enough, too, to stop Pauly, who was by now ten feet away. He turned around, a big question mark on his face. 'Betty Jo?' he called back.

'I'm coming,' she called to him, making to move around the woman.

The woman grabbed her arm. 'Whose man you got tonight?' Her lipstick was smeared all over her face, like she'd been kissing a horse.

'Lady, I don't know you,' she said.

Pauly had come back. A gentleman – a true gentleman.

'At least one of us is a lady,' the fat woman said.

'Beatrice,' the stick man said, 'I told you: I made sure nothing happened.'

And then she understood. The sly stick had been puffing up his image with his lady, inventing someone young who'd come on to him previously, all horny.

She gave the stick man a pitying look. 'You ought to know better,' she said, grabbing Pauly's arm to head to his car.

It was late, almost closing time, and other nuts, full of booze and hot for trouble, were percolating in that parking lot as well. The two punks sitting at the bar had come out and were giving some guy crap about his highly waxed red Pontiac. 'We could run right over you, dipshit,' one of the punks was saying. 'Steamroller that red Pantyac.'

For an instant, she pitied the two punks as much as the Pontiac's owner. They were dirt poor farm boys, facing nothing but another sunup on a broke farm. She knew their anger. She felt it herself, every time she crossed the river for another suffocating night at the phone company.

Another couple of men, whose faces she couldn't see, were hanging back at the edge of the parking lot, sitting on the hood of an old junker car. By the way they were aiming their heads they weren't watching the spectacles of the punks or the drunk woman and her stick of a man. They were watching her and Pauly. It creeped her out.

'Fine place for a drink,' Pauly said as they got in his car.

'Every night is freak night in Grand Point.'

They pulled out onto the highway, but no sooner had they crossed the bridge into Grand Point proper than Pauly started driving funny, speeding up then slowing down. He ran a red light at the courthouse, punched the gas for two more blocks then swung onto a street lined with houses, cut his lights and stopped. He reached to tilt the rearview to better see behind.

'Car trouble?' She turned around to look, knowing it wasn't.

'Someone's following us. He pulled out of the Hacienda with his lights off, staying back, but I saw flashes off his chrome. When I sped up, he sped up. When I slowed, he slowed.'

'An Important thinks he owns me,' she said, her voice all quivery.

For a moment he said nothing, and she was afraid he'd push her out of the car. Then he gave out a sigh. 'Well, it could be me.'

'That debt? You owe it here, in Grand Point?'

'So long as it's paid back by dawn I'm OK,' he said, not really answering. He started up the Buick.

She quickly brushed away a tear before Pauly could see. Part of her wanted to tell him to drive her home, but a bigger part wanted to stay with him, no matter what. He could change her life.

'OK, then,' was all she said.

FIVE

They drove without talking, him checking the rearview, her watching through the back window. No headlights lit the night behind them, which meant exactly nothing.

He turned into a gravel parking lot just before Big Pine Road and killed the engine. For a moment, they watched without talking, the only sound the tick-ticking of the wasp's big motor cooling down. The road behind them stayed dark.

'False alarm,' she said, not really believing it.

'My overactive imagination,' he said, not likely believing that either.

The long, low building across the road was a blurred dark shape, almost invisible against the slightly lighter night sky because it had no windows. Sitting at the town line between Grand Point and absolutely nothing to the south, east, and west, everybody knew the Wren House was a Jekyll and Hyde sort of place. It was good enough for eating during daytimes and early evenings, but after that it welcomed a rough crowd – gamblers and workers at the sulky track north of town, folks who liked dark places. There'd been two stabbings there in the past year.

'I come here to play dice sometimes,' Pauly said.

And probably to lose the money he owed the debt for. 'How long will you be?' she asked, hating herself for sounding so scared and seventeen.

'There are always guys in there packing lots of cash. I'm going to roll a few times to be friendly, then find someone to cash my check.'

'The gambling's in the basement, I heard.' She didn't like the idea of waiting alone upstairs, especially if they'd been followed.

'Have a drink at the bar. I won't be long.'

Nothing appeared as they walked across the road. Still, she couldn't help asking, 'Ten or fifteen minutes?'

'No more.'

The Wren House was almost as dark inside as it was out. The walls were dark wood, shiny in spots from old grease. Cheap bird pictures, the kind on calendars from insurance companies and muffler shops, covered some of it, but most were curling off their thumb-tacks. More women than men, most of them fat and greasy like the walls, sat smoking in twos and threes at the red-checkered tables, sucking on whiskey mixes and longnecks, likely waiting on men downstairs gambling.

Downstairs, too, was the drain. There wasn't a kid in town, Pinktown or snooty Grand Point regular, who hadn't heard about the drain. Past the gambling rooms was supposed to be something the public never saw – a room with a special sloped floor stained with blood. Most said it was for quartering beef for the restaurant upstairs, but plenty believed more than livestock had been cut to bleed down there.

She did not like this place. 'Only fifteen minutes, for sure?' she asked again, making sure to take a stool where the mirror behind the bar would show anyone coming up on her.

'Twenty minutes, tops.' He took one of the two gin bucks he'd ordered and disappeared down the hall.

'Alone tonight?'

She almost jumped off the stool. Her attention had drifted after some minutes, or else she would have smelled the man's oily mix of Brylcreem hair jizz and Jade East cologne slithering up on her. He was about forty, had a gold front tooth, and wore an honest-to-mercy lime green leisure suit with white threading at the collar.

The wood handle of a gun bulged from the white-piped waistband of his green pants.

'My boyfriend's just downstairs,' she said quickly.

'I'm nice, when you get to know me,' he said.

It was as far as he got. Pauly had come up and pushed between them.

'Ready to go?' he said straightaway, sweating like he was fevered.

Gold Tooth stepped back, but only a little. 'I'm getting to know the lady,' he said.

'Fuck off,' Pauly said, turning his back to the man.

'Cash your check?' she asked Pauly.

'No need.' He pulled back his front pants pocket to show a wad of bills. 'They think I'm going to the john. No way I'm letting them win all this back.'

'Pay your debt?'

'Later.' He glanced, nervous, down the hall, toward the stairs that led to the basement.

They hurried to the door, and out into darkness.

BOOK II: RIDL'S STORY

SIX

J onah Ridl eased the open old Volkswagen to a rattling stop and shut off the engine. The shoulder of the road, high above the river and the town beyond, would be good for the first pictures.

He held his hand out, palm down. Steady. Eddings might have been right; maybe it was finally time for crime.

He lit a cigarette and studied the scene below. 'Bucolic,' Eddings had said. 'Bring me bucolic.'

That looked to be no problem. A pristine cement bridge, as bright a white as if Tom, Huck and the gang had painted it just that morning, crossed a sparkling Royal River. Bright green leafy trees, lush with full summer, lined the bank beyond, shading what was sure to be a picturesque burg, dozing in the mid-afternoon heat, beneath a sun as happily yellow as the un-rusted portions of his convertible. It all reeked of bucolic.

He grabbed the old Canon FT-QL, hefted himself up to half-standing and fired four fast shots over the windshield. He knew the cheesy caption Eddings would love: 'American pastoral: June, 1982. The day death came to bucolic Grand Point, Illinois.'

The editor had called Ridl into his office three hours earlier. 'Another cat, Your Lordship?' Ridl asked. Earlier that morning, Eddings had sent him to photograph a white cat some fool had dyed red and blue in honor of the upcoming Fourth of July. Such had things deteriorated – for the cat, and for Ridl's career at the *Chicago Sun-Times*.

Eddings held up Ridl's sheet of double-spaced type. '"The dye job is so expert,"' he read aloud, '"one can envision the cat on its hind legs, playing the flute, marching alongside patriots holding flags and muskets and beating drums."' He started laughing.

'The picture's even better,' Ridl said, trying to summon a grin. The cat had been only the latest in his lunatic assignments.

Laughing even harder, his eyes wet, Eddings read on. '"Perhaps the cat's owner" – oh, I so love this – "should be dyed in the spirit of celebration as well.'" He wiped at a tear that was running down his cheek, crumpled the copy and threw it at the wastebasket in the corner, missing by a foot. 'It's time, Jonah. Absolutely, it's time.'

Ridl reached for a cigarette.

'This, just off the wire,' Eddings said, shifting into the staccato, old-newsreel voice he sometimes fancied. 'Murder on lovers' lane.'

Ridl focused on steadying his hands enough to light his cigarette. Special Features didn't do murders and, sure as hell, *he* didn't do murders – not anymore. Special Features did the fillers that puffed up the paper: safe stuff like nonsense about dyed cats.

The editor leaned forward. 'Just after midnight, under the fullest of moons,' he whispered, almost in a moan, 'a man was shot dead in the bucolic—'

'That's for Front Section, or Metro,' Ridl said.

'It gets even better. The man's car was moved, and his girlfriend is missing.'

'The girl he was trying to rape shot him with his own gun, pushed his body out, used his car to drive away and is hiding out? She'll show up, dripping snot, warranting sympathy. Metro for sure, if Front Page takes a pass.'

'This is perfect.'

'It's crime. We're Special Features.'

'More enticement.' Eddings reached in his desk and took out a white envelope. 'Being ever mindful of the pay cut you took to join us in the basement, I offer forty-five in expenses.'

Special Features never covered crime, and Eddings never offered expenses. 'Where, exactly, did this horrific event occur?'

'Grand Point, Illinois, population 4,032.'

'That's a hundred miles west.'

'A little vacation. Talk to the local sheriff. Stay overnight.' Eddings leaned back and laced his fingers behind his head. 'Tomorrow, maybe interview every shopkeeper in town.'

'To con them into thinking we're going to become a presence that far west of Chicago, so they'll run ads with us.' It was subter-fuge, but there was even more. Eddings was testing to see if Ridl was ready to return to Metro, and crime.

'You've been down here what, six months?' Eddings asked, but really saying that six months was long enough.

'You'd run the piece with my byline?' Ridl asked.

'Who pays attention to bylines?' Eddings said, evading the

question but meaning yes, they were going to test run Ridl's name to see if it still attracted wolves.

Ridl owed the *Sun-Times* for those six months of cover. He should have been fired, if only to silence the community activists and local pols that wanted his head. Instead, the deputy managing editor got Eddings to create a place for him to lay low in Special Features.

He crossed to Eddings's desk and picked up the expense envelope, damning the way his hand shook.

Eddings noticed. 'Piece of cake, Jonah. A drive in the country, for advertising.'

Meaning this time Ridl could get no one killed.

'We'll talk about the byline when you get back,' Eddings went on. 'If you're not ready, we'll run it under my name.' Then, grinning, 'Just don't forget the bucolic. We want our new advertisers to know that one lousy murder won't stop us from showing their surroundings as idyllic.'

He drove to his apartment, packed a small bag and headed west to a small town a hundred miles west of Chicago.

Ready enough, at least, to commit bucolic.

SEVEN

The Peering County Sheriff's Department was in the basement of a hundred-year-old red brick and gray limestone courthouse, set smack in the middle of a square surrounded by equally ancient storefronts, some laid up in the same sturdy red brick, others in cautiously painted white clapboard. The bricks were faded; the paint was chalking. It was another hot day.

Despite the heat, the courthouse lawn was lush and green, obviously tended by people who understood fertilizer. A farm couple – him in a seed cap, her in a sundress, both of them tanned and creased – idled near the sheriff's door.

He went down the outside stairs. All four of the beige metal desks beyond the counter were empty. A pretty, slender, dark-haired girl in an orange University of Illinois T-shirt and cut-off blue jeans sat in the waiting area.

She looked up at him angrily, and mumbled something.

'What?' he asked.

'You'll have to yell, damn it.'

'Anybody?' Ridl shouted toward the wood door behind the desks.

'Louder,' the girl said.

Ridl turned. 'Who are you?'

'The press. Who are you?'

He ignored her. 'Which paper?'

'*The Daily Illini.*'

He thought he ought to call Eddings to say he was chasing the same story as a girl reporting for a college newspaper and no one else, but instead he screamed across the empty office. 'Hey! Anybody? Anybody at all?'

The door opened a few seconds later. A sheriff's deputy, no older than the college girl, stuck out a narrow head on a scrawny neck. 'What?'

'Jonah Ridl, *Chicago Sun-Times.*' He held up his old Metro press card, pretty sure no hick cop this far from Chicago would recognize the name after six months. 'You got a release?'

'A what?'

'A press release.'

'About what?'

Ridl felt an instant's nostalgia for the straightforwardness of the morning's dyed cat: he'd gone; he'd photographed; he'd scurried back. 'Maybe about the lovers' lane killing that just happened?'

The young cop stepped out from the darkness behind the rear door. Though he couldn't have weighed more than a hundred and twenty pounds, and wore neither a badge nor a gun, it was his too-large uniform that really killed the act. It was stiff and new and so oversized that his body seemed to wobble independently within it as he attempted a swagger across the office.

'Well, I guess I'm the press what-cha-ma-call-it,' he said, when he got to the counter.

'Like hell, Jimmy Bales,' the girl muttered.

'Did I not tell you to leave?'

'I'm press, same as him.' She gestured toward Ridl.

'You got no credentials, girl. Scoot.'

She made no move to get up.

The deputy's face flushed deep red. 'Shall I arrange to have you escorted out?'

'By whom? There's nobody around except you.'

'Laurel Jessup!'

She swore under her breath and got up. She was six inches taller than Ridl's five-five, all tanned skin, bone and no curves. And stunningly beautiful. She slammed the door behind her.

'Damn college girl, thinks she's so smart,' the young deputy said.

'How old is she?' Ridl asked, before he could think not to.

'I dunno; two or three years older than me. Why?'

'Never mind. Tell me about the killing.'

'Not much to tell. A man was found murdered on Poor Farm Road. His name was Paulus Pribilski, ex-Marine and, more recent, telephone lineman. He was twenty two, from Rockford, Illinois. We're investigating.'

'And . . .?' Ridl asked, when the deputy stopped.

'That's it.'

Ridl took out his narrow spiral notebook. 'The girl with him that's now missing? What's her name?'

The kid took a step backward. 'Have to check with Clamp on that.'

'Who's Clamp?'

'Chief Deputy Wilbur Reems. Sheriff Milner assigned him to head up the investigation.'

'Where is he?

'Out investigating, of course.'

Ridl made a show of flipping to a fresh page. 'Bales, is it? Give me the correct spelling so I can report how little you, as the press what-cha-ma-call-it, know about what's going on.' Hearing himself, he had the sudden thought that he sounded exactly like he used to: steady, confident, focused.

Jimmy Bales's face reddened. He looked around the office, then spoke in a low voice. 'Betty Jo Dean's her name. She's a good girl, built a little too mature for her own good, maybe, but a good girl.'

'She's the killer . . .?'

Bales dropped his voice even further, to a whisper. 'Clamp told the sheriff that if the Polish was packing, and he got too fast with her, she coulda got hold of his gun to stop him. That would explain her hiding out, scared nobody will believe her.'

It was ordinary, just as he'd told Eddings. He'd do some interviews and shoot some photos that evening, chat up two-dozen shopkeepers the next morning and be gone from Grand Point by noon.

'How well do you know her?'

Jimmy Bales inhaled deeply, as though trying to inflate himself to fit his too-large uniform. 'Spoke to her myself, last night. I keep a close eye on things after dark, and was on patrol outside Dougie's. I talked to both her and that Polish guy. As I'll probably write in an official report, they were getting along amenably.'

'No problem between them?'

Bales shook his head.

'Dougie's?' Ridl asked.

'The Constellation. It's a bar right across the street from here. I also observed them later at the Hacienda, out on the highway. The Polish was trying to get his paycheck cashed. We heard they went to the Wren House after that. According to witnesses, the Polish won a large amount of money gambling in their basement.'

'The money's missing?'

'I don't know what's missing.'

'Other than Betty Jo.'

'Yeah. She's missing, all right.'

'Where's the Wren House?'

'Follow Second Street down to the very south end of town, just before it becomes Route Four.'

'Poor Farm Road is the local lovers' lane?'

His face flushed. 'A half-mile past the Wren House.'

'Easy enough for someone to follow Pribilski?'

The deputy's eyes brightened at the inference. 'See, that's what the sheriff told Clamp could have happened. Best you shouldn't jump to conclusions about Betty Jo being a killer.'

'Pribilski's car wasn't found near his body?'

'No. It was found in the parking lot across from the Wren House. Clamp thinks there were two of them – one to drive Pribilski's car, the other to drive their own. All the more reason to think it was gamblers, since Betty Jo wouldn't have driven Pribilski's car back to the Wren House then left it. She has no car of her own.'

'Who found Pribilski?'

'A fisherman from here in Grand Point. He was driving east down Poor Farm Road, fixing to drop a couple lines in the Royal like he does every morning. A hundred yards in he saw a shoe lying in the middle of the road. No big deal, one shoe, except that, getting closer, he saw a dark red stain next to it, looking exactly like dried blood. He got out and saw drag marks on the gravel that could have been made by feet being dragged off the road. It didn't take more than a few steps to see a man lying face up alongside the cornfield, and he wasn't breathing. Well, he got right back in his car and hightailed it here to report directly to Sheriff Milner because, as the sheriff likes to remind folks, everybody knows he's always at work early. The sheriff called Ruskin, the coroner, told him to get out to Poor Farm Road, and headed out there himself with two deputies. They saw the shoe. They saw the blood. And at the edge of the corn, just past the ditch, they saw a man dead from gunshot.

'Coroner Ruskin arrived within thirty minutes, him being an early riser too, and the sheriff radioed Bud Wiley at the funeral home. After a brief examination of the deceased – there was no doubt he was dead, being as he was already stiffening – Coroner Ruskin authorized Bud to remove the body to Wiley's funeral home.'

Bales's head jerked up as the outside door opened. A sixty-year old man walked in. He wore a tan and green uniform just like Jimmy Bales's, except that his was tight across the belly and had a star on it that said sheriff. He was red-faced and sweating.

'Sheriff Milner? I'm from the *Chicago*—' Ridl said.

'Not now,' Milner wheezed, banging open the gate in the counter. Jimmy Bales spun around and followed him through the empty office.

'Did you find Betty Jo Dean?' Ridl shouted.

'Beat it!' Milner yelled, charging through the open door at the back wall. Jimmy Bales slammed it closed behind them.

Ridl touched the back of his neck. It was prickling, like back in Metro when he tumbled onto something significant. This time it was telling him that cops almost always talked to the press, even when they had nothing new to report, because they wanted to come across smart. They never wanted to look rattled, or like they didn't know what was going on.

Not so, the sheriff of Peering County. He'd been too upset to care what a reporter thought.

Ridl rubbed hard at the back of his neck until the tingling stopped, and went out the door.

EIGHT

Laurel Jessup, college girl, was waiting at the top of the stairs. 'Jonah Ridl,' she said.

He gave her no nod of acknowledgement, no forced smile. They'd probably studied his case in one of her journalism classes last semester. He'd been national news.

He jammed his hands in his pockets in case they got nervous. *'The Daily Illini?'*

'It's a real paper. Fifty thousand students are down at the U of I. How's this killing so special that it summons someone so famous?'

'Not famous.'

She failed at suppressing a grin. 'Infamous, then?'

'The story looked interesting.' He'd never admit he was sent to snag advertisers.

'You've got a good nose. From what I hear, Betty Jo Dean is not the type to be cowering somewhere, scared to come home.'

'You don't know her?' Laurel Jessup looked to be almost the same age as the missing girl.

Her eyes flashed, but for only an instant. 'I'm twenty-one, a senior. Besides, I live miles away, in DeKalb. I came here hoping to see reporters in action. So far, it's just been a TV woman from Rockford and . . .' She stepped back a foot and pretended to inspect him. 'I figured you'd be older.'

At five-five and two hundred pounds, she probably figured he'd be taller and thinner, too. 'What else have you heard?'

'I've got a source.'

'Then what's your source telling you?' he asked, not believing her.

'Chief Deputy Reems is scattering his deputies too far and wide.'

'A small town cop, panicked, lost his focus?'

'I don't know. How old are you anyway?'

Her directness was enchanting. 'Twenty-nine,' he said, 'but some days I'm a hundred.'

She checked her watch. 'I've got an interview.'

'Your source?'

'I might get you in, but it would have to be later . . .' She left the proposal unstated.

'If we share the byline?'

She gave him a huge smile and walked away, all long strides and energy.

The farm couple he'd seen earlier had moved to the shade of a tree. They stood together, not speaking. They were waiting for something.

The man had taken off his seed cap and was twisting it in his hands. 'You a reporter?' he asked when Ridl walked up.

'*Chicago Sun-Times.*'

'We just saw Sheriff Milner go in. Is there news?'

'Your sheriff doesn't like to say much.'

'Usually you can't shut him up,' the woman said.

'We only came to the courthouse for a copy of a quit claim,' the man said quickly.

It was strange, the denial, and unnecessarily defensive. 'Terrible thing,' Ridl said to the woman, hoping for more words from her.

She looked down.

'Do you know Betty Jo Dean?' he asked her.

'She's dead,' the woman said to the ground. 'If she didn't come home, she's dead.'

'Martha, you don't know any such thing.'

Martha raised her head, looked her husband in the eye and shook her index finger at the sheriff's door. 'I do. And they damned well know it.'

'Hush now,' the man said to his wife. He turned to Ridl, his face anxious to explain. 'Martha's a friend of Betty Jo's mama.' He grabbed his wife's elbow and steered her away.

Ridl looked across the street, searching for the bar Jimmy Bales had mentioned. The Constellation was narrow, jammed between an insurance agency and a one-man law office. Though the sun still beat bright on the town its sign was lit, alive with little stars winking on and off. Jimmy Bales had said it was one of the places Betty Jo Dean and Pauly Pribilski had gone to drink, before Pribilski's own life winked off for good. The Constellation could wait. He wanted to take pictures of Poor Farm Road while there was still good light.

He drove slowly through several blocks of century-old, pale-painted wood houses before speeding up past a McDonalds, a Shell station and sparser blocks of fragments of prairies. He didn't come to a stop sign until he got to the southern outskirts of town, where Second Street intersected with Big Pine Road and became Route 4.

A windowless, long brown barn-like structure loomed dark on the northeast corner. A white, backlit sign on wheels advertised a Friday night fish fry special for $2.99, and Harvey Wallbangers for a dollar. He'd tried the drink once on a date several years before. It was the yellowish green of anti-freeze and tasted sickly sweet. He hadn't liked it, or his date. Her name was Nancy, and she was obviously embarrassed at being fixed up with a man substantially shorter and wider than she was. She covered that by accusing him of being egocentric when, making conversation, he'd said newspapers were all that protected the world from chaos. He'd never had another Wallbanger, nor had he ever called her again.

Attached to the wheeled sign was a pole, on top of which the clever restaurateur had mounted an oversized red plywood birdhouse, which had become splattered with white drips. The restaurant was the Wren House. It was the last place Paulus Pribilski had been seen alive. Except by his killer.

He raised his camera. Nothing was more bucolic than a birdhouse, even strafed white by bombardier birds. He took a picture, and another of the restaurant hulking dark behind it.

Jimmy Bales had said Poor Farm Road was only a half-mile ahead. He drove up a concrete overpass that spanned a pair of railroad tracks and stopped at the top. Down below, a police car blocked the entrance to a gravel road that ran off to the left from Route 4. A hundred yards in, people milled about in clusters, talking. A news van was parked alongside the road. A woman in yellow and a cameraman in black jeans and a black T-shirt stood at the edge of a large patch of flattened corn. Behind them, ragged rows of searchers moved slowly through the field toward the west, flattening more corn.

He snapped three photos, drove down and parked across from the Peering County sheriff's car blocking Poor Farm Road. Two deputies leaned against the hood. He wondered if they were embarrassed to be guarding a crime scene that people were trampling.

An image of such a loosely managed crime scene might matter. He pointed his camera dead at the two officers, making sure to center the news crew and one of the trampling search teams in the background between them. Both cops frowned as he snapped their picture.

'How's the hunt for Betty Jo Dean?' he asked, walking up.

'Progressing,' the taller of the two said.

'I'm with them.' Ridl pointed at the news van.

Neither cop had more words. Ridl walked around them.

The news van belonged to the NBC affiliate in Rockford. The woman in yellow, studying notes on a clipboard, was in her mid-twenties, and dressed television perfect in a soft skirt and blouse that matched her sunny blonde hair – and, Ridl supposed, the faded, sunny yellow paint on his car, except where it was rusted. Certainly there was no rust eating at her, and might never be – at least, not the kind that had been corroding his insides for the past six months.

Her cameraman was even younger, about twenty-one. His black T-shirt, ripped under one arm, advertised an Allman Brothers concert from a dozen years earlier. He stood behind a camera on a tripod, where clothing didn't matter, waiting for the reporter to memorize her lines. They were recording a segment for later broadcast.

She raised her microphone and nodded at the cameraman. 'After leaving the Constellation,' she said, 'the couple went to Al's Rustic Hacienda, a local bar, where they were seen having a drink and attempting to cash Pauly Pribilski's check. Local sheriff's deputies received reports that the pair got into an altercation with a man and a woman in the parking lot before heading to the Wren House, where Pribilski might have won money gambling. Presumably, the couple then drove here, to Poor Farm Road.'

She lowered the microphone, consulted the clipboard and gave the cameraman a new nod. 'A fisherman found Pribilski, a former Marine, at six-thirty this morning, lying here.' She pointed to a spot five feet to her left. 'According to Coroner Ruskin, one shot entered his left side and penetrated his heart, causing instant death. Another struck him in the abdomen. His 1970 Buick was found in the parking lot across from the Wren House, a half-mile north of here. The sheriff's department confirmed that they were familiar with the car, a distinctive GSX model, from times when Pribilski, a lineman for the DeKalb-Peering Telephone Company, stayed after work to enjoy a beer before returning to his home in Rockford. It's routine, sheriff's sources said, to notice strangers in their small community.'

As she stopped to check her notes, Ridl again mulled the aberrant thought: sunny yellows were everywhere in Grand Point. The news reporter's hair and clothes, the dead man's car, even the backdrop of the cornfields, though those yellows were only inferred, shrouded

as they were in green husks. Still, nothing would make Eddings's
eyes glisten more than to work all those yellows into his piece.

The reporter continued, 'Pribilski's wallet is missing. Police
believe it contained a fair amount of cash from gambling winnings,
along with the paycheck he wanted to get cashed. Found on the
ground, near where sheriff's personnel believe Pribilski's car was
parked, was a fresh cigarette butt with lipstick on it. It was a Tareyton,
the brand Betty Jo Dean, the young Grand Point woman seen in
Pribilski's company last night, is known to smoke. She is missing.
Sheriff's department personnel declined our request to speak on
camera, citing their need to devote all their manpower to locating
Miss Dean.'

She said sign-off words and lowered her microphone. Ridl stepped
forward.

'The sheriff's department declined to speak, instead devoting all
their manpower to locating the young woman?' He cocked his head
toward the two deputies idling at the entrance to Poor Farm Road.

She grinned. 'Those two?'

'They're not bothering to protect the crime scene.' He gestured
toward a team of searchers.

'Supposedly, the scene's been processed. Maybe those two cops
are waiting to see who comes back to linger—?'

'The proverbial killer returning to the scene of his crime? Nah,
those two are just killing time.'

'You are?'

'*Chicago Sun-Times*,' he said, skipping his name, 'but I told the
cops I was with you.'

'Then you'll be watched. The sheriff is real sensitive about the
town's reputation. Those deputies tried to stop us from coming in.'

'How did you change their minds?'

She nodded toward her cameraman, loading their gear into the
back of the van. 'He started setting up right in the middle of Route
Four. They didn't want to be taped obstructing our access. They
relented.' She opened the van door and got in. 'Good luck getting
along with the people here,' she said through the open window.
They drove away.

He stood for a minute, watching fifteen, maybe twenty search
teams plod through the fields, as far west as he could see. They
didn't believe Betty Jo Dean was a murderer. They believed Betty
Jo Dean was dead.

He walked back to the county cruiser. 'You think Betty Jo Dean is on the run?'

'Have to ask Clamp,' the tall cop said.

'Where is he?'

'Checking a lead.'

'If she's not running, why wasn't she killed too, and left right here with Pribilski? She was a witness to Pribilski's murder – why would a killer risk taking her away in Pribilski's car, only to leave the car such a short distance away? Why risk driving her someplace else?'

Neither cop bothered to respond. It enraged him further. 'Are you thinking Betty Jo can't be a suspect because Pribilski was an ex-Marine, and no seventeen-year-old girl could get him down?'

The shorter cop shrugged. 'Don't take strength to fire a gun,' he said.

'Why don't you tell those searchers they're wasting their time, like you're wasting yours, guarding this road? She's not in that field. She must be running.'

'You little shit,' the tall cop sneered, taking a step toward Ridl.

His partner stepped between them. 'Have a good evening, sir,' he said, and then, strangely, both cops laughed.

It only took the short walk across the street to understand why. A pink ticket was stuck under his windshield wiper. It was for illegal parking. The 'Amount of Fine' section had been filled in with a ballpoint pen. It was fifteen dollars, more than any such violation would cost in Chicago. He looked at the cops, both of whom were staring right back at him.

He lifted his camera and fired off six fast pictures, each one identical. It was all he could think to do to make them frown.

NINE

Only ten cars were parked across from the Wren House. Few of the locals had thought to gather there to seek comfort in bargain-priced Wallbangers.

Then again, it might have been the stink of the murder, committed so close by, that was keeping them away.

There was little light inside, just a few dim wall fixtures. But there was art. Calendar pictures of colorful birds were thumbtacked, unframed, to dark pine plank walls sparkling with grease. A small stage with a lone stool was set up in a far corner for anyone bent on bursting into song, or perhaps just to warble for a moment, like a cardinal or a blue jay. It was a place for crackers. And birds.

Only one of the booths surrounding the empty tables in the dining room was occupied. Jimmy Bales said gambling went on down in the basement. That's where the owners of the few cars parked outside must be, and where Pauly Pribilski had gone to win the last bucks of his life.

A hostess came up with a menu. 'One for dinner?'

'The killing's kept everyone away?'

'Booth or a table?'

'I'll have a drink first.' He walked past a wall of spindles that resembled prison bars. Three men sat at the bar. Each wore thread-bare denim overalls. All looked too broke to gamble on anything other than their small glasses of tap beer. He sat in the center, between two guys who paid him no attention.

'Is the fish good here?' he asked the man to his left.

'Never tried it.'

'How about the Wallbangers?'

'Shit,' the man said.

The bartender came over and asked to see his ID.

'Twenty-nine?' he asked, studying the driver's license photo taken when Ridl was nineteen.

Ridl had heard it before. Being short didn't help. Being fat didn't, either.

'And old for my age,' Ridl said.

'You a reporter?'

'*Chicago Sun-Times.*'

The bartender handed the license back and Ridl ordered a tap beer. 'What are you hearing about the killing?'

'Clamp's in Freeport, checking out two guys that were hanging around the Hacienda.'

'Two guys, or a man and a woman?' Ridl asked, remembering what the television reporter had said for broadcast. She'd mentioned a mixed couple, not two men.

'I heard two guys.' The bartender set the beer on the counter. 'Seventy-five cents,' he said.

It was cheaper than a Wallbanger, and less green. He laid a dollar next to the beer. 'Those two guys were hassling Pribilski and Betty Jo?'

'Mister Reporter, all kinds of rumors will be checked out before this is over.'

'You know Betty Jo Dean?'

'Nope.'

'She was in here last night, with Pribilski.'

'No way I know her. Or him, if that's your next question.'

'You think the killer is local?'

'Jesus, mister.' The bartender grabbed a towel, went down to the end of the bar and began polishing a beer glass that already looked clean.

One of the men sitting alongside Ridl looked over with red eyes. 'Fifteen years ago, we had outshiders,' he said, slurring the word. 'Whores, military off the train for a hoot, punk kids from every dink town around. People who run this town got fed up and hired Clamp Reems as chief deputy. Clamp grew up at the sulky track north of town, a bad ass himself. He got rid of it all. This killing's a surprise.'

'Local, then?'

'Could be.'

The bartender came up. 'Last call, Vince. Finish your beer.'

'Sun's still out.'

The bartender leaned across the bar. 'Last call, Vince.'

The man saw through his fog and gave Ridl a lopsided grin. 'Local?' he asked loudly. 'No way in hell. Foreigner, for damned sure.'

Ridl left his beer untouched, went out and crossed to the parking lot. No one else at that bar was going to say another word to him.

A new pink rectangle was stuck beneath his windshield wiper. This time, the ticket was a twenty-five dollar fine for a missing rear license plate.

He walked to the back of his battered Beetle. They hadn't even bothered to be cagey; the license plate screws lay in plain sight beneath the back bumper. Only the plate was missing.

The sheriff's deputies had followed him from Poor Farm Road. They wanted him gone.

The back of his neck was tingling. He headed toward town.

No signs outside Al's Rustic Hacienda advertised anything, let alone Wallbangers. Nor was there any hint the place served fish. That, especially, was a good thing. The Hacienda was a hovel of splotchy brown stucco and peeling, red-painted roof shingles, a dump that looked as though anything marine it might offer would have been snagged whiskered, crudded and diseased from the bottom of the Royal River roiling not twenty feet away.

Yet unlike the Wren House, the Hacienda's parking lot was crammed full of cars. At least twenty teenagers clutching long-necked beers surrounded a young man in a bowling shirt who was leaning against the hood of a battered black Jeep. He was pointing toward the door of the Hacienda.

'As soon as they come out, Betty Jo and the Polish guy, this black-haired broad steps in front of Betty Jo. The broad is shit-faced, angry, dripping sweat. The man with her, a skinny squirrel, is hanging back. He wants no trouble.

'The broad starts giving Betty Jo crap about coming on to the squirrel. Betty Jo's no slouch; no drunk broad is going to push her around. She stays cool, gives the broad a smile and says something pitying to the squirrel.'

'What?'

'Couldn't hear.'

'Who were they?' a red-haired girl, barely sixteen, asked.

'The broad and the squirrel? Not from here. Rockford, maybe.'

'Where was the Polish guy during all this?' a kid with sideburns descending into serious acne asked.

'He was in a hurry, hustling ahead to unlock his car, but when he realized Betty Jo wasn't keeping up he turned and started coming back. Betty Jo waved him away; she was doing fine without him. And she was. She left the woman in her dust. But it was crazy here, that night. There was this other pair, a couple of dorks leaning against an old beater Mercury, hassling a guy about his Pontiac – red, ragtop, real shiny wheels, saying their old Merc could steam-roller the ragtop like it was tin. The dorks were just as shit-faced as the broad with the squirrel. I couldn't see who they were, on account of the shadows, but one of them . . . his voice was sort of familiar. Next thing, I hear the Polish guy's GSX pulling out of the lot. Nice exhaust, custom pipes, nothing factory installed.'

'Someone else pulled out after them?' the young red-headed girl asked.

'Maybe.' Bowling Shirt said more softly, his swagger slipping, 'I didn't pay it any mind.'

'Jesus, you could have seen the killers take off after them,' Sideburns said.

Bowling Shirt snorted, but it was forced. 'It was just someone leaving.'

'You hope it was only that,' Sideburns said.

'Bet your ass,' Bowling Shirt said.

Ridl went inside. It was packed, full of smoke, clanking glass and people shouting to be heard above the din.

Surprisingly, it was also full of cops. Eight uniformed sheriff's deputies sat at one end of the bar, including the two who ticketed him at Poor Farm Road and, later, at the Wren House.

Heads turned to look at him. The noise level fell away. A stranger, an interloper, had invaded their filthy little place.

It took no imagination to believe the cops who'd ticketed him earlier would wander outside to write something new, perhaps for his missing back plate, bad parking, or any of a thousand other imagined infractions. Mostly, though, he'd be ticketed for not being smart enough to get out of town. And this time, they might call for a tow truck and impound his car. Such were the way things played out for reporters in Grand Point.

He went back outside.

TEN

The sallow-faced young man behind the bar looked up with a huge, hungry smile. The Constellation was empty.

'Dougie?'

'Yeah?'

'*Chicago Sun-Times*.' Ridl sat at the bar and ordered a Coke.

'It's Doug, actually,' the young man said, serving up the Coke.

'What?'

'I hate everybody calling me Dougie. They should have quit that after high school.'

'And how long ago was that?' It had to be four years, tops.

'Eleven years.'

Ridl took a sip of his Coke. 'The man that got killed was in here last night with Betty Jo Dean?'

'I identified the body this morning,' Dougie said, giving his importance a long nod.

Ridl set his Coke down and took out his notebook. 'You knew Pribilski well?'

'He stopped in here first most evenings, when he was working in Grand Point.'

'"First?"'

'He liked gambling down at the Wren House. Too much, he said once. Most nights he stopped in here first, to relax a little before heading down there. "Getting loose," he called it.'

'Because your sheriff's department keeps an eye on strangers, they knew to call you to identify the body?'

'Actually, it was me who called them. Once I heard he'd been shot, I called the sheriff's department to say he and Betty Jo had been in here last evening. They said to go find the sheriff or Clamp at Wiley's Funeral Parlor. Saw more than I wanted, that's for sure.'

'Like what?'

The big smile he'd greeted Ridl with bloomed again. 'Want a sandwich? I made up a bunch for when you reporters came.'

'Business good?'

The smile wavered. 'Nobody came except some girl from the University of Illinois pretending to be a reporter, but she didn't have any money. Got ham and cheese, plain cheese or plain ham.'

'How much?'

'Eight bucks,' Dougie said, watching Ridl's eyes.

Ridl would have laughed if he wasn't desperate for information. Eight dollars was double what a sandwich would cost, even on Chicago's overpriced Michigan Avenue where Ridl never hung out.

'Includes the Coke,' Dougie added, sweetening the deal.

'Ham and cheese.' The shakedown was minor. He laid one of Eddings's tens on the counter and the plastic-wrapped sandwich materialized almost instantly.

'Yes, sir, I seen plenty,' Dougie said, making no move to find two bucks for change.

'Keep the change,' Ridl said, as though that were a choice, too.

The sandwich was stiff inside the wrap. Opening it revealed rye bread that was abrasive, like a scouring pad. Dougie was a conniver; he'd gotten a deal on old bread to maximize his expected windfall.

'They had him barely covered by a sheet, all bloody in the middle,' Dougie went on, the tariff having been paid, 'but not so's I couldn't see everything right off, soon as I walked in. Luther quickly covered him up all the way, except for the face, so's I could do the identifying. They said it was a necessary formality, if I wanted.'

'"Luther?"'

'Luther, Bud's nephew, was the only one in the room. Bud – Mr Wiley, it's his funeral home – was in the other room. I heard him talking with some others.'

'No trouble recognizing Pribilski?'

'Go ahead – eat,' Dougie said, looking at the sandwich Ridl had kept poised outside his mouth, hoping for humidity.

He took a bite. It was like sand-papering his tongue.

'Think the rest of the sandwiches will last another day?' Dougie asked.

Ridl took a sip of Coke to soften the lump in his mouth. 'I'm positive they'll taste the same for quite some time,' he said. Then: 'Pribilski?'

'His face was still damp. Sheriff had told them to clean him up quick so's his Rockford kin wouldn't see.'

Ridl managed to swallow. 'The sheriff directed them to wash the body?'

'Maybe not Sheriff Milner himself, but somebody from the department. Why not?'

Destruction of evidence was why not, like allowing people to tramp all over the cornfield, but he didn't need to share that with this idiot. 'Did you know Betty Jo Dean?'

'She's a sweetheart.'

'Is she a killer?'

'Hell, no. She's beautiful.'

'She's a suspect, right? She was in Pribilski's company. He turns up dead, his car gets moved, possibly with her driving, and now she's disappeared.'

'You ever see a picture of her?'

'Not yet.'

Dougie pulled out a small photo from his wallet.

'I was showing this to that college girl reporter before a deputy came in and said she was illegally parked. This is Betty Jo in high school, freshman year.'

It was not an official school photo. Betty Jo Dean sat on a blanket in a park, wearing a modest bikini. She was young, pretty and over-ripe for a high-school freshman.

'She gave a picture just to you?'

'I don't guess that,' Dougie said. 'Lots of guys liked her.'

'She prefer older guys, guys from out of town, like Pribilski?'

'Pribilski was only twenty-two.'

'You're older than that. Did she like you?'

The man who forever was, and would forever be, a Dougie actually blushed. 'Likely enough, I suppose, but I never made moves on her.'

'They came in together last night, her and Pribilski?'

Dougie looked down at Ridl's almost-intact sandwich. 'Another? Cheese this time?'

'I'm on a diet.'

Dougie nodded – too accepting.

'They came in together?' Ridl asked again.

'He got here fifteen, twenty minutes before her shift was over at the phone company. She works part time, in the evenings.'

'How did she act? Normal?'

'A little nervous. Kept turning around to look at the door.'

'New date jitters?'

Dougie shrugged. 'All's I know, she kept looking at the door.'

'Like she was afraid of seeing someone?'

'I don't know.'

'And him?'

'Pauly? No way was he nervous. He used to be a Marine and then climbed poles for a living. Huge shoulders, big biceps. I don't expect he was afraid of anybody.'

'I'm confused about something you said earlier,' Ridl said. 'Luther said you could identify the body if you wanted?'

Dougie's face reddened. 'Actually, it was more like Luther saying I could have a look if I wanted.'

'He was the only one in the room, other than you? He was doing you a favor, giving you a peek?'

Dougie's face darkened even more. 'That don't have to get out, does it? Look, they didn't need me to identify anything. They already knew who Pribilski was.'

'Because your sheriff's department was already keeping an eye on him, right?'

'Clamp keeps the town safe that way,' Dougie said.

'Or did, before the killing.'

Dougie Peterson had stopped listening. His eyes had gone vague. 'Poor bastard, all them shots,' he said, half under his breath. 'Think what you will, it was good they tried to clean him up before his folks got there.'

'Yeah, you said . . .' Ridl paused. 'What do you mean, all those shots? One to the heart, one to the abdomen?'

'Pribilski's pants were off, and I saw, before Luther pulled the sheet all the way up . . . No way in hell Betty Jo could have done that,' Dougie said, his eyes once again focused on Ridl.

'Did what?'

Dougie looked away. 'Shots down below.'

'What are you telling me, Dougie?'

'I'm telling you there's no way Betty Jo could have done that.'

'Shoot him?'

'Shoot him like that. Bastard was shot in the nuts, four, five times. Someone blew his balls off.'

ELEVEN

He ran down the sheriff's stairs and banged open the door, holding up his *Sun-Times* I.D.

'Nothing's new,' one of the two duty deputies said. Both had their feet up on their desks.

'How many times was Pauly Pribilski shot?' He was wheezing, out of breath, sweating from running across the street.

'You're getting nothing tonight.'

'Multiple gunshots to the groin? You know damned well that's passion.'

Both deputies switched out their smirks for glares. 'Beat it,' the second one said.

'If it wasn't Betty Jo Dean who killed him, then it was someone emotionally involved with her, or with Pribilski. No one else would shoot him like that. Who's jealous? Who's enraged?'

'We're investigating.'

'Looks like it's going real slow, here and at the Hacienda.'

'It's nighttime.'

'There's a seventeen-year-old girl somewhere out in that night, running, hiding or dead. Why aren't you looking for her?'

One of them got up and started moving toward the counter. 'I can find a reason to arrest you, round boy.'

'Thanks so much,' Ridl said, and left.

His hands shook a little as he stood on the lawn and lit a cigarette. The night was more vivid than any he'd known in months. Though the air was heavy, it smelled purer, and despite the humid haze the stars seemed to shine a million watts brighter. He took a deep drag on the cigarette. There was no doubt: the night felt right because things felt so wrong in Grand Point.

A figure stepped out from the shadows along the building. 'What do you know?' Laurel Jessup, student journalist asked, trying to sound casual.

'You're watching the sheriff's door to see who goes in?'

'You've been it, so far.'

'It's too late to be walking around this town by yourself,' he said, surely sounding like the girl's mother. 'How did that interview go, after I saw you?'

'I told you: I've got a great source. Shared byline?'

'That depends on what you've got.'

The sheriff's door opened down below and two sets of footsteps began climbing the stairs. Ridl tugged the girl around the corner of the building and stubbed out his cigarette. Neither of them spoke.

Unseen cigarette lighters clicked faintly in the night. The two deputies had come out for a smoke.

'Where's your car?' he whispered.

She pointed to a dented red Dodge Dart parked directly under a street lamp, in easy view of the cops. Two window decals were centered in its rear window. The first was a blue-and-orange graphic masterpiece of the University of Illinois mascot Indian holding a beer stein; the other a row of three identical gold Greek letters, triangles.

'Sorority girl?' he whispered.

'Tri-Delt.'

She was so different than him, a kid who'd commuted to a second-rate Chicago city college from his ma's two flat.

'Walk your way around and come up to your car from across the street so they don't think you've been hanging around the court-house,' he said.

'Why?'

'I'm a reporter.'

'So am I.'

He gave her a sigh. 'They don't like reporters here. I'll tell you more tomorrow if you leave now.'

'Damn,' she said. But she left, of a fashion. She marched straight out from the shadows, crossing the lawn directly in front of the two cops. One whistled softly at her.

She threw a lot of flounce into her walk as she passed beneath the street light next to the phone booths, and took too long to get into her car. The only thing she hadn't done was thumb her nose at the two cops.

He waited a full five minutes, then crossed Second Street far enough down so the two cops couldn't see him. He drove back up on a parallel street, clear of the courthouse.

The ticket seller at the movie theater in the next block was lit brightly in her booth, a glassed-in exhibit of a gray-haired woman alone. She raised her head abruptly at the clattering sound of his car driving by. He almost waved. Grand Point, that night, was deserted.

He passed into a residential block, looking for the sign he'd spotted earlier. It was three blocks farther on. Hand-painted on thin plywood and faded by a dozen seasons, it was stuck on a stick in the lawn of a two story, clapboard Victorian. 'ROOMS,' it read, faint in the light from the street lamp at the corner. He parked and walked up to a porch lit low by a single small bare bulb. An elderly woman answered the bell.

'How much are the rooms?' Ridl asked.

'How many nights?' she said through a clicking pair of dentures.

'Just tonight.'

'Ten bucks. You a reporter?'

'*Sun-Times.*'

'Never heard of it.'

'It's a scholarly journal, read mostly by Hollywood types.'

She nodded like that made sense, and said, 'I'm expecting a bunch of reporters once they find Betty Jo Dean.'

'You think she's a victim, or the killer?'

She dodged the question, a persistent businesswoman. 'There ain't but one motel in Grand Point, and it's got bugs. You want the room?'

'Air-conditioning?'

'Rooms rent fine without it. You want the room?'

He shifted his feet only slightly, reaching for his wallet, but it was enough to enlarge his shadow disproportionately against the pale clapboards of the house. He looked up at the sky. The moon was full. It would have been just as bright the night before.

He found a ten and handed it to her. 'I'll be back,' he said, and hurried to his car. He had a need – no, an obsession – to see the murder scene in the full light of the moon, as it must have been.

'You best be quick!' she shouted. 'I won't leave the door unlocked, and I go to bed right after Johnny Carson.'

He sped south, past the houses, McDonalds, the Shell station, fragments of prairies and the almost empty parking lot that signaled the Wren House was still taking a beating on unserved Wallbangers. He slowed at the top of the overpass. The milky light of the moon chalked Poor Farm Road into a flat white alley between two endless black fields. He drove down and turned left.

A car was parked where Pauly Pribilski's body was found. Courageous neckers, or perhaps thrill-seekers, come to park under the same full moon that had lit the bullets fired into Pauly Pribilski.

He cut his headlights and coasted to a stop a short distance back. As his eyes adjusted to the gloom, he saw that some of the beaten-down stalks of corn had begun wrenching slowly back up, contorting to clutch at life again, but the field would never be the same. Too much was dead.

A woman moved in the trampled corn. She wore a long dress or coat, despite the heat of the night. Beneath a soft, shapeless hat, her face was indistinct, and shifting. She might have been wearing a veil.

She moved slowly in a tight little circle. Her head was tilted downward and she seemed oblivious to Ridl, parked not fifty yards away. Several times she stopped and stretched out her arms in front of her, as though seeking something from the ground.

He watched her for fifteen minutes, then his curiosity could wait no more. He started his engine, turned on his headlamps and eased forward. The woman looked up. She was indeed wearing a long black dress and a long veil. She walked to her car, in no apparent haste, got in and drove away.

Sometimes nuts came out to play after a killing. This one had come costumed, right down to a long black veil. He drove back to the rooming house and took his small duffel bag to the front door.

As the landlady led him upstairs, she reminded him that it was a good thing he'd snapped up a room, as they were going fast. He asked how many others she'd rented. None yet, she said, but it was bound to happen.

The room he'd snapped up belonged to her son, now apparently grown and gone. He'd decorated it with hanging model airplanes. Ridl stripped to his shorts and lay on an itchy wool blanket that felt even hotter than the air trapped in the closed-up room. Opening the window by the bed set some sort of monstrous bug, unseen, banging on the window screen – trying to get in instead of out, he hoped. He turned out the light and the bug gave up.

As he lay in the heat in the dark, he let himself wonder if he were mountain-building. It was still most likely that the girl had been attacked by her date. She'd fought back and ended up killing him. Unhinged, she'd gone into hiding. Even at the end of the day, it reeked of ordinary.

Except that too many bullets had rained into Pauly Pribilski's groin. That wasn't ordinary, and the growing belief that he'd tumbled onto a good story began to calm him.

So, too, did the softer image of a tall and slender girl, tan and beautiful, who was not too many years younger than him.

Soon, he found sleep.

TWELVE

The sound of a small airplane, flying low, woke him at seven-thirty the next morning. He swung too quickly out of bed and got hit by another airplane, this one much smaller and dangling from the ceiling. Keeping his head low to avoid the rest of the mismatched squadron, he slipped on a fresh golf shirt and his khakis, went into the hall and found the bathroom. It was a place of Ivory soap and furry pink bath mats. He showered quickly and was downstairs before eight. By then, he'd heard the airplane – the real one – four more times.

'Coffee's on the counter, Mr Ridl,' the landlady said. No doubt braced for the onslaught of reporters needing rooms, she'd donned a pink blouse that matched her bath mats.

Another woman sat with her at the chrome-trimmed, white Formica table. Ridl took a cup from the counter, filled it with coffee from the percolator – no new-fangled Mr Coffee, not for this landlady – and joined them.

'Mr Ridl, this here is Blanche.'

Blanche nodded.

'Mr Ridl is an important reporter for a Hollywood newspaper,' the landlady said.

Blanche looked at Ridl with narrow-eyed interest. 'You know movie stars?'

'Too many to count,' he said.

'That your yellow convertible on the street?' Blanche asked. 'Doesn't look like a Hollywood car.'

'It's a rental.'

'It's got an awful lot of rust on it,' Blanche said.

'Keeps me from appearing too Hollywood.'

'It's got a ticket on it. I looked: no parking is the offense,' Blanche said.

Ridl caught the profanity before it got loose from his tongue, and said instead, 'How much?'

'Forty-five, because it says it's a third offense,' Blanche said. 'More than usual.'

'What's usual?'

She made a noise of disgust in the back of her throat. 'Zero. Delbert Milner is an elected man. Foolishness like parking tickets will get him thrown out as sheriff.'

'I heard an airplane,' Ridl said.

'Searching for Betty Jo Dean,' Blanche said. 'Besides the airplane, and me and others going door-to-door, there are teams crisscrossing fields all the way west to Big Pine State Park.'

Ridl gulped the last of his coffee and got up.

'Want me to hold your room?' the landlady asked. ''Course, you'll have to pay in advance.'

'I hope I'll be leaving after I do some interviews in town,' his mouth said, but his head already doubted this. The fresh ticket on his windshield went beyond a sheriff hassling a reporter. He'd been tracked, found on a side street. They wanted him gone, fast.

He got in his car and headed south, toward Poor Farm Road.

*　　*　　*

The intersection of Route 4 and Big Pine Road was clogged in every direction by cars and trucks. He had to drive a quarter mile west before he could park.

He shot pictures of the long, ragged lines of people moving west through the fields of tall grass. Though it was still early, the temperature was already in the upper eighties. He didn't want to think about what shape the girl was sure to be in if she'd been lying in such high heat for over a day.

He moved into the field to join the closest line of searchers. 'You a professional photographer?' the woman closest to him asked.

'Reporter, *Chicago Sun-Times*.'

'She's not going to be found here,' the woman said, waving vaguely at the prairie grass surrounding them. 'All this was searched yesterday.'

'How about the state park?'

'Big Pine? That's four miles ahead. Park rangers are doing that because some of the paths are dangerous. It'll be hard, slow work. Years of leaves, mounded up. You could hide a body good . . .' Her voice trailed away.

'You're thinking she'll never be found?'

'Not there, not in the Royal, either.' She pushed at the grass in front of her. 'That river is just a few hundred yards east of where Mr Pribilski was found, and it's deep and runs fast. Wouldn't you rather weight a body to disappear instead of leaving it in these weeds to be found?'

'Assuming she wasn't the killer, why abduct Betty Jo Dean?'

She gave him a weary look. 'The killers might have had additional need of her.'

'Rape?'

'I heard she excited plenty of men.'

They came to an access road.

'Then we have this,' the woman said, stopping to wipe her forehead. 'Care to guess the name of this particular road?'

'I wouldn't have a clue.'

'It's called the Devil's Backbone because of the way it's twisted. Up there is the Materials Corporation. Sand and gravel pits, some of which have been flooded for years. They've got divers checking them out, but I imagine there are a hundred little crags and nooks in every one. If Betty Jo's in there, she's likely never coming out.'

They crossed the access road and passed under a gnarled, stunted

tree, the only tree within several hundred yards. 'If you don't think
she'll be found, why are you doing this?' he asked.

The woman looked straight ahead, at the miles of open prairie
that stretched ahead of them.

'You can't not do it,' she said simply. 'A girl's gone missing.
You have to keep searching until you know what happened to her.'

He joined a dozen different search teams that morning. They'd come
from Grand Point and from Rockford, Dixon, Rochelle and tinier
towns he'd never heard of. Occasionally they talked; mostly they
just pushed ahead through the grasses, swarms of insects and the
heat, their faces set in grim determination. By noon, the temperature
was ninety-four degrees.

At twelve-thirty, a woman left the road to push into the weeds.
She was waving her arms frantically, trying to shout, but her voice
was too weak to be heard.

The searchers broke their lines to move toward the woman. When
she got close, she cupped her hands to her mouth. 'Sheriff's making
an announcement in fifteen minutes.'

'What about?' someone yelled.

'I heard big news, nothing more,' the woman shouted, and pushed
forward to reach those who had not heard.

THIRTEEN

A hundred cars heading up simultaneously from Big Pine Road
made for a maddeningly slow crawl to the courthouse. By
the time Ridl parked and ran back to the square, the courthouse lawn was packed.

Sheriff Milner appeared in an arch on the second floor two minutes
later. Unlike yesterday, when he'd blown into the sheriff's department, beet red and sweating, today Delbert Milner was ashen-faced,
his skin the pale gray of a corpse.

He pasted on a smile, held up his arms like a politician declaring
victory, and shouted, 'Neighbors, I have news! I believe Betty Jo
Dean is alive!'

It set off a cacophony of shouted questions. Milner waited until the last of them died down, then continued, 'I've received a tip. A truck driver, heading north on Route Four at about the same time Mr Pribilski was killed, caught a car in his headlights just past Poor Farm Road, headed south. Its driver was steering with his left hand and using his right to beat a young woman in the passenger's seat.'

Fifty hands shot into the air. Milner shook his head. 'There's no time for questions. You need to help. I think Betty Jo Dean is being held captive somewhere south of Poor Farm Road. Get down there and help search that whole area.'

'Those cabins along the river?' a man in a business suit shouted.

'Ideal spots!' And with that, gray-faced Sheriff Milner went back into the courthouse.

He must have expected pandemonium, and he got it. He'd set loose a mob, running for their vehicles. Within only a minute or two, Route 4 was a parking lot again, this time pointed back south.

It took Ridl thirty minutes to get down to the overpass, and another fifteen to turn where most of the cars were turning, onto Poor Farm Road. All continued past the spot where Pauly Pribilski was found and followed the curve south along the river. Parked vehicles already lined both sides, narrowing the road to a bare single-car width. He found a parking spot between a white Ford Econoline van with a red Diver Down decal on its rear window and a black-and-white sheriff's cruiser, then headed through woods of maples and oaks to the bramble that grew alongside the water.

A dive team worked from a small blue, square-fronted boat anchored off the opposite bank. A man in a black wet suit sat at its stern, resting his hand lightly on a slim slack rope dangling over the side. It was a signal line, tied to a partner below.

Down river, fifty of Milner's energized citizens were darting about like crazed insects through a long row of run-down shacks that lined the riverbank. Ridl walked up to a man who'd hung back at the edge of the clearing to talk to newcomers. 'We got no warrants,' he said. 'We can't ask to see inside. Just look anywhere you can.'

Ridl nodded and walked ahead.

There were twenty-one cabins spread unsociably apart in that deep shade along the Royal. All had started out as small shacks, little more than lean-tos, constructed haphazardly of whatever scrap wood had been around for the taking. Some had been expanded into large shacks as more material – wood crating, old fence lumber and the like – became available. Most had outhouses, except for three that had been modernized, of a fashion, with straight pipes aimed from indoor toilets right into the river. All were unadorned, except for one whose mildewed plank siding had been decorated with several fish heads, which in turn had long since been picked clean by the ancestors of the hundreds of flies that now buzzed around Ridl's head.

It was dark, dank and perfectly isolated for holding a girl who'd witnessed a murder. The cool of its shade might have been equally perfect for holding a corpse for some brief time as well.

He worked alongside the other searchers, peering under cinder-block pilings down into the pits below the fetid outhouses, and beneath upside-down boats and canoes set on low wood bucks. They scrutinized the moss-slicked ground for signs of recent digging, and knocked on the doors of every cabin. Few people answered, of course, and that made it dumb work, for if anyone in those cabins knew anything about the girl's disappearance, they would have already come forward. Unless they were a killer or a kidnapper, in which case they would have simply lied.

More people came as the afternoon wore on. Some helped search while some stayed by the river, watching the divers who might dislodge the girl at any moment.

He spotted Laurel Jessup staring at the water, and walked up. 'What are you seeing, *Daily Illini*? Frogs, or a Pulitzer for investigative reporting?'

She gave him an odd smile. 'Don't look around, but I'm seeing a cop who's been watching me all afternoon.'

'Young cop? Maybe it's lust.'

She put her arm through Ridl's. 'Then this'll give him something to stew over.' Embarassingly, she had to bend down to kiss Ridl on the cheek.

'I should sputter,' Ridl said, only half kidding.

'Wait 'til I'm gone,' she said, laughing, and walked away.

He did look around after she'd gone several yards, but by then the cop had disappeared.

The divers came out of the water at seven, and carried their gear and square-fronted blue boat through the woods to the road. The searchers followed them. By then, everything had been searched as well as it could be without warrants.

Ridl stayed behind as the woods went silent, looking at the river rippling white in its hurry to get down to Biloxi or Baton Rouge or wherever it was headed. He would not have wanted to be a diver in that fast current, though he supposed the water might be moving slower below the surface, calm enough to hold a weighted body in place.

'That your Volkswagen, parked on the road? Yellow thing, black top?'

A round-bellied sheriff's deputy who was maybe thirty-five had come up on him, silent as a panther. The man's substantial jowls surrounded a jaw clenching a corncob pipe. A torn cigar stood ludicrously in the bowl of the pipe. He could have been mistaken for a hick, a cracker cop, except for his eyes. There was nothing comical about the way they didn't blink, or the way he'd appeared so soundlessly.

The name on his shirt tag read Reems. He was the chief deputy who ran the law in Grand Point.

'You're Jonah Ridl, *Chicago Sun-Times*.'

He met the man's unblinking eyes. 'Why try to shoo me out of town?'

'You're asking questions that are meant to make us look like fools.'

'You're being dishonest.'

Reems pulled out a chrome Zippo lighter and lit the dead cigar. 'How so?'

'Pribilski got shot once in the heart, then multiple times in the crotch. That's rage, not robbery.'

The chief deputy rocked back on his heels. 'New leads are popping up all the time, just like this here,' he said, nodding toward the row of cabins. 'We just learned of a gray-haired gent who parks his car on Poor Farm Road, usually around midnight. According to one person, he was there Monday night into Tuesday.'

Ridl took out his notebook. 'Was he alone, this man?'

'Yes. Maybe he just likes to watch the moon, or maybe he likes to watch others. Or maybe he's a wienie-wagger, bringing his privates out to delight in the night. We'll find him.'

'Not a local?'

'Don't even know that, yet.'

'What else?'

'There was a Pontiac on Poor Farm parked just ahead of Pribilski's car.'

'I thought it was a couple of guys in a heap, hassling a guy who owned a Pontiac at the Hacienda.'

Reems smiled, releasing a puff of smoke. 'There you have it: we heard it both ways and more. We're checking everything out.'

'Along with every man or boy that ever went out with Betty Jo Dean?'

'And every girl that went out with that Polish, and every boyfriend of every one of those girls. Problem with jealousy is that it's everywhere. It's a long list of leads we've got.' He started walking toward the road.

'You think you'll ever find her?' Ridl called after him.

Reems turned around. 'Betty Jo's reputed to have more than a touch of the Devil in her. I'll settle for her being someplace safe, laughing her ass off, though at what I can't yet imagine.'

Watching the chief deputy move silently away, he knew it would be a mistake to dismiss the man as a buffoon. The extra fifty pounds he was packing and the cigar jammed ridiculously into his pipe were camouflage. Clamp Reems was no bumpkin.

Likely as not, he was Betty Jo Dean's best hope.

FOURTEEN

The landlady banged on his door rapidly. 'Mr Ridl, Mr Ridl!' she yelled.

For a moment, he fought the racket. He'd been soul deep in a sweet dream about a too-tall girl and the flavor of a kiss.

'Hey, Mr Reporter!'

He sat up too fast, striking his head on the underbelly of a cargo plane, which then set the whole plastic squadron jangling like giant Chinese door beads.

'They found her!' she yelled above the clatter. 'They found Betty Jo Dean!'

He stepped into his khakis. 'Alive? She's alive?' he shouted, grabbing yesterday's shirt and socks.

'She's—' Her words disappeared in the beat of her orthopedic shoes thumping down the stairs.

He stepped into his unlaced Pumas, grabbed his notepad and banged down after her. The wall clock at the base of the stairs said it was eight-fifteen.

Blanche, the bearer of all news, was again seated at the kitchen table. A quick glance at the look on both their faces told him what they didn't want to say.

He'd stayed another night; of course he had. And now he was going to hear what he'd begun to hope he never would. He busied himself too long pouring a cup of coffee before joining them at the table.

'Dennis Poe found her at around five-thirty this morning,' Blanche said. 'He was running empty up the Devil's Backbone to pick up a load at the materials plant.'

He remembered the road. He'd helped search there yesterday. 'That's a half-mile west of the Wren House, right?'

Blanche nodded. 'The Devil's Backbone is narrow, and it's custom for the empty truck to make way for someone coming out full. Dennis pulled over to let a full truck pass. He smelled or saw something in the weeds, and hightailed it ahead to the plant to call the sheriff. Delbert Milner got there in five minutes flat.'

'*Smelled?*' Something oily worked up the back of his throat. 'Surely you're not saying she'd been out in the heat for some—?'

Blanche raised her hand, stopping him. 'Maybe it's just that Dennis Poe saw her from the cab of his truck.'

He ran for the door.

Two sheriff's cruisers blocked traffic from turning onto Big Pine Road. He left his car by the Wren House and walked the short half-mile to the dozen cop cars clustered at the base of the Devil's Backbone.

Fifty onlookers had gathered around a deputy. Ridl snapped a couple of photos, not necessarily looking through the lens for a tall girl, and started up the access road.

'No press,' the deputy said.

He stepped back and took pictures of the men standing loosely together thirty yards up the Devil's Backbone. He recognized the exact spot because it was next to a twisted, half-dead tree – the only tree within a hundred yards. He'd searched under that tree, with others, the day before.

He turned to the deputy. 'Her body was found under that tree?' he asked, disbelieving.

'Yes.'

'You're sure: under that tree?'

The cop nodded.

'She still there?' he asked.

The deputy glanced uneasily up the Devil's Backbone. No one was looking back. 'I heard she was in bad shape,' he said. 'Clamp took one look and had Mr Wiley take her to his funeral home.'

'How bad?'

'Shot once in the back of the head, clothes thrown down on top of her like rags, then out for two days in this heat? Bad enough, I'd say.'

'Two days? You're sure – under that tree, for two days?'

'That tree is mostly dead and doesn't throw off much shade, if that's what you're wondering. Like I said, once Clamp saw the decomp, he had Mr Wiley quick take her out of there.'

'You said she was nude?'

'Partially.'

'The sheriff will hold a press conference?'

'Maybe not Delbert.'

'Milner isn't there?' He looked up the few yards again.

'He got taken sick suddenly and left. Look, Mister, anything else you need, ask Clamp.'

Ridl raised his camera and took another photo of the men up the road, standing beneath the tree where so many people had searched just the day before.

Word spread fast. Television news vans from Rockford, East Moline and Dubuque were parked close when he got back to the court-house, and he supposed it was print reporters who were jamming the phone booths out front. He drove across the river to the pay phone he remembered in the Hacienda's parking lot. He lit a cigarette after he'd fed in the dimes.

Eddings started yelling as soon as he picked up, culminating in, 'And thanks again for not showing up for work this morning.'

'This is bigger than you thought,' he said when the editor paused to gulp air. 'A man gets killed at one in the morning on Tuesday, then his date shows up dead on Thursday in a field that was thoroughly searched on Wednesday.'

'You're missing the point of why you're there.'

'They're having a press conference.'

'Have you excited any potential advertisers?'

'Only sheriff's deputies.' He told Eddings about the tickets he'd collected.

'Trying to run you out?'

'That'll end. There's press everywhere, now.'

'When's the damned press conference?'

'I might stick around afterward. Something's real wrong here, Eddings.'

'Yeah. Two dead and three tickets.'

'More than that.'

'Because you think the girl was dumped later?'

'Or freshly killed after being held for forty-eight hours.'

'What if I threaten to fire you?'

'You won't find anyone as good with dyed cats.'

'On my desk tomorrow, Jonah,' Eddings said, and hung up.

He opened the phone booth door, lit another cigarette and savored a play on words: Jonah Ridl had risen from two dead.

FIFTEEN

ate that afternoon, a hand reached from the throng of people going up the stairs and grabbed his forearm. It was Laurel. She'd gotten dressed up for the press conference, sort of. She still wore cut-offs, but she'd traded her university T-shirt for a white blouse, and was wearing lipstick that wasn't at all necessary.

'How sure do you have to be?' she asked, tugging him from the crowd when they got to the top.

'What do you mean?'

'How much should you know before you ask a question?'

'At a press briefing?' Ridl said. 'They're questions, for Pete's sake. You're not expected to know the answers.' Then: 'What do you suspect?'

'It's OK to fire away, no matter what?' she pressed, ignoring his question.

'You can ask anything.' He'd leaned closer, he told himself, only because he was tired of getting jostled by the crush of people pushing into the courtroom.

'And the shared byline? It's still on?'

He nodded.

'I'll see you later,' she said. And then she was gone.

They packed into a small courtroom, full of news people and

townspeople – several of whom, standing stiffly together, were dressed so identically in short-sleeved white shirts and dark ties that he wondered if they were the town council – and plenty of cops, though Milner was not there. It was a stately room with massive ceiling beams, white-plastered walls and oak wainscoting made black by a hundred years of waxing.

It was a proper room for dispensing justice and, as Chief Deputy Reems must have hoped, formal enough to discourage shouting. He had not presumed to sit up on the judge's dais. He stood below the raised bench, separated by a thick wood railing from the television crews and print reporters and, behind them, as many locals as could squeeze in. Reems wore his tan and green uniform, but he'd ditched the corncob pipe and genial air of country folksiness he'd laid on Ridl by the river.

'Good morning,' he began. 'I am Chief Deputy Wilbur Reems. Let me explain what's happened here before I answer questions.'

Ridl looked around. He didn't see Laurel.

'This morning,' Reems went on, 'we recovered the body of Betty Jo Dean, age seventeen, of this town. She'd been shot once in the back of the head. She was found lying on her stomach, fully dressed except for her slacks, which were neatly folded and placed upon her. Now, let me put this unfortunate development into the context of what we believe.'

He raised a pointer to the top of an L-shaped map he'd chalked on a wheeled blackboard. 'At approximately one o'clock on Tuesday morning, Paulus Pribilski, age twenty-two, of Rockford, was killed on Poor Farm Road. He was shot five times with a .38 revolver as he stood next to his car, a Buick GSX, while a second assailant held Betty Jo Dean helpless in that car. After Pribilski's killer had dragged him to the edge of the cornfield, he drove his own vehicle to the Wren House parking lot. The second assailant followed in Pribilski's car, with Betty Jo in it.' He moved the tip of the pointer straight down, to the left corner of the L's base.

'Abandoning Pribilski's Buick in the Wren House parking lot, the two assailants drove Betty Jo to the Devil's Backbone Road,' he said, moving the pointer to the right, along the base of the L, 'where she was shot once in the back of the head and left in the tall weeds by the side of the road.'

Hands shot up. 'Not yet,' Reems said. 'I want you to be clear why we're sure two individuals perpetrated this crime. First of all, when a gunman approached Mr Pribilski's Buick, jerked open the door and pulled him out to shoot him, Betty Jo's reaction would have been to run. A second person had to be there to restrain her from taking off into the cornfields.

'Second, two people had to be involved because one was needed to drive Pribilski's Buick to the Wren House while the other drove their own car.

'Third, our most promising leads involve eyewitness accounts of several pairs of individuals behaving in hostile fashions. Coming out of the Rustic Hacienda, Mr Pribilski and Miss Dean got into an altercation with a woman and a man. The woman was quite angry with Betty Jo about something. Also in that parking lot were two young men loafing next to an older car. This pair was looking for trouble, threatening another couple, owners of a red Pontiac convertible, but they might well have turned their attentions to Pribilski and Betty Jo.

'There's also a report of a third duo, one of which may have once had local ties, hanging around the Hacienda's parking lot that night, though there's confusion about that.

'Finally, we have reports that Pribilski might have won a substantial amount of money from gambling with several men after leaving the Hacienda. Two or more of those men might have taken offense at Pribilski leaving before they had a chance to win their money back. There's also an unsubstantiated report that Pribilski owed large debts to gamblers down at the Wren House, debts he neglected to pay.

'Add to all this, we've learned Pribilski was very active on the social scene up in Rockford. Betty Jo Dean, of course, was known to have a number of male admirers not just here, but in surrounding communities. Jealousy might well have been the motive for these killings.'

He set the pointer on the tray beneath the blackboard. 'We have a tremendous number of leads. We're casting a wide net, using every resource available, but this is going to take some time. Now I will take your questions.'

'A local woman said she heard from Betty Jo the day after Pribilski was killed,' a man with a print reporter's narrow notebook said.

Reems patted his pocket, like he missed his pipe. 'Your source is Miss Abigail Beech?'

The reporter said nothing.

'Never mind.' Reems looked around the room. 'For those of you who haven't had the pleasure, Miss Beech is our local psychic, or whatever. She's been prowling the ground along Poor Farm Road hoping for signals, I guess.'

Reems was referring to the woman in the long dress and veil that Ridl had seen in the moonlight.

'It's cruel, her saying such nonsense,' Reems said. 'Next question.'

'What about the older man seen driving southbound, struggling with a girl in a car?'

'That tip was a hoax. For those of you who haven't heard, Sheriff Milner got an anonymous phone call about some trucker seeing such an incident. A hundred searchers combed the cabins and the river bank south of Poor Farm Road, but nothing came of it.'

'Was she raped?' an older woman in a blue dress asked.

Reems's eyes flashed with anger. 'She most certainly was not,' he shot back. 'Doc Farmont conducted a thorough examination this morning. Betty Jo's body was unfortunately decomposed, having been out in the heat for over two days, but he is certain she was not sexually molested.'

'Were she and Pribilski having consensual sex at the time they were attacked?' the same woman asked.

Reems stepped forward to the edge of the rail. 'Where the hell are you from?'

'*Des Moines Sentinal Register.*'

'Let me tell you something, Miss *Sentinal Register*. What Betty Jo Dean was doing out on Poor Farm Road is none of our damned business, beyond it being a date. Her family lives in this town. We're respectful of our neighbors here. And of their memories.' Reems pointed to someone else. 'Next question.'

'She was shot once, in the back of the neck?'

'And fell forward, yes.'

'Does the bullet match the ones recovered from Pribilski?'

'It's the same .38 caliber. I'll be taking that bullet with the five we recovered from Mr Pribilski to the Illinois State Police lab, but I expect they're from the same gun.'

'Wasn't that excessive, removing all five from Pribilski?'

'I insisted every one be extracted, in case there were two shooters.'

'.38 is a common caliber, correct?'

'Unfortunately, yes. We're not going to bother checking ammunition suppliers, since there are a million of them around.'

When Ridl raised his hand, Reems called on him with a nod of recognition. 'The man from the *Sun-Times.*'

'Any thoughts on why Betty Jo Dean was taken from Poor Farm Road? If the objective was to get rid of an eyewitness, why not shoot her and leave her with Pribilski? Why risk driving her someplace else to kill her?'

Reems grimaced. 'I hate to speculate, but the intent must have been rape. It's small comfort, but they must have changed their minds after they took her.'

'That doesn't explain risking moving the Buick. All three could have simply piled into the perpetrators' car.'

'My own theory is they moved the Buick to delay the discovery of Pribilski's body. They didn't know they'd left a shoe on the road and a puddle of blood.'

Ridl followed up with: 'You're certain Betty Jo was lying along the Devil's Backbone Road since very early Tuesday morning?'

'It isn't me that's certain. It's the coroner.'

'He didn't do the autopsy. You just said Doctor Farmont from right here in Grand Point did the examination.'

'OK, it's Doc Farmont's who's certain she's been lying there the whole time. What's your point?'

'Hundreds of people searched that area by the Devil's Backbone Road, beginning Tuesday. I helped search there myself, on Wednesday, and distinctly remember walking past that gnarled tree. How was she missed?'

'If you were down there, you saw those tall weeds.'

'Yet this morning she's seen by a man in a truck, farther away than we were?'

'The driver was sitting high up in his cab. He had a better view than you. And if you must know, he also mentioned smelling something bad, like a dog or something had died at that spot.' He held up his hand in admonishment. 'I'd appreciate you not dwelling on that. It's a fact, and you're entitled to report it, but decomposition's one of those details that's a horror to the family.'

Reems pointed to a reporter on the other side of the room.

'Milner was first on the scene?' Ridl shouted. 'It made him sick?'

Reems looked back, his face darkening. 'People get sick, damn it. Our sheriff's got a touch of the flu. He stayed, securing the crime scene, until I got there with Mr Wiley from the funeral home.' He checked his watch. 'Now, let's give other people a chance.' He pointed to a hand raised against the opposite wall. 'Yes, miss?'

'Who was the man that slapped Betty Jo outside the Hacienda, last Friday night?' It was Laurel Jessup's voice, high and nervous.

'Who the hell told you that?' Reems shot back, furious.

'Was it that man's fetus that your Doctor Farmont aborted from her?'

'This damned briefing is over,' Reems yelled, striding angrily through the side door.

SIXTEEN

'Jonah Ridl, I'll be damned,' the voice called out behind him.

Ridl, jittery from Laurel Jessup's grenades back in the courtroom, spun around. 'Spetter,' he said. He hadn't seen him inside.

The *Chicago Tribune*'s investigative reporter, dressed also in khakis and a golf shirt, was Ridl's counterpart at the *Trib*, or rather, Ridl had been Spetter's, until Ridl parachuted into the basement anonymity of the *Sun Times's* Special Features.

'We talk about you, Jonah,' Spetter said.

'Bad stuff?' Ridl said, producing what he hoped was a real smile. He shot a glance over Spetter's shoulder, looking for Laurel.

'Bad circumstances, Jonah. It could have been any one of us.'

It wasn't, though. It had been only Ridl, and something he should have let go.

'Let's have a drink,' Spetter said.

'I'd better pass.' He wanted to find Laurel.

'I'll buy.'

'It isn't that; I can afford a drink.'

'Just a Coke, then? Your byline just disappeared, man. I'll come back a hero if I say I ran into you.'

Ridl hesitated. He didn't want to lie, but he didn't want to admit he'd spent the past six months hiding in Special Features, either. Spetter, though, had been about the only one who'd checked up on him those first days after Ridl himself had become news.

Ridl pointed to the Constellation across the street. 'It's quiet there.' It had a window that faced Laurel's Dodge Dart, parked at the curb.

The place was empty. Dougie Peterson showed happy teeth when they walked in. Recognizing Ridl, perhaps. More likely, smiling at the prospect of peddling a couple of the sandwiches still curling in plastic wrap on the bar.

Spetter got a Scotch, Ridl a Dr Pepper.

'Sandwiches?' Dougie asked. 'Made fresh.'

'Expense account,' said Spetter, a man new to Grand Point, buying two.

Ridl led them to a table with a view out the front window.

Spetter took a bite of his sandwich, then set it down fast to reach for his drink, obviously needing the moisture.

'It's good to see you,' Spetter said, when he could. 'This story here, though . . . waste of a day.'

Laurel was crossing the street, walking slowly as though dazed. Ridl got up and went out the door.

'Laurel,' he said.

Her eyes glistened and her lips were trembling. 'I screwed up, didn't I? Shut things down cold?'

'I was the one who said you should ask anything, but Jesus, Laurel . . . How solid was that business about a man hitting her and an abortion?'

'Like a rock, I think.'

'Who was the father?'

'My scoop, Jonah.'

'One of those white-shirt businessmen in the courtroom?' Ridl asked.

She shrugged.

'I told you I'll share the byline if you give me what you have. We'll split the writing.'

Her face worked at smiling.

'You could go back to campus this fall waving a clip from the *Sun-Times*,' he added. 'That's big time for a journalism major. Just make sure the information's solid.'

'I'm on my way to do that now.' She gave him her home phone number. 'Call me tomorrow, after noon,' she said, getting in her car.

'Wasn't that the girl who stopped the show?' Spetter asked when Ridl came back. He'd watched through the window.

'Journalism major, University of Illinois.'

'God save us from the determination of the young. Think she was right about the man slapping the Dean girl, and the abortion?'

'No idea,' he lied.

'I tried telling my editor that we get better murders in Chicago every single day,' Spetter said. 'No dice; he saw intrigue in the girl not being found for two days. But it's a wilderness out there, lots of big weeds.' He checked his watch. 'I gotta go.'

'Why don't you take your sandwich?' Ridl asked, offering up a smirk. 'It'll last for weeks.' His own lay untouched, but then, he'd been to the Constellation before.

Spetter laughed, and left.

Ridl stayed at the table, ate the dry ham, the brittle Swiss and only those fragments of gritty rye bread that wouldn't come off the cheese. Then he shifted in his chair to call across the empty bar. 'Who knocked up Betty Jo Dean, Dougie?'

Dougie's face froze, but he wasn't looking at Ridl. A sheriff's deputy stood in the doorway, a dark shape backlit by the sun lowering behind him.

Ridl got up. 'Guess I'll shove off,' he said, moving around the cop and out the door.

He drove south, turned right at the Wren House and parked where he'd parked when he'd helped search the fields. Several people milled about the gnarled tree. He took pictures as he walked up. He'd study them when he got back to Chicago, but there was no way they'd convince him Betty Jo Dean had been laying there when that field was searched.

He stopped, shocked. The weeds surrounding the gnarled tree had been mowed.

'Why was this cut?' he asked a man standing nearby.

'Clamp ordered it, to search for evidence.'

'They find anything?'

'All I saw was the guy doing the cutting.'

And destroying evidence.

The Materials Corporation was five hundred yards up the road, a scattering of several small house trailers used as offices. Six huge haulers were parked in a row at the end of the gravel lot. Though it was well past quitting time, three men stood smoking nearby.

'Jonah Ridl, *Chicago Sun-Times*,' he said, walking up. 'Mind if I ask how many trucks come out of here every day?'

'You mean just ours, or customers, too?' one of the men said.
'Total trucks.'

'I'd guess, what,' he looked at the others, 'two dozen every day?'

'At least,' another man said. 'June is high season for us.'

'So maybe fifty trucks came in and out of here since early Tuesday
morning?'

'You're wanting to know why not one of them drivers saw her
in the weeds until this morning?' the first man asked.

Ridl grinned. 'They had to concentrate on their driving, and not
the side of the road?'

The man spit on the ground. 'Drivers aren't blind.'

'I'll bet no one here is stupid, either,' Ridl said.

None of the three asked what he meant, and that spoke plenty about
what they didn't believe coming from their sheriff's department.

He walked back down the road, deciding against taking any
more pictures. No matter how many he took, none would convince
him that fifty drivers had missed seeing a body lying so close to
the road.

SEVENTEEN

I t was dusk, mercifully too late to lie to shopkeepers. He'd make
one last stop and head back to Chicago.

He crossed the river and swung into the parking lot of Al's
Rustic Hacienda. Like last time, there was a crowd of underage
drinkers lounging around the cars in the parking lot. Also like last
time, inside there was a raucous mix of clinking glasses and liquored
laughter. The place smelled of thick smoke and booze. Ridl worked
his way through to the bar and ordered a ginger ale.

A smudged blonde in her early thirties was sitting on the stool
next to him. 'You're new,' she said. Her eyes were bloodshot. Most
certainly she'd been perched at the bar for some time.

'Yes,' he said.

She cocked her head. 'Reporter, or boy scout?'

'Reporter.'

'I thought . . . you'd all been run off by now.' She shook her
head. 'Stupid.'

'Some of us are more tenacious than others.'

'No point,' she said. 'Ish done.'

A brunette of the same vintage, though less smudged, nudged herself between Ridl and the blonde. 'For God's sake, Evie.'

Evie tilted forward until her elbows steadied on the bar. 'Ish true, goddammit. Nothing more to be learn.'

'There seems to be leads pointing to the patrons of this establishment, or at least your parking lot,' Ridl ventured to the brunette.

Her face tightened. 'Plus gamblers down at the Wren House, a peeper parked just off Poor Farm Road and God knows how many jilted lovers. You can't lay it all here.'

'You think any of the leads will pan out?' Ridl asked.

'Never, bet your ash,' Evie said, peering around the brunette. 'Damn whore, that Betty Jo Dean.'

The brunette put her arm around Evie and walked her away.

'Ginger ale or gin buck?' Clamp Reems filled the space vacated by the two women.

It was no real surprise. 'Gin buck?'

Reems pointed to Ridl's glass. 'A buck looks like plain ginger ale, but it's got gin in it. It was Betty Jo Dean's favorite drink.' He paused, obviously enjoying the confusion on Ridl's face. 'We're not hillbillies, Mr Ridl. We're being thorough.'

'You thought to find out what she drank?'

'No, I said that to show off. She dated the bartender here for a time.'

'She wasn't in that field yesterday, Deputy Reems. I was there. I searched around that tree myself.'

'Too many people say she was easy to miss, covered with last year's leaves.' Reems pointed to a small group of men sitting at tables in the back, barely visible through the smoke. 'Go ask them directly.'

'Who are they?'

'Doc Farmont and his assistant, Randy White. Bud Wiley, our mortician, is at the next table with his nephew, Luther, and Horace Wiggins, our crime scene photographer. Any of them will tell you Betty Jo was covered with debris, and had spent quite some time exposed to the elements.'

'There'll be a more formal autopsy by your coroner, or the Illinois State Police?'

'No need. Cause of death is obviously gunshot wound to the

back of the head. Because of the decomposition, the Dean family wants her buried tomorrow.' He pulled out his pipe and fished in his pants pocket. Coming out with a freshly torn cigar, he jammed it in the pipe and lit it with his Zippo. He grinned, comfortably Colonel Cornpone again. 'Don't worry about them parking tickets. Being as you're leaving tonight, I'll get the fines waived.' He walked away.

'Best be careful, mister,' the bartender said after Reems had disappeared in front of his own smoke. 'You never want him paying too much attention to you, and that goes double when you're talking to his wife.'

'His wife?'

'That blonde you were talking to. She's Evie Reems.'

'She's rattled.'

'We're all rattled.'

'You went out with Betty Jo?'

The bartender looked wistful for an instant, then his face went blank. 'We got along, for a time.'

'When was this?'

'I forget.'

'All the boys liked Betty Jo Dean?' Dougie Peterson over at the Constellation had said it. Evie Reems had said more than that, calling Betty Jo a whore.

'Mister, we all liked her, about as much as we hated liking her. She was beautiful, too young and too old simultaneously. Be careful, is all.'

There was no point in hanging around to finish a ginger ale that would now taste like something left by a murdered girl. He'd call Laurel from Chicago the next day and write up what he had. He went out to his car.

As he pulled up to the highway another engine started up loud behind him. He waited, uneasy, but no headlights came on. It was paranoia; he'd spent too long in Grand Point. He turned east and eased the rattling Volkswagen up to a sedate forty miles an hour.

His headlamps lit a black-on-white sign five minutes later: 'Leaving Peering County, One Mile.' He chanced a last glance in the rearview. Something shiny glinted on the road, well behind him. Certainly there were no headlamps; it was unlikely to have been an automobile.

He watched the mirror more than the road, but nothing showed in the darkness. To be sure anyway, he killed his lights when he crested the hill at the county line, downshifting to a stop on the shoulder so as to not flash his brake lights. He shut off the engine, jumped out and ran back up the hill.

He saw and heard nothing for a few seconds, and then the rumble of a big engine grew louder in the night. There was no glow of lights, front or rear. The car was running dark. Good people did not run dark on a highway in the night.

He moved to the shoulder of the road and dropped onto his stomach. It was a damned dumb thing he'd done. There was no time to run back to the Volkswagen and accelerate away to safety.

The engine was almost deafening now. Only a big V-8 sounded that full and throaty. People hadn't bought expensive, thirsty engines much since the energy crisis sent gasoline prices to the moon a decade earlier.

Except cops. Cops still liked the big engines.

The engine rumbled as loud as thunder; the car was climbing the rise. He pressed himself down as hard as he could. In a second, the driver would crest the hill. Even running without lights, its driver would see Ridl's car in the moonlight, parked below.

The night went red from the taillights. The engine quieted, a little. The car had stopped.

He lifted his head just enough to see. The car was barely ten yards in front of him, idling, a beast hungry in the darkness. He pushed his cheek down hard into the dirt and tried not to breathe. A moment passed, and then another.

The transmission snicked softly as the driver shifted into another gear, and then the tires squealed softly, turning on the asphalt. He lifted his head. The car was backing into a turn. Headlamps came on, sweeping across the field on the other side of the highway, and the car roared back toward Grand Point.

He stood in time to see the vague shapes of bubble lights on the roof. Reems, or another of Milner's men, wanted to make sure he was gone.

He went back to his car.

EIGHTEEN

The *Peering County Democrat*'s offices were above the True Value Hardware, across the highway from the courthouse.

'Good morning,' he said to the sour-faced woman at the gray metal desk. 'I'm Jonah Ridl, of the *Chicago Sun-Times*.' Eying the other gray desk in the small room, fortunately vacant, he added the lie: 'My office called?'

'Never heard of you,' the woman snapped.

She was barely in her thirties, but already her face had hardened with the squinting eyes and deep frown lines of a woman angry at being lied to for decades. There was also the possibility she'd sensed that he'd slept in his car on a farm road a safe mile past the outskirts of Peering County, and shaved by a stream.

He pulled out his wallet, brimming with bits of paper. 'I'm to meet with ah, ah . . .' He made a show of fumbling through the scraps of old notes.

'Horace Wiggins, our publisher,' the woman said impatiently. 'He's the only other one who works here.'

Ridl smiled with what he hoped looked like gratitude. 'Yes. Mr Wiggins, of course. It's about the murders.'

'Can't help you now. Horace is out, photographing the funeral.'

'Betty Jo Dean is being buried so soon?' he asked, faking surprise at what Reems had told him the night before. 'I figured the police would want her body for at least another day.'

'Doc said it was best.'

'Yes, of course. That would be Doctor Romulus Farmont? I'm here to speak to him as well.'

'I could swear I've seen you before. In town, earlier than today.'

'I must have an evil twin,' he said.

'At the Hacienda, last night,' she said, with the certainty of a woman who's never been wrong. About anything. Ever.

'That's a lovely brooch,' he said, trying to ingratiate himself with her by feigning interest in the enormous cut-glass abomination that hung on her bird-like chest like a fallen window sash.

A slight smile twitched at the frown lines guarding her mouth. 'Anyway, Horace is not here,' she said, less harshly.

He took the chance. 'I was supposed to see the crime scene photographs.'

'Says who?'

'Said my office. They arranged it with Mr Wiggins.'

'I don't know anything about that. Besides, there's only the one.'

'Pardon me?'

'Horace brought in only the one picture.'

'You saw it, then?'

'Wasn't supposed to, but I did. Horrible.' She fingered the weight of the glass brooch.

'Badly decomposed, I heard.'

'I couldn't see that, for the leaves, but then I only looked for an instant.'

'Leaves?'

'There were leaves all over her head, completely covering it up. I suppose that's just as well – spares the family from seeing.'

'I'm only here for the day. I don't suppose you . . .' He let the plea dangle like the glass on the plain of her chest.

She glanced at the door nervously and stood up. 'You must promise to tell no one I showed you, because you should really wait for Horace.'

'Not a word,' Ridl said.

She walked to the other desk, took an eight-by-ten black-and-white picture from an envelope, and brought it back to Ridl.

'Mr Wiggins doesn't shoot in color?' No one shot crime scene photos in black and white anymore.

'Not this time.'

At first, all he saw were leaves, just as she'd said. But then he made out an upper torso, lying chest down on the ground, and the top half of a pair of white panties, partially covered by the folded dark slacks Reems had mentioned at his press briefing. The girl's patterned blouse had been tugged up, exposing her skin up to the back strap of her white bra. The upper portion of her right arm and her elbow were also visible; the rest of the arm and all of her head were hidden under the cover of leaves.

The photo looked arranged, as though the profusion of leaves had been meant to obscure any meaningful details.

'You're sure this is the only photo?' Ridl asked.

'Horace said any more would only distress the family unnecessarily.'

Ridl stopped himself from telling the lame-headed woman that crime scene photos were not given as keepsakes to the victim's family. 'I can't see any decomposition,' he said.

'Doc Farmont wouldn't be wrong about such a thing, nor would Bud Wiley. If they say it was there, it's there.'

'There's no bloating at her back or on the part of the arm that's visible. Bodies bloat up after death, especially in heat like we've been having.'

'That's a question for the doc.'

'And supposedly, the excessive decomposition is why they hurried to bury her today?'

'No supposedly about it,' she said, bristling. 'You best talk to Doc and Bud if you want to learn more.'

He thanked the woman, gave another smile to the brooch on her chest and went down the stairs.

Too much was wrong. The cops were making too little of too many bullets fired into Pribilski's crotch. Too much evidence had been destroyed, through trampling and mowing and washing. The cops were too insistent that Betty Jo Dean had lain a long time along the Devil's Backbone, when too many searchers would attest to that not being true. Betty Jo Dean was being hustled too quickly into the ground. And the one photo taken of Betty Jo Dean's corpse smacked too much of being staged to obscure anything meaningful at the discovery site.

Perhaps most of all, though, Sheriff Delbert Milner might have gotten too sick after seeing the most sought-after corpse in his county.

He looked across to the row of phone booths in front of the courthouse. A telephone directory dangled below the stainless steel shelf in the closest one.

He walked across the highway.

NINETEEN

The directory had listed Delbert Milner as living on the western outskirts of Grand Point. It was a tidy beige brick ranch house brightened by green shutters, set on an expansive, freshly mowed corner lot. Carefully trimmed yews and a long row of purple and white flowers ran along the front.

Ordinarily, it would have looked like a happy house, but today a red-and-white Cadillac ambulance was backed crooked in the driveway, and a Peering County sheriff's car had been left at a haphazard angle out on the street. Both had their lights flashing.

A young sheriff's deputy stood stiffly outside the front door. He was holding his wide-brimmed hat in front of him, as though he were in church. Or at a funeral.

The top was up on Ridl's convertible, but it wouldn't buy him invisibility. The deputies knew his car. He parked three houses back, behind a brand-new Ford F-150 pickup truck, and had just slumped low behind the steering wheel when a second sheriff's car raced up and slammed to a stop in the middle of the street, next to the first cruiser. A haggard-looking, middle-aged woman in a white nurse's uniform got out of the back and ran through the front door the deputy had hurriedly jerked open. An instant later, it must have been her who screamed.

The deputy who'd driven the nurse looked out his window at Ridl's car. Ridl recognized him. It was the tall cop he'd seen on Poor Farm Road on his first day in town – one of the pair who'd ticketed him for illegal parking and then for missing a rear license plate. The cop was speaking into his radio handset.

Two ambulance personnel came out, wheeling a collapsible gurney. They did not hurry. The body on the gurney was zipped to the scalp in a black vinyl bag.

The nurse came out fast behind them. Her face was wet with tears and red with rage. 'Murphy's in DeKalb, not Wiley's, you hear?' she shouted to the ambulance crew. 'Murphy's Funeral Home in DeKalb!'

'You sure, Mrs Milner?' one of the men shouted back, opening the ambulance's back door. 'The sheriff played cards with Mr Wiley.'

Mrs Milner was not a large woman, but she raised her fist and came toward him. 'You need me to drive the damned ambulance?' she screamed.

'No, ma'am.'

As the two men collapsed the wheels and slid the gurney into the back of the ambulance, Mrs Milner doubled over and fell to her knees. The young deputy left the front door and ran across the lawn.

'We'll go to DeKalb,' the ambulance driver shouted. 'Clamp says whatever you want.'

He climbed in and they drove off, lights flashing but in no hurry. The young deputy got Mrs Milner to stand, and together they walked into the house.

The tall cop got out of the second cruiser and began walking toward the Volkswagen. His face looked angry. Ridl gave him a faint wave and drove away.

Most probably, Milner had been dropped by a heart attack. He was overweight, and had been sweating too hard the first time Ridl had seen him down in the sheriff's office. He'd looked no better the next time. He'd been ashen-faced addressing the townspeople from the arch in the courthouse, reporting a trucker's tip and encouraging them to search the land and the cabins south of Poor Farm Road. That Milner had gotten sick at the sight of Betty Jo Dean at the Devil's Backbone fit too. Clearly, the man had not been well.

Mrs Milner was a nurse, a medical professional. She'd have known, more intimately than anyone else, how sick he was. Even so, her shock and her screams were understandable. Her husband was dead.

Only one thing nagged: she'd insisted hysterically that her husband be taken out of town, away from Wiley's, to another funeral home in DeKalb.

He caught up with the ambulance three miles east, and hung back the thirty minutes it took to get to DeKalb. Murphy's Funeral Parlor was on the main drag. He parked in front of a Rexall pharmacy, two doors down, where he could see when the ambulance left, and called Eddings from a booth out in front.

'The prodigal deigns to call,' Eddings, ever the wordster, said. 'You do recall you and your story were supposed to be in my office today at noon?'

'Too much is wrong here. The sheriff just got carted away, dead.'

'Murdered?'

'Probably a heart attack.'

'Now who's talking ordinary, Jonah?'

'I have to hang around.'

'For what? Spetter at the *Trib* gave it barely a hundred words this morning.'

'I'll have at least two thousand for openers. I can call later, to dictate?'

Eddings sighed and gave him the name of the night man to call.

'One more thing,' Ridl said. 'I've got someone working with me. Laurel Jessup.' He spelled it out. 'I told her we'd share the byline.'

He smiled, imagining her strutting on campus with a well-worn clip from the *Sun-Times*. And for the first time he felt the weight of the last six months start to lift. It was slight, to be sure; he'd never be completely free of a kid shot dead in a Chicago alley, but Laurel was a start, a way back. Maybe even an amends.

'Never heard of her,' Eddings said.

'Journalism major at Illinois. She's got a source – lines into a motive that no one else knows about. I'm calling her this afternoon.'

The ambulance, emptied of Delbert Milner, appeared at the end of the street and turned toward Grand Point. He told Eddings he'd call the night man and walked to Murphy's front door.

A man and a woman were seated in an office to the right, their backs to the door, facing someone across a desk. The man's shoulders were hunched. The woman's were shaking. She was sobbing.

A white-haired man in a black suit came out of a viewing parlor and crossed the foyer to close the office door. 'Always especially terrible when a young person dies,' he said. 'May I help you?'

'I said I'd follow along behind the ambulance but I got stuck behind a truck.' It was only the first of the lies he'd planned.

'You're here about Sheriff Milner? Not to worry. He's safe in our hands.'

Ridl chewed at his lip. 'Terrible, terrible thing.'

The white-haired man put on an appropriately consoling face. 'We'll oversee every possible detail, though it will have to be a closed casket viewing . . .'

Closed casket. Words too searing for a death by heart attack.

'Closed casket,' Ridl repeated.

He hadn't kept the question out of the words. The funeral director's eyes narrowed from consoling to cautious. 'Forgive me; I thought perhaps you were a son. You are family, sir?'

'I wasn't at the house.' It was all he could think to say.

'Wiley's is a fine establishment, to be sure.'

He almost wanted to laugh. The funeral director wasn't being protective of Milner's family; he was worried about being accused of poaching a stiff from another mortician's turf.

'You're wondering why we're not using Wiley's?'

The man in the black suit smiled, obviously relieved that Ridl understood the delicacy of the situation.

Because Grand Point's own funeral director was up to his own formaldehyde in covering up big things, along with the town's doctor, newspaper publisher and maybe half its sheriff's department, Ridl wanted to say, and the newly widowed Mrs Milner didn't want any of their dirty hands touching what was left of her husband, who perhaps hadn't wanted to conspire anymore.

'I'm fully prepared to put in a reassuring word,' Ridl said instead, 'so long as I'm comfortable with your decision-making.'

The mortician beamed.

'To best communicate the need to restrict the viewing,' Ridl went on, 'and for my information only . . .' He cleared his throat. 'Exactly how bad is the . . .?' He let the question dangle – a guess, but one he had to make.

The funeral director leaned forward. 'You do understand, reconstruction in the case of gunshot is tenuous at best?'

'How close was the shot?'

'There is no doubt.'

'That close?'

'Oh, no, no, no,' he said, trying to soothe. 'I merely meant . . . well, you understand, depression's a disease.'

The office door opened and the bereaved couple came out, accompanied by a younger version of the white-haired funeral director.

'She's safe in our hands,' the younger mortician said to the couple, echoing the same line his father had used with Ridl. The woman sobbed. The man's face was tight, but dry. He carried a purse. The victim must have been a woman.

The older director touched Ridl's elbow and nudged him ever so gently away. 'There are papers . . .?'

'The family will be contacting you shortly,' he said, and left. Sheriff Milner had died of gunshot. Whether it had been a suicide or murder wasn't something he was likely to learn on his own, anytime soon.

Someone with better sources might know. And it was time anyway. He stepped into the phone booth outside the Rexall, fed in a dime and called Laurel Jessup.

TWENTY

The phone rang nine times before a child answered. It was her younger sister, perhaps.

'Laurel Jessup, please.'

The girl started crying. A soft thud came then, as though she'd dropped the receiver.

An older woman must have picked it up. 'Yes?' she asked softly.

'Jonah Ridl, calling for Laurel Jessup.'

'For God's sake . . .' The line went dead.

Faces he'd just seen blended into a blurred kaleidoscope in his mind: a father with shoulders hunched in grief, a mother sobbing, and a young solicitous mortician murmuring practiced words that wouldn't do anything at all.

Suddenly there was no air. He pushed at the folding metal door and stumbled out of the phone booth. He made it back to Murphy's by concentrating on the symmetry of the lines between the squares of the sidewalk. He did not dare to think.

The white-haired man was still in the foyer, straightening a flower arrangement on a small table.

'Sir?' he asked, startled by what he must have seen on Ridl's face.

'The other person that was brought in . . .'

'Miss Jessup.'

And there it was.

'I knew her,' he managed.

The white-haired man nodded because, after all, it was what he'd trained himself to do.

'Tell me,' Ridl said.

'Sir?'

'Tell me how she died, goddamn it, and don't give me any shit about her being in safe hands.'

'I'm afraid . . .'

Ridl advanced. He wanted to hit. Hard. 'Murder? Was she shot, like Milner?'

The funeral man stepped back, his pale eyes horrified. It was so very good that he was afraid.

'Oh, no,' he said. 'My goodness, no. It was a car accident.'

His mind scrambled back to his own dark drive the night before, when he'd been tailed by a deputy.

'Where?' he demanded.

'West of here.' The old man named a different highway.

'But still Peering County? Yes?'

'Yes, yes.'

'What was odd about the crash?'

'Nothing.' The funeral man stepped back hurriedly.

'There had to be something odd about the crash, damn it.'

'Not really. The deputy who brought her purse said she must have fallen asleep. It was late. She ran off the road and hit a tree.'

It made horrible sense. 'Was anything taken from Laurel's purse?' Like a notebook that contained the name of a source . . .

'Please, sir, you must calm yourself. The purse spilled open from the impact. Its contents were scattered all over the inside of the car. A deputy brought it here. We gave it to the family. I'm sure everything was returned safely.'

That old weight came again, as crushing as when he'd gone to the morgue to see the pale skin and fuzzy beginnings of a mustache on a kid too young to be in a gang.

He bought two tablets of lined yellow paper at the Rexall and sat in his car. He wrote deliberately and slowly, pausing time and again to make sure it was all of what he knew, and all of what he suspected. There would be no redoing the story, not ever.

It took all of the afternoon and into the dusk. When he was done there were only a few sheets left on the second tablet. He threw them away. He never wanted to write on lined paper again.

He went back into the Rexall. He bought an envelope big enough for all the lined sheets of paper, and enough stamps from a rectangular machine on a stand to mail it twice to the moon.

He put her name on it and tried to push the sheets into the envelope. They would not fit, not all at once. Some had curled up from his rereading. Many were damp.

A young girl, not much younger than Laurel, came out from behind the counter and asked if he was all right. His voice sounded normal as he said, 'Yes,' but he knew then that he would never be all right again.

She took the papers from him and slid them in smaller batches into the envelope. She did not speak of their dampness.

There was a mailbox at the next corner. He let the envelope slide from his hands.

BOOK III: THE MAYOR'S STORY

TWENTY-ONE

The Present

Mac Bassett sat at his usual booth in back, waiting for nobody to come. Marveling, again, at how quickly it had all come apart.

He'd decided, right after he was sworn in as mayor, that the Willow Tree would be a better place to meet with constituents than the city's offices over at the courthouse. At mid-morning, the restaurant was good, quiet, neutral turf. The lawyers, dentists and shop-owners had left to face the commerce and conflicts of the day. The retirees had gone, too, shuffled off to start their lawnmowers or oil their door hinges or do whatever they did to pass the time until lunch, before maybe taking a trip south to the Wal-Mart. By ten-thirty only the waitresses were left in the Willow Tree, and they were too busy setting up for the lunch rush to mind folks coming in to brace their new mayor about a neighbor's sagging fence, an uncollected tree limb or a puddle of rain water in the middle of their street that just wouldn't drain away.

Right off, April told him he was being a damned fool. Again. Patronizing a competitor's restaurant was a boneheaded idea. Their own Bird's Nest was the smart place to meet with constituents. Mac could listen just as well in his own place, and there was always the chance they'd come back to buy dinner. Had he forgotten the place had been killing them financially in the year they'd owned it? Any business advantage they could eke from him being mayor ought to be pounced on, squeezed and wrung for its very last nickel.

Mac joked it away, saying he wanted to keep his two lives – brand-new mayor and failing restaurateur – separate. What about him being a pie-eyed optimist, she asked – didn't that qualify as a full life, too? Three lives, he corrected, allowing her that.

For the first month of his mayoralty, it had worked just as he'd hoped. People had come to the Willow Tree to slide in the booth opposite him and tell him of minor breakdowns in the creaking machinery that passed for government in Grand Point, Illinois. He'd

listened. And later, he'd made calls. And sometimes, the trolls over
at city hall or at the city garage, all of them put in place years
before by the man Mac defeated for mayor, had listened. Sometimes,
even, things got done.

But that was in March, three months before. In April, he'd been
indicted. And quick as a thunderclap, the good citizens of Grand
Point decided that living with sagging fences, uncollected tree limbs
and puddles that never went away was more practical than wasting
time sitting in a booth opposite a man headed for prison.

And so, on an otherwise fine day at the beginning of June, Mac
Bassett sat alone, waiting only for the chance to order the coffee,
eggs and crisp bacon that he hoped would ease him into a peaceful-
enough mindset to drive south, to the crossroads, to face his own
restaurant – that long, low, dying thing he'd bought for reasons he
no longer understood.

'How's things legal-wise, Mac?'

Pam Canton, the plump, blonde waitress, always brought an
observation or two, something national in scope, to go with the first
fill of caffeine. She always said it fast, then left. Never before had
she looked to start a conversation, particularly about his legal
troubles.

And never before had she set a dog-eared manila folder on the
table. She slid into the booth, like his constituents used to do, to
talk more.

'My lawyer says we'll win. Their indictment is sour grapes politics, but proving that in a court of law takes time.'

'And big money, I'll bet.'

'Yes.' He sipped at the coffee, waiting for what was on her mind.

'I've got something I want you to look into,' she said.

It couldn't be much. Pam wasn't a constituent. She'd only recently
moved to DeKalb, a few bumps in the road east, from somewhere
down south.

'Betty Jo Dean,' she said.

'Betty Jo Dean,' he repeated. The name was familiar. Maybe he'd
seen it in the paper.

'A teenage girl. She was murdered.'

'I'm sorry. A friend of yours?'

'No. It happened in 1982. I wasn't even born.'

His mouth went dry. '1982? A teenage girl killed in 1982?'

'Yes,' she said, a bit uncertainly.

'How old, exactly? Do you know?'

'Pardon me?'

'How old was she?'

She pushed back in the booth. Something crazy must have been showing on his face. 'Sev . . . sev . . . seventeen,' she stammered.

He'd frightened her with his rapid-fire words. 'Born in 1965, probably?' he asked, more conversationally. He hadn't had to do fast math; he'd already known.

'I don't know, Mac. Jeez, why does it matter?'

He took a breath. 'It doesn't; I'm sorry. Sometimes I ask too many questions, is all.'

Her face relaxed. 'Last place Betty Jo Dean was seen alive was leaving your restaurant.'

He remembered, then. The wife-half of the couple that sold him the restaurant, called the Wren House at the time, had taken him aside after the real estate closing. Glancing nervously at her husband, who was talking to their attorney down the hall, she'd taken a folded tan envelope from her purse and pressed it into his hands.

'It wouldn't be right, you not knowing about Betty Jo,' she'd said, talking low like she was passing on state secrets.

He'd asked what she meant. The woman had murmured something about a young girl and her date being murdered after leaving the Wren House. 'But some say she comes back.'

'I thought you said she was dead—'

'Shhh.' The woman had looked down the hall. Her husband was walking toward them.

'Betty Jo Dean,' the wife whispered. 'She comes back.'

The husband must have recognized something in his wife's eyes. 'Don't be filling Mac's head with old nonsense,' he'd said, working a smile onto his face.

Mac had jammed the woman's tan envelope in with the rest of his closing papers and wished them both a happy retirement in Florida. Within minutes, he'd forgotten all about Betty Jo Dean.

'The people I bought the restaurant from mentioned something about her,' he said now.

'She and her date, a man named Pribilski, left the Wren House and drove south the half-mile to Poor Farm Road.'

'A lovers' lane back then also?'

'Yes. Pribilski was dragged from his car, shot and left by the side of the field. Betty Jo was driven away in his car by one of the killers, who left it in your parking lot across the street. She was found dead in the tall grass along the Devil's Backbone, two days later.'

That road, too, was only a half-mile from his restaurant, though west instead of south.

'There were all kinds of leads,' Pam went on. 'Before Betty Jo and her date went to the Wren House they'd been drinking at Al's Rustic Hacienda.'

'Never heard of it.'

'It's that abandoned, dirty stucco place with the peeling, painted red roof shingles, on the east bank of the Royal.'

Mac knew the building. It was an eyesore. He'd hoped to get it torn down after he got elected, liked he'd hoped to do all kinds of things.

'All the town's honchos used to drink there,' she said. 'That night, Pribilski and Betty Jo got into some hassles in the parking lot. There were several couples hanging around out there and being confrontational: a woman with a man, who yelled at Betty Jo; two brothers, one from Iowa and one who used to be from here; and another two men in a beat-up old car who'd been hassling another couple. All this couple stuff is important because the theory has always been that two people had to be involved to drive away the two cars – Pribilski's and the one belonging to the killers – from Poor Farm Road.'

She was talking about killings that had occurred decades before. He needed to order his eggs.

'There were other suspects, too,' she droned on. 'Old boyfriends, old girlfriends, men Pribilski beat at dice that night, right there in that basement of your place, Mac.'

He took an obvious look at his watch, hoping to hurry her along. 'They never caught the killers?'

'Some folks wonder if anyone really tried.'

'How can you know that? You said there were all kinds of leads. Certainly they were chased down.'

'Maybe there were just too many of them.'

'Someone was deliberately trying to mislead the investigators?'

'Not "someone"; maybe some *people.*'

'More than one?'

'Maybe those big shots from the Hacienda, together.'

'A conspiracy?' Pam's story was getting wilder by the minute.

'Could be.'

Voices came from near the door. Early lunchers were starting to arrive. It was almost eleven o'clock.

It was too late to order breakfast now. 'What do you want me to do, Pam?'

She looked across the dining room at the people coming in. One of the other waitresses glared back at her.

'Last week, I went to the library here in Grand Point, trying to find information they might have about the crime.' She bit her lower lip. 'The librarian asked why I wanted to go digging around in that old case. I said it was just curiosity. She said, fine; microfilms for the Rockford Register were in the basement. And they were, only not for 1982.'

'Misplaced?'

'Every other year was there, just not 1982.' She nudged the manila folder across the table. 'I went to my own library. This ran in 2007, on the twenty-fifth anniversary of the killings.'

He flipped it open and saw a photocopy of a DeKalb newspaper article. 'This crime is so old. Why are you so interested?'

She gestured slightly toward the other side of the room. 'See that door?'

He knew the door, and the banquet room behind it. He'd been in there several times when he was running for mayor. 'The banquet room,' he said. 'It can hold a hundred people.'

'Except on Tuesdays and Fridays, at eight in the morning. Then it holds only a handful – the people that run this town. I've never much paid attention to them; one of the other girls takes their breakfast orders, so I don't know if it's always the same exact bunch. Always, though, the door is kept shut, and no one – and I mean no one – is supposed to go near it. They like their privacy, is what we're told.'

'How does this fit with that murdered girl?'

She glanced across the restaurant. The manager was staring at her, obviously willing her to get up and work the tables.

She slid out of the booth. 'One morning, a couple of weeks ago, the restaurant was especially quiet. I was passing near that door. Except that morning, someone had left it open, more than a crack. And I heard them.'

'Heard them?'

'They were saying her name: "Betty Jo Dean."'

The manager had had enough. He was walking over.

'Pam, people are coming in,' he called from a few tables away. She nodded. The manager turned back around.

'Listen,' she said, 'I asked some of the regulars here about the crime. Nobody wants to talk. I'm new here, barely getting by. I can't be pushing this.'

'What's to push?'

'It's not right.'

'What isn't right?'

'They weren't just saying her name. They were laughing.'

She tapped the manila folder she'd left on the table.

'I think one of them in that room killed Betty Jo Dean.'

TWENTY-TWO

D riving south to the Bird's Nest, biting at an Egg McMuffin – an abomination, but fast, filling and on his way – Mac told himself he didn't need to add a waitress's fantasy about an overheard laugh and the mention of a dead girl to the vile stew of things that kept him up at night. At fifty, his life was cluttered enough, verging as it was on total collapse.

Front and center, of course, was the nightmare of the grand jury indictment.

Not much more than a year earlier, he'd been a good Republican, county board trustee and head of the judiciary committee in neighboring Linder County, and getting along well enough by running a dinner theater out of his converted barn. But then he'd been out-politicked and defeated for reelection.

The loss had stung, but the dinner theater – barely profitable productions put on by a local amateur group, with food prepared by Mac and April – would continue to be his life. Or so he'd thought, until a neighboring farmer had offered to lease Mac's Linder County land and buildings. He'd offered a premium buck, almost double what Mac was making on the dinner theater.

More money than he'd been making, and all he'd had to do was move.

And he'd just heard of a roadhouse restaurant for sale in Grand Point, in neighboring Peering County.

'Are you frickin' nuts? Run a restaurant?' April had said.

'We've been serving food for years.'

'That's different, and you know it.'

'It's a great opportunity. I can smell it.'

'You don't do well with opportunity,' she'd said, offering up the towing company, the insurance agency, the mini-golf park, the auto repair shop and the dozen other schemes they'd lost money at before they got divorced.

'This is different. Besides, there'll be rent money coming in from the farm.'

'I don't like it,' she'd said, but had offered to go look at the Wren House with him. The place had been half-full that night. They'd learned later that half was as full as it ever got.

'I don't like it,' April had said as they drove back, because her instincts were good, and it was what April always said, anyway.

'We can do things: karaoke, theme nights, dinner theater.'

'Have you ever given up on anything once you started obsessing on it?'

'Let me think.'

'Never mind.' She'd lit a cigarette, blown smoke at the car window she hadn't bothered to open, and said, 'What the hell, I'm in.' She almost always said that, too. Blonde, beautiful and blunt, she was a hell of an ex-wife.

And so, at what seemed now to have been at warp speed, they'd bought the restaurant in Grand Point the month after he lost his bid for reelection to the Linder County Board.

A niggling detail had remained: he'd had seven months left on his term as a Linder County trustee. He'd gone to the board chairman, to resign. But the board chairman had talked him out of it, saying Mac's resignation would unnecessarily inconvenience everyone. Serve out the term, the chairman said; it's only seven months.

Mac had stayed on the board. He'd spent his mornings clearing out of his farm and his afternoons and evenings refurbishing the restaurant he was going to reopen as the Bird's Nest. Seven days a week he'd made the commute from Linder County to Grand Point, except sometimes when he was simply too tired to drive home. He'd joked about that at his last meetings on the Linder County Board – how he sometimes slept like a homeless busboy on a fold-away cot behind the tables in his new restaurant. It was funny, open and upfront.

One man, Ryerson Wainwright, had had to force his laugh. A more than occasional invitee, he'd been Linder County's new State's Attorney. Slender and middle-aged, he'd had an appreciation for fine things and had quickly demonstrated a fondness for gilt-edged, dollar-a-page official stationery; a four-thousand-dollar leather desk chair, and other extravagances that belonged nowhere on a public official's expense report.

As head of the judiciary committee, it had been Mac's responsibility to review the new state's attorney's expenditures. Since a reporter from Linder County's largest newspaper routinely attended the meetings, Mac's challenges to Wainwright's excesses had been reported, along with the board's directives that he return what he could and personally reimburse the county for what he couldn't. Wainwright had stopped his indulgent spending, but the damage done to his political career was fatal.

Linder County, like all counties in Illinois, had a residency rule: its trustees must live within the borders of the county. To live elsewhere, while drawing even the few hundred dollars that trustees were paid for expenses, was against the law.

The more times Ryerson Wainwright heard Mac Bassett joke about having to spend yet another back-breaking night sleeping in his restaurant, the more notes he remembered to make.

It had only been in the last month of his term as a Linder County trustee that Mac had bought a cottage in Grand Point. He hadn't moved until the day after his term on the Linder County Board ended.

Ryerson Wainwright hadn't been in a rush. In fact, he'd probably thought it was better to wait until Mac Bassett became more entrenched in his new community. Things had developed better than Wainwright hoped.

Three months after Mac moved to his new home, the then-mayor of Grand Point had decided he needed Mac Bassett's parking lot to widen the southernmost intersection of the town. He'd had the city attorney file a suit to seize the land. It was only coincidence, the mayor had said, that property he himself owned, a field kitty-corner from Mac's newly reopened restaurant, would become much more marketable if it faced a widened intersection.

Mac had been outraged at the bald arrogance of the play. He'd fought back, garnering local support by petitions circulated in the Bird's Nest. Enough people backed the new restaurateur that the city council dropped its lawsuit. Mac's parking lot would stay intact. He'd won.

But to everyone's surprise, except April's, Mac Bassett wasn't done. He'd announced he was going to run for mayor.

'Are you frickin' nuts?' she'd asked. 'We just moved here. Running for mayor will convince people you're a lunatic.' She'd grinned. 'Except me, of course. I don't need more convincing.'

'A committee of townspeople came by today. They see me as Abraham Lincoln.'

'He was ridiculously impulsive and struggled to run a restaurant, too?'

'They said I'm precisely the sort of man to bring honesty to the mayor's office.'

'Ah, hell, I'm in,' April had said.

Ryerson Wainwright, watching from Linder County, would have voted for Mac if he'd been allowed. He could only delight at the heightening of his target's profile.

The election turnout was low. Mac had won, shocking himself, and shocking April. And as Mac had been about to learn, positively thrilling Ryerson Wainwright.

'Politics ain't beanbag,' some ancient Chicago pol had croaked, a hundred years before. And so it went well west of there, too. Ryerson Wainwright had hardly been able to contain himself before holding a news conference: Mac Bassett had violated the conditions of his Linder County trusteeship. He'd been living in Peering County while still drawing expense pay as a Linder County trustee. As state's attorney, Wainwright was required to send the matter to a grand jury.

Mac's first reaction had been disbelief; surely a few nights spent sleeping in his restaurant did not constitute living in Grand Point. His second had been to hire an attorney, Jim Rogenet, who'd told him that in the spirit of the law, the charges were preposterous: the trustee expense reimbursements were barely over a hundred dollars a month; Mac had gone to the board chairman, intending to resign but had been persuaded to remain; Mac had been upfront and open about the occasional nights he'd slept in Grand Point, and that they'd been few of them.

'Very, very few, right, Mac?' Rogenet had asked, pressing the question.

'My back couldn't tolerate many nights on a folding cot.'

'You must assemble a calendar of all the nights you spent at your home in Linder County, just in case.'

'Just in case?'

'Find gasoline receipts, landline telephone charges, appointments for doctors, dentists . . . anything in your business diary that will show your ongoing presence at your home in Linder county.'

'You think they're going to indict me?'

'I think I want to be prepared.'

The grand jury had indicted Mac Bassett in April, one month after he'd been elected mayor of Grand Point, Illinois.

Gone went the little cash and few stock funds Mac had set aside to grow for retirement, handed over to the lawyer to help grow his own retirement. Gone went the camper van and the almost new Corvette. These days, Mac drove an old red Ford F-150 truck he'd found that had been about to be scrapped for parts.

Gone, too, went the goodwill of the people of Grand Point. Fewer and fewer came to the Bird's Nest for the fish fry on Friday night or the chicken bonanza all day Sunday. The Bird's Nest was teetering even more wildly, about to go down.

No, Mac Bassett thought now, as he pulled into the parking lot that had set off so much trouble little more than a year before, he didn't need a waitress's vague suppositions about an overheard laugh and the mention of a dead girl's name adding to the toxic clutter in his life.

TWENTY-THREE

Mac sent the bartender home at eleven-thirty, locked the door and poured the customary last whiskey for Farris Hobbs. Farris had been drinking at the roadhouse for forty years, and somewhere in there a tradition had been established. He sipped four whiskeys each night. Three he paid for, and one, the last, was poured free to warm the man's walk home. Farris used to drive, but that was before five DUIs, all ticketed before he'd barely weaved out of the parking lot, cost him his driver's license. Fortunately, walking was no hardship; Farris lived in a two-room cottage across the street, just north of the parking lot. Still, to be sure Farris arrived safely home, it was Mac's custom to walk him across the highway and then point him the few last steps to his door.

It was no chore. Farris was good company, steady or wobbling, a genial man who greeted the world with a sleepy smile. And except for one instance when he overshot the men's room and mistook the ice machine for a urinal, he never caused a problem. Even that one slip-up was explainable, friends pointed out. It had been Farris's birthday, and well-wishers had treated him to much more than his usual load.

That night Mac poured himself a short knock as well, and asked, 'Farris, you've lived here your whole life, right?'

'Every one of my blessed sixty-four years,' Farris said amiably.

'Betty Jo Dean.'

Farris's face froze, and for the first time that Mac had ever seen, Farris's smile disappeared. Just as surprisingly, for Farris had never been known to hurry the taste of whiskey, he gulped down the last of his drink and slipped off his stool like a man late for a bus.

Mac's hand on the bottle was just as fast. Now much intrigued, he clanked the bottle neck loudly against Farris's glass, pouring him an unprecedented – excepting those that had ended up in the ice machine on that long ago birthday – fifth drink. 'On the house,' Mac said, leaving the bottle on the counter as a promise of even more to come.

Farris wavered, standing next to the stool. 'I don't need that,' he said, perhaps to Mac, more likely to the refilled glass.

'OK, I'll walk you across.'

Farris eyed the fresh whiskey, free and waiting. He got back on the stool. 'I don't hardly know anything.'

'No big deal. It's just the name came up in conversation today.'

Farris took a sip, and must have decided its taste was sweet indeed. 'What kind of conversation?' he asked, in no apparent hurry now.

Mac lied. 'Someone mentioned the summer a girl, Betty Jo Dean, got killed. I didn't let on that I didn't know about that, because as mayor, I'm supposed to know the town's history.'

Farris looked at the door, as though afraid of eavesdroppers. 'Betty Jo was from Pinktown, across the river. In 1982, just before the Fourth of July, she was out with an older guy, Polish, down from Rockford. They were parked on Poor Farm Road in his Buick, maybe necking, maybe more. The way the sheriff's department told it, two people came up to their car, pulled him out, shot him once in the heart and several times in the nuts. They dragged him off into the ditch. One drove off in their car; the other drove away in the Polish's Buick with Betty Jo still in it. They left the Buick in your parking lot, across the highway. He was found the next morning, alongside Poor Farm Road. Betty Jo was found two days later up on the Devil's Backbone, shot by the same .38 revolver. There was talk of all kind of leads: jealous girlfriends; jealous boyfriends; people Betty Jo pissed off at Al's Rustic Hacienda; people the Polish pissed off right here on these premises, gambling. Our cops were running every which way. Headless chickens, they were, chasing them leads. They botched every damned one of them.'

'What do you mean?'

'None of our boys was used to working a murder scene. Take that Polish's car keys, because that I saw myself. Like I said, the Buick was found right across from here, its keys still in the ignition. Lots of folks were hanging about, including yours truly, admiring that car. Yellow it was, with black stripes – a real hot hauler. Anyway, Clamp reaches in for the keys, so nobody would get a notion to see how such a big engine might sound. Pulling them out, he dropped them in the dirt. When he picked them up, they were filthy. And so were his hands, when he got back in to drive it to the municipal garage. Whatever prints was on them keys or the steering wheel were gone, smudged away. Then Clamp had the whole inside stripped, looking for clues, and getting all sorts of new fingerprints everywhere.

'Clamp was just nervous; they all were. Well, the whole case went like that. Our boys were overwhelmed; no leads ever worked out.'

He finished his drink in one last, fast swallow, slipped off his stool and headed quickly for the door, as though afraid of hearing Mac pour him a new drink.

'I'll walk you, Farris,' Mac called to the man's back, jangling his keys to show he was coming to unlock the door.

Farris shook his head. 'Tonight I'll see myself home.'

Mac unlocked the door and held it open.

Farris paused before stepping outside. There was none of the usual redness in his eyes; nothing watery to show a night of drinking. They'd become stone-cold sober.

'How long you been living in Grand Point?' Farris asked.

'I've owned the Bird's Nest for over a year,' Mac said carefully, mindful of the indictment he was under.

'Over a year, and you ain't never heard the story about Betty Jo?'

'Not a word of it.'

'That tells you something right there, don't it?' Farris Hobbs said, and walked off into the night.

TWENTY-FOUR

F inally it was morning. There would be no more than three hours sleep. Mac gave it up and pushed himself out of bed.

It had been a fool thing to talk to Farris Hobbs about Betty Jo Dean. The man's nervous secretiveness, piled on top of Pam's overly suspicious fantasies, had only agitated up new questions he did not need.

He'd poured himself his usual Scotch before going to bed. But instead of sipping it in the dark to calm the chimpanzees in his head that shrieked at nighttimes, about the indictment, the failing restaurant, and the horror from further back, he'd left the light on and read the *DeKalb Advocate's* twenty-fifth anniversary account of the deaths of Pauly Pribilski and Betty Jo Dean. When he finally slipped into sleep, around five, it had been to a fitful, temporary place. The image of a seventeen-year-old girl lying face down in a field, with a bullet hole blown in the back of her head, kept jerking him awake.

He made coffee and took it into the living room to read the article again. He knew the reporter. Jen Jessup freelanced for the small papers in Peering and DeKalb counties. During the mayoralty campaign she'd found a hundred hot ways to call Mac an interloper, a carpet bagger from another county out simply to settle a score over a parking lot. And, since the indictment, an outright crook.

Her 2007 piece about the murders, though, was coldly clinical. She recapped the events leading up to the discovery of Pribilski's body, and traced the two-day search that led to discovering Betty Jo Dean in the tall grass up the Devil's Backbone. She recounted some of the leads that had arisen from the investigation – noting, as Farris had said, that the most promising of them centered on the several pairs of people hanging around Al's Rustic Hacienda. But, as Hobbs had also said, there were others of interest – an older man, perhaps a peeper, who liked to park near the lovers' lane, and an almost unlimited number of social acquaintances of the murdered couple. Betty Jo and Pauly had gotten around; each had dated aggressively.

The piece ended abruptly, with a single sentence saying that despite the high number of leads, none had ever pointed conclusively toward a suspect. No mention was made of what, if anything, successive sheriffs had done with the case in the ensuing twenty-five years.

Mac set the article on the lamp table, wondering if its abrupt end came from coarse editing – small-town newspapers were not always known for prizing quality in the prose they published – or whether the piece had been chopped for some other reason.

The phone rang. It was Jim Rogenet, Mac's lawyer in Linder County. 'Wainwright's not returning my calls. Obviously he's not anxious to offer you the chance to plead out.'

'I won't plead out,' Mac said. 'I didn't do anything wrong.'

'I think we ought to countersue to get his attention.'

'Charging him with what?'

'Irresponsible, malicious and politically motivated prosecution.'

'How much would that cost?'

'What will it cost if we don't counter?' The lawyer was inferring the wretchedly obvious: a conviction would lead to prison. 'I'd like you to come in so we can get this counterpunch filed.'

Mac told him he'd be in the next day.

'One more thing,' Rogenet said. 'How good are your press contacts out there, Mac? I'm having no luck interesting anyone in Linder County about Wainwright's standoffishness. They're afraid of him.'

'Like Jen Jessup?'

'She just hates you, period.'

'We'll have no luck in Grand Point, either. The local publisher is still loyal to the man I beat for mayor.'

'Nuts. I was hoping the announcement of a countersuit might pressure Wainwright to return a call. Listen, Mac, bring in what you've got that proves you spent most of your nights in Linder County.'

That was a problem. He'd pulled together nothing at all.

He drove to the Bird's Nest. It was shockingly cold inside, almost like a crypt. And that triggered a memory: '*The girl comes back, you know. She comes back to the Wren House,*' the former owner's wife had said, pressing an envelope at him. An envelope he'd never opened.

His office was upstairs, a pair of rooms cut into the attic. A yellow, lined pad of paper lay on his desk next to his old appointment calendars. Rogenet told him to list everything – dentist and doctor appointments, board meetings, car repairs – that would prove he'd spent the overwhelming majority of his nights in Linder County. The lined tablet was blank. So were most of the pages in the appointment book. Mac never had been one to write much down.

'*The girl comes back, you know. She comes back to the Wren House.*'

He knelt to rummage through a bottom file drawer, found the woman's envelope mixed in with real estate documents and brought it to his desk. He shook out an old Wren House menu, a Grand Point Chamber of Commerce booklet and several yellowed newspaper clippings.

The menu listed specials for late June and early July, 1982. The Wren House had offered a Patriots' Platter of fried fish; a Bunker Hill burger topped, predictably, with American cheese; and a potentially disgusting Independence salad of red cabbage, white onions and bleu cheese served warm, if it had ever been served at all.

He set the menu aside and picked up the slim Chamber of Commerce booklet. It was a typical booster piece, eight pages featuring lists of local restaurants, shops, and services. The first two pages showed photos of the town's leaders. Someone had made little checkmarks above some of the photos.

The newspaper clippings had been cut from the *Peering County Democrat*. Each had to do with the murders of Pauly Pribilski and Betty Jo Dean.

Mac arranged them in order. The first had been published on Wednesday, June 23, and reported the discovery of Pribilski's body the previous morning. Thursday's clip summarized the leads that had been gathered and detailed the search to find Betty Jo Dean. The same photograph of Betty Jo Dean was run at the top, both days. She wore a two-piece swimsuit, and was semi-reclining on the grass in a sunny park, smiling seductively. She'd been in her mid-teens, trying hard for older. It was a wrong photo to run of a missing girl. It made her look like a tramp.

Friday's clip reported Thursday's discovery of Betty Jo Dean alongside the Devil's Backbone Road. As in each of the previous clips, someone had underlined, in soft pencil, the mention that the couple had been last seen leaving the Wren House.

He picked up the Chamber of Commerce booklet again. As he thought, the publisher of the *Peering County Democrat* was pictured. Then, as now, it was Horace Wiggins. His photo was one that had been marked with a tiny check.

The fourth clip, run on Saturday, reported Friday's sudden death of Sheriff Delbert Milner. Milner was described as a caring man. Some speculated that distress over the discovery of Betty Jo Dean had overtaxed his already diseased heart.

The last newspaper article ran on July 8, and reported testimony at the coroner's inquest. The dead man's brother described Pauly Pribilski's last evening at home as being ordinary – dinner as usual before leaving for Grand Point. A local man described the different couples that had been hanging around the parking lot at Al's Rustic Hacienda. A young trucker told of discovering Betty Jo's body. Bud Wiley spoke of removing Betty Jo from the field. Doc Farmont discussed his brief examination, saying a formal autopsy was not needed because the cause of death was so obvious. Finally, the then-acting sheriff, Wilbur 'Clamp' Reems, gave an account of the scant evidence found at both murder scenes.

The coroner's inquest adjourned in short order. Causes of death were obvious. The investigation would continue.

Slam, bam; thank you, ma'am. All wrapped up nice and tidy, except that no one knew who might have done the killing.

He picked up the Chamber booklet again. Two of the town's trustees, Doc Farmont and Bud Wiley, had testified before the coroner's jury. Wiley's wife was the jury's secretary. All three pictures had gotten checkmarks, along with Wiggins's.

He rootled in his center drawer, and found the slip of paper. He dialed the Florida number of the restaurant's previous owners.

Phil answered on the first ring.

'Phil? Mac Bassett.'

'How are you?' The retired restaurateur sounded genuinely pleased to hear from him.

Mac filled a sociable first minute with bromides about the restaurant and the town, and then eased into the reason for his call. 'I was cleaning out my file cabinet and came across an envelope. It contained some old news articles, one of your old menus, and a Chamber of Commerce booklet, all from the summer of 1982.'

'I'm sure I don't remember,' Phil said. But he'd said it too fast.

'The news accounts were about a couple of murders.'

'Throw them out.'

'Someone saw reason to mark a few photos of the town's trustees with little check marks.'

'I'm late for bridge,' Phil said in a nervous voice, and hung up.

Mac set down the dead receiver. He wasn't really surprised.

Then he picked up the phone again. Rogenet, his attorney, had given him a thought that could kill two birds.

TWENTY-FIVE

M ac had two hours before April and Maggie would arrive to resuscitate the Bird's Nest for another evening. April would yell hell if she caught him tilting his lance at anything except what Rogenet needed to prove Mac's full-time residency in Linder County. Maggie wouldn't; the dining-room hostess would simply roll her eyes.

He started online. The *Rockford Register-Star* had put the old story in its Web archives. Pribilski had been a local boy, and the accounts were respectful. He'd honored himself with the U.S. Marines, and was well liked by his fellow workers at the DeKalb-Peering Telephone Company. A photo in uniform showed him to be nice-looking, with a broad Slavic face and blond hair.

The Rockford paper had ginned up their depiction of Betty Jo Dean. They'd used the swimsuit photo *The Democrat* had run, and reported that the killings had occurred under a full moon, in words that subtly inferred Betty Jo had been a temptress who'd lured the innocent, unsuspecting young man to his death on lovers' lane. The paper had reported the seemingly endless list of leads Chief Deputy Reems was pursuing, noting that all were coming up dry.

Mac leaned back in his chair. He always felt uneasy around Reems the few times he'd talked to him. The man projected a false heartiness, an artificial bumpkin's smile that never got to his eyes. Clamp's eyes were coyote's eyes, always searching, always registering, always hunting. Still, it must have taken such eyes to chase out the unsavory elements that had dirtied Grand Point for so many years.

It must have been particularly galling to those eyes to have never found the murderers of Pauly Pribilski and Betty Jo Dean.

He switched off the computer, went out and drove to the courthouse. The sheriff's department was in the basement.

'Clamp around?' he asked the desk sergeant.

The middle-aged man smiled. 'Clamp's never around. He likes to keep moving.'

'I need to talk to him about an old case.'

'Which case?'

'Betty Jo Dean.'

The desk sergeant's smile went away. 'Clamp still takes that one personally.'

'Nothing's ever been learned?'

'Why are you digging in that?'

'A constituent asked about it.'

'I'll tell Clamp you dropped by,' the sergeant said, finding something to look at on his desk.

Mac went up the stairs, crossed Second Street and walked two blocks south. Like all the buildings close to the courthouse, the brown brick library was old. The plaque outside said it had been built with funds donated by Andrew Carnegie in 1908. The poster inside said their collections had outgrown the facility and they needed new benefactors.

'May I help you?' the woman behind the desk asked. Her curt tone suggested she was interested in no such thing.

She wore no nametag; everyone knew everyone in Grand Point. Except Mac. He didn't know the woman's name, but he recognized the curtness. After the indictment, it was everywhere.

'You've got the *Democrat* on microfilm?' he asked.

'Nope.'

'How about the *Rockford Register-Star?*'

She got up with a sigh, led him down to the basement with a sigh and unlocked an old oak door. With another sigh. A solitary microfilm reader sat on a chipped, gray metal table. She switched it on to warm it up and walked to a beige metal cabinet. Opening the twin doors, she asked, 'What do you need to see?'

'June, 1982.'

For an instant, she seemed to freeze in front of the rows of small boxes. The she said, 'Here we go,' and handed him a box.

He looked at its label. 'This says 1981.' He handed it back to her.

Her hand shook, taking it from him. 'My mistake.' She put it back, and made a show of looking again.

Even standing well behind her, Mac could see the obvious gap in the row of film boxes. The first and second half-years of the Rockford paper for 1982 were missing, just as Pam the waitress had said.

The librarian made a nervous little laugh. 'I surely don't understand this.'

'No matter, I'll come back,' he said.

She was obviously lying. She'd known those films were missing. Likely enough, she knew they were never coming back, either.

He walked north to the True Value hardware store and climbed the adjacent stairs to the office of the *Peering County Democrat*. He'd gone there once to be interviewed during the mayoral campaign. Horace Wiggins hadn't bothered to conceal that his interest was a sham, a formality. Like Jen Jessup, the *Democrat*'s publisher had made no secret of his support for the then mayor, Pete Moore.

Only the assistant, a dour woman in her sixties, was in the office. It was rumored that she was the publisher's mistress. That had to be well back in the day, for it was hard to imagine the pinched-face woman writhing beneath anyone, even one as equally pinch-faced as Horace Wiggins.

'Horace be back soon?' he asked her.

'Lunch,' she said, adding pointedly, 'with Pete Moore.'

'Lunch with an ex-mayor certainly sounds like fun,' Mac said, with a grin.

The assistant made a frown, deepening her already descending crevasses.

'You've been here since Horace took over the *Democrat* from his father, right?'

'1979.'

'The library says they don't have microfilms of your old issues.'

'We've got them going back to 1937.'

'On microfilm, or disc, or file?'

'Actual issues. Horace keeps them in his garage.' She took a long, weary breath to show annoyance. 'How can I help you, Mr Bassett?'

'I thought Horace might like to hear my side of the indictment story.' Wiggins had run the Linder County state's attorney's indictment verbatim, but hadn't bothered to call for Mac's response.

'Bit late, aren't you?'

'Truth is always timely.'

'I'll be sure to pass that along.'

He walked down the stairs before the poor woman's face cracked into pieces.

It was only when he got to the Bird's Nest that he realized he'd blown off his constituent hour at the Willow Tree. Maybe it was time. No one was going to show up anymore.

The two women in his life were readying the restaurant for the dinner hour, except they no longer called it that. Now they called it the prayer hour, that time of day they prayed for people to show up.

April, the ex-Mrs Bassett, was in the kitchen. Tall and statuesque, she towered over their head cook, furious at his most recent infraction, whatever that might have been. She didn't bother to nod at Mac as he passed through.

There was no nonsense to April. Except for agreeing to marry Mac – something she rectified with divorce as soon as she came to her senses, she liked to say – she was a high-speed practical woman, long on concentration, short on tolerance. Seeing her now, berating their cook, Mac was reminded of the first time two priests from the local parish stopped in for a drink. They'd been fishing in the Royal River and were dressed in shabby clothes. 'April,' Mac had called out when she'd breezed into the bar, focused on a clipboard, 'I'd like to introduce you to two Fathers from town.' April had looked up, made a quick study of their clothes and their unshaven faces. 'If they're priests, then I'm the frickin' Virgin Mary,' she'd said without breaking stride on her way into the kitchen.

The priests had had the good humor to laugh. Mac had had the relief to laugh, too.

April's domain was the kitchen. She was comfortable in heat and chaos, amid things that had sharp edges or banged loudly.

Maggie Day moved more softly. Shorter than April, and thinner, she favored straw cowboy hats, tinted rimless glasses and loose, black clothing. He and April had known Maggie for years. She'd been the hostess at a popular Linder County restaurant and had helped out, from time to time, at their dinner playhouse. They'd considered themselves lucky when she'd agreed to come out to Grand Point to run their dining room.

That day, as usual, she moved purposefully through the room, straightening each silverware setting. There was never a day, Tuesday through Sunday, that the restaurant didn't welcome customers with immaculately arranged silverware, tables and chairs, and a soft hello from Maggie Day.

April managed the kitchen; Maggie the dining room. Both had long ago given up trying to manage Mac.

Maggie frowned when he came in, and pointed toward the far wall. A woman sat at one of the tables, with her back to the door. She was sipping coffee.

Maggie arched an eyebrow under the bent brim of her hat. 'Can you believe the brass on that woman?' she whispered. 'She had the nerve to say you invited her.'

'I suppose I did,' he said.

TWENTY-SIX

'Jen Jessup, it's a pleasure,' Mac said, sitting down with his own cup of coffee.

The slender newswoman, auburn-haired, dark-eyed and at least ten years younger than Mac, studied him. 'You really mean that?'

Mac smiled. 'Not a chance in hell.'

'Why an interview about your indictment now? You've been avoiding me since it was first announced.'

'You've been biased against me ever since I ran for mayor.'

'You were a carpetbagger, seeking to settle a personal score.' She took a tiny, digital recorder from her purse. 'No matter. Give me all of it.'

He took her through it all, ending with his most recent conversation with his lawyer.

'You're really going to countersue?'

'Ryerson Wainwright distorted my occasionally being too tired to drive home as a means of political payback.'

'For pinning him to the mat for questionable expenses?'

'It's pathetic.'

'It seems simple. You violated Linder County's residency law for trustees by residing here, albeit on a cot.'

'For a few hundred in expenses? It's an obvious sham.'

'Were you planning to run for mayor of Grand Point while you were still collecting compensation as a Linder County trustee?'

'Of course not. My decision to run against Pete Moore came after I'd left the board and moved here. He tried to slice off part of my parking lot for a turning lane – which, by the way, would improve egress from his own vacant land across the street.'

'You're using me now to announce your countersuit, firing a warning shot across Ryerson Wainwright's bow.'

'You bet.'

'Fair enough.' She switched off the recorder and put it in her purse.

'Betty Jo Dean,' he said.

'I've heard you've been asking around about her,' she said.

'Does the case stink?'

'Why ask me?'

'I was given the article you wrote on the twenty-fifth anniversary of the murders.'

'Lots of deaths that summer of 1982.'

'What do you mean?'

'Never mind.'

'Nobody wants to talk about it,' he said.

'Go see your current sheriff, Jimmy Bales. Or better still, Clamp Reems. He was in charge of the investigation.'

'I stopped in to see Reems. He wasn't in.'

'And now you're waiting for his call?' She smiled.

'I'm not that naive. There's precious little on the Web. The Rockford newspaper microfilms have disappeared from the library. All I have is that article you wrote in 2007.'

'Bella asked me to do that.'

'Bella?'

'Bella Dean Telkin, Betty Jo's older sister. She called me, saying I should write something about why the murders were never solved. I was in sixth grade when they happened, so I had to research, like you're doing now. I had difficulties, like you're having. No one wanted to talk, not in Grand Point. Sheriff Bales said the case was too old to fuss with. Clamp Reems talked to me, but he didn't give me anything that hadn't been in the papers. I drove to Rockford and looked at their police files. They were filled with discounted leads. I went to the *Register-Star*. None of their old reporters from back then is still working. I read every bit of their old copy. It was a sensational case in 1982, and it went nowhere.'

'The case that died too fast?'

'They say none of the leads panned out.'

'Your piece was choppy, at the end.'

'Horace Wiggins, here in Grand Point, wanted no part of it. I got it run only in DeKalb, where I live, but even there they insisted on whacking off the last couple of paragraphs.'

'Why?'

'I editorialized, questioning why the case had been allowed to die. The editor was right to cut that. It was opinion, not journalism.'

He walked her out, but she called an hour later. 'We're set to meet with Sheriff Bales tomorrow morning. You can ask him what happened to the investigation.'

'Why did you set it up?'

'I'd like to do an update.'

'That nobody might want?'

'I'll still get to see the look on your face when Jimmy Bales comes across the desk at you.'

TWENTY-SEVEN

'Bullshit, absolute bullshit,' Sheriff Jimmy Bales yelled at Jen Jessup. Then, turning, purple-faced, to Mac, 'You ought to know better, too, even for a damned—' Suddenly, Bales shut his mouth.

'For a damned what . . . upcoming convict, perhaps?'

'Choose your own words, Mr Mayor.' He slurred the title – may-yore – like it was profane.

'You had so many leads,' Mac said.

'Clamp did; it was before my time. And he chased down every damned one of them. Why don't you go ask him why this case fell apart?'

'I will. But it's your department now. What have you done recently?'

'I was eighteen when Betty Jo got murdered.'

'Same age as her, about?'

'A year older. I knew her. We all knew her.'

'All the more reason you'd want to find her killer.'

'With what money and what personnel? We've got budget cuts. People would have my head if I dropped current crimes to go sniffing around an old case that couldn't be solved even when the clues were fresh.'

'You'd rather they believe anyone can get away with murder in Peering County if they just wait it out?'

Bales snuck an anxious glance at Jen Jessup, no doubt afraid she'd use that in print. 'You're twisting my words. You know damn well what I mean.'

'What's in the case report?'

Bales opened a side desk drawer and pulled out a brown accordion file. 'Not much,' he said.

He spread the contents on his desk. There was a thick stack of typed, 'City of Rockford – Department of Police' letterhead sheets, bound together by a large black clip. Another twenty sheets of handwritten notes, in different sizes and colors, were loose. There was one black-and-white photograph.

Bales waved at the mess on his desk. 'Be my guest,' he said, with just the slightest smile.

Mac looked at Jen Jessup, who so far had said nothing. She shook her head. 'I went through it all for that piece I wrote. Other than the crime scene photo, there's nothing there but dead leads.'

Mac flipped through the sheaf of Rockford police reports. Each was an officer's report detailing follow-up on a particular tip. The leads were widely varied, and ranged from a report that Pauly Pribilski once dated the ex-wife of an army sharpshooter to the incidence of a seventeen-year old Rockford boy caught trying to steal a box of .38 caliber bullets. Most of the leads had been sent up to Rockford by Chief Deputy Wilbur Reems.

'Clamp sent leads to the Rockford police?' Mac asked.

'Pauly Pribilski was one of their locals. They were anxious to help,' Bales said. 'Being as our department was understaffed then, like now, Clamp laid anything he could on the Rockford boys. Besides, this department had plenty of local leads to deal with, not to mention the town being up for grabs, what with all the reporters and nervous townspeople. And don't forget, Delbert Milner died right at the beginning of it.'

'Died of what?' Mac remembered Milner's name from Jen's article.

'Heart attack, almost right after he was called to where Betty Jo was discovered.'

Mac set down the Rockford reports and picked up a few of the loose, handwritten notes. One, written in black fountain pen ink, reported that Pribilski had met Betty Jo Dean at the Constellation, a bar Mac had never heard of, the night of the murders. Several others also referenced the Constellation, and a bartender named Dougie Peterson.

'Dougie Peterson?' he asked Bales.

'He imagined himself a sort of expert in the case, constantly coming up with new theories. A real pest, I heard.'

'He still around?'

'Drowned.'

Jen Jessup inhaled sharply and leaned forward. 'When?'

'End of that July, I think. That summer was hot. Damned fool must have been cooling off under the bridge. That's where they found him, bobbing, his head bashed up against the cement.'

Another sheet, this one pink and torn, summarized a rambling interview with a boy Betty Jo had dated once. Mac flipped through a dozen more notes. Most were soiled, like they'd been handled often, and equally vague. He set them on Bales's desk. 'Worthless,' he said.

'Nothing that's usable now,' Bales agreed, settling comfortably back in his chair.

'Why weren't these notes catalogued, taken better care of?'

'Lots of people pawed through them over the years, trying to solve the case.'

'Crap,' Jen said.

'Whoa, now, miss,' Bales said.

'It's true. What little is in your file has been treated like trash paper.'

'That photo?' Mac asked, pointing to the black-and-white picture that Bales had kept at his side of the desk.

The sheriff slid it across. 'Betty Jo Dean, as she was found.'

She lay face down in tall grass. Her blouse was hiked up, exposing the white back strap of her bra. The top two inches of her white panties showed above a tangle of weeds. Her right hand was outstretched in front of her, as though she'd tried to crawl away. The fingers of her left hand peeked out from beneath the right side of her body.

Her neck and head were completely obscured by the leaves.

Mac set the photo down. 'Where are the rest?'

'That's it, just the one,' Bales said.

'Only one crime scene photo?'

'Horace only took the one.'

'Horace Wiggins? The publisher of the *Democrat*?'

'Saved us a fortune over the years, not having to hire someone else.'

'Surely he was told to take more than one photo.'

'Why? Everybody knew who was lying there and how she'd died.'

Mac stared at the fool, but Bales wouldn't meet his eyes.

Mac pushed the Rockford sheets, torn notes and lone photograph back across the desk. 'This file has been gutted.'

'Ya think?' Jen Jessup said.

Bales ignored her sarcasm. His round face was calm. 'Betty Jo Dean got killed a long time ago. Things got lost.'

It was time to fire into the dark. 'I've heard talk there was a cover-up,' Mac said.

Bales's face flushed. 'Who the hell said that?'

'I heard some of the town's heavy operators put a lid on things.'

Bales stood up, fast as a rocket. 'We . . . we're done,' he stammered.

Jen Jessup followed Mac up the stairs. 'Nice bluff,' she said when they got outside.

'Nice rage, yourself, about that empty file. And nice gasp when you heard the Constellation's bartender drowned so soon after the murders. What's going on?'

'Are you going to ask Wiggins why he took only one picture?' she asked, dodging his question.

'Did you, when you wrote your article?'

'Wiggins said what Bales just said: one was all they needed.' She looked across the highway at what once was the phone company building. 'Old-timers will tell you this town used to be full of gambling, hookers, lots of drunks brawling on the sidewalks. Clamp Reems ran all that out. The heavy operators, as you call them, were respectful of him and of his investigation back then. Maybe they simply accepted that not all cases can be solved.'

'Or he was too respectful of them?'

'Meaning Clamp knew to keep quiet about their dirty laundry?' She nodded. 'Of course. It's a symbiotic relationship. They feed well off each other.'

'You think he knows more than he's told about Betty Jo Dean?'

'A good cop always does. There have been so many stories about who killed that young man and Betty Jo.'

'Your article reported couples, former boyfriends, former girl-friends and a peeper.'

'I could have mentioned dozens more. For instance, there was a teenage boy who had a reputation for sneaking up on cars parked along Poor Farm Road, for a little look-see at what was transpiring inside. Supposedly, this kid made no secret of being in love with Betty Jo. She wouldn't give him the time of day because, essentially, he was a twerp.' Jen arched her eyebrows. 'Know who that kid was?'

Mac shook his head.

'Jimmy Bales,' Jessup said.

'Jeez.'

'Jimmy wasn't the only one. Betty Jo had other admirers.'

Mac thought back to the check-marked photos in the Chamber of Commerce booklet. 'How about the heavy operators themselves, guys like Horace Wiggins, Bud Wiley or Doc Farmont?'

'And Luther Wiley, who took over the funeral home after his uncle Bud drank himself to death. Heck, I even heard that Clamp Reems himself had a thing for Betty Jo Dean. I'm not saying any of them were involved with her, but one thing's for sure: they were and are powerful men, and rumors bloom like flowers in fertilizer in this town. When it came to Betty Jo Dean, there were more flowers than most.'

'She must have been something.'

'They were young and ripe with life.'

'"They?" Aren't you just talking about Betty Jo Dean?'

She looked again at the old phone company building. 'I hope you don't give up on this, Mac Bassett.'

'There's nothing I can think to do.'

'Then think harder,' she said and walked quickly away, as though she'd said too much.

TWENTY-EIGHT

It was eleven o'clock. His stomach was doing loops from not having breakfast, perhaps. Or from too much Betty Jo Dean, more likely. The Willow Tree was just down the street. He took his usual booth but the usual waitress didn't come over.

'Where's Pam?' he asked the red-haired woman who came with coffee. The pin on her uniform said she was Alta.

'She quit. She's moving. Something about her mother being sick. Strange, though . . .' She paused.

Something fluttered in his stomach. 'Strange?'

'She told me both her parents died when she was young.'

'You remembered wrong?'

She gave him a look that said she'd done no such thing. Ever.

'You think there's something wrong about her leaving?'

'I didn't say that,' she said quickly.

'You've lived in Grand Point for a while, right?'

'My whole fifty-one years.'

'Remember 1982?'

'Betty Jo Dean?'

'Yes.'

'I saw you talking with Pammy last time. Don't know what set her off, but all of a sudden she got goofy about those old killings. Boss had to tell her to stop pestering everybody.'

'You knew Betty Jo Dean?'

'Not well. She was Pinktown and I'm regular Grand Point. I was a year ahead of her in high school. And, of course, I graduated.'

He caught the inference. 'Pinktown? Trashy houses, trashy people?'

'Some say.'

'Betty Jo was a little trashy, too?'

'She liked the boys, and gave them reason to like her.'

'You tell Pam that?'

'Told her no good would come from poking into those old killings,' she said. 'You know what you want to order?'

He'd lost what little appetite he'd brought in. 'Just one scrambled egg.'

Alta wrote it down.

'One more thing,' he said. Alta would know who came to have breakfast, Tuesdays and Fridays, in the private dining room.

'Yes?'

Something vague cautioned his mind. 'Never mind,' he said.

'Damn it, is this really the time?' April fumed when he told her of needing to see Pam in DeKalb.

'She cared enough to get interested in the case of a murdered girl.' He tried a smile, but it wasn't getting him past April's eyes. They'd narrowed.

'Making sure there's nothing sinister in Pam's leaving is more like it.'

'That, too.'

'Waitresses quit because of personal emergencies all the time. You've seen it here.'

'Her phone's disconnected. I got her address from another waitress. I'll swing over to her place, give her the news and be back in a couple of hours.'

'Chances are she's left town.'

'I want to chase this down. I think there's a chance she quit because of the questions she was asking.'

'About the killing of a teenage girl?'

'Sure.'

'How old?'

'I'm not sure how old Pam is.'

'No – how old was the murdered girl?'

'Seventeen, I think.'

'Seventeen, you think? Or seventeen you damned well know.'

'All right, seventeen. And yes, she was born in 1965.'

She nodded, satisfied she didn't need to say anymore. 'Friday is our biggest night.'

'You supervise the kitchen, like always. You've got Maggie for the dining room, like always. If I'm late getting back all you have to do extra is watch the bar.'

'Ah, hell,' she said, a positive sign. 'You'll try to be back early?'

He could only nod.

Pam Canton's address was a brown wood two-story apartment building in DeKalb. Several cars were parked on the graveled-over backyard. It was cheap housing for students at Northern Illinois University, just across town.

According to the mailboxes inside, Pam lived in the basement level at the rear. Her door was wide open.

'Anybody here?' Mac called in.

'Looking to rent?' a man's voice answered. 'This will be ready tomorrow.'

Mac stepped into the two-room efficiency apartment. An

unmade bed stood against the far wall. The only other furnishings were a television and a straight-back wood chair.

The landlord was in the bathroom, throwing toiletries into a plastic garbage bag.

'I'm looking for Pam,' Mac said.

'She left. She called me this morning at work, said her brother was having complications from an appendectomy and that she had to go take care of his kids. She was gone by the time I got here.'

'Her mother, you mean? Pam told her boss it was her mother who was sick.'

'You know her?'

'A little.'

'She told me it was her brother.'

'She beat you out of any rent?'

'Not a dime. She said she was taking classes in the fall and paid up through the end of the month. Here's what else I don't understand: it was obvious she was close to broke, yet she left clothes, sheets, towels.'

'And that television?'

The landlord made a show of eyeballing Mac carefully. 'Who are you, exactly?'

'A friend from Grand Point. No idea where she might have gone?'

'I don't know anything, except I got to rent this place again. Damn; I figured her for staying more than two months.'

Walking out, he noticed two cabinets over the kitchen counter. Both were filled with dry food; energy bars, a full box of Cheerios, a dozen cans of soup, a can of coffee – stuff that could have been swept fast into a shopping bag, even by a woman in a hurry. She'd taken none of that, either.

Pam Canton, a woman working for tips to go to school, hadn't left to help an ailing mother or brother.

She'd fled.

TWENTY-NINE

ac got back to the Bird's Nest earlier than expected, which met with April's approval. She told him the bartender had called in sick, which also met with her approval, for it saved an evening's base wages. For the next hours he tended the bar and watched the replay of an old NBA semi-final on a sports channel. When it was over, the thin group at the bar thinned even more, down to three old-time Grand Point men – Farris Hobbs and two others – who talked slow and drank even slower.

Business hadn't been any better in the dining rooms. The regular fifteen couples who came to the restaurant for fish every Friday, come rain, shine, or nuclear war, Mac always used to think, had thinned too, down to only ten other couples, making it one of the worst Fridays they'd ever had. Maggie sent the three waitresses home at eight o'clock.

After she closed the kitchen, April motioned for him to step into the hall. 'Rogenet called this afternoon, looking for you. He said you were going to stop by. How much is this countersuit going to cost?'

'As he put it, "What's the cost if I don't do it?"'

'Frickin' bloodsuckers.'

'It's worth a shot if it puts Wainwright on the defensive.'

'But it won't alter the facts, will it? Those basic facts you still haven't put down on paper?'

'How can I say where I was sleeping on any given night? I spent a lot of days here, but who can prove anything about my nights?'

'Don't be naive. Wainwright will get testimony, even if it's manufactured, from all the friends you made here in Grand Point defeating Pete Moore.' The sarcasm was true.

'I'm innocent until proven guilty. Wainwright's got to prove I wasn't sleeping in Linder County.'

She rolled her eyes. 'Mac Bassett, ever the believer in justice. Tell your over-billing bastard lawyer we need a discount.'

He took a breath. 'I'm thinking about going into Chicago tomorrow,' he said.

'Oh, Christ.'

'Just for the day.'

'Does this have to do with that waitress leaving her Grape Nuts behind?'

'And a television,' he said, knowing in an instant it sounded lame.

'Frickin' evil's afoot, for sure, Holmes.'

'Something's wrong, April.'

'Wrong enough to prevent you pulling together information that might keep you out of jail? Wrong enough to keep you from finding time to sign papers for your countersuit? You bet something's wrong. You've become obsessed with this teenage girl, seeing a link—'

'I'll only be in Chicago for the day.'

'—to another girl who was also born in 1965,' she finished.

'Chicago's Washington Library has a huge collection of old newspaper microfilms.'

She pointed to the few men sitting at the bar. 'There are three old-timers who'd probably love to jaw about an old crime, especially if you pour on the house. Cheaper than driving all the way to Chicago.'

'I want to read what the Chicago papers reported. I'll see Rogenet on Monday about my countersuit.'

'This little trip will make the obsession go away?'

He nodded as though he believed it.

Her face relaxed a little. 'I'll take the deal. Go to Chicago tomorrow; stay overnight if you have to research more on Sunday. But come Monday, without fail, you're with Rogenet, plotting to keep your ass out of jail.'

He nodded, and she marched back into the kitchen.

By then, the last of the diners left. On her way out, Maggie motioned for Mac to walk her to the front door.

'Something's not right here,' she whispered.

He looked at the empty dining room. 'Really?'

She didn't laugh. 'I don't mean that,' she said. 'Are you sure you want to disturb the Betty Jo Dean thing?'

'You've been talking to April.'

'April hasn't said a thing. Word's starting to filter around that you're nosing into an old crime, and I'm getting a feeling. Just . . . I don't know. Be sure of what you're doing, I guess,' she said, and went outside.

He walked back into the bar area, silenced the volume on the overhead television that no one was watching and said, 'Grand crimes in Grand Point, Illinois.'

Farris Hobbs groaned. 'Here we go again: Betty Jo Dean and the Polish guy. He grilled me about that, night before last,' he said to the others. 'Bought me an extra drink, on the house, he did.'

The prospect of free booze should have set all their glasses to tapping on the glossy counter. It didn't. To a man, they stared up at the muted television screen, not speaking.

'All right, all right,' Mac said, as though he'd been met with a clamor. 'I'll buy the next round.' He lined up fresh glasses and poured each man another of what he'd been drinking.

No one reached for the new booze.

'The mere mention of a crime from 1982 stops you cold?' he asked.

'Not much to tell, is all,' said the man who used to run the movie theater. He was eyeing the new, full glass in front of him apprehensively, as though touching it would obligate him to say more.

'The case got stalled years ago,' said the town's tow truck driver.

'But there were so many leads,' Mac said.

'So many dead ends.' Farris Hobbs pointedly pushed his new drink a couple inches away, a master of self-control.

The tow truck driver stood up, his drink untouched. 'Rumor was most of them tips were made up by our own deputies to keep the Rockford coppers the hell out of the way.' He headed for the door.

'Ever hear that the killer might have been local, someone influential enough to stop the investigation?' Mac asked.

That did it for the man who used to run the movie theater. 'Sweet shit, don't talk like that.' He, too, headed for the door.

Farris Hobbs pulled his drink back to within clutching distance. 'It was so long ago,' he said.

The tightness on his face showed that nothing more was going to come out of his mouth. Mac turned up the television.

THIRTY

The highway heading east out of Grand Point was deserted at seven-thirty on Saturday morning.

Mac had barely gotten four hours sleep. His bedside Scotch had begged another, and that begged still another, to dull the churnings in his mind about a waitress who disappeared and men sitting at a bar, too afraid of thirty-year-old killings to sip a free drink.

A car charged up behind him. Mac recognized the shape of the grill. It was a Cadillac Sedan DeVille, so shiny it looked like it had just been polished.

He knew someone who owned a car like that. That bastard, Ryerson Wainwright, drove a DeVille. His was bright red, to attract the most attention. Wainwright kept it highly polished. He lived by sparkle.

The car swung out into the oncoming lane, pulled abreast and blew past his laboring truck. In an instant it was only a dark speck in the distance.

He'd not gotten a glimpse of the driver, but he recognized the red.

What he couldn't figure was why Wainwright had been in Grand Point at such an early hour.

The Harold Washington Library was an enormous mausoleum of bricks and granite in Chicago's downtown Loop. The newspaper microfilms were kept in long rows of putty-colored cabinets on the second floor.

The *Chicago Tribune*'s coverage, on the inside pages, was terse and dense with facts: many leads were being chased down; low-flying planes had aided ground search teams; Pauly Pribilski had been found in a field, shot multiple times; Betty Jo was discovered under a tree with one bullet embedded in her skull.

The *Tribune* had run four photos in five days. He'd already seen the first, of Pribilski in his Marine uniform. The second, of Betty Jo wearing a plaid top and smiling into the camera, was taken in seventh grade. The third picture showed the Devil's Backbone the morning she was found, crowded with cops. The final photograph was of her father, dressed in a light-colored suit, helping his wife into a car to ride to the funeral.

The *Tribune*'s last report ended with a bit of poignancy. Betty Jo was buried in the dress she was to have worn to her brother's upcoming wedding.

The *Daily Reporter*'s first piece was more lurid. A front-page headline trumpeted, 'Murder at Moonlight Tryst,' reporting that Pribilski had been shot once in the heart, then four times, fast, in the lower abdomen. They'd run two photos – Pribilski's Marine picture, and the swimsuit shot of Betty Jo that Wiggins had run in the *Peering County Democrat*.

A day later, the *Daily Reporter* had reported that a psychic, Abigail Beech, had contacted the Dean family to tell them their daughter was alive, and in the company of a dark-haired man.

Mac leaned back from the microfilm reader. He knew Abigail Beech. He'd hired her to do a dinnertime psychic act a couple of times the previous winter. She'd been a hit, moving from table to table, asking a little, telling a little, making the customers laugh. His customers enjoyed her, and he planned to have her back. She came in, now and again, for dinner. Maggie often joined her for a moment, in a booth.

The *Daily Reporter*'s third report offered titillating details: Betty Jo Dean had been discovered almost nude, dressed only in a girdle, and was known in the community as a girl of many loves. According to one of her friends, Betty Jo thought of all her boyfriends as good Joes, and used to say, 'I love 'em and I leave 'em,' also quoting an anonymous local bartender who said, 'Betty Jo didn't care whether a man was married or not.' Clamp Reems was also quoted, saying only that 'the murders may be hard to unravel because beautiful Betty Jo Dean led such a complicated life.'

His head ached from squinting at the microfilm reader. He put the rolls away. Jen Jessup had recapped everything of value. He'd learned nothing new other than an act he'd hired for the restaurant had once passed herself off as a legitimate psychic.

He went out into the bright sunlight of mid-afternoon. Though it was a Saturday, traffic headed toward the outbound expressway was choked to a standstill. He walked down to a striped-awning restaurant that sold small things on rolls at prices the Bird's Nest couldn't get for a whole meal. Thinking to wait until traffic died down, he ordered coffee and a smoked ham sandwich, and rationalized while he ate: people got murdered every day. Some of them were young, seventeen years young, and some of those cases would never be solved. That was the horror of the world he'd known since he was nineteen.

An hour later, traffic was still not moving. He went back to the library to kill another hour, and took out a microfilm spool labeled, '*Chicago Sun-Times*, May–July, 1982.' He forwarded it to the last ten days of June.

Unlike its competitors, the *Sun-Times* had reported nothing in the first days following the murder. He kept his finger on the advance button, only half interested in watching bygone times scroll by, until he got to Tuesday, June 29, 1982, a full week after the discovery of Pauly Pribilski's body.

He jerked his hand away like he'd been jolted by electricity.

A huge headline ran across all of pages two and three: 'WHAT'S WRONG IN GRAND POINT?' Underneath were thousands of angry-looking words.

It wasn't the text, though, that dried his mouth like it had been chalked. It was the name of one of the reporters, up at the top in the byline.

Jessup. Laurel Jessup.

THIRTY-ONE

An editor named Leon Eddings had prefaced the piece: 'The *Chicago Sun-Times* is proud of the wide-ranging, hard-hitting, fact-based coverage it extends to its readers throughout all of Northern Illinois. Our reporter, Jonah Ridl, submitted the following immediately prior to embarking on a national assignment. Because Mr Ridl's report raises disturbing questions and infers actions and motivations that are still being examined, we are offering what follows as editorial content, and not as our usual, doubly-verified presentation of facts.'

It was an odd beginning, written as though the editor was trying to keep the *Sun-Times* from being sued.

Odder still, the editor had not mentioned the second reporter, Laurel Jessup. It seemed beyond coincidence that she shared a last name with Jen Jessup.

Much of the *Sun-Times* piece read like the other newspaper accounts, though there was far more detail. Published a week after the discovery of Pribilski's body, the reporters had had the benefit of hindsight. They'd carefully summarized the case through the manhunt for Betty Jo Dean, the sheriff's department's announcements of an almost unfathomable myriad of leads, Thursday's discovery of the young girl's body and Friday's death of Sheriff Delbert Milner.

And then the straight-up reporting ended and the piece adopted an accusatory tone.

'In the days to come,' it went on, 'it is likely that a public clamor will rise up to demand answers from the Peering County Sheriff's Department about many inconsistencies in this matter.

'Why hasn't much been made of the shots to Pribilski's groin? Why was his body hurriedly washed and his fingernails trimmed, without a forensic examination for incriminating traces of his assailant's blood that may have been lodged on his person?

'Why does the sheriff's department insist that Betty Jo Dean's body was dumped alongside the Devil's Backbone Road the same night Pribilski was killed, when teams later on that Tuesday and

Wednesday (including one in which a *Sun-Times* reporter participated) searched the very spot where she was subsequently found? How could she have been missed repeatedly?

'Why was only one photograph taken of Betty Jo Dean at the site where she was discovered? Why is her head completely obscured beneath leaves in that lone photograph? Why were the leaves not removed for subsequent photos that would show the condition of her body, especially the entry wound of the bullet(s) that killed her?

'Why were so many onlookers allowed to trample the sites where the bodies were discovered? Why did the sheriff's department not cordon off the areas for examination?

'Why does it appear that the sheriff's department is rushing in so many different and contradictory directions?

'What did Sheriff Delbert Milner suspect? How did Milner really die?

'Finally, was anyone else murdered because of what they knew about these killings?'

A voice came over the library's speakers. It was four forty-five. The library would close in fifteen minutes.

He forwarded quickly through the next issues. The *Sun-Times* hadn't run any more articles about the murders in Grand Point. That was strange. Even more odd, there was nothing more written, on any subject, by either Jonah Ridl or Laurel Jessup.

He printed the article, returned the spool to the microfilm cabinet and ran to the information desk. He'd left his smart phone in the truck. 'Where are your general-use computers?'

'There, but we're closing,' she said, pointing to an alcove. A dozen computer stations stood in a row.

'The access code,' he said.

'Nine minutes,' she said, hurriedly writing the code on a slip of paper.

Mac logged on at the closest one and Googled, 'The *Chicago Sun-Times*, Jonah Ridl.' Hundreds of listings appeared, but all seemed to refer to a gang slaying earlier in 1982.

'Six minutes,' the librarian called across the cavernous, empty room.

He keyed in the online white page directory for Illinois. There was no Ridl listed in the entire state. Typing fast now – only five minutes were left – he expanded his search to the national pages. There were eleven Ridls in the United States.

Across the room the librarian was noisily clearing off her desk. He started writing down the phone numbers.

'Sir!' the woman shouted across the room.

The white page numbers were probably a long shot anyway. Too many people had jettisoned landlines for unlisted cell phones.

'Sir!' The woman had stood up and was jangling her keys. The huge ceiling fluorescent lights were clicking off, one row at a time.

He reached to turn off the computer. And had a thought.

He typed in the editor's name. Leon Eddings.

There was only one. He was in Chicago.

He ran the three blocks to the parking garage, grabbed his phone and started calling the Ridl numbers.

It went fast. Of the eleven, only six were home. None had ever been a reporter; none had ever known a reporter.

He called Leon Eddings. A robust voice answered.

'Did you used to be an editor of the *Chicago Sun-Times*?' Mac asked.

The man chuckled softly. 'At last I've won the Pulitzer?'

Mac laughed, almost giddy with relief. 'My name's Bassett, and I'm the mayor of Grand Point, Illinos,' he said. 'I'm calling about—'

The editor cut him off. 'You're calling about Jonah Ridl.'

'Yes. He was a—'

'I know who he was, damn it. It's just that I'd almost given up.'

'Given up?'

'I've been waiting over thirty years for someone from Grand Point to ask me about Jonah Ridl.'

THIRTY-TWO

Leon Eddings lived in a northwest suburb of Chicago, in a green-sided house directly beneath a flight path to O'Hare International Airport.

The editor was short and stocky, with a ruddy complexion and a fringe of white hair surrounding a bald head. Mac guessed his age to be eighty.

He led Mac into a small living room filled with overstuffed furniture, magazines stacked on the floor and the day's newspaper spread open on the couch. A lace doily had fallen off the arm of one of the chairs and lay on the worn carpet like a monstrous snowflake. Eddings picked it up and put it back on the chair. 'Things get messed up, now that my wife has passed on,' he said, motioning for Mac to sit down.

'I'm sorry. Recently?'

'Five years ago,' he said with a sheepish grin. 'I can make coffee, unless you'd like Scotch?'

'What am I going to need?'

'Scotch,' the man announced. He went into the dining room, came back with two glasses and a bottle of generic Scotch. He poured two inches into each glass, set the bottle on the cocktail table between them and sat on the sofa.

'Thank you for driving out,' Eddings said. 'As soon as you mentioned you were the mayor of Grand Point, the old juices got running and I wanted to put a face to the voice.'

A plane thundered overhead, low enough to rattle the bottle on the table. The old man didn't seem to mind, and used the moment to savor a slow sip of his Scotch.

When the plane had passed, he said, 'As I told you on the phone, I've been waiting years for someone to come and ask me about Jonah Ridl.'

'You were very cryptic.'

Eddings nodded his head approvingly. 'Cryptic? There's a fine word, and not used much anymore. Yes, I suppose I was cryptic. I didn't want to say too much on the phone without knowing exactly why the mayor of Grand Point would come around, after all this time, to ask questions.' He raised his glass, signaling Mac to speak.

'A waitress asked me about two murders. There was little on the Internet, and nothing in our local library. I came into Chicago to use the newspaper microfilms at the Washington Library, and ran across Ridl's story.'

Eddings leaned forward. 'That's it?'

'Pretty much.'

Eddings tapped his nose. 'Smells like bullshit.'

'All right, there's a little more. The waitress who asked me about the killings said some of our influential locals get together for breakfast twice a week. She overheard one of them mention the name of the murdered girl, and then they all laughed. She thinks one or more of them knows more than was ever reported. She asked me to look into it.'

'And . . .?'

'Ridl and his co-writer went further than other reporters. They cited the same facts, but then they made big accusations.'

'Let me tell it chronologically,' Eddings said. 'I sent Ridl out to Grand Point on the Tuesday the young man's body was discovered. He was to gather facts on Tuesday, spend Wednesday chatting up local potential advertisers and be back in the newsroom with copy on Thursday morning. Thursday morning came; no story, no Ridl. He called that afternoon, saying he needed more time. We argued. I reminded him he'd been sent out to make us look, to advertisers, as though we covered the whole top of the state, clear out to Grand Point. I told him to take another day if it was so damned important, but I needed copy by Friday afternoon. Unspoken, but understood, was that I also needed a list of merchants our advertising people could contact.

'Friday came; again no Ridl, no copy. Again, a phone call. He said the story had grown even bigger, and he was going to write it long, at least two thousand words. He said he'd dictate it to a night man. And he said he had a kid working with him, a journalism student named Laurel Jessup, and that he promised her a byline credit. I said OK.'

'You cut Ridl a lot of slack.'

'A talent like Ridl doesn't come ordinarily to a basement operation like Special Features; he got hidden in us. He'd been part of a team of reporters investigating a street gang. The gang was big into drugs and prostitution. One of Ridl's sources bragged he was planning a hit on a member of a rival gang. Ridl wrestled with what he'd heard and decided he couldn't just stand by. He tipped the target, anonymously, thinking the guy would lay low for a while. The target didn't; he killed Ridl's source, the source's girlfriend and her four-year-old child. Hell broke loose, as you can imagine. Ridl became the news.'

Eddings held up the bottle. Mac shook his head. He had a long drive back to Grand Point.

The old editor rewarded himself with another two inches. 'The big bosses could have fired him; *should* have fired him, as a show of journalistic responsibility. They didn't. They were better than that. They dumped him into the anonymity of my domain, where he wrote trifling little pieces under my name that we used to fill the spaces between real news and ads. Ridl was traumatized, but he adapted. The furor died down; people became enraged by different things and quit writing to the paper, demanding that Ridl be let go.

'Six months passed. Outwardly, Ridl appeared all right, but if you caught him in an unguarded moment you could see the pain was still there. And so I, in my infinite wisdom, seized upon the brilliant idea of sending him to Grand Point. It was an advertising mission and the story looked ordinary, a run-of-the-mill lovers' lane tragedy. It was right up his old alley but without potential for controversy, a way to get a sniff of what he used to be so good at. Of course, I was secretly hoping he'd come back raring to get transferred back up to Metro, where he rightfully belonged.'

He reached for the bottle, shook his head and set down his glass instead. 'There was a message waiting from our night man when I got in Monday. Ridl never called. Turns out he mailed in the story handwritten, on tablet paper. We got it on Tuesday. I tried calling his apartment. No answer. I tried tracking down the Jessup girl, found a family of that name in DeKalb. She'd fallen asleep at the wheel and been killed in a single car accident, late the same Thursday Betty Jo Dean had been found. I didn't need to intrude upon their grief to find out about Jonah.'

'Ridl must have learned of her death after he talked to you on Friday.'

'And that's why he mailed his piece. I think Jonah was in love with her, in some small, beginning way, and her death shut him down for good. He must have felt he got her killed, like he got that gang kid, the girlfriend, and the kid killed six months earlier. I never spoke to Jonah again.'

'He quit?'

'He vanished. His last paycheck never got cashed.'

'He never showed up at another newspaper?'

'I kept an eye out for years. He never surfaced again.'

'And the article? Did it make the splash you'd hoped?'

'Nothing beyond a few letters. I never had the heart to assign another reporter to follow up. The investigation died.' He smiled. 'At least, until now.'

'I don't know anything beyond what I've told you. No progress was ever made on the case.' Suddenly he felt impatient, anxious to be gone. He didn't want to think any more about the killer of another teenage girl getting away. He set down his glass. 'I really should be going.'

'Not so fast.' Eddings poured another inch into Mac's glass – the same stunt Mac had pulled on Farris Hobbs. 'As a resident – hell, as mayor of the town – you'd never heard of the murders until a few days ago?'

'Not a word. Either everyone's forgotten . . .' He let the rest of the thought dangle. No one had forgotten, not really.

'More likely, your townspeople are afraid to talk about it?' Eddings asked, finishing Mac's thought. 'And now that Betty Jo Dean has got your interest?'

'I don't know what I can do. The trail is cold.' He stood up. 'I have a long drive.'

'You don't want to know where Ridl is?'

Mac dropped back into his chair like cement. 'You know?'

'Twin Lakes, Wisconsin. An hour from here.'

'How did you find him?'

'I didn't. Someone in the newsroom had a cottage up there, years ago. He was driving to town and chanced to see a short, fat guy cutting grass at their city hall. He'd grown a beard, but damned if it wasn't Ridl. He tried to talk to him but Ridl wouldn't shut off the mower.'

This time Mac got up, anxious for a whole different reason.

'I've got just one more question,' Eddings said at the door. 'You really came because a waitress heard some old men laugh?'

Too much was spinning in his head. 'No,' Mac said. 'I think I'm here because I keep hearing a dead girl scream.'

What he couldn't say, because now he didn't know, was which one.

THIRTY-THREE

He'd found a cheap motel several miles north of O'Hare Airport, because he was too agitated to do anything else, and had gone to bed with a belly full of Eddings' Scotch and a head full of Jonah Ridl. When he awoke the next morning the Scotch was gone, but Ridl remained. And the agitation still throbbed like something wild.

The map showed the drive would take an hour, as Eddings had said. It took two, because the highways going north to Wisconsin were clogged with summer Sunday traffic – cars and trucks and SUVs towing boats filled with laughing people headed north for picnics and water skiing and shrieking good times. Not a one of them looked to be an indicted, failing restaurateur, frittering what might be his last free days away on a murder most everybody had long quit caring about.

He turned off the highway at a sign that said Nippersink and drove along roads marked with letters and numbers instead of proper names. He came to an old-fashioned, full-service gas station and pulled in. A young man was working under a truck on a lift in one of the two service bays. 'Everybody knows Jonah,' he said. 'Been working for the city for forever. You a friend?'

'An old acquaintance.'

The young man grimaced. 'You haven't seen him in a while?'

'Quite a long time, actually,' Mac lied.

'You might want to brace yourself. Jonah's not looking too healthy these days. Nobody knows if he's seen a doctor. He keeps to himself – never did like talking much. One thing's for sure: he's lost a ton of weight, and he's got a cough.' The young man gave him directions that followed more roads designated with numbers and letters.

Ridl lived on a narrow road shaded with old trees. His house trailer was set on blocks in the middle of a clearing that had gone to the same sort of tall grass that grew along the Devil's Backbone.

An old yellow Volkswagen convertible was parked on the ruts that served as a drive. It was splotched with red and gray primer as though badly afflicted with two kinds of measles. A bicycle pump leaned against the flat front driver's side tire. The rear hood was up. An emaciated gray-haired, gray-bearded man was bent over the motor, doing something with a screwdriver. The last inch of a cigarette dangled from his mouth.

He didn't look like he'd ever been the round fellow Eddings had described.

Mac got out of his car. 'Jonah Ridl?'

The man straightened up with effort. He was only five foot five and looked to be at least seventy. 'I suppose,' he said.

'I'm the mayor of Grand Point, Illinois. You remember Grand Point?'

Ridl took the cigarette from his mouth and stubbed it into the dirt next to a thousand others. He coughed, deep and wet, spat onto the ground and lit another cigarette. 'Why are you here?'

'You dug deeper than the other reporters.' Mac told him about the waitress hearing men laughing behind a closed door about a dead girl, and of the current sheriff who didn't give a damn about an investigation that had gone no place at all. 'I came to Chicago to look at newspaper microfilms,' he said, 'and that got me to the piece you did for the *Sun-Times.*'

'The crowning glory of my journalism career,' he said. He coughed again and bent back to the car's engine.

Mac took the chance. 'There's only one person who's followed up on the crime.'

'Go away.'

'A part-time reporter named Jessup. She would have been a kid back then.'

Ridl took a long time to straighten up, as though he were shouldering all the pain in the world.

He suggested a beer.

THIRTY-FOUR

T he old man had begun wheezing like he was panicked for breath. They went to the front of the trailer where a lone webbed lawn chair was set next to a dented aluminum cooler. Ridl motioned for Mac to take the chair, reached into the cooler for two blue cans of Point Beer, handed one to Mac and sat on the lid.

'Not a damned thing has happened?' he asked when his breathing calmed.

'I didn't even know about the killings until a waitress mentioned them a few days ago.'

'It validates things, I suppose.'

'What?' Mac asked, startled.

Ridl offered up a weak smile. 'Sorry. I meant my rationalization for not hanging around your crooked little burg. I figured those murders would never be solved, and right now, I'm looking for all the rationalizations I can find.' He took a pull on his beer. 'Your waitress didn't give you the names of those men?'

'Maybe she didn't know them. She'd only been working there a few weeks.' Mac offered up his own weak smile, 'I didn't ask. I thought she was paranoid.'

'Why not ask her now?'

'She's gone. She grabbed some clothes and took off. Left an apartment full of food, bed sheets and towels.'

'She got threatened.'

'Or worse.'

'Or worse,' Ridl agreed. 'You could hang around that restaurant some morning, see who comes out of that private dining room.'

'I'd be noticed. These days I've become quite conspicuous.'

Ridl didn't ask what he meant. 'No matter. I'll bet I can still tell you who those men are: the newspaper publisher, the funeral home director and his nephew, any one of the number of sheriff's deputies who controlled the crime scene, perhaps a couple of bartenders from back in the day, some guys who gambled at the Wren House and anybody who conducted any autopsies, like the coroner or that local doctor, what's-his-name.'

'Romulus Farmont.'

'It's been some time. Everybody's still alive?'

'The funeral director drank himself to death.'

Ridl made a laugh that turned into another cough.

'You posed very specific questions.' Mac said, pulling the folded copy of Ridl's *Sun-Times* article from his pocket.

Ridl glanced over. 'I've never seen that.'

Mac held it out.

'No need, I remember.' Ridl closed his eyes. 'First, I questioned why the cops weren't bothered about Pribilski being shot multiple times in the groin. That indicated a crime of passionate rage, a shooter with an emotional tie to one of the victims. Neither Milner nor Reems expressed much interest in that line of inquiry.

'Next, I asked why the mortician was allowed to wash Pribilski and trim his nails without a forensic examination being conducted.'

'To destroy evidence, or can it be innocently explained as preparing the body for burial?' Mac asked.

'Either way, Bud Wiley had to get approval first. A bartender named Peterson was at the funeral home. He told me the place was crawling with people. Maybe Pribilski was thoroughly examined, though I doubted it.'

'Peterson?' Mac asked, recalling the name from his meeting with Jimmy Bales and Jen Jessup. 'Dougie Peterson?'

'"Dougie" it was,' Ridl said.

'He drowned, a month after the killings.'

Ridl closed his eyes again, and for a moment, Mac wondered if the man was breathing. He opened them, finally, and looked down toward the road. 'Poor, stupid Dougie. He saw the body and told the tale. His buddy, Luther, was the funeral director's nephew, and he snuck him in for a peek at the body. Dougie was the one who told me Pribilski had been shot in the groin multiple times.'

'Betty Jo was washed carefully, too?'

'No doubt, and her nails clipped as well. They hurried her into the ground the day after she was found, saying they were sparing the family since she was so decomposed.'

'You challenged the sheriff's department's belief that Betty Jo's body had been lying beside the Devil's Backbone since that Tuesday morning.'

'Search teams combed that exact area on the same morning Pribilski was found. I was with them on Wednesday, when they searched it again. She wasn't lying there then.'

Mac looked down at the *Sun-Times* article. 'You questioned why only one crime scene photo was taken of Betty Jo Dean. I've seen that photo.'

'Then you know her head was completely obscured by the leaves that had fallen off that tree. The photo was worthless, deliberately.'

'A cop directed that only one be taken?'

'Or the coroner, or someone from the funeral home. Or Wiggins might have taken several, but reported that only one turned out.'

'Blackmail?'

'Or he kept better ones in reserve, thinking he might need them to protect his own ass someday.' Ridl took a short pull on his beer. 'One more thing about those leaves: how could her body have laid on the ground for all of Tuesday and Wednesday, and through the night into Thursday morning, without those leaves getting disturbed by an animal attracted by her decaying, odiferous flesh?'

'It all adds credence to your belief that she was dumped after the search teams had been through on Wednesday, and those leaves were used to conceal evidence in a photograph.'

'Then again,' Ridl said slowly, 'covering her with those leaves could have been an act of tenderness.'

'My God,' Mac said.

'Remember how she was found? Her slacks were folded neatly on top of her, not just tossed down, as you'd expect from a killer. Those leaves might have been placed just as carefully to cover her head, her wound.'

'An act of passion, of consideration, like folding the slacks?'

'Pribilski's was a passionate kill as well, only that was rage.'

'The cops suspected this?'

'They allowed people to stomp all over Poor Farm Road, and they actually directed that the grass be cut along the Devil's Backbone. Whatever evidence might have existed in both places was destroyed.'

'A cop,' Mac said.

'Any one of several?' Ridl grinned, but there was no mirth in it. 'Could have been, but there again, not necessarily. It could have also been the coroner or the doc, or someone else with authority.'

'What about all the leads that fizzled, the couples and pairs of brothers and others, old boyfriends and old girlfriends?'

'You're asking if that, too, was the work of a cop, deliberately misdirecting? You're thinking Sheriff Milner and Clamp Reems kept everyone running around, chasing their tails, to obscure any real leads?' Ridl shook his head. 'I always thought Milner was the most intriguing character in the melodrama.'

Mac read aloud from the *Sun-Times* article on his lap. '"What did Sheriff Delbert Milner suspect? And how did Milner die?"'

'I think Milner was a good man, but a politician in over his head, trying to direct career cops. Did you read of a car seen speeding south from Poor Farm Road, being driven by an older man struggling with a younger woman?'

It had been mentioned in the Chicago papers. 'About the time Pribilski was killed? Clamp Reems said it was a hoax, a false lead,' Mac said.

'I think Reems was right. It was a false lead – made up by Milner.' Ridl stood up, reached to pull two new beers from the cooler, and sat back down. 'One of those cabins down by the river would have been a fine destination for a man abducting a girl. But Milner didn't have cause for warrants. He couldn't send people inside those shacks. I think he did what he could do in a hurry, and set off a ground search to send a message to whomever might be holding her in one of those cabins: "We know she's there, we're closing in. Release her while you can still cut a deal."'

Mac saw the horror of where Ridl was heading. 'But sending people down to those cabins had the opposite effect? Instead of triggering Betty Jo's release, it forced the killer's hand because he knew the searchers would be back soon with warrants?'

Ridl lit a cigarette, looked down toward the road for a minute. 'Sometime before dawn on the morning she was found, he took her to the Devil's Backbone and shot her.'

'That would have triggered Delbert Milner's heart attack, for sure.'

Ridl coughed fiercely, smoke and spit and maybe a little blood. 'Who the hell said it was a heart attack?'

'The current sheriff, Jimmy Bales.'

Ridl wiped his mouth with a stained handkerchief. 'I got to Milner's house early that Friday morning. Milner's widow was hysterical, insisting that her husband be taken out of town to a mortuary in DeKalb. I followed the ambulance, went in after they left . . .' Ridl stopped. A tear ran from his eye.

'How did Milner die, Jonah?'

'Gunshot to the head,' he said, in a whisper.

'Suicide? Grief at what he set in motion with that false tip?'

'I've always wondered. Now that you've told me about Dougie Peterson, I'm thinking maybe not. Maybe it was murder, for what he suspected.'

They sat for a time, saying nothing, and then Ridl asked, still in that same whisper, 'Is she tall? Is she almost too skinny? Fair complexion, coal-dark eyes, brown hair?'

'Jen Jessup is beautiful. She's in her early forties now.'

Ridl looked away. 'I egged Laurel on with the promise of a shared byline. She had an extraordinary source, someone who told her about Betty Jo getting slapped just a few days earlier. And about having an abortion – likely it was her killer's baby – some weeks before that.'

He turned to Mac. 'Supposedly Laurel fell asleep driving home from Grand Point, and I've so wanted to believe that, but I could never convince myself.' He reached to touch Mac's wrist. 'Do you see what your next step must be?'

'Yes,' Mac said.

THIRTY-FIVE

Mac was at the courthouse the moment it opened, and went first to the county clerk's office. Part of Ridl's story, one of his questions, seemed too incredible.

The mouse-like woman who handled vital records brought him a thick ring binder. It only took a minute to find Delbert Milner's death certificate. Dr Romulus Farmont, M.D., certified that the cause of death was a coronary embolism.

Not a gunshot wound.

That didn't prove anything, unless it pointed to a conspiracy to shroud Milner's cause of death, as Ridl had said.

He went down to the recorder of deeds office. 'I'd like to check land titles,' he told the orange-haired woman behind the counter. She was sixtyish, quite heavy, and looked to be unhappy about both.

Her eyebrows, dyed unnaturally to match her hair, moved closer together in confusion. 'You're thinking of staying?'

'I am,' he said, trying to beam. 'I'm thinking about buying a little weekend place, something along the river.'

'Don't you think you ought to wait . . .?' She let the thought trail off.

'Until my indictment is dismissed?'

'There is that; yes.'

'We're countersuing,' he said to her, and to the dozens of people she'd tell. 'Things are going to get interesting.'

'I heard that restaurant of yours is in difficulty.'

'Thank God for my trust fund,' he said, as though he had one.

Her eyebrows were almost touching in consternation now. 'What property do you have to see?'

'All of them along the river, south of Poor Farm Road.'

'Them old fishing cabins?'

'Some have been fixed up.'

'That area has changed some,' she allowed. 'Used to be that nobody wanted them old shacks for anything except to keep bait and maybe a fold-up cot for napping. You got a particular property in mind?'

'I might approach more than one owner.'

'I surely don't have time to guide you, property by property. You can do your own research.'

She left and came back with a large book held together with aluminum screw-posts. Flipping halfway through the pages, she turned the book so Mac could see. 'Every one of them's on this one page.'

She disappeared around the back row of shelves. A moment later, a chair groaned as her voice began murmuring. Jungle drums were beating; Mac Bassett was countersuing.

The left side of the ledger showed a drawing of irregularly shaped land parcels running parallel to the Royal River. A faint note at the top showed that the land was first subdivided twenty years before the Civil War. The first parcels had been large, but as the years went by, the parcels were divided, and divided again.

For over a hundred years, the dollars they fetched at sale were small. No one wanted to pay much for land that must have routinely flooded. But in the 1950s the dollars went up, and so did the assessments. Mac guessed that was when the dam was built, twenty miles up-river. No longer would the land along the river flood with every strong rain.

There were twenty-one properties, of which twenty had been developed with some sort of structure. Some of the names on the titles were familiar, doctors and dentists and druggists and merchants, sons and grandsons. But the names he was looking for, Wiggins or Farmont or Wiley, weren't there. Clamp Reems owned a property, but he'd bought it in August, 1982, six weeks after the murders.

Also that year, late in November, the largest of the parcels, a property at the extreme southern end of the string, had been reclassified and its taxes substantially reduced. 'Country Club Partners' was its listed owner.

'Excuse me?' Mac called to the murmuring woman.

'What is it now?' she yelled back, invisible.

'A question, and then I'm done,' he shouted.

'Hold your horses.' She materialized from behind the shelves.

He pointed his finger to Clamp Reems' property. 'Clamp told me he'd been down there longer than since August, 1982.' Reems had told him no such thing, but it was not a time for truths.

'Every mark in that ledger is right. I've been keeping it myself since 'seventy-five.'

'Well, someone's wrong.'

'He might have meant he was one of them belonged to the country club, before it burned,' she said.

He looked down at the ledger. 'That large property that got its taxes reduced?'

'It wasn't anywhere near an actual country club, leastways not in the way people think of such fancy places. That's just what they called it for the title. It was nothing but a shack, like the rest of the places down there.'

'Clamp owned it?'

'Don't know for certain whether he was one of them.'

'Come to think of it, I heard Clamp, Horace Wiggins, Bud Wiley and Doc Farmont all had a piece of that cabin.'

Her face slipped naturally into an expression of distaste. 'No telling who came and went down there, drinking, fishing, doing God knows what. Quite naturally, they didn't want to advertise their membership.'

He squinted at a brief notation. 'It burned on the Fourth of July, 1982?' That was just a few days after the murders.

'Fire took it in a flash. Punks, most likely, playing with fireworks.'

'It says Country Club Partners still owns the parcel.'

'Thought you were looking for a cabin.'

'Vacant land would do; I could build exactly the kind of place I have in mind.'

'Can't help you with who owns it. Money order comes twice a year for the taxes, saying the remitter is Country Club Partners.'

She closed the ledger and picked it up.

He left, thinking that Pauly Pribilski and Betty Jo Dean were still coughing up dead ends.

THIRTY-SIX

'**Y**ou can run, but you can't hide,' Rogenet said when Mac answered his phone.

'I'm in my truck. I can come over right away.'

'No need. I filed first thing this morning.'

'I thought you wanted to discuss it first.'

'April didn't tell you she called me Saturday?' Rogenet chuckled. 'After cussing me out for my invoices, we talked everything through. She's a smart woman, Mac. She knows the case as well as you. She said you talked about it, and I should go ahead at my discretion. This morning we filed on official misconduct, but we can always allege additional counts later. That's OK, right? She said what with the break-in and all—'

'The break-in?' Mac asked, suddenly the dumbest man in town. 'How bad was it?'

'Let me call you back,' he said.

April's car was in the parking lot. It shouldn't have been. The Bird's Nest was closed Mondays.

The kitchen door had a fresh square of plywood screwed where glass had been. The door was locked. He pulled out his key. It didn't work. He bent down to the cylinder. It was shiny, new. He pounded on the new plywood.

'I just talked to Rogenet,' he said when April opened the door.

'I should have told him you were too frickin' absorbed in playing detective to worry about staying out of prison. Lucky for you, I had the break-in to explain why you didn't call him.' She picked up two shiny keys from the counter and handed them to him. 'Things are crashing down, Mac. If you pull your head out of your ass, you'll see that.'

'What's missing here?'

'Nothing, as far as I can tell. We emptied the registers before closing on Friday night, of course. It might have been kids, looking for booze, but every bottle in the bar and in the basement seems to be here. Maybe they got scared off.'

'When?'

'Sometime before I got in at ten, Saturday morning. I saw the broken back door glass right away.' She stopped. 'What's that look on your face for?'

He told her about seeing Ryerson Wainwright speeding out of Grand Point, very early Saturday morning.

'You're sure it was him?'

'No, but how many bright red Cadillacs have you seen?'

'You're getting paranoid. Why would he risk smashing your back door? There's nothing here to find.'

'Strategy for the countersuit, maybe.'

'I looked around upstairs, too, and saw that strategy. One blank yellow pad of paper containing no times and dates to prove you were at home, in Linder County?' She bit her lip in frustration.

He told her about Jonah Ridl, and going to the courthouse just an hour before.

She threw up her hands. 'You went all the way up to Wisconsin, and then now to the courthouse to see who *might* have owned a cabin where Betty Jo Dean *could* have been kept?'

He nodded.

'What the hell for, Mac? Why don't you wait until you're in prison? You'll have all kinds of time then.'

'A girl was murdered.'

'*Thirty-two years ago.*'

'No one seems to care.'

'Which girl are we talking about? The one here, in Grand Point?'

'Of course.'

'Then here's who cares, Mac: the librarian, who's surely been blabbing about you pestering her for missing microfilms. The old bat at the newspaper office, who must have told Wiggins you didn't like the crime scene photo he took. Jimmy Bales, the damned law in this county, who you accused of negligence. The old gin bags who come here to drink in peace, who you badgered about things they want to forget. And God knows how many waitresses at the Willow Tree who are telling their customers – customers, can you imagine? – that you're a lunatic, looking into an old murder when you should be defending yourself against an indictment and trying to keep your own restaurant from bankrupting us all. That's who cares, Mac. We might as well light up the sign out front: "Mayor

Bassett is trying to piss off everybody in Grand Point. Come on in, he'll do you next.'"

'April—'

'Let me ask you something else. During your little weekend vacation, did you find time to stop at a cemetery?'

'Damn it.'

'Just tell me: did you stop?'

He knew better than to lie. 'I was driving almost right by it, Sunday morning.'

'How long has it been since you were there?'

'I don't remember.'

'How long?'

'Two, maybe three months.'

She started across the kitchen. 'Oh, by the way,' she said, stopping at the broken door. 'Some crabby old woman called for you, probably wanting money we owe. Her number's on your desk, next to the blank paper you prepared for Rogenet.' She slammed the door behind her, and a few seconds later her wheels spun as she gunned her car out of the lot.

April was right. To seize upon Betty Jo Dean when an indictment and a collapsing restaurant were set to ruin him was beyond lunacy. Perhaps she was right about the other thing, too. Maybe Betty Jo Dean's killer wasn't really who he was chasing.

He grabbed the liquor inventory sheet and went down to the basement. April had been right about the inventory. Nothing had been taken.

He went up to the office. A pink message slip was tucked under the phone. He didn't recognize the name, but didn't doubt it was someone looking for an old bill to be paid.

He prepared a new liquor order and paper-clipped a check to the form. As with all his suppliers, the liquor distributor demanded cash upfront.

He worked next on his quarterly payroll report. When that was done, he took the restaurant's copy to file in the cabinet across the office. And saw.

The bottom drawer was open, barely an inch.

He wasn't always a careful man. But when it came to keeping that particular drawer closed he was conscientious to a fault. Right after they'd bought the restaurant he'd skinned his leg and drawn blood on that drawer because he'd left it open. He'd never made that mistake again.

Now it was open.

He bent down to look at the folders. The payroll records and building documents were in their usual order, as were the closing papers at the very back. All were where he'd left them, including the tan envelope the previous owner's wife had given him. He pulled it out and took a look inside. The menu, the Chamber booklet and the news clippings were all there. He put it back and closed the drawer. He couldn't imagine there was anything in that drawer, or in the entire restaurant, that was worth breaking in to look at.

Still, he didn't suppose an intruder would have known that.

He dialed the number April had left, ready again to fake good cheer and make false promises of improving financial health.

The woman answered on the second ring. 'What?' April was right; the woman was a crab.

'This is Mac Bassett—'

She cut him off. 'You need to stop this damn foolishness over my sister's death.'

THIRTY-SEVEN

'I may no longer live in Grand Point, but that doesn't mean I don't keep up with the goings-on,' Bella Telkin said. 'Stop using my sister's death to draw attention away from your own troubles.'

'Someone asked me to look into it.'

'I don't care. Stop it. No one needs any more talk about Pinktown and her dropping out of school, and the men she might have known. It's over; she's dead; it's done.'

'Yet you wanted a newspaper article done on the twenty-fifth anniversary of your sister's death.'

'Who told you that? That damned newspaper only reopened old wounds.'

'We're talking about the same article? Jen Jessup's?'

'I told her – no, *implored* her – to leave things alone. But no, she had to dredge it all up again.'

'Maybe I can give the sheriff another nudge.'

'The way I hear it, the law's nudging you straight into prison.'

'One question, please?'

'Goodbye, Mayor Bassett.'

'Did anyone from the family view the body?'

'If you're suggesting it wasn't Betty Jo lying there, you're as crazy as people say.'

'I'm bothered that there was only one crime scene photo taken, and that shows her head completely covered with leaves. That doesn't seem to be proper police procedure.'

For a moment she said nothing, then: 'I still have nightmares about going down to identify her remains. She was so badly decomposed.'

'You saw her?'

'They said it was a formality, but someone from the family had to sign. I was older than Betty Jo by twelve years, but I was still only twenty-nine at the time. I—'

Mac interrupted. 'You actually saw decomposition?'

'Bud Wiley, or maybe the nephew, Luther, told me the sight of her might torment me for the rest of my life, that she'd been lying in that field for two nights and there'd been animals and all. They were most considerate over at Wiley's. I was spared from having to see too much.'

'But you did see her?'

'I saw all I needed. I recognized the slacks and the belt they showed me. And I recognized my mother's wedding ring on her right hand. My mother quit wearing it when she got the arthritis so bad, and Betty Jo, God knows why, took a fancy to it. The ring alone was enough to identify her.'

'You never actually saw her body—?' He stopped. He was talking to dead air. Bella Dean Telkin had hung up.

The crime scene photo didn't show much, but it didn't show decomposition. There'd been no obvious swelling of her forearm and the skin around her lower back, as would be expected on a corpse left out in summer heat for two full days. One of the Wileys had lied to Bella, covering something up by making sure Betty Jo Dean was *covered* all the way up.

But there'd been another lie, much fresher. He called Jen Jessup.

'I don't want us to start getting along,' she said.

'When's your interview with me going to run? I want the word out that I'm countersuing Wainwright.'

'I haven't finished writing it.'

'And then you'll have trouble placing it?'

'Maybe.'

'My lawyer filed this morning, accusing Wainwright of official malfeasance. More charges will follow.'

'I'll put that in.' Then, too casually, she asked, 'How are you coming along with Betty Jo Dean?'

He was just about certain now that she'd never had any intention of mentioning his countersuit in her piece about him. No matter; it was time to float a lie. 'I'm thinking I'll talk to that sister, the one who begged you to do a twenty-fifth anniversary piece on Betty Jo, to recharge the investigation. What was her name?'

'My God, don't call her,' Jen said, too fast. 'I heard the article woke old nightmares. Leave her alone.'

There was no doubt. Jen Jessup had lied; she was the one who'd wanted the investigation reopened, with that article she'd written.

'When you researched that piece, did you run across a reporter named Ridl?'

'No,' she said quickly.

'Did you check out the Chicago newspaper morgues?'

'Why are you asking these things?'

'Idle curiosity.'

'No. Rockford, DeKalb and Grand Point gave me what I needed.'

'And Bella.'

'What?' she asked, confused.

'Betty Jo's sister,' he said. 'The one who insisted you write that article.'

'You'll keep me updated on your progress?'

'You mean about my countersuit?' he asked, playing dumb as a brick.

'And the other?'

It was enough. He said he would and left it at that. He didn't blame her. Her sister was dead, perhaps murdered, and that trumped everything.

He rummaged in his desk until he found the voice-activated digital recorder he'd bought when he'd been so full of hope for Grand Point, the restaurant and the rest of his life. He'd carried it everywhere, afraid of letting even one good idea slip away. It was long ago.

He thumbed it on. The batteries were still fresh.

Not daring to pause even for an instant to consider what he was about to do, he got up and drove into town.

THIRTY-EIGHT

Horace Wiggins leaned back in his chair, his feet up on his desk.

'Mr Mayor,' Wiggins said, with no trace of enthusiasm at all.

'Mr Publisher. I stopped by last week.'

Wiggins shot a glance at the dour assistant and rumored squeeze. 'You were looking for old copies of the *Democrat*.'

'The microfilms for the *Rockford Register-Star* from 1982 have disappeared from the library.'

'Pity, that,' Wiggins said.

'I'd like to read your coverage of the Pribilski-Dean murders.'

'Horrible, that,' Wiggins said.

'You have the back issues?'

Wiggins made an exaggerated show of looking around the mess in the cramped room. 'Somewhere in my garage, maybe. Would take a year to find them.'

'Pity, that,' Mac said.

It was confrontation, at ultra-low speed.

'Your crime scene photo of the Devil's Backbone was troubling.'

Wiggins dropped his feet to the floor. 'What the hell does that mean?'

'It doesn't show anything. I'm wondering why you didn't remove the leaves from the back of her head and take a photo that shows the wound.'

'No one needed more.'

'Who decided that?'

'It's been a long time,' Wiggins said.

Mac left. The first visit had gone well.

Death had come again to Wiley's. A row of cars with orange funeral stickers on their windshields was lined up behind a gray hearse.

Luther Wiley was in his office. 'Hello, Mac,' he said, looking up.

Luther's office, like the rest of the funeral home, was embedded thick with the scent of decades of dying flowers. Mac supposed Luther must have become embedded that way too, over time, though he might have personalized his own scent with the spray that gave his pompadour a soft sheen. It was hard to tell. Certainly his cheeks were unnaturally red, and Mac had the unflattering thought that Wiley used rouge. He could only hope that the man wasn't dipping into the powders that were kept for the clients.

'Betty Jo Dean,' Mac said.

Wiley's smile remained carefully in place, but his cheeks darkened beneath the rouge. 'A horrible thing. So many years ago.'

'You were involved.'

The smile tightened. 'What can you mean?'

'Her body was brought here directly from the Devil's Backbone.'

Luther's smile relaxed in relief. 'I only drove the hearse. That's all I did. My uncle loaded and unloaded her.'

'No ambulance?'

'One wasn't necessary.'

'The autopsy was done here?'

'Not really an autopsy. The wound was obvious. We – my uncle, I mean – merely prepared the body for interment.'

'The next day.'

'Pardon me?'

'She was buried fast. The next day.'

'After a brief service here, yes. Closed casket, of course.'

'To be sure: the coroner conducted no examination?'

'Doc Farmont and Randy, his assistant, came over and spent time on her. Other people could have been in and out, but I wasn't around to notice. There was no doubt as to the cause of death, Mac.'

'She was decomposed, her sister Bella said.'

'Badly, according to my uncle.'

'Bella said she never actually viewed the body.'

The pasted smile flickered. 'I wasn't around when Bella came by.'

'She said you were.' Bella hadn't been sure, but it wouldn't hurt to jab Luther. He was dodging.

'Bella's memory is playing tricks. Obviously, she'd been distraught.'

'A shame, that Betty Jo's body was in such bad shape. There was no chance to learn what had happened to her?'

'Doc Farmont said she wasn't raped, if that's what you're getting at.'

'It's this fuss about decomposition that bothers me, Luther. I saw the discovery site photo. There was no bloating, no signs of animals marking her. Just a bunch of leaves arranged to hide her head.'

'Arranged? Surely not, though I've never actually seen the photo.'

'It's a strange picture, worthless as documentation of a crime scene.'

'What are you doing, Mac? Why the sudden interest?'

'Some constituents are concerned.'

'About those old murders?'

'I'd never heard about them.'

'You're new. Us old-timers want to forget.' Again, the smile.

'She was dirty, like Pribilski?'

'She was lovely—' He stopped. 'What do you mean?'

'Was she cleaned up fast, too?'

'We always do what we can.'

'I think you folks did much more than that, with both of them.'

Mac left without looking again at Luther's red face.

The second one had gone well, too.

Mac had never met Doc Farmont. The doctor had retired several years before Mac moved to Grand Point. He lived north of town, in a white cottage along the river. Mac found his way around the back.

A tall, thin man with white hair, dressed in paint-splattered khakis and a yellow T-shirt, was brushing white paint onto the wood hull of an old cabin cruiser set up on rusty metal racks.

'It's going to be a fine boat,' Mac said, walking up.

'I've been expecting you, Mr Mayor,' Farmont said, keeping his eyes on his brush.

'You've heard?'

'That you're sniffing around those old murders? The whole town's heard. People are upset. Few, I'm sure, have been encouraging.'

'Will you be encouraging?'

'I won't be around to be anything. I'm putting this in the water next week and sailing downriver to balmier climes.'

'You did the autopsies.'

'I never saw Pribilski. I briefly examined Betty Jo. She'd been shot.'

'What did you conclude?'

'That she was dead. Since I was in the county's employ for that examination, you'll have to see Sheriff Bales if you want to know anything more of what I found.'

'Speaking of sheriffs, how did Delbert Milner die?'

The doctor started toward the other side of the boat without answering.

'And Dougie Peterson? Was his head bashed before or after he drowned?'

The doctor had moved out of sight.

There was no point in chasing him around the boat. Mac walked away.

The third one had been a draw.

He called the sheriff's department from his truck. They told him Clamp Reems was off that day.

The chief deputy lived on a horse farm in a faded gray farmhouse two miles northwest of Grand Point. Red flowers bloomed in stone pots on either side of the green front door.

The curtains were drawn against the summer heat. He walked up to the front door and rang the bell. After a minute, he knocked twice. No one came. He went back to his car.

As he backed out of the drive, something white flickered low in the house. A curtain had fluttered on the first floor. Someone was home, someone who might have been alerted by a telephone call. The only question was whether there'd been one caller, or two, or all three.

Mac didn't know whether to call that a win, a loss, or a draw.

It was four o'clock, and time. He drove to the Willow Tree. As he expected, the restaurant was deserted. He sat at his usual booth, in the back, and ordered coffee and a club sandwich.

As the waitress walked away, he got up and walked toward the men's room, but stopped short. The door to the empty private dining room was open, as it always was, except when there were private banquets. Or those special breakfasts on Tuesdays and Fridays. He looked around the restaurant. No one looked back. He ducked inside.

As he'd told Pam Canton, not that many days before, he knew the room. He especially remembered one wall, where large, antique toy trains were lined up on a high shelf. He pulled the digital recorder out of his pocket, set it to the voice-activated mode and hid it behind a red-painted boxcar. Its microphone was sensitive; it would catch anything said in the room.

He went back to his booth. His club sandwich had arrived. He ate what he could and left.

He'd poked at the publisher, the mortician and the doctor. He'd parked in front of Clamp Reems' house long enough to flutter a curtain. Likely enough, two or more of them would show up tomorrow for their usual Tuesday breakfasts. Likely enough, they'd be talking about why the mayor was sticking his nose in where it surely did not belong.

He could only hope they'd say something more.

THIRTY-NINE

M ac sat upstairs in the Bird's Nest the next morning, Tuesday, reshuffling invoices to see who could be put off and trying not to imagine what was being said into the voice recorder he'd hidden at the Willow Tree.

A car crunched onto the gravel lot across the highway. He got to the window in time to see a second car, a beige Crown Victoria, pull in and park next to an older red Mustang fastback.

The driver of the Mustang got out. He was tall and lanky, and in his mid-thirties. He wore pressed denims, an embroidered western shirt and a NASCAR cap.

Sheriff Jimmy Bales got out of the Crown Victoria and the two men walked together across the street.

Mac went to the door and held it open. 'Good to see you again so soon, Jimmy.'

Bales came in first. 'We're wondering if we might chat for a few minutes, Mac.'

The younger man said nothing as Mac led them to a table in the darkened dining room.

Both declined Mac's offer of Cokes or coffees. They weren't expecting to be there long.

'Mac, this here's Reed Dean, Betty Jo's younger brother.'

'Welcome, Mr Dean,' Mac said.

'That Pam Canton over at the Willow Tree stirred all this up?'

Bales said abruptly. 'Hell, Mac, she didn't even live in Grand Point, let alone Peering County.'

'You do keep your ear to the ground, Jimmy. You also heard she took off fast?'

'Don't make it sound so sinister. Everybody at the Willow Tree knows she had a sick relative, just like they knew she'd become interested in Betty Jo. She agitated that interest on to you and now you're obsessed. When Reed phoned to tell me you'd pestered Bella, I thought we'd best come right over and answer your questions – though you'd do better talking to Clamp – and be done with this nonsense.'

'Clamp's off today. I stopped by his house but no one came to the door.'

'The case has been investigated, Mac.'

'There were lots of leads, for sure,' Mac said. He looked over at Reed Dean. The man's face was impassive.

'The killers are dead,' Bales said. 'There's no way of bringing it to final justice.'

'You know who killed Mr Dean's sister, and you said nothing about it when I was in your office?'

Bales glanced at the man sitting next to him. 'I've known Reed since he was a boy. When he called last night, asking if I'd go with him to get you to stop pestering his family, I had to finally admit I've known the identity of the killers for quite some time. Like I just said, they're both dead, and what I don't want is to punish their relatives, who are innocent of any wrongdoing.'

'Who were they, Jimmy?'

'Two brothers. One worked on a farm west of here. The other was visiting – no; make that staying away from – Iowa, where there was a warrant outstanding on him for battery. That terrible night, those two boys were hanging around the parking lot of Al's Rustic Hacienda. When Pribilski and Reed's sister left, they did too, coming down here to the Wren House as well. What's for sure is that the Iowa brother got into a dice game and apparently lost a good bit of money to Pribilski. When Pribilski and Betty Jo left the premises, the brothers followed them.'

'How long have you known this?'

'I conducted my own investigation real quiet when I first became sheriff. I found a witness who saw both brothers drive onto Poor Farm Road, cut their lights and get out of the car. That same witness heard gunshots not two minutes later.'

'They never reported it?'

'Too scared.'

'The motive was robbery?'

'As I said, Pribilski won considerable money that night shooting dice. His wallet was never found.'

'Your local farmer and his Iowa brother weren't known to the investigators back then?'

'Sure they were, along with other suspects, but the eyewitness was not. I was the one discovered him, upon becoming sheriff.' He paused dramatically. 'Remember, Mac, it had to be a pair of killers, since two cars had to be moved. That narrows the number of suspects down to a few.'

'Not necessarily,' Mac said.

Reed Dean, silent since he'd come in, sat up straighter in his chair.

Mac went to take an aerial photo of Grand Point from the wall. Using a pencil as a pointer, he put the tip at the intersection of Rural Route 4 and Big Pine Road. 'We're here. This is where Pribilski and Betty Jo were last seen.'

'And the brothers, don't forget,' Jimmy Bales said.

Mac moved the pencil point south, to Poor Farm Road. 'This is where Pribilski was shot. It's less than a half-mile away.'

'So?' Bales said.

Reed Dean leaned forward. He understood.

'That's walking distance,' Mac said.

Reed Dean nodded. 'Walking distance, for sure.'

'A lone killer could have followed Pribilski and Betty Jo down from the Hacienda,' Mac went on. 'He didn't need to come in here and risk being seen; he could have waited outside for them to come out. If he was a local, which I'm guessing he was, he would have known where a young couple would be headed if they left here driving south. He could have left his car in the lot across the street and hoofed it down to Poor Farm Road. It wouldn't have taken more than ten minutes. He could have snuck up on the car, killed Pribilski, dragged him to the ditch and driven Betty Jo back up here in Pribilski's car, and then took her away in his own car.'

'It explains why Pribilski's car was moved,' Reed said. 'He needed it to bring Betty Jo back to the parking lot.'

'And all the while, during the killing, during the driving back here, she's quiet as pie?' Bales said.

'He had a gun,' Mac said. 'More important, I think Betty Jo stayed quiet because she knew her abductor. She could have been hoping to talk her way into being let go, or escaping. I think she knew her abductor loved her and was going to take her someplace to try and reason with her, to keep her mouth shut.'

'He took her straight to the Devil's Backbone, to kill her,' Bales said.

'No way in hell did she lay in that field for two days, decomposing, untouched by animals and unseen by searchers. She was alive those two days.'

Bales broke into a sweat. 'You believe that false tip about an older man fighting with a younger woman, driving south on Route Four? That's why you were checking deeds at the courthouse, to see who owned those cabins down there? Hell, Mac; those cabins were searched.'

Bringing up Ridl's theory that the tip had been Milner's ploy would only bring more knee-jerk denial. 'Check the one crime scene photo, Sheriff. No decomp; no animal damage. She wasn't lying there for two days, undisturbed under a blanket of leaves.'

A drop of sweat fell from his forehead as Bales turned to Reed Dean. 'This is bullshit.'

'You're sure of that, how?' Reed asked.

'Because of that witness, damn it. And because it had to be two people, no matter what Mac says.'

Reed Dean picked up the old aerial photo. 'One man could have done it, easy.'

'Damn it, Reed,' Jimmy Bales said.

Mac got up, saying he had to check on something in the kitchen. Reed Dean appeared willing to consider what Mac was suggesting. If Reed could influence Bales, a new investigation could be launched.

Mac dawdled for ten minutes, to allow Reed time to work on Bales, before coming back to the table.

Jimmy Bales was gone. Reed Dean sat alone, still staring at the aerial photo.

He looked up. His eyes were wet.

'Will you help me?' he asked.

FORTY

He didn't have truths to tell Reed Dean. He couldn't even mouth solid suspicions. 'I don't know how I can help,' he said. 'So much time has passed.'

'I was only six when she died,' Reed said. 'For months after, anytime there was a knock on the door, my mother made me hide behind the sofa. Didn't matter if it was only kids, come to see if I could play. Sometimes I stayed behind that couch for hours just because people were out in the neighborhood. And when that bad summer was over, my mother wouldn't send me to school. She was terrified someone would come for me, too.'

'Who did she think would come for you?'

'She didn't know. Nobody knew. All she could think was to keep me hid in the house until she got so bad they had to stop her.'

'Stop her?'

'I didn't just lose my youngest sister – I lost my mother, too. She wasn't right from the moment they found Betty Jo. Finally, my father, brother and oldest sister decided they had to institutionalize her in East Moline. I was sent to live with Bella, who was married and living down in Dixon. And you know what was strangest of all? When I came back, I saw that none of what we'd been through seemed to matter. We were still Pinktown.'

He spoke like he was shouldering the weight of a hundred hard years. 'Pinktown. It's a filthy old name but still whispered, painting you the same as the builder once painted the houses. The builder used the one color because he got it cheap; people use the one word because they're mean. You know what? There isn't a damned one of them places got a trace of pink left on it. If somebody did paint something pink over there, even if it's just a red that looks a little pink, on a shutter or a birdhouse or some other damned thing, it wouldn't be long before one of the neighbors marched up in broad daylight with a can of black or brown or green paint and a brush, to paint that pink away. No pink, no more, not anywhere in Pinktown. But people west of the river, Grand Point proper, will always see folks from east of the Royal as trash. Born pink, always pink.'

'Meaning it was no big deal your sister got killed?'

'Meaning no real need to investigate her murder.'

'Do you believe Bales about those two brothers?'

'I believe he could have made it up yesterday or today.' He pulled out a pipe, slipped the bowl into a plastic pouch. His hand shook as he tamped the tobacco with his thumb.

'Did anyone in your family ever talk about who killed Betty Jo?'

Reed lit the pipe with a blue plastic Bic. 'They never mentioned her at all. Keep in mind, I was six when I was sent to live with Bella. At first, I figured that was because I was a kid. Yet even when I was full grown, they didn't talk about her. Not to me; not to each other. My brother, Fred Junior – he was the one supposed to get married that summer – he never said a word. The shock of it all shut Fred up for the rest of his life. He died a couple of years back, in an auto accident.'

'As you know, Bella didn't want to talk when I called.'

'She's spent out. By the time I got to my teens I'd heard all kind of things about Betty Jo. People came up to tell me their own theories about who killed her. I'd repeat them to Bella; she'd shush me and tell me it was best forgotten. That's how she coped; that's how everybody in the family coped. So when that reporter, Jen Jessup, called in 2007, Bella told her to drop it cold. Of course, that Jessup woman did no such thing, and the story caused Bella a lot of pain.'

He set down his pipe and lit a cigarette. 'When you called, she saw it all beginning again. She called me. I called Jimmy Bales, thinking we'd ask you to drop your investigation. Now your aerial picture has got me seeing other things, like why nobody before figured it could have been a one-man job, though I don't see how knowing that will help at this late date.'

'Maybe there was a lid on the investigation.'

'What do you mean?'

Mac excused himself, went up to his office and came down with the tan envelope the restaurant's previous owner had pressed upon him. He shook out the old news clippings and chamber of commerce booklet. Opening the booklet, he pointed to the checkmarks above some of the photos.

'Importants, my dad used to call them.' Reed said, squinting at the yellowed old photos. 'You think they covered something up?'

'I don't know. The woman who co-owned this restaurant gave this to me at the closing. I think she was linking the check-marked photos to the newspaper clippings.' Then: 'You're sure your father never said anything about the killing?'

'Not to me.'

'He's dead now?'

Reed Dean nodded. 'Most mercifully. He suffered. Dad worked at the Materials Plant. Blacksmith work, repairing the chutes and machines. Someone once told me Clamp Reems made a point of telling Dad that he must have passed Betty Jo's body on his way to work that Tuesday and Wednesday morning. Passed within a few feet of his own daughter, Clamp supposedly said, rotting dead just off the Devil's Backbone. Must have torn at Dad, hearing that, especially from that shit chief deputy, but he never said.'

'Your father didn't like Reems?'

'Everybody's afraid of him.' Reed blew smoke up at the ceiling. 'But Dad, I think he had a special dislike for the hick.'

'Any idea why?'

Reed crushed out his cigarette. 'I've got the damnedest recollection from right before Betty Jo died. I see the two of them, Dad and Reems, out in front of our house, yelling at each other, with Dad doing the most of it. I can see Dad's finger jamming that bastard's uniform shirt.'

'You sure it was Clamp Reems? You were awfully young.'

'I can see it like it happened today. The reason I'm sure it was Clamp Reems was because of that damned fool corncob pipe, always with a ripped piece of cigar jammed into it. That's the kind of thing a kid would remember.'

'You're sure it was before your sister disappeared, and not after? Your father would have been impatient with Reems afterward for not making any progress.'

'Reason I'm pretty sure is I remember looking up at the house and seeing Betty Jo watching from behind the bedroom curtain.'

'You never asked your parents about it?'

'They'd been damaged enough, especially my mother. She came out of East Moline wrecked. She told me they gave her electric shocks, made her bite down on a rubber thing so she wouldn't bite off her tongue. She kept pointing to the door.'

'The door?'

'Our front door. She kept saying Betty Jo was due to come through it any time. Said she'd gone off to be a nun in a convent, that she'd come back when she was trained and things would be like before. At first, my dad would say nothing when Mom got to talking like that. And me being so young, I didn't understand, so I started watching the door myself, thinking Betty Jo really was going to come on through, even though I'd been to her funeral. But Dad wouldn't let Mom go on too much that way before he'd have Doc Farmont come over and give her something to quiet her, though he couldn't stand that bastard any more than he could stand Reems.'

'Why?'

'I never knew, other than Dad said once that Doc just knew too much.'

'About what?'

'About every damned thing, I suppose. He was like Reems; he knew where the bones were buried. Doc was the only medical man in town. Took care of things and kept 'em quiet.'

'What sorts of things?'

Reed shrugged, looked away.

'Abortions?'

'They were legal then. I checked,' Reed said.

'You think Doc Farmont gave Betty Jo an abortion?'

'No sense talking that way now. Look, Mr Bassett, now that you've acquainted yourself with the events about my sister, isn't there anything you can do?'

'I don't know.'

'Then why are you doing it?'

'I didn't intend to go this far. I'd just set out to ask a few questions.'

Reed stubbed out his cigarette. 'Before she died, my mother made me promise to find out where Betty Jo had gone. Until now, I never figured anything could be done. Now we've got Jimmy Bales saying he's known for some time it was two brothers.'

'That came awfully fast.'

'Jimmy Bales is not known for independent thinking.' He tapped the page of photos in the Chamber of Commerce booklet. 'Somebody put those words in his mouth.'

He stood up and said he had to be at work.

Mac walked him out to his fastback Mustang. He had to be someplace, too.

He ordered a burger at the Willow Tree's front counter and walked down to the deserted end of the dining room like he was going to the washroom. The door to the private room was open. He ducked in and reached up behind the red-painted boxcar on the high shelf. The audio recorder was right where he'd left it. He took it down, jammed it in his pocket and walked back out to the counter.

His burger came up five minutes later. Mac drove home. In his living room, he sat in the big overstuffed chair and thumbed the recorder to Play.

There was a brief click, and then the static of a blank recording.

He rewound the instant of noise, then pressed Play again.

Again the click; again the static.

He knew what it was. It was the sound of the recorder being lifted up and switched off.

Someone had known what was hidden high on the shelf in the private dining room.

FORTY-ONE

Mac never bothered to go to bed on Tuesday night. He spent the evening and into the middle of the night in the big chair in the living room, sipping Scotch to dull the memory of the ominous click of his voice recorder, signaling he'd been found out, like perhaps Delbert Milner, Laurel Jessup and Dougie Peterson had been found out. It didn't work. He jerked alert at every creak of the half-dead ash tree in the back yard, every brush of a tendril of a bush against the clapboards of his house.

It was almost a relief when the telephone jangled him out of his soft fog at three-fifty in the morning.

'Mac Bassett?'

'Yeah.'

'Fire Chief Tare. There's a fire at the Wren House.'

Mac pushed himself more upright. 'You mean the Bird's Nest,' he said, muddled by the Scotch.

'Best you come down,' Tare said, clicking off.

Mac pulled on his sneakers and half ran, half hobbled out to his truck. He sped south through the town, leaning forward over the steering wheel to look for any glow of orange in the sky. There was only darkness.

And then he was there, and there was relief. The Bird's Nest was intact. He waited for the lone fire truck to pull away from the back door, and drove in. The fire chief's red sedan was parked in the back, by the Dumpster. Mac made a wide turn to sweep his headlamps across the back of the restaurant. All looked well.

He left his headlights shining on the back of the building. Chief Tare was standing next to the Dumpster, in front of the steps that led to the kitchen door.

'We got it right away.' Tare pointed to a scorched section of the cedar siding. 'No real damage.'

The wood was charred in an almost perfect rectangle, running three feet up from the ground and five feet across.

'Unusual to see such a regular pattern?' Mac asked. His head was clearing.

Tare stepped back, probably from the Scotch on Mac's breath. 'Accelerant, poured or squirted in a horizontal line, to run down the wood,' he said. 'Could have been kids with gasoline.'

Mac concentrated on speaking distinctly. If Tare thought he'd arrived drunk, word would spread that Mac had got tanked and tried to torch his place for the insurance.

'It might not have been kids.' Mac pointed to the plywood covering the broken kitchen door. 'That broken window was round one. This fire is round two.'

Tare frowned in the glare of Mac's headlamps. 'Someone is sending you a message?'

Something new and frightening swept through Mac's mind. Paranoia fueled by the Scotch, perhaps. He said it anyway: 'You got here fast.' Too damned fast.

'We got a call. Indistinguishable voice, man or a woman, adult or child, saying there was a fire at your restaurant.'

'You didn't call the cops?'

'I didn't think it was necessary.' He looked up again at the kitchen door. 'Of course, I didn't know you'd already had an incident.'

'It's unusual, isn't it? You, the chief, coming to such a small fire?'

'I like to keep my hand in, make sure things get handled properly.'

'In the middle of the night?'

Tare started toward his car. 'Best you heed what these messages mean, Mac.'

Mac walked around the restaurant, checking to make sure the doors and windows were locked. Everything was secure.

He went back to his truck, got in and shut off the lights. He didn't want to go back to his house; he didn't want to go inside the restaurant. He didn't want to be penned up anywhere. He sat in his truck behind his restaurant until the sun rose enough to lighten the rectangle that had been charred onto the back of the Bird's Nest.

He had a thought. He got out of the truck, walked to the Dumpster and lifted the lid.

Lying bright and obvious on top of the black bags of garbage was a blue and white plastic bottle of charcoal starter. No one could have missed it, if anyone had been interested enough to look.

The fire hadn't been meant to send a message. It had been meant to send two.

The first was the most obvious: this time, the fire was carefully limited, to scorch only a small rectangle. Next time, it wouldn't be confined. It would be higher and hotter. The whole restaurant would be destroyed.

The second message was even more chilling. The arsonist hadn't bothered to conceal the accelerant; he'd set it in plain view inside the Dumpster. In almost any circumstance, the chief or one of his firemen should have thought to look there. They hadn't. They weren't curious – that was the message.

'No cops?' Mac had asked the fire chief. 'None needed,' Tare had replied.

Not now, not in the future, not for any harm that would come to Mac Bassett.

FORTY-TWO

Things got better that evening, for a time.

The Bird's Nest was busy. Two-hundred and seventy-three heads showed up to eat and, more profitably, to drink in front of the television sets Mac had set up around the restaurant. Ordinarily, Mac would have credited the crowd to Chicago's Crosstown Classic, that annual baseball contest between the Cubs and the White Sox. That night, he figured there was another contingent – Bassett watchers, who'd come for a last meal before the restaurant, and perhaps Mac himself, went up in smoke. He mentioned it to April.

'Whatever it takes to make a profit, Mac,' she said, trying to tease, but there was no mirth in her eyes.

Mac made his first round through the crowd at six-thirty. When he'd first taken over the restaurant, he'd tried to work the room at least twice each evening, stopping at each of the tables to greet the people he knew and introduce himself to those he didn't. He'd enjoyed it. After his indictment, it instantly turned into rough, awkward work. People didn't want to talk much to someone headed for jail.

That evening, as usual, a brief 'How's it going, Mr Mayor?' meant, 'You going to prison, Mr Mayor?'

'Fighting back,' he said a hundred new times. 'Countersuing.'

'Countersuing?' most asked in surprise. Jen Jessup hadn't published anything about Mac's countersuit. He still doubted she'd tried.

'The whole thing's political retribution, and that's going to come out,' he said those hundred times.

'Political here, or political back in Linder County?' more than one asked.

Mac was careful then, because a good number of the diners were friends of his predecessor, Pete Moore. 'Political everywhere,' he said, smiling, hurrying on to the next table before his mouth could bring more grief.

Jen herself called midway through the evening. 'Heard there was a fire.'

'Surely not at your desk.'

She took a breath. 'No one wants the piece. Horace Wiggins turned it down without bothering to explain, of course. The papers in DeKalb, Rochelle, and Dixon said they won't be party to your grandstanding. Even the Rockford paper I string for said they'll give you space only when you get sent to prison. I'm really sorry, Mac.'

'Thanks for not sugarcoating.' He waited for her to ask about Betty Jo Dean.

'That fire?' she asked. 'Deliberately set?'

'Charcoal starter. Fire Chief Tare showed up but didn't bother to look inside the Dumpster.'

'Be careful, Mac,' she said, and surprised him by hanging up without asking about Betty Jo Dean. Jen Jessup was a puzzle, beautifully wrapped.

A sallow-skinned man in a green sport coat, bright blue shirt and dark olive tie sat alone in the booth farthest from the door. He was around sixty, and sweating as though with a fever. His thin, graying hair was pasted back on his skull, and shiny with tonic.

An untouched glass of Coke lay on the table in front of him, next to a closed menu.

'Welcome to the Bird's Nest,' Mac said.

The man offered a faint smile.

'From here?' Mac asked.

'My whole life.'

'You must have seen some changes, then,' Mac said, offering casual, meaningless words.

The man shifted his eyes nervously to look at the door. Mac thought of Farris Hobbs the night Mac had first brought up Betty Jo Dean. Farris's eyes had shifted like that.

'Some things change; some things are best left alone,' the man said.

April was crossing the dining room toward him. She looked worried.

'Want to know what I know?' the man asked.

'Sure,' Mac said, watching April. No doubt, something was wrong.

The man mumbled something Mac didn't hear over the clatter of the other diners.

April got to the booth. 'The vent fan again . . .'

She didn't have to finish. The circuit to the exhaust fan had blown. The kitchen would fill with smoke, activating the alarms, emptying the restaurant and summoning the fire department. Between skipped checks and the fire department's charge, the evening would be a thousand-dollar disaster.

Only sometimes could Mac jiggle the circuit breaker in time.

'1982,' the man said meaninglessly.

'Absolutely,' Mac said just as meaninglessly, and left to hurry after April through the dining room.

He ran down the stairs to the labyrinth of small rooms beneath the restaurant. The original building had been built in the late 1800s and had been expanded over the years. Each time, new foundations had been made, first of fieldstone, then of block and, finally, of poured concrete. The result was a basement warren of dank little rooms. The smallest of them was especially creepy to April and Maggie. It contained a raised cement platform, pitched to a center drain, and stained a dark, rust color. 'The blood-letting room, for slaughter,' the previous owner had joked when he'd first given Mac a tour of the building. It had been the place where whole carcasses had been butchered for meat, decades earlier. Mac had tried to scrub away the old blood, but even Muriatic acid couldn't remove it. Maggie Day refused to go in the room. She said it contained bad spirits that chilled her bones.

The fuse box was in that room. He turned on his flashlight and jiggled the switch to the kitchen fan. Luckily, on that night of live baseball and two hundred and seventy-three paying customers, the fuse reoriented itself, and the big vent fan clattered back into life above his head. Disaster had been staved off once again.

On his way back up, he remembered there was something he wanted to ask Maggie, but the baseball game was playing, the cash register was ringing, and the thought flashed away in an instant. He spent the next two hours hanging out in the bar, enjoying the sounds of paying patrons.

The game ended at nine-fifteen. Ten minutes later, the bar was empty except for Farris Hobbs and his two friends.

'Dining room is empty—' Maggie Day said, finding Mac in the kitchen twenty minutes later.

He remembered what he'd wanted to ask her about: her friend, Abigail Beech, the psychic who'd been mentioned in the old articles about Betty Jo Dean.

'—except for one guy sitting in that hidden booth the teenagers like,' Maggie went on. 'He finally ordered a hamburger, and he's been stretching it. It's like he's killing time, waiting for a train.'

'Thin guy in a green sport coat?' Mac remembered the man.

Maggie smiled. 'Shiny hair, stuck to his skull.'

'1982,' the man had called after him, as Mac raced for the breaker box. He'd said it like it was supposed to mean something.

It did, Mac now realized. It meant murder, two, three, four, maybe even five times over.

He picked up one of the pitchers of Coke the waitresses used for refills and walked into the dining room.

'Was the burger OK?' he asked the man in the back booth. The table had been cleared except for his glass. Mac refilled it and sat down.

'Very, very good. Exceptionally good. I haven't been in this place since it was the Wren House.'

'We've been careful to not change too much,' he said.

'You removed the bird pictures. I liked them. They were pretty.'

They'd been ripped calendar pages. 'They were in bad shape,' Mac said.

'My name's Randall White,' the man said. 'That mean anything to you?'

It sounded familiar, but Mac couldn't place it. 'No.'

'Folks call me Randy.'

It came then, in a fiery instant. Randy White had been Doc Farmont's assistant. Someone had said White had been at Wiley's funeral home the day Pribilski had been brought in and likely for Betty Jo Dean as well.

White smiled at the recognition he now saw on Mac's face. 'I understand you've become interested in the murder of Betty Jo Dean.'

'How did you hear that?'

'From Farris Hobbs, and others. You've brought considerable attention to yourself.'

'How may I help you?'

'It's me who can help you.'

Mac tried to keep his voice even. 'How?'

'I know who killed Betty Jo Dean.'

FORTY-THREE

Mac waited until the man appeared satisfied that he'd shocked him.

'You know who killed Betty Jo Dean?'

'Sure,' White said.

'Others know, too?'

'Some. Not many.'

'Doc Farmont knows?'

'I'm only telling you this because it would be a real tragedy if all this gets stirred up again.'

'For the town?'

'For the family,' White said. 'See, Doc made up his mind the family should suffer no more, so he swore me to secrecy. I'm not saying he told no one else. He might have told some, to shut down troublesome inquiries. But until this moment, I've never breathed a word. I'll ask you to be just as discreet.'

'About what?'

'Doc Farmont's a crusty old sort, but he took care of the people in this town, yes sir. And he knew how to keep his mouth shut.'

'Abortions,' Mac said, impatient to speed up the man's leisurely pace.

'Like I said, Doc always had everyone's well-being at heart. It was four years after the killings. One day, Fred Junior came to see the doc.'

'Fred Dean, Junior? Betty Jo's older brother?'

'By six years,' White said. 'I was Doc's assistant, back then. Nothing legally medical, you understand, since I had no licensed training. But I assisted in procedures where it wouldn't technically be illegal, when a situation called for an extra pair of hands.'

'And in that capacity you became aware of something Fred Dean, Junior consulted Doctor Farmont about?'

'I was never invited to sit in on a consultation, you understand, but Doc's office had thin walls, and on occasion, in spite of my every effort to allow privacy, I'd overhear things. And so it was on the day young Fred came in with concerns.'

'Concerns, Mr White?'

'About genital warts. Seemed he'd sprung one or two on his privates.' White smiled slyly. 'Pinktown boys often engaged with Pinktown girls. And Fred Junior did belong to a group of young hellions who used to orgy up the river a piece.'

'Orgy?'

'Young Roosters, they called themselves, frolicking about in the woods with young women, local and imported. They thought it perfectly normal, their goings-on. They were a bunch of sick-minded young men. Now and again, one of the Roosters would come in to see Doc about a result of their excesses. Usually it was the drips.'

'A sexually transmitted disease?'

'If that's what you want to call it, sure. There were all kinds. Anyway, Young Fred's concern was about warts, and about the exact nature of the procedure that would be used to remove those, ah . . . things. In particular, he wanted to know about the type of anesthetic

Doc would administer during the procedure. He'd heard the knockout was sodium pentothal.'

'Truth serum?'

'*Exacto-mente*,' White said. 'He didn't want to be put under, unless he was sure that Doc was obligated like a lawyer to keep anything he heard during the surgery confidential.'

'What did the good doctor tell him?'

'Doc said he always kept his mouth shut, no matter what.'

'What about you?'

'I ordinarily kept lots of stuff quiet, but as I mentioned, on this occasion Doc took the extra precaution of swearing me to secrecy anyway. Then – and this is the most interesting part – he swore me to secrecy a second time. Brought it up right out of the blue a couple of weeks later. I took that to mean the procedure was done when I wasn't in the office. I'd only overheard the consult.'

'Yet you're violating that oath now?'

'Only because you've created an extreme situation. I'd like to stop things before they get out of hand, reputation-wise.'

An impossible thought flitted in Mac's mind. 'Are you implying Fred Dean, Junior murdered his sister?'

White offered another sly smile.

Mac spoke slowly, hesitant to even say the words. 'Surely you're not suggesting young Fred contracted an STD from his own sister . . .?'

'I'm suggesting this entire matter ought to be dropped,' White said.

'Fred Junior got his warts from Betty Jo? Her own brother killed her in rage?'

White leaned across the booth so he could whisper. 'They were Pinktown, pure and simple. It's best to leave all that alone, so people don't get to conjecturing like you're doing now.'

It was too fantastic. 'You actually heard no such thing, did you? You merely heard Fred Junior questioning Doc Farmont about confidentiality in general?'

'Best leave all this alone, Mr Bassett.'

'What about the autopsy you and Farmont did on Betty Jo?'

Randall White took a sip of Coke and wiped absently at his brow. 'That was Doc's show at Wiley's. And it wasn't just me in there with the Doc, anyway . . .'

'Who else was there?'

'I don't think I remember.'

'The coroner?'

White made a snorting sound. 'Another damned politician. Most he was good for was signing death certificates, when he got around to it.'

'Tell me about the autopsy.'

'That's confidential, on account of it was police business.' It was the same excuse Doc Farmont had hidden behind.

'Are you saying there was nothing unusual about that autopsy?'

'What was done was necessary.'

It was a strange statement. Mac decided to throw a hard curve. 'Why wasn't Bella, the older sister, shown Betty Jo's face when she was asked to formally identify the body?'

Randall White pushed himself out of the booth so fast he nearly knocked over the pitcher of Coke. Standing over Mac, he said, 'I'm trying to make you understand the sensitivity of this case. My God, man, Betty Jo's older sister and younger brother are still alive. If they were to get even a whiff of what I just told you, their memories of their departed sister and brother would be ruined forever. The autopsy was necessary. Betty Jo's deep in the ground.'

And with that, Randall White, a sweating man in slick skin, walked out of the restaurant.

Mac sat for a moment, reached for a clean glass from an adjacent table and poured himself a couple inches of Coke.

He'd struck nerves – big, throbbing nerves. He'd asked questions all over town, and even been caught hiding a voice recorder at the Willow Tree. Messengers had been dispatched to stop him. First, Jimmy Bales had showed up with Reed Dean, to spout a story about two mysterious brothers. Then others had come to break a window and scorch a wall. Now Randy White had come to deliver a sick story about a brother who was no longer around.

After a moment, or maybe ten, he got up and walked back to the bar. The cash drawer had been emptied; the side doors and back door were all locked. The kitchen lights had been turned off.

He came back into the dining room. As he turned off the last of the lights and the room darkened, pulsing red flashes came in through one of the side windows from the highway. He hurried out of the front door.

The flashing lights came from a sheriff's car and an ambulance, parked at the shoulder of the road. There'd been no siren.

He ran across. A body, zipped in a black nylon bag, was being loaded into the ambulance.

'Randy White?' he yelled at the emergency technician.

'Randy White?' the man asked, confused.

'Is that Randy White?'

'No. This here's Farris Hobbs.'

FORTY-FOUR

'What the hell, Mac?' Rogenet mumbled on the phone, coming out of sleep. 'It's two in the morning.'

'Farris Hobbs talked to me, and now he's been killed across the street. No sirens, just nice and quiet; something else that's going to go away. A waitress disappeared before him, just up and gone. The sheriff maybe got murdered. And before him, Betty Jo and Pauly, and Laurel and Dougie, of course. People are coming at me with strange stories about everything, and they're all lying. Someone tried to set fire to the restaurant – they only burned a square onto the back.'

He knew he was babbling, his voice skittering high and tight, but he had to get the words out. He gulped air, and went on: 'Someone broke into the Bird's Nest. It had to be someone sent by Wainwright, Ryerson Damned Wainwright—'

'Whoa!' Rogenet yelled, having finally had enough. 'First of all, who just got killed?'

'Farris Hobbs. He drank here every night. He lived across the street.'

'He died leaving your place?'

'Nobody from the ambulance would talk to me. Just whisked him away, cold meat.'

'He was drunk?'

'Maybe. Probably. He gets – got – comfortably mellow, is all.'

'OK, now we're getting somewhere. You're in shock, worrying about being sued for overserving him.'

'No, damn it. He got killed for talking. It's a message to everybody in town: steer clear of me.'

'The sheriff got murdered tonight, too?'

'No. That was years ago. They passed it off as a heart attack, but it was a gunshot wound to the head.'

'You want me to believe Ryerson Wainwright is somehow involved in all these crazy things?'

Mac made his next words come out slow. 'Of course not, but I think he hired someone to break in, to see what I'd pulled together for my defense.'

'Well, he can sure as hell relax. You've done nothing to keep yourself from prison.'

'Maybe I'm too high profile to kill, but the others – Pam and Farris . . .'

'Start at the beginning, but slowly,' Rogenet said easily, as he would to a hysterical child.

So Mac did, from the beginning.

'You really think you put yourself into some trick bag with those old killings?' Rogenet said when Mac was done. 'That this recent stuff goes back to all that?'

'Sure.'

'Let me make a call. I'll call you back in fifteen minutes.'

'Don't be blowing me off on this, Jim.'

'You mean like you've been blowing me off to work on some old murder case that no one except you seems interested in?' He hung up.

Mac looked out the dining-room window. The ambulance and the sheriff's cruiser were gone. The highway was dark. He poured himself a Scotch.

Rogenet called back. 'Good news. April said you're not as crazy as you sound. She's quite aware of your obsession with those old murders, and that you've been pissing time away playing detective instead of working the restaurant and, oh, yeah, giving any thought to keeping yourself out of prison. But she also said you're acting, and I quote, "absolutely no frickin' crazier than you've ever been." It's good enough for me, Mac. Here's what you do. If you're sober enough, drive home and go to bed. I'll call you tomorrow morning after I've made more calls. And Mac?'

'Yes?'

'Don't talk to a soul.'

But of course, Mac already had.

Rogenet called at ten the next morning. 'I just spoke to Jimmy Bales, your beloved sheriff. I started to pass off my interest in Farris

Hobbs as concern for any liability the Bird's Nest might have, but he brushed that away. He wanted to talk about the trouble you're stirring up. He doesn't like you, Mac.

'Hobbs was hit by a car traveling southbound on Route Four. Bales got an anonymous tip at about three in the morning from someone who sounded distraught. The tipster said that just after midnight he saw Hobbs stumbling into the path of that car, and that he could have been pushed. It wasn't a high-speed hit. Nonetheless, the driver had no time to react to Hobbs suddenly falling in front of him. The driver panicked and sped away, according to the tipster.'

'I suppose Bales mentioned I'm known to walk Farris partway home every evening he drinks here?'

'He did mention that, three times at least.'

'The inference being I did the pushing?'

'He left that conclusion to my imagination.'

'I didn't walk him last night. I sat with a customer until past closing time, and then I sat alone some more. I lost track of time. I didn't see Farris leave. Hell, I didn't see April or Maggie or anyone else leave either.'

'That customer? Was he Randall White?'

'How do you know that?' Mac asked.

'First thing this morning, he says, he heard about Hobbs getting killed. So he did what any righteous citizen would do: he marched into the sheriff's office and offered himself up as a sort of witness, seeing as how he'd been very close by, spending time with you, until probably just before Hobbs got struck down.'

'How thoughtful.'

'He said you'd become quite agitated when he mentioned Hobbs's name. Said you kept pestering him about what Hobbs knew, about you and about the murders on Poor Farm Road.'

'So agitated I pushed Hobbs down in front of a car?'

'That's what Bales inferred. Look, Mac, you were talking crazy last night. That business about Ryerson Wainwright sending someone to break into the Bird's Nest makes no sense.'

'I admit I was squirrelly, but I'd just found out about Hobbs. As for Wainwright, I saw his red Cadillac speeding out of Grand Point early the morning of the break-in.'

'*His* red Cadillac, or one that looks just like it?'

Mac said nothing.

'Mac, that's too crazy.'

He started to say something about the partially open file drawer he'd discovered afterward, but decided against it. He had no proof. 'Still no word from him about our countersuit?' he asked instead.

'He must be thinking he's got a slam-dunk case. That's all right; we'll beat him in court. Be on good behavior, Mac. Don't do or say anything stupid.'

Mac took a breath. 'About that . . .' He told the lawyer what he wanted him to do.

The lawyer's breathing quickened. 'Did you hear any damned thing I just said?' he asked, no doubt stunned.

'Only more truth will end this.'

'Reed Dean – he's on board?'

'I woke him up last night before I woke you. He's expecting your call.'

'You understand our countersuit works only if it makes Wainwright look reasonable. He'll slam the door on any agreement if it makes it look like he negotiated with a mad man.'

'I won't settle if it requires an admission of guilt. I did nothing wrong.'

'You must come across as merely assisting poor Reed Dean, something you're doing as his friend.'

'Fine.'

'According to April, you don't have the money to be indulging in any nonsense.'

'You know what they say about a fool and his money? Mine and I have already parted. I'll pay you when I can.'

'Let me call Reed Dean.'

FORTY-FIVE

Rogenet worked magic. He got them an appearance before Judge Tinley the following Monday morning. Rogenet met Reed Dean and Mac fifteen minutes beforehand, in a meeting room one floor above the courtroom. Even though the building was air conditioned, the lawyer was sweating.

'Some ground rules,' Rogenet said, dabbing his face with a

handkerchief. 'First of all, Mr Dean, this is your action. I am here representing you alone, and Mac is here at your request.'

'Got it,' Reed said. He'd been nervous ever since Mac had proposed the idea, and had called Mac at least a dozen times to be sure this was the only logical next step.

'Second,' Rogenet said, 'we're here to discuss this action only, and solely in terms of its potential to help solve Betty Jo's murder.'

Reed worked his throat. 'So long as Mac can speak for me.'

'We don't mention theories about townsfolk who might have had something to do with the killings,' the lawyer said, turning to look at Mac. 'And we sure as hell don't utter anything about Ryerson Wainwright.'

'Of course,' Mac said.

'They, on the other hand, might bring those things up. They're going to go right at your motivation, Mac. They're going to accuse you of showboating, of trying to use Mr Dean to cloud your more immediate problem in Linder County. You've got to keep your mouth shut and let them sling their manure.'

'Understood.'

'Finally, we must come across pure as the driven snow, open and above-board, anxious to cooperate. If we don't, the judge will rule against our petition. The murders are unsolved, so are technically still the object of an ongoing investigation. What you're seeking is access to key evidence – evidence they're required to protect under the law. Evidence they'll say they might need someday.'

'They've done nothing for three decades,' Mac said.

'That has no bearing today. We cooperate. They see, touch and impound anything they want. That's the only way Judge Tinley will go along with it.'

'They won't safeguard the evidence if it points to someone in town,' Mac said.

'Agreed, damn it?' Fresh sweat had broken out on the lawyer's brow. No question, the lawyer was ill. Mac and Reed agreed, and the three walked down the stairs to the courtroom.

Peering County's State's Attorney, Roy Powell, and its sheriff, Jimmy Bales, were already seated at a table in front.

Jen Jessup was also there, sitting at the back. She gestured for Mac to hold up for a moment, and they walked to a far corner of the courtroom.

'What on earth are you hoping to learn by all this?' she asked.

'You must have excellent lines into the courthouse,' he said, glancing pointedly at Powell.

'You're not answering my question.'

'It's the best I can do.'

A door opened at the front of the courtroom. The judge came out.

Mac moved to sit behind Rogenet and Reed, both of whom remained standing to face the judge. Several feet away, State's Attorney Roy Powell also rose.

'Let us be informal, but informing,' the judge began. 'Mr Rogenet, precisely what is the urgency of this matter?'

'The petitioner, Mr Dean, is aware of new information—'

'New information, or innuendo?' Powell cut in.

'Real information,' Rogenet shot back, 'that has stabbed at a wound that has not healed for the Dean family.'

'Mr Dean?' the judge asked.

Rogenet spoke. 'If I may, Your Honor, Mr Dean requests that Mayor Bassett present the matter on his behalf. This has moved so fast, not even—'

'Your Honor,' Powell interrupted, 'nothing need move so fast that we can't employ common sense.'

Roy Powell was but the latest peacock in a family of finely feathered lawyer-politicians, a tall man with carefully sprayed gray hair and an even more careful tailor. Mac had heard rumors that Powell's suits cost three thousand dollars apiece.

Judge Tinley held up his hand. 'Let's listen to the petitioner first, shall we, Mr Powell?'

'Yes, Your Honor.'

'Fine, fine. Now, Mr Dean, you wish Mayor Bassett to speak on your behalf?'

Reed Dean had worn his customary denim and western shirt, but today's outfit had been severely starched and pressed, in honor of the court. Even his NASCAR hat, which he held in his hand, was almost funeral – all black, with no trace of red or yellow flames or silver, fast-rolling wheels.

'Yes, Your Honor,' Reed Dean mumbled.

'Speak up, sir,' Judge Tinley said.

'I'd appreciate if Mr Bassett would speak for me,' Reed said, almost shouting.

'And so it will be,' the judge said. 'Mayor Bassett, will you proceed?'

Mac rose to stand next to Rogenet. 'Thank you, Your Honor. Someone in Grand Point asked me if I knew about a pair of murders that occurred here back in June, 1982. I told her I did not. She asked if, in my capacity as mayor, I could look into the case, and report whether there had been any developments in the investigation since 1982.'

'You are referring to the Betty Jo Dean and Paulus Pribilski homicides, is that correct?'

'Yes, sir.'

Judge Tinley turned to the court reporter. 'Let the record reflect that I may have to refer to the sheriff's files on these homicides before issuing a ruling.'

'You'll find nothing, Your Honor,' Mac said. 'The files have been decimated.'

'Decimated, sir?'

'The information that remains in the sheriff's files from 1982 is worthless. There's nothing left.'

'Is this so, Mr State's Attorney?'

Powell, surprised, looked at Bales.

Bales, red-faced, stood up. 'Much of the original material from the investigation has been misplaced, Your Honor.'

Judge Tinley, annoyed, motioned for Mac to continue.

'I have spent the past week trying to ascertain whether the sheriff's department has made any progress on the case at all. They have not, Your Honor.'

'Granting Mr Dean's petition will do what, exactly?'

'Subject his sister's case to a modern forensic examination.'

'A private investigation can't be allowed because of the risk it presents,' State's Attorney Powell said. 'Granted, the case has not progressed as everyone hoped, but because it is still unsolved, it is an active investigation. To allow evidence to be transferred to private hands, especially those of someone who is currently facing criminal charges in another county . . .'

'This is Mr Dean's action, and not Mayor Bassett's, right, Mr Powell?' the judge asked.

'Everybody knows who's behind this action, Your Honor.'

'You're suggesting that Mr Dean or Mayor Bassett will corrupt any evidence that arises?' the judge asked Powell.

Jimmy Bales stifled a laugh.

Judge Tinley frowned, and looked down at Reed Dean. 'Forgive me, Mr Dean, I meant no pun with my unfortunate choice of that last word.'

He turned back to Powell. 'What new efforts have you undertaken to investigate these murders?'

Powell touched his necktie, making sure it was perfectly vertical. 'I'd have to refresh my memory.'

'Enough of this.' Judge Tinley checked his watch, a pointed gesture since there was a large clock on the wall. It was ten minutes to twelve. Rogenet had told Mac that Judge Tinley was known for not suffering long hearings. Nor was he known for being late to lunch.

'One more thing, Your Honor?' Powell asked hurriedly. 'The county is concerned about Mayor Bassett's standing in this matter. He's been traipsing around town, casting aspersion and innuendo at the offices of the *Peering County Democrat*, Wiley's Funeral Home and elsewhere. There's even a report that he bugged the private dining room of the Willow Tree restaurant.'

Judge Tinley leaned forward. 'Bugged? He set up microphones to record people eating?'

'Not merely eating, Your Honor.'

'What then? Drinking, too?'

Roy Powell turned from the judge's sarcasm to glare again at Jimmy Bales.

'More than that, Your Honor,' Bales said.

'You have proof, Sheriff?'

'It's under investigation, Your Honor.'

'Like the Dean-Pribilski murders, or more actively?'

'I suppose more actively,' Bales, the fool, said.

'There's also the burden of cost, Your Honor,' Powell said. 'The county's budget is strained. To incur expense in such an old and perhaps unsolvable case would be an unwelcome burden to the taxpayers of Peering County.'

'Unsolvable? So you do feel you can learn nothing more?'

'I meant merely we don't have the money.'

'Did not Mayor Bassett, speaking for himself and Mr Dean, assert in their filing that they will bear the cost?'

'Well, yes.'

The judge again checked his watch. 'There's a reason why there's no statute of limitation on murder,' he said. 'We must never give up on such cases.'

He hunched over his desk and wrote for a time. Then he looked up and said to the two lawyers, 'You may sign this now and pick up copies from the clerk this afternoon. Here's what it says: "Petitioner Dean's request is granted. It shall be conducted as a cooperative effort, to be jointly supervised by the Illinois State Police, the Peering County Sheriff's Department, the Office of the Peering County Coroner and any such other law enforcement authorities as collectively deemed necessary by the foregoing parties. It shall be accomplished within sixteen days. Peering County shall bear the cost of implementing this order. Any matter or material found as a result of the granting of this petition shall be turned over to the forensic laboratories directed by the assigned State of Illinois forensic pathologists. Attorney Rogenet and Reed Dean may be present for any and all proceedings that result from this order. In consideration of the state's attorney's concerns, Mayor Bassett is denied access to the resultant proceedings. Attorney Rogenet, Reed Dean and Mayor Bassett shall be privy to the subsequent findings that result from this order."'

'Surely . . . surely not sixteen days, Your Honor,' Powell stammered.

'Yes, indeed, Mr State's Attorney. Enough time has been wasted.'

A clatter came from the back of the courtroom. Everyone turned.

Randall White had slipped into the room. He'd pitched forward in a dead faint, and now lay face down in the aisle.

Jen Jessup rushed to help him.

'Exhumation is to be effected within two weeks and two days,' the judge said, standing up. 'Up she comes, gentlemen.'

FORTY-SIX

Two weeks and two days.

The words of the judge's order to exhume Betty Jo Dean flew from Grand Point like bullets, striking television and radio stations and print newsrooms as far away as Iowa City, Springfield, Milwaukee and Chicago. Within hours, reporters began calling Reed Dean at home. He referred them all to Mac.

Mac read each the same statement: "'The Dean family has suffered three decades of not knowing who killed their beloved Betty Jo. It is hoped a modern forensic examination of her remains will aid the Peering County Sheriff's Department in renewing their investigation into the murders of Betty Jo and Paulus Pribilski.'"

Jim Rogenet had written the statement, admonishing Mac to not stray from it. 'Remember what we discussed. Some reporters will recall your indictment and accuse you of using the Dean case to grandstand for publicity on your own behalf. I've put in another call to Wainwright, hoping to block what's sure to be his negative reaction.'

'Especially if he's mixed up in what's been happening to me.'

'Don't go beyond the statement.'

When Jen Jessup called, Mac read her the identical words.

'All right,' she said, 'now tell me the rest.'

'Saying anything more could worsen my chances in Linder County.'

'I hear Farris Hobbs was pushed in front of that oncoming car.'

'A lot of people knew Farris drank at the Bird's Nest.'

'I also heard you always walked him across the highway.'

'Not that night.'

When he didn't say more, she asked, 'Did you ever get to talk to Clamp Reems?'

'That's down the line, after the exhumation.'

'Ever hear how he got the nickname "Clamp?" It seems that Wilbur, as he was known when he was young, was a hard-drinking, cigar-chomping hellion. One night, he got in a fight at Al's Rustic Hacienda. Wilbur's jaw got broken, and they had to wire it so tight there wasn't room for his beloved cigars.'

'So he started using a corn cob pipe to hold his cigars, because its mouthpiece was thin enough to jam into his wired jaw?' Mac laughed.

'There's an unfunny part. The guy who broke his jaw?'

'Yes?'

'Best-case scenario? He got run out of town alive.'

'Worst case: he was killed and his body was never found?'

'I don't know why I'm telling you this,' she said, and clicked off.

Two weeks and two days.

News of Betty Jo Dean's upcoming exhumation helped the Bird's

Nest stagger along. Old-time customers who'd fallen away after the indictment came back to eat, drink and dust off their memories of the place and the case. Curious newcomers came too, for a look at the last roadhouse Betty Jo Dean had ever seen.

And some came, though not nearly as many on the night of the Crosstown Classic, for a glimpse of Mac Bassett, the man behind the whole business of raising up Betty Jo Dean.

They left disappointed. Rogenet had been explicit about Mac not risking any untoward comment that Bales or Powell could use to null the exhumation. So he holed up in his office upstairs, staring at mostly blank old calendars, doctor and dentist bills and precious little else, seeing nothing that could prove he spent most of his nights as a board trustee sleeping at home in Linder County.

Two weeks and two days.

Somewhere in there, Maggie Day made up her mind about strangeness.

One afternoon, setting up the dining room, she said to Mac, 'Abigail Beech stopped in last night.'

'I'd forgotten to ask you about her. She was mentioned in an old news account, insisting Betty Jo was alive for two days after Pribilski was killed.'

'Isn't that what you believe?'

'Well, sure, but . . .'

'She still believes she was right.'

'She's an entertainer, Maggie.'

It was difficult, sometimes, to gauge Maggie's facial reactions because her low riding, broad brimmed cowboy hat and large tinted glasses obscured so much of her face.

She smiled a little. 'She went out to Betty Jo's grave in Maryton. She said something's wrong.'

'Wrong, how?'

'She doesn't know, just that it's wrong.'

Mac let it go. Abigail Beech was likely just looking to build interest in another gig.

Two weeks and two days.

Three days after the judge had issued his order, Mac began stopping into the sheriff's department. It was his only violation of Rogenet's admonishment to keep a low profile.

'When?' he asked, each time.

Bales was always in, always available, and always semi-reclining in the chair he'd worn almost all the leather off from all that semi-reclining. Always, he mouthed the same words: 'We're on it, Mac.'

'When exactly, Sheriff?'

'Just as soon as we can get everybody singing out of the same hymn book. Lots needs to be done. We've got to get the proper paperwork out to the custodian at Maryton Cemetery. We need to do a soil test of the ground, arrange for a backhoe operator to open the grave and get someone with a hoist to haul her out. We need a flatbed truck to bring the vault to wherever the state forensics people say. But first, we've got to hear from the state, so we know the forensics experts they're going to assign, and just exactly when they plan on doing this thing.' Bales would then sigh. 'Such a muddle, Mac. Lots to do, but we're working on it.'

After hearing this for the sixth time, Mac said, 'I'm going to beat my indictment, Jimmy. I'm not leaving.' Bales and whoever tugged his leash were stalling, hoping to drag their feet until Mac got caught up in standing trial, getting convicted and being sent away. They could then work on Reed Dean to withdraw his petition for exhumation.

'I surely hope you win,' Bales said, without a trace of sincerity on his face.

Two weeks and two days.

April brought up the exhumation only once. She was standing by a counter in the kitchen. Her face was rigid, absent of any of the bravado she used to keep the world at bay.

'Why expose us to all this on top of everything else?' she asked. 'Do you really need retribution or justice? Is it really for a girl you'd never heard of until a few days ago?'

He looked at her face, this woman of such quiet strength, and realized it mirrored the doubt that kept him clutching a glass of Scotch most nights.

'I don't know,' he said.

FORTY-SEVEN

On the second Thursday following the judge's order, after Jimmy Bales again smiled and shrugged when Mac stopped in to find out what progress had been made, Mac took a copy of the court's exhumation order down to the cemetery.

Mac had never had occasion to go to Maryton. He knew the town had prospered in the late 1800s as a crossroads trading center, but had withered after the railroad was put through Grand Point, five miles to the north. Houses and stores were abandoned; its few streets crumbled. Folks could not make a living. They'd left.

The dead began coming, then, in abundance. County-owned Maryton Cemetery, surrounded by acres of suddenly worthless land, became the cheapest place to bury the departed of Peering County. Among them were interred the members of the Dean family, going back three generations. Including Betty Jo, in the summer of 1982.

The gray-faced custodian's name was Gerald. He sat in a clammy stone storage building, surrounded by muddy water hoses, rusted lawn rakes and a not-quite-closed desk drawer full of skin magazines.

Mac handed him the exhumation order, which Gerald pointedly set down without reading.

'Never mind these papers, Mayor Bassett,' he said. 'Sheriff's got to set it up. He's paying for the exhumation.'

'Almost two weeks have passed. I'm trying to speed things along. Who will you use for the digging?'

'Ralph, but the sheriff's got to approve.'

'Give me Ralph's number. I'll call him.'

'You need a soil test before anything,' Gerald said.

'Who does that?'

'Ralph. He's got to make sure he don't sink into the beloveds.'

'Let's call him now.'

'I'll have to hunt up his number.'

A large, smiling man in faded overalls appeared in the doorway.

'Wait outside,' Gerald snapped.

The large man extended his hand to Mac. 'Name's Ralph,' he said.

'Damn it,' Gerald muttered. Then: 'Ralph, this here's Mayor Bassett of Grand Point. He's here about the Dean exhumation.'

'Heard about the court order,' Ralph said.

'Nothing's happening,' Mac said.

Ralph looked at the custodian. 'We're waiting for the sheriff, right, Gerald?'

'How's the soil?' Mac asked.

'Shit,' Gerald said.

'Worse than that, maybe,' Ralph said. 'Like to step outside?'

Mac followed him around to a second door. Ralph went in and came out with an eight-foot steel rod. They walked several hundred feet to a small headstone cut with Betty Jo Dean's name. It was small and modest, and hinted nothing at how she must have screamed on Poor Farm Road and, if Ridl was right, in the two days that followed.

Ralph set the steel rod perpendicular to the ground.

'Gerald in there,' he said, cocking a thumb back at the stone building, 'he's been running this cemetery for nigh on forty years. He ain't going to push the sheriff for papers because he don't want no part of any exhumation. Worried hell will pay.'

'Why?'

Ralph wrapped both of his ham-like fists around the rod and pushed down. It quickly slid three feet into the earth.

'Mush,' Mac said.

'That ain't the only problem,' Ralph said. 'Gerald's records are incomplete.'

'About the soil?' Mac asked, confused.

'About how your Miss Dean was buried.'

'I've got a court order. Nothing more is needed.'

Ralph gave him a pitying look. 'Soon as I heard I'd be doing an exhumation, I came out with this here steel rod to get a little heads-up on conditions. I've never done an exhumation, see, but I've dug plenty of holes for burials. Lots of spots around here are as wet and soft as this one, and plenty fill up with ground water before I finish digging. That's a bastard; it's never good dropping beloveds into water.'

He pushed on the rod again. It went down another foot. 'And as you can see,' he said, 'this here is one of the spongy places.'

'You can still do it, right?'

'Diggin's diggin'; I can dig anywhere.' Ralph scratched his chin. 'Look, can we speak confidentially? It might save everybody a ton of grief.'

'Of course.' Mac would have said anything to speed up the man.

'What I'm asking is whether you checked to be sure she's in a vault. You'd want no part of digging up an unprotected casket, right?'

Mac swallowed, trying to force down the queasiness rising in his throat. 'I thought every casket had to be put in a cement vault.'

'You being mayor, you know lots of people around here are poor. Sometimes corners get cut to accommodate their circumstances.'

They'd been putting caskets, unprotected, directly into the ground.

'How do we find out if corners got cut for Betty Jo?'

Ralph turned to unmarked ground to spit. 'Right after we heard we'd be doing the dig-up, we checked our records. They didn't show squat, so we called Wiley's. Luther said all his Betty Jo Dean records are lost. Then he said there'd be lots of press at the exhuming. If things don't go right – meaning no vault – not only would we be disturbing that poor girl for nothing, but we'd be exposing charitable practices right in front of news people with cameras. Burial business workers can do jail time, Luther Wiley said, for not making poor folks come up with money they don't have for vaults.'

He tugged the steel rod out of the ground. Its bottom half was shiny with muck.

'So there you have it,' he said. 'If she's got no vault, there's nothing down there but specks of bone and rotted pine and unnecessary legal trouble for God-fearing people.' He raised his eyebrows. 'And from what I hear, you understand about unnecessary legal trouble?'

'Luther Wiley said it was best if Betty Jo doesn't get disturbed?'

Ralph nodded. 'He'd be liable too, just like Gerald and me, if he can't lay it off on his dead uncle.'

'I'll talk to the family,' Mac said.

He called Reed on his way back to Grand Point. 'You were too young, but do you think Bella remembers whether Betty Jo was buried in a vault?'

'Everybody's got to be buried in a vault.'

'They're telling me at Maryton that isn't always so. Sometimes people can't afford—'

'Sweet shit; you're suggesting Betty Jo was put into the ground without a vault?'

'I'm trying not to think that.'

'I'll call Bella.'

Reed called back in five minutes. 'She doesn't remember.'

Mac called Rogenet. 'If there's no vault, the state will shut down the whole cemetery,' the lawyer said. He was out of breath, like he'd just climbed steep stairs. 'They'll begin digging everywhere. If there are corpses, or what little is left of them, staring back from the holes, things will get crazy. Since the cemetery is county-owned, your sheriff is going to be in the middle of it, along with that funeral director since, from what you've just told me, they both know about this little problem.' The lawyer inhaled deeply. 'For now, Bales has got no choice but to comply with the judge's exhumation order. I'll call him and say I just heard the most fascinating little tidbit about what lies beneath the ground at Maryton. Or not. I'll infer that the best way to keep my mouth shut is for him to proceed pronto, hoping Betty Jo is in a vault.'

Reed phoned late that afternoon. 'Someone named Brown from the State of Illinois just called. Said he was a forensics examiner and wanted to confirm that the exhumation was set for Monday, at eight in the morning.'

'Rogenet worked at warp speed.'

'Not at all,' Reed said. 'I asked Brown how long he'd known. He said he'd arranged things with Jimmy Bales a week ago.'

Mac whistled softly at the sheriff's audacity. 'Bales was going to use his own diggers and exhume without telling us or the press. That would solve the problem of anyone being around to notice whether folks were buried without vaults, and it would give him the chance to use his own fast, friendly doctor. No doubt he planned on re-interring her without the kind of thorough examination we want, hoping the State would then back off, since the work had already been done.'

'Clever bastards,' Reed said. 'Brown said Betty Jo will first be taken to the municipal garage, where she'll be transferred to an ambulance and driven to Rochelle for X-raying at the hospital. Afterward, she'll be returned to the sheriff's examining room in Grand Point, where Brown will collect samples from her fingernails and mouth, whatever.'

'We're almost there, Reed.'

'You think we'll learn anything?'

'We already have.'

'You mean about the sheriff?'

'And Luther Wiley, Horace Wiggins, Doc Farmont and others we don't know about yet. People don't want us anywhere near that forensic examination.'

'We'll know more come Monday morning,' Reed said, and hung up.

It didn't take as long as that.

That night, Randall White, sweat-faced, charged into the Bird's Nest. 'We need to talk, outside,' he said.

Mac led him through the kitchen and out to the Dumpster.

White grabbed Mac's arm. 'You need to stop this foolishness.'

'You mean about me killing Farris Hobbs, as you suggested to the cops?'

'She's coming up, Monday?'

'Eight a.m., but I imagine you knew that before I did.'

'You don't know what you're doing,' White said. 'Folks are going to suffer.'

'They want to know the truth.'

'Leave the truth alone.'

'What the hell . . .?'

'There was a mad panic to get that bullet out of Betty Jo. She was in such bad shape, lying so long out in that field, everybody was hurrying.' Spittle had formed on White's lips.

'What are you talking about?'

'The damned bullet everybody was so anxious to get at.'

'They got it, right?' Mac asked. 'They got the bullet?'

'Doc Farmont slipped away this afternoon,' White said. 'He was painting his boat just this morning. Next thing, someone saw him passing beneath the highway bridge, heading south.'

'He told me he was planning on sailing that boat to the Mississippi, then down to the Gulf of Mexico, but that wasn't going to be for another week or so.'

'You're not listening,' White said. 'I saw Doc just this morning, painting his boat.'

'Doc put the boat in the water while the paint was still wet? That sounds like he's as afraid of the exhumation as much as you are.'

'No good will come from it.'

'I'll remember that,' Mac called out to the man's back. Because by then, White was hurrying away like a man fleeing an avalanche.

FORTY-EIGHT

Mac got to Maryton in the first gray mist of Monday's dawn, edgy with fear that the ground beneath Betty Jo Dean's tombstone was mush and contained nothing but black slivers of decayed pine, a loose collection of bones, and nothing to point to the men who laughed at the sound of Betty Jo's name.

He parked his truck outside the fence, walked through the gates and headed toward the grave. A quick last look, a murmured word of apology to Betty Jo Dean, and he'd be gone.

A dark figure knelt in the distance. It was a woman, dressed in a black gown. Oddly, for the day was already warm, she wore a dark, broad-brimmed hat with a long black veil.

He got closer and saw she was kneeling on Betty Jo Dean's grave. She stood up. 'The child is not at rest,' she said.

Mac knew that voice. 'Abigail?' He couldn't see her face through the veil. 'Abigail Beech?' She'd worn the same sort of costume, minus the hat and the veil, at the Bird's Nest.

'The child is not at rest,' she repeated. 'Her face is wrong.'

'She's being exhumed today.'

'Her face . . . it's wrong.'

'What do you mean?'

She said nothing, and started toward the gate.

Doubt clawed at him as he watched her walk away. Perhaps he hadn't the right to set loose the men and machines that would rip into the ground to get at Betty Jo Dean. Perhaps he hadn't the right to call forth reporters who would resurrect details of her death and likely invent lurid new ones about her life. Perhaps he had no damned right at all to create a spectacle that drew the likes of Abigail Beech, murmuring behind a black veil.

For the first time since Judge Tinley's courtroom, he was grateful that State's Attorney Powell and Jimmy Bales demanded he be barred from the exhumation. He didn't want to watch. He didn't want to be seen.

He hurried back to his truck.

Two men drove a large stake truck into the cemetery at seven o'clock. They stopped well back of Betty Jo's grave and unloaded long metal poles. They built the skeleton of a temporary fence, unrolled long gray plastic tarps and stretched them between the poles. The tarps would shield the site from the road.

Two Peering County sheriff's cruisers rolled up at seven-thirty. The first drove between the gates and continued up to the blue temporary fence. The second stopped at the entrance and a deputy got out to stand guard. Only authorized people could get in now.

Through the wrought-iron fence, Mac saw Jimmy Bales and State's Attorney Powell get out of the first cruiser. Bales's uniform was rumpled, as though he'd already wilted in what was sure to be a very hot day. Powell wore a crisp, blue-and-white-striped seer-sucker suit that would never look wilted. They disappeared behind the gray plastic wall.

Big flatbed trucks drove into the cemetery ten minutes later and pulled close to the gravesite. The first carried a backhoe. The digger got out, pulled down a ramp and offloaded the yellow diesel machine.

The second truck was fitted with a high, long I-beam that ran from its cab back past the rear bumper. A winch with a thick cable was mounted at the tail end. It would be used to hoist out whatever was in the ground, should there be anything solid enough to lift.

Several private cars arrived next. Most appeared to be reporters, and were denied entrance. Only two men shouldering big camera bags were allowed inside. Mac guessed they were state photo-graphers, there to record the exhumation.

Jen Jessup arrived in her blue Neon. She got out and marched up to the gates like she belonged. Mac waited for her to be stopped, but she never even slowed. She flashed a smile at one of the depu-ties, he touched the brim of his Smokey hat with a forefinger in a small salute, and she walked right into the cemetery. One of the reporters who'd been denied access swore.

Reed Dean arrived in his red Mustang at the last possible minute. He parked on the road outside the fence. He wore jeans as always, a starched dark shirt and a bright red NASCAR cap, as if for courage. Spotting Mac, he gave a faint wave and walked through the gates to watch what remained of his sister being dug up.

The diesel backhoe fired at precisely eight o'clock, sending up big puffs of black smoke from behind the gray screens. Mac watched through the side window of his truck, imagining the spongy ground being torn open by the long steel teeth of the backhoe's bucket. The backhoe labored for twenty minutes before the smoke thinned, and its engine lapsed into a soft, loping idle. Then it went silent.

Mac shut his eyes, not wanting to think that, behind the gray screen, the sheriff, the state's attorney, the diggers, the hoisters, the photographers, Jen Jessup and Reed Dean were looking down at nothing but bits of rotted pine amid a jumble of skeletal parts.

Another diesel started, different, quieter. He watched the gray tarps for black smoke, but none rose up. It was a good sign; it was not the backhoe, filling the hole back in. It was the truck with the winch.

Ten minutes passed, then ten more. And then, with a clash of gears, the truck carrying the hoist rumbled through the cemetery gates and onto the road. It turned north toward Grand Point.

On it rested a coffin-shaped rectangle, covered in blue plastic secured with silver tape. A vault.

Jimmy Bales and Roy Powell followed in the sheriff's cruiser. Jen Jessup walked out with the official photographers.

Reed Dean came out last, walking faster than Mac had ever seen him move. His forehead was glistening. He came over to Mac's truck. 'Cement vault,' he said. 'Solid, no cracks. She's been preserved.' He hurried to his Mustang.

Mac waited for Reed to pull onto the road, then followed him north to where they were taking his sister.

FORTY-NINE

The four big overhead doors were raised. Thirty people milled within the high metal garage – sheriff's deputies and state police officers; a damp Jimmy Bales talking to the ever crisp Roy Powell; photographers and reporters and the simply curious who'd drifted in to see what had become of Betty Jo Dean. A man in cut-off jeans and a white T-shirt waited by an open-topped orange tool cart. In the corner, half hidden in shadow, Jen Jessup stood talking to the city clerk.

The truck rigged with the huge I-beam and winch was the only vehicle inside. A man stood on its flatbed. He'd removed the blue tarp and was attaching the hoist cable to a four-pointed sling wrapped around the damp, mud-encrusted vault.

One of the photographers waited behind a video camera mounted on a tripod. He'd aimed it at a square canvas tarp spread out on the floor, behind the truck.

There were no deputies guarding the door. Mac eased in to where Reed was pressed against a far wall.

'They'll take her out of the vault here,' Reed said, 'drive her to Rochelle for X-raying and bring her back to the county's medical examining room next door.'

Bales had spotted Mac. He left Powell and hurried over. 'You're not supposed to be in here.'

'Doc Farmont took off.'

'He left on a planned vacation.'

'He put his boat in the water with its paint still wet.'

'Get the hell out of here, Mac.'

'I'm filling in for Rogenet,' he lied. 'Besides, this seems to be open to everybody,' he said, pointing to the reporters and locals watching the two men working to lower the vault.

Bales worked up a smile. 'You're satisfied with your little diversion?'

'Little diversion?'

'Shifting the focus from your own difficulties?'

'I'm downright excited at the prospect of uncovering something that points to Betty Jo Dean's killer.'

Bales walked away.

The winch on the flatbed groaned as the cable tightened around the concrete vault. 'Easy does it,' the worker by the tool cart yelled.

The man on the flatbed nodded, raised the vault slowly until it was a foot off the truck bed, pivoted the hoist and lowered the vault gently onto the tarp.

The man on the floor took a thin crowbar from his cart and began scoring the vault's lid to loosen any grit that might hold it closed. When he'd gone all the way around, he grabbed a hammer, inserted the blade end of the crowbar into the seam and went around again, gently tapping into the seam. Finally, he inserted a larger crowbar into the seam at a corner and struck it hard. A crack like a gunshot boomed off the metal walls as a piece of the lid broke off and bounced to the tarp.

The second photographer stepped up with a digital camera and took several pictures of the broken corner. After he stepped back, the man with the hammer swung again. Another piece of the lid fell away.

Reed pointed to a tall, gray-haired man and a short, stout woman standing together in the pool of sunlight, just inside one of the big open doors. 'That's Doctor Brown, the state's forensic M.D. The woman is his assistant.'

The man with the hammer swung at the crowbar again. More pieces of the lid fell onto the floor.

'Everybody stand back,' Powell, cool in seersucker and in command, called out. People stepped back, but not much.

The worker hit the vault again. This time the entire corner disintegrated, exposing wire mesh molded into the concrete. He pulled away the loose pieces and set down his tools. The man who operated the winch came up and they lifted off the lid and set it on the floor.

The still photographer moved around the opened vault, snapping photos of the casket inside. Suddenly he stopped and bent to snap a fast series of shots of one corner.

He lowered the camera and pointed to something wedged between the casket and the vault's inside wall. 'Come here,' he called to State's Attorney Powell.

Powell and Jimmy Bales hurried up. Bales started to reach where the photographer pointed.

'Not without gloves,' the photographer said quickly.

Bales dropped his hand. Dr Brown, the state's forensic M.D., pulled on thin surgical gloves and walked up to the vault. He reached into the gap, removed what looked like a large cloth wrapped in newspaper and carried it across the room to an empty table against the far wall.

Mac and Reed stepped closer to the vault. The coffin inside was covered thick with chalky grit, the same color as the cement vault.

The man who'd opened the vault picked up the hammer and pry bar, and split the arched casket top into large pieces. It took only a moment to remove the top half of the casket lid.

White silk fabric lay across what was inside. The lining of the casket lid had fallen down after so many years.

'Your turn,' the worker said to the doctor.

Dr Brown, still wearing gloves, stepped forward and gently lifted the white silk just enough to peer beneath it. Shaking his head, he motioned for his assistant to come up.

'I don't know why the hell this is, but we'll send her this way.'

Mac turned to Reed, and was surprised to see him looking at the table where Dr Brown had set the partially wrapped fabric recovered from the vault. Reed was trembling.

'I need to be sure,' Reed said, and started walking toward the table.

Mac followed him across the garage.

The fabric, a dark print, had been folded neatly inside the newspaper.

'Don't touch,' someone called out from across the garage.

'No need, damn it all to hell,' Reed shouted back. 'I know what it is.'

'What is it, Reed?'

'My sister's dress.'

'You can remember that? You were only six when she died.'

'I got photographs of that fabric.' Reed Dean clenched his fists, unable to continue.

'Why, Mr Dean?' Jen Jessup said. She'd seen Reed's eyes fill with tears and come over.

'That's the dress Betty Jo was supposed to wear to Fred Junior's wedding,' he said. 'My mother and Betty Jo both got identical dresses. Mother insisted Betty Jo be buried in hers, and Mother wore hers when the wedding finally took place, later that year. Mother said Betty Jo wearing that dress was sort of like her being there at the wedding. I have the wedding pictures, everybody trying to look happy.' He looked at Mac. 'Don't you understand? Those bastards at Wiley's threw her in her casket naked, like some dead animal.' He gripped Mac's arm. 'Who does that?'

Mac could only shake his head. He couldn't find words good enough to mean anything.

Reed turned to Jen Jessup. 'What kind of sons of bitches bury a young girl naked?'

Jen was looking past Reed, toward the center of the garage. The cavernous space had gone quiet.

'And in that,' she said, pointing.

FIFTY

She'd been zipped in a dark vinyl body bag. It was wet at the
bottom.

Two sheriff's deputies and two state troopers each grabbed
a corner, lifted the bag onto a gurney and wheeled it to an ambulance
that had backed into the garage. They loaded her in, slammed the
door and the state troopers ran to their cars. One pulled in front of
the ambulance, one tucked in behind, and together they formed a
small motorcade to drive the girl to the hospital in Rochelle.

At least there was respect in that.

Reed watched it all in a stunned silence. 'Naked, in a damned
bag?'

Mac walked over to Bales. 'You better hope that was just ground
water, or Reed's going to start thinking he ought to sue everyone
in the county.'

Bales had lost his bluster, shocked like the rest of them by the
sight of the wet bag. 'We won't know about damage until they come
back,' he said, almost too quiet to hear.

'That small bundle wedged in the vault?'

Bales looked at Mac, confused. 'What?'

'That fabric wedged between the casket and the vault? Get it
photographed some more, for the record. Right now, before it gets
disturbed.'

'Why?'

'It's the dress she was to be buried in.'

Bales nodded vaguely. It was obvious he didn't understand. Mac
went to get the still photographer, and led him to the table. Bales
followed behind, slowly, like his feet hurt.

Reed stepped in front of the sheriff. 'Get your sorry ass over to
Wiley's and find out why the hell they buried her like an animal.
Find out what was so damned important they couldn't take the time
to prepare her respectfully.'

'Now, Reed, nobody's going to know that after all this time.'

'Luther was part of it, back then. Ask him, or I will. He'll be a
hell of a lot happier if you do it.'

Bales looked outside, no doubt thinking that to get away, down
to Wiley's, would be wise.

Mac turned to the photographer, who shot two fast pictures of
the parcel on the table and walked away. He wasn't being paid for
confrontation.

Reed's face was now within a foot of Bales's. 'Something you
don't understand about what I just said?'

'The sheriff's department had nothing to do with the burial,'
Bales said.

'You'll be going over to Wiley's,' Reed said.

'It could . . . could have been just ground water,' Bales stammered.

'It's not just about the wetness, you idiot. It's about the dress.'

Bales headed outside.

Through it all, Jen Jessup had stood silently by, taking notes and
saying nothing.

'How about an early lunch, Reed?' Mac asked. 'Or just a drink?'
The best thing he could do was to get Reed out of there. 'She won't
be back for a couple of hours.'

Reed shook his head and moved closer to the dress wadded in
newspaper on the table. 'I need to stay here.'

Mac went outside, crossed the highway and walked the three
blocks to the funeral home.

Luther Wiley was in his office, seated behind his immaculate,
empty desk. As before, the thick, cloying smell of flowers worked
at masking everything. But that morning, the office smelled stronger
of something more. Whiskey.

It was no surprise that Jimmy Bales was not there.

'Tell me again how you weren't involved in preparing Betty Jo
Dean for burial,' Mac said from the doorway.

'I don't know what you mean.'

'My guess is you've already heard about Betty Jo Dean's vault
being opened.'

'She's on her way to Rochelle for X-raying.'

'You didn't bother to put clothes on her. Her dress was jammed
between her casket and the vault.'

'My uncle handled everything.'

'She was jammed in a body bag that's now wet. Did you even
bother to embalm her?'

'What the hell do you want, Bassett? She was badly decomposed.
She'd been lying in that field for days.'

'Searchers said otherwise. She wasn't there the day they found Pribilski, or the next.'

'My uncle prepared her for Maryton, not me.'

'You've put plenty of others into that ground since then.'

'What are you talking about?'

'Vaults, Luther, or rather, the lack of them.'

Luther's face paled under the rouge.

It was a fine day for feeling mean. 'I'm thinking you'll do time, Luther,' Mac said, and left.

Crossing the courthouse lawn, he stopped to face the panorama of the town. The old building, decked out with banners for the Fourth of July, seemed to be especially mocking that day with false promises of justice. The ancient fronts surrounding the square seemed to be a sham as well. He'd once seen them as stable embodiments of solid values, built to last for all time. Now they looked false, flimsy things built to obscure. One had shrouded the goings-on of Doc Farmont. Horace Wiggins still worked behind another, churning out his strange mix of truths, half-truths and outright lies. And just a few blocks north, in a fancy old Victorian house, the Wileys – uncle and likely his nephew – had perpetrated a last act of desecration, throwing Betty Jo Dean unclothed into a vinyl bag. Somehow, that last, indifferent act seemed the most galling of all. Reed Dean had been right. They'd buried her like an animal.

Someone stood across the street, half-hiding behind a tree, watching the road from Rochelle. It was Randall White, waiting for Betty Jo Dean.

The bile he'd been fighting all day rose in the back of his throat. He came up on White from behind.

'Waiting for Betty Jo?'

White spun around, his face pale.

'I couldn't help noticing your interest in the road, Mr White. I expect it will be some time before they bring her and her secrets back, though already there have been interesting developments. The sheriff and the state police will want to speak with you.'

'I tried to warn you.'

'Genital warts?'

'Opening her casket. She was in bad shape.'

'Too bad to dress? Too bad to do anything but treat her like a Pinktown slut and throw her in a bag in a box?'

White blanched. 'I don't know anything about that. Those things happened at the funeral home.'

'You were at that funeral home, Mr White. You liked to assist Doc Farmont.'

'Others were there, too. I only did what Doc said.'

'And what, exactly, was that?'

'What Clamp said. The bullet, mainly.'

'Doc's gone. Everything falls down on you, now.'

Sweat sparkled on White's forehead. 'I did nothing wrong.'

'What else are they going to learn today, Mr White?'

White turned and looked down the road in the other direction, a rat trapped in the sun.

'What else, Mr White?'

'There was a mad panic to get at her bullet.'

'Who was in a mad panic?'

'I had nothing to do with that. Nothing, you understand?' He hurried down the sidewalk, away from the courthouse, away from the metal garage and away from the truth he feared, that was on its way back from Rochelle.

FIFTY-ONE

The ambulance brought her back after two hours and forty-nine minutes. Only then did Reed leave the dress at the table and come to stand with the cops and the curious as she was carried into the examining room. She'd been put inside a new body bag, this one made of a beige, synthetic material.

A sheriff's deputy stopped Mac from following the official personnel in. 'Only those with permission, Mr Bassett.'

'He's with me,' Reed said.

'Doesn't matter,' the deputy said.

Mac stepped back, motioning for Reed to go in without him. Jen Jessup came up and, getting a nod from the deputy, went into the room. Through the doorway, Mac saw her approach Roy Powell. They spoke for a moment, and Powell came to the doorway.

Without looking at Mac, he spoke to the deputy. 'So long as

Mayor Bassett remains at the back, he is welcome to attend the proceedings.'

Such was the power of the press.

The examining room was large and painted a deceitfully cheerful light green. White cabinets and white Formica counters lined two of the walls. The floor was glossy white tile.

Reed stood braced against the rear wall as though he was trying to push himself back into the cinderblocks.

His sister lay on a stainless steel table at the front of the room.

Dr Brown and his stout assistant were laying out shiny utensils on the stainless-steel table. They'd put on blue cotton coats and fresh, thin green gloves. They'd not gone to Rochelle. Presumably they'd consult those films later, after their examination.

Their faces were expressionless, their hands sure. No doubt they'd done this a thousand times.

One photographer stood at each end of the table. The video man had again set his camera on a tripod, the still photographer held his Canon at the ready. It was reassuring. The state was meticulously documenting everything.

Several uniformed officers stood loosely lined up between the table and the spectators. The two state police cops were the ones who'd escorted the ambulance to Rochelle. Three others were county deputies. Clamp Reems, the chief deputy, said nothing, and looked at no one.

State's Attorney Powell stood away from the table, talking with Jen Jessup, the only reporter in the room.

Mac glanced at Reed, who stared straight ahead. He wondered whether Reed was seeing anything at all.

Dr Brown unzipped the new beige body bag, exposing the original black bag inside, and paused briefly so both photographers could record the first step. No one spoke. Other than the fast clicks of the digital camera, the only sound in the room was the irregular thrumming of a bad bearing in the exhaust fan overhead.

'There is fluid accumulated at the bottom of the original black vinyl enclosure,' Dr Brown dictated into the overhead microphone. 'It has leaked into the new body bag.'

The new bag was meant to contain whatever was leaking from the original. Mac snuck another look at Reed, wondering how many more such horrors the man was going to have to endure that day. The doubt he'd felt at the cemetery that morning struck at him again. Ripping Betty Jo out of the earth might answer nothing, and traumatize her family in ways he'd never imagined, particularly if she'd begun to dissolve.

Dr Brown unzipped the black body bag that had enshrouded Betty Jo Dean since 1982, and folded back the flaps. For an instant there was no sound. And then his assistant gasped, and dropped her long metal probe to clatter loudly on the white tile floor.

'My God,' he whispered, disbelieving, dropping his hands to his sides.

One of Bales's deputies stepped forward. 'Jesus,' he said.

'Please!' Brown recovered to say. 'You must all remain back from the table. I will ask the troopers and deputies to eject anyone approaching the table. There is to be no talking, as that will interfere with the recording of this proceeding. Let us all do our jobs. Let us conduct our examination and collect our samples. Only then may you come forward to view this most unfortunate young woman.'

Reed Dean had gone pale. 'What the hell is going on?'

Mac shook his head, unable to imagine what had unnerved the forensics team. The young deputy who'd looked into the bag had turned to stare at a side wall. His chin was trembling and he was taking long, deep breaths.

Dr Brown reached into the unzipped black body bag with a tweezers. 'Pubic hair,' he said, depositing a sample into a plastic bag his assistant was holding open.' Then: 'Finger nail, right index,' 'finger nail, right middle,' and 'thumb nail, right hand.'

The sheriff's deputy who'd seen her hurried to the door and pushed it open. His face had gone pale and he was sweating like he was about to throw up.

Mac could take no more. He charged past the uniforms and up to the steel table. The air left his lungs. Never had he imagined this.

Her flesh had turned gray and mottled, and glistened with moisture that shouldn't have been there. Years of decomposition had done that, from the carelessness of those who'd raced to hide her beneath the ground. But that wasn't the horror.

It was the skull. It was loose. It lay at the top of the bag, its top slightly dislodged above the eye sockets, canted crazily like a poorly fitted lid of some grotesque cookie jar. The jaw hung open in a ghastly silent scream.

Impossibly, it was missing even the barest speck of flesh.

'Get him the hell out of here!' Jimmy Bales yelled.

Boots shuffled behind him and strong arms gripped both his arms. They spun him away from the girl.

'You damned fools! Can't you see?' he shouted, struggling to face the hatred in their eyes.

The troopers half-lifted him, propelling him toward the door. Bales raced to jerk it open.

'Can't you see?' Mac shouted as he was shoved into the hall. *'That's not her head.'*

FIFTY-TWO

One of Bales's deputies took up a post outside the door to block Mac from trying to get back in. It was a laugh, if laughs could be gotten that morning, so close to the horror that lay on the stainless steel table inside. He never wanted to get near that loose, screaming skull again.

He took off across the green of the courthouse square. Vague, nonsensical thoughts floated in his head. Stronger than any of them, the morning's dark specter of Abigail Beech, entertainer, psychic, and – please, God – part time lunatic, came back to him. 'There's something wrong with her face,' she'd murmured, rising up from Betty Jo's ground.

'Indeed there is, Abigail,' Mac thought, calmer now. 'Someone cut it off.'

But there was more than that. Even if his mind did not yet see, his gut had known enough to give it words: 'That's not her head.'

He reached the highway and slowed to a walk, the image of what he'd just seen still on fire in his brain. The skin on her body had deteriorated to a soft, gray, paste-like substance, but the skull was devoid of even the smallest particle of flesh. And it was loose.

Footsteps charged up loud behind him. 'Happy now, you damned fool?' Randall White sneered.

'Explain the butchery.'

'Doc had to remove her head to get at the bullet.'

'There's no flesh on the skull like there is on the rest of the body.'

White's face relaxed, his confidence growing. He actually smiled, showing the stubs of dark teeth. 'Doc dissolved the flesh away. He moved her head back and forth from one bucket of lye water to another, loosening the soft stuff off to get at the bullet.'

'He could have used a probe.'

'I wasn't there.' White smiled even more broadly now. 'All I heard was the bullet was embedded deep, and there was a mad panic to get at it.'

'Why panic?'

'Because of the decomp. She needed to be buried to ease the family's suffering.'

Mac had the errant hope that nothing supernatural had happened that morning, that Abigail Beech had simply learned of Betty Jo's decapitation, back in the day. She'd used that to whisper her ethereal visions to Mac that morning. She'd been showboating, trying to pass as a psychic; she'd been hustling for a gig.

'Who else knew Doc Farmont removed her head?'

White smirked. 'Have to ask Doc.'

'He's gone, leaving you to explain everything to the sheriff.'

'Like Jimmy Bales ain't already heard?'

'Bales knew her head had been removed?'

'Ain't saying yes; ain't saying no. I only know I wasn't in the room when the cutting was done.'

'You'll need to tell this to state police.'

'Say I *heard* Doc Farmont removed Betty Jo's head, sloshed it in lye water to get that bullet to plop out, kerplunk, on the floor? You tell them for me.' White spat once on the sidewalk and walked away.

He went back to the courthouse. The deputy was still guarding the door. Mac leaned against one of the sheriff's cruisers. He didn't have to lean long.

Fifteen minutes later, the guard moved aside, and two state troopers, each carrying a large insulated cooler, stepped out. Dr Brown and his assistant followed close behind. Roy Powell and Jen Jessup came next, followed by Jimmy Bales, who was talking to Reed Dean. Clamp Reems came out last, alone.

Mac fell in step alongside Dr Brown. 'Were her fingernails clipped?' he asked.

'What?'

'Could you tell if her fingernails had been freshly clipped?'

'If only . . .' Brown shook his head.

Bales had been steering Reed toward the corner of the building, away from everyone. But when he saw Mac walking with the doctor, he hustled over.

Bales grabbed Mac's shirt, allowing the forensics team to walk on. 'Leave those folks alone.'

'You've got a problem with that skull, Jimmy,' he said.

'It's bullshit, you yelling out it's not Betty Jo's. Lots of things can explain it.'

'Randy White just tried. He said there was a panic to get at the bullet, so Doc Farmont cut off her head. That's preposterous, but he inferred you already knew that.'

'I know no such thing. The staties are taking her skull, vertebrae, femur and all the other samples to their lab. They'll straighten out your stupid theories.'

Reed Dean walked over. 'They said they'll put the hurry-up on it, and report by the end of the week,' he said to Mac.

'That's awfully fast,' Mac said.

'You saw the fluid in the bottom of the bag,' Bales said. 'Those fingernails you're so curious about? They've been soaking all these years. The doctor doesn't think he'll get anything from them.'

Jen Jessup had come to stand next to Reed.

'Doesn't it bother you that Pribilski's corpse was cleaned,' Mac asked Bales, 'and that his fingernails were clipped before he was released to his family?'

Jen had pulled out a thin notebook. 'How do you know these things?' she asked Mac.

'Old newspaper microfilms in Chicago. One was especially informative, written in part by a DeKalb girl.'

Jen Jessup's face changed, just a little.

'People need to be careful what they write,' Bales said.

'You're not curious about any of this, Jimmy?' Mac asked.

'Staties will analyze everything.'

'Will the staties tell you why her head was cut off?'

'Like you just said, Doc needed to get that bullet.'

'Did you notice how the top of the skull was slightly dislodged?'

'There was a cut, yes,' Bales said.

'Doc did that, to get at the bullet?'

'Let's wait for the staties.'

'Odd, isn't it, to have to remove the whole skull when the top was simply removed?'

'Maybe the top was removed after,' Bales said.

'Why not ask Doc Farmont?'

'Doc's on vacation.'

'So I heard. Still, he's sure to have a cell phone.' He looked around. Clamp Reems was gone. 'In the meantime, you can question your own chief deputy. He might shed light on all sorts of things.'

'Clamp tried for years to hunt down the killers. It's the biggest failure of his life.'

The flatbed hoist truck rumbled by, taking Betty Jo in a new cement vault back to Maryton.

'She's safe now,' Bales said. 'New casket, new vault, all courtesy of Peering County,' he said to Reed Dean.

'And still buck naked, except for her underwear,' Reed said. 'My mother brought that bridesmaid's dress to the funeral parlor so she could be dressed proper. Old man Wiley just jammed the dress into the vault.'

'Not jammed, Reed,' Mac said quickly, flirting with a new realization. 'It was carefully wrapped in newspaper, then placed almost respectfully between the vault and the casket.'

Everyone, Reed and Bales and Jen Jessup, looked at Mac like he'd lost his mind.

'What the hell are you talking about?' Reed asked.

'Respect,' Mac said, seeing leaves placed to cover a murdered girl's head, and slacks folded neatly on her body. And now, a dress placed carefully inside the vault.

'Some odd, fast, last gesture of respect,' he said again.

He wondered if that proved Betty Jo Dean's killer had been at Wiley's just before she'd been sent off to Maryton for the first time.

FIFTY-THREE

Mac couldn't push it from his mind. Under the guise of searching for a bullet, they'd cut off her head and replaced it with another.

None of it could make sense.

Working in his office, calculating bills he couldn't afford to pay, or struggling to think of anything that would prove he'd spent most nights in Linder County, suddenly seemed easier than wondering about the skull.

Rogenet called as he was approaching the Bird's Nest. 'I heard the autopsy just ended.'

'You've got good ears.'

'No; I called Powell's office. His secretary said he was on his way back from the autopsy. How did it go?'

'Powell let me in.' He told Rogenet about the skull.

'Based on only a brief glance, you announced it wasn't hers?'

'I like to think I lost my head, too,' he said, offering a joke.

Rogenet wheezed into the phone, not laughing. The man was still sick.

'You've got to put that out of your mind for now,' the lawyer said. 'Wainwright finally called. He wants to meet me the day after tomorrow, at two in the afternoon. That's because, the day after that, he and I are up before the judge for a status hearing, and Wainwright wants to pretend he's tried diligently to get this pled out. I want you in the hall outside his office, dressed nice, clutching a thick sheaf of papers that prove you spent almost every night sleeping in Linder County.'

'I'm not taking a plea.'

'Work with me, damn it. We have to show the court we want this resolved without a trial, too.'

'No plea, but I'll be there.'

'You've got another problem. Remember I said I called Powell's office?'

'What now?'

'There's a rumor he's looking to indict you in Peering County.'

Mac cut the truck's engine and closed his eyes. 'What for?'

'Theft of honest services.'

'What's that?'

'A vague, some say unconstitutional, law that prohibits public officials from providing less than full, honest service to their constituents. Its constitutionality is under challenge, but for now it's being used as a catch-all for prosecutors fishing to indict.'

He opened his eyes and looked at the back of the Bird's Nest. The roof was sagging more than before, the windows were losing paint. And now, there was that rectangle charred onto the siding, warning Mac to back away from Betty Jo Dean – warning diners, too, to stay away from a restaurant likely to go up in flames.

'How can Powell use theft of honest services against me?' he asked.

'I'm guessing he'll allege inappropriate use of your mayoral power in the Betty Jo Dean case.'

'That's crap.'

'It's push-back by those who run Grand Point. Powell's one of them.'

'And Wainwright's helping him. It was him I saw, in that red Cadillac speeding out of Grand Point.'

'Concentrate on proving you spent most of your nights in Linder County. See you Wednesday afternoon.'

'Ruminating?' Maggie Day stood in the doorway to his office. He hadn't heard her come up the stairs. It was closing time.

'Jim Rogenet is going to meet with Wainwright Wednesday afternoon. I'm supposed to bring proof positive I spent most of my nights in Linder County.'

She glanced down at the dozen sheets of tablet paper he'd filled up. 'That's encouraging,' she said.

'I don't have receipts. All I can do is summarize my case.' He told her that Roy Powell was readying an indictment against him.

'Pushback for Betty Jo Dean, or for defeating Pete Moore for mayor?'

'Either, or both.'

'You're sure you have no receipts or charge card statements from Linder County?'

'I made a point of buying here in Grand Point, to get to know the local merchants.'

She brightened with a thought. 'Gasoline receipts?'

'I always pay cash. And I filled up here.'

'I need to think on that,' she said, pursing her lips. 'April told me the autopsy didn't go well.'

'She was in bad shape, Maggie.'

'Is she happy?'

He would have laughed at that if that question had been asked by anyone other than Maggie Day. He knew she was dead serious.

'Maybe she's the only one who's pleased. Her story is finally getting out.'

She sat down in the chair across from his desk. 'Abigail called me earlier today. She said something about Betty Jo's face, but nothing about her whole head being removed.'

'Abigail was at the cemetery first thing this morning, kneeling at the grave. She's strange, Maggie.'

'But she's not stupid. And in spite of what others say, she doesn't seek publicity.'

'Your Miss Beech was all over this case back in 1982.'

'Trying to help the family.'

'Or trying to get publicity.'

'Didn't that reporter, Jonah Ridl, tell you Betty Jo couldn't have been lying dead off Devil's Backbone Road from the get-go, because he himself searched that field and she wasn't there?'

'Yes.'

'Plus you yourself saw no decomposition in that one photo?'

'Yes, again.'

'See? Abigail was right, back then, about Betty Jo not being killed at the same time as Pribilski, just like she was right this morning about something being wrong with her face. She's theatrical, and she puts on a good show. That doesn't mean she's a fake or a hustler. She believes.'

'Abigail could have heard about Betty Jo's decapitation, back in the day.'

'Speaking of hearing things, that state's attorney, Roy Powell, your baddest new enemy?'

'Yeah?'

'He used to sleep with your newest reporter friend, Jen Jessup.'

'Shit.'

'Be careful what you tell her.' She got up. 'Stay out of prison, Mac. Betty Jo needs you around.'

FIFTY-FOUR

The state's report on Betty Jo Dean's death came fast, like something nasty hurriedly scraped off a shoe. It was emailed mid-Wednesday morning, simultaneously, to State's Attorney Powell and Sheriff Jimmy Bales.

Bales called Reed Dean. Reed called Mac.

'The report's in,' Reed said. 'Sheriff wants me to come at one o'clock, so he can put it to bed.'

'Those were his words: "put it to bed?"'

'Sounds like whitewash,' Reed said. 'I need you to come along.'

'I've got a meeting in Linder County at two.'

'It shouldn't take but five or ten minutes. Still, I'll call Bales and tell him we'll be there at twelve-thirty.'

When Mac came out of his house he saw a thick white business envelope under his windshield wiper. His name was written on a lavender sticky note attached to it. He recognized Maggie's handwriting.

He peeked inside and laughed at the childlike, naive cunning she sometimes threw at the world. She'd been caring, concerned and preposterous. He jammed the envelope into his suit jacket.

Jimmy Bales was out to lunch at twelve-thirty. Reed told the duty officer they were there to pick up a report. The duty officer told them to wait.

'I talked to him personally, Mac,' Reed Dean said as they took chairs. 'I told him you had a meeting in Linder County at two, and that we'd be here at twelve-thirty.'

'That might be why he's late, but we'll give it a few minutes.'

Jimmy Bales didn't walk in until one-fifteen. 'Mac has no reason to be here, Reed,' he said as he led them to his office.

'I told you he'd be here as my representative,' Reed Dean said.

'Representative for what?'

Reed looked to Mac.

'Representative for what happens next,' Mac said carefully. 'And that will depend on what is, and is not, in the state's report.'

Bales turned to the computer behind him, pressed one button, then another. The small printer came alive and ejected two sheets. Bales handed them to Reed.

Reed held them up so they could both read. Most of the space on the pages was white. The verbiage was slight. There were three conclusions:

'One individual is represented across the skeletal remains.' The first sentence was clearly directed at Mac's outburst during the autopsy, when he'd shouted that the skull did not belong to Betty Jo Dean.

'Nothing usable for chemical analysis was extracted from the body. It had not been embalmed. The hands and fingers, in particular, have been resting in liquefied material for some long period of time.' The second conclusion was no surprise.

'A bullet entered the cranium through the left side of the anterior nasal aperture, then traveled across the foramen magnum and struck the posterior left rim of the foramen magnum.'

Mac looked up from the report. 'What's the *"foramen magnum?"*'

Jimmy Bales was smiling, an indulgent man. 'I had to look it up, too. It's the base of the skull, where the spinal cord enters to join the brain.'

'This report says she was shot through the nose, and the bullet traveled downward to lodge at the back of her skull, at the base of her brain?'

'You got it, Mac. Like this.' Bales raised his chin so that his face was angled sharply upward. He then pointed his forefinger, as though it was the barrel of a gun, downward against his left nostril. In that position, a bullet would angle down, from front to back, through the skull.

'You now have the official results from the Illinois State Police,' Bales said, dropping his hand.

Mac looked at the signature line at the end of the report. 'Someone named Darrel Thompson prepared this,' he said.

'So I saw,' Bales said.

'Why not Doctor Brown?'

'He must have given his notes to this guy, Thompson, to write up.'

'A lot must have gotten lost in translation.'

'Like what?'

'The press accounts in 1982 quoted the coroner, Sheriff Milner, and your own chief deputy, Clamp Reems, as saying Betty Jo Dean was shot from behind, at the base of the skull. None said she was shot through the nose.'

'Obviously they were misquoted, because we got fresh, official results that say different. Betty Jo Dean was shot through the nose, with the bullet coming to rest at the base of her skull.'

'Clamp see this yet?'

'I'll show it to him next time our paths cross.'

'This report doesn't speculate why the head needed to be removed.'

'That's still so obvious, Mac: to get at the bullet. And as regards your little outburst in the examining room, about that not being Betty Jo's head because it had no skin? Randall White came to see me. He confirmed he told you Doc had to remove the head, and that in the process of extracting the bullet he used a lye solution which washed away her flesh and other soft tissue.'

'Randy White is lying.'

'Why would he do that?'

'To avoid being named a co-conspirator in covering up the identity of the killer.'

'Well, aren't you something special?' Bales said, leaning across his desk. 'You been looking into this matter for but a few days and already you've identified a grand conspiracy?'

Mac's phone vibrated in his pocket. He pulled it out. Rogenet had sent a text. He put the phone back in his pocket.

'We need to find out how qualified this Thompson fellow is,' Mac said.

'We don't need to find out anything. Obviously our state police has confidence in Thompson.'

Mac's cell phone vibrated again. He pulled it out and caught sight of the time. It was ten past two. He opened the display.

Rogenet had texted again.

'PRISON,' he wrote.

FIFTY-FIVE

April was the first to call, five minutes after he sped east out of Grand Point. 'Where the hell are you? Rogenet called three times. The first two, I told him I was sure you were on your way.'

'I am.'

'If you are, you're damned late. The third time, he said he left you a message, and that it was no joke. What was it, Mac?'

'Cryptic.'

'Is Betty Jo Dean making you late to the most important meeting of your life?'

'The report came in this morning. Reed Dean called, asked me to go—'

'Ah, Jesus,' she said, seeing it all, like she'd always seen it all. 'You blew off Rogenet because Reed Dean called you to come fetch?'

'I didn't think—'

'Damned right,' she said, hanging up.

Maggie Day phoned one minute later. 'Listen, Mac . . .'

'You talked to April?'

'She's scared. I am, too. Your priorities are a mess.'

'I'm on my way to see Rogenet right now.'

'You better hope you're not too late. That state's attorney hates your guts.'

'Which state's attorney: Wainwright or Powell?' he asked, trying for a laugh.

It didn't work. She didn't laugh.

'Nice of you to join us,' Ryerson Wainwright said, not bothering to stand up as his assistant escorted Mac and Rogenet into the office. 'Seventy minutes ago Mr Rogenet arrived on time, saying you were going to join us. He began checking his watch. I told him that made me uncomfortable and suggested he wait in the hall, which he has done, for those seventy minutes.'

And that was where Mac had found him, sweating and out of breath. Wainwright's assistant popped out before they could talk and escorted them both inside.

'I was unavoidably detained,' Mac offered up.

'I'll be honest,' Wainwright said, leaning back in the chair that had cost too much. 'I don't know what you people think we can accomplish here. We're set for a status hearing tomorrow. I suggest we discuss a plea—'

'What sort of plea are you envisioning?' Mac said.

The state's attorney frowned; he didn't like being interrupted. Rogenet reached to touch Mac's arm.

'Three years, minimum security facility,' Wainwright said.

'For whom? You or me?'

'Damn it, Mac,' Rogenet tugged at his necktie like it was choking him.

'For what crime in particular?' Mac said.

'For an obvious felony,' Wainwright said. 'You misrepresented yourself as a resident of Linder County in order to maintain your status as an active county board member and collect income as such.'

'No. This is about my arm on your frivolous spending when I headed the judiciary committee. This is about you blowing four thousand dollars on your chair. This is about your gilded, embossed personal stationery that cost a buck a sheet. This is about your sloppy, self-aggrandizing—'

Rogenet's fingers clenched weakly at Mac's knee, then fell away to fish a handkerchief from his pocket.

'Office supplies?' Wainwright asked, sneering. 'I'm supposed to be an expert on office supplies? My office made mistakes. So what?'

'They go to your embarrassment in front of the county board, your enmity toward me, and now your motivation.' He held up the narrative he'd written. 'They go to you willfully ignoring my openness and honesty about my purchase of a restaurant in Grand Point. You know I kept the board chairman and my fellow trustees completely aware of what I was doing. They saw no problem with it.'

'Our concerns will be developed more fully in our countersuit,' Rogenet said too softly.

Mac looked over at Rogenet. The color had drained from his face.

'Three years, minimum security facility,' Wainwright said.

Mac stood up. 'Not a chance, you hack,' he said, and walked out.

He waited at the door to the parking garage. Rogenet shuffled up fifteen minutes later. His pallor was gone. Now he was red-faced, but still out of breath.

'You all right, Jim?'

'I'm sure glad you were there,' the lawyer said, trying to smile.

'I disguised my residency for a few bucks in expenses? I was straight up with everyone. This is all such crap.'

'The law is technical and usually precise. This may be one of those times when we don't want precision. I want you to consider the deal.'

'Three years in prison?'

'Less than two, most likely.'

'Never.'

'It beats fourteen.'

'Not a day; not a deal. We go to court, for their case and for my countersuit.'

'Wainwright's motivation will be hard to impugn. It's his job to enforce the laws of Linder County.'

'We go to court.'

'And you go to jail?'

Mac caught his breath.

'You better think fast, Mac. We're in court tomorrow morning at ten. I want you there, in the hall and on time. It's a status hearing, and Wainwright will push for an expedited trial date. We could be at trial within a month, and the trial itself might only take half a day, unless . . .'

'Unless?'

'Unless he needs more time to build a bigger case. Maybe you really did see him in Grand Point that Sunday morning. Maybe he was having breakfast with Roy Powell and perhaps other good citizens of Grand Point, friends of the man you defeated for mayor or those you've simply pissed off over this Betty Jo Dean business. They might all want to lie their asses off, testifying that you spent all kinds of nights in their fair, crooked little town while you were still on the Linder County Board.'

'Shit.'

'Shit, most absolutely, yes. That coupled with the distance itself . . .'

Rogenet didn't have to finish. The miles between Grand Point and Mac's farm in Linder County were irrefutable; Mac's new restaurant was far enough away to make anyone question whether he'd returned home every night. Coupling that with testimony from people who'd swear Mac spent many nights in Grand Point would make for a slam-dunk conviction.

'Fourteen years?' Mac asked.

'Maybe less.' Rogenet took out his handkerchief and wiped his forehead. 'Go back to Grand Point. Think about your priorities.'

Mac didn't bother to hand him the narrative he'd written. There was no point.

FIFTY-SIX

Rogenet's words reverberated as he walked to his truck: *Prison. Fourteen years.*

Other voices jumbled in, but they spoke no words. They merely laughed, as they'd laughed in the banquet room at the Willow Tree, only now they were laughing at something new: Mac Bassett was going away.

His hand shook as he called April. 'Wainwright needs vengeance.'

'Oh, Mac.'

'Take the restaurant tonight,' he said.

'You're going to plan strategy with Rogenet?'

'He told me to think. I need to drive, clear my head.'

He wondered if prison might bring relief from murdered girls. He wondered if he were going mad.

He drove without paying attention to where he was headed. But once he crossed into Wisconsin, he realized it was where he'd been headed from the moment he left Linder County.

God help him.

The primer-splotched yellow Volkswagen rested right where it had been. The bicycle pump still lay on the ground next to the flat front tire.

Ridl sat outside, on a lawn chair. He'd set up another on the other side of the cooler.

His face looked even more drawn, the cheeks beneath his thinning beard more gaunt and hollow. Whatever cancer was eating him had grown more voracious.

'I've been expecting you,' Ridl said, gesturing through a curl of cigarette smoke at the second lawn chair.

Mac sat down. 'Really?'

'Your face had the look I used to see in the mirror. Commitment or lunacy, I never was sure. Care for a beer?' He reached into the cooler between them, gave Mac a Point and a wicked grin. 'I can vouch for the fact that these don't seem to be fattening.'

'I got her exhumed.'

Ridl sat motionless, as though summoning strength, then raised his beer in salute. 'What did she show you?'

'They cut off her head.' He described the autopsy. 'I yelled out that it wasn't her skull.'

'Because there was no flesh?'

'It was unthinking, but now I think it was because Randy White had already made a point of saying there was a mad panic to get the bullet.'

'Squirrelly little guy, used to be Doc Farmont's assistant?'

Mac nodded. 'White was fast with an explanation once Betty Jo was exhumed. He said Doc Farmont had to remove Betty Jo's head, then soak away all the flesh and tissue before the bullet fell out.'

'Like shaking a coin bank to get at a penny?' Ridl laughed a laugh that quickly convulsed into a deep cough. 'Randall White is covering his ass.'

'He's trying to cover a bunch of asses.'

'What does the good doctor say?'

'He took off in a hurry before the exhumation.'

'Your sheriff saw nothing unusual in that?'

'He said he'd talk to him when he returned.'

'Your sheriff is in on the cover-up.'

'It gets worse. There's an official report from the state lab. It boils down to three sentences. The first said, "One individual is represented across the skeletal remains."'

'Understandable, if they were simply being sloppy. What was the second?'

'"No usable material was extracted from the body." She hadn't been embalmed, and her fingers were resting in liquefied matter.'

'Unfortunate, but it makes sense. The third finding?'

'"The bullet entered the left nostril, angled downward, and came to rest at the base of the skull."'

Ridl set his beer down on the grass like it weighed ten pounds, and took a long time to light a cigarette. 'And that's why you found your way back here?'

'Yes. I need to be sure.'

'No way in hell.'

'You're certain?'

'Everyone spoke of her being shot from behind, through the base of the skull. Even the lone discovery site photo supports that. She was found on her belly, pitched forward from the impact.'

'Shot by someone who might have loved her enough to protect her head with leaves and fold her slacks neatly on top of her?'

'So I always thought,' Ridl said.

'Now there's something new along that line.' He told Ridl about the dress wrapped carefully in newspaper, tucked between the casket and the wall of the vault.

'That places your killer at the funeral home,' Ridl said, 'narrowing your list of suspects.'

'Not by much. All sorts of people could have been in and out of Wiley's.'

'Did you check out who owned those cabins south of Poor Farm Road?'

'Again, too many people. The largest of the cabins was owned blind, by something called the Country Club Partners. It was used by a bunch of prominent locals.'

'Damn it.'

'It burned down, right after the murders.'

'To destroy evidence showing Betty Jo had been kept there,' Ridl said.

'Obliterated forever,' Mac said.

'Have you caught up with Clamp Reems?'

'I haven't tried further. Jen Jessup interviewed him about the case a few years back. He gave her lip service, nothing more than what had been in the papers back in the day.'

Ridl's voice dropped to a whisper. 'What has she said about her sister?'

'I threw her a hint that I knew they were related, but she didn't respond.'

Ridl coughed – a low gurgle that quickly built into a loud hacking that shook his worn body. When it was over, he leaned back, and sucked air for a moment.

'I'm running out of time,' Mac said. He told the old reporter of his indictment, and the likelihood that he would be tried and convicted within a few weeks.

Ridl reached into the cooler, handed across another beer. 'You're a noble man, Mac Bassett.'

'I can't figure who would have benefitted from switching the skull.'

'You don't believe Randy White's story?'

'That the good doctor removed her head to get at the bullet? White might have been told that, but I'm bothered by the circular cut around the top of the skull. The bullet could have been extracted that way, without beheading her.'

'Work backward,' Ridl said. 'Who would have known the head was switched?'

'Doc Farmont cut off her skull at Wiley's, according to Randy White. That means Bud Wiley knew, since he put her in the bag before burial. Likely enough, so did Luther, his nephew.'

'Besides those four, the coroner?'

'I don't think he ever came to Wiley's.'

'Neither did Sheriff Milner,' Ridl said. 'I was told he went home sick after he got a look at Betty Jo on the Devil's Backbone.'

'Clamp Reems.'

'Possible. I remember he was everywhere those days, hard to track down.'

'And Horace Wiggins. He had to know everything that was going on . . .' Mac stopped to stare into the distance, only dimly aware he'd suddenly stopped talking.

'Mac?' Ridl asked.

'Wiggins is the key. Wiggins is the leverage,' Mac said slowly, thinking it through. 'He knows why no other crime scene photos ever surfaced.' He stood up, edgy with the sudden sense of what he was thinking. 'That one photo showed nothing except a covering of leaves, right? And perhaps a perverted last act of tenderness, or at least a staging to obscure the condition of her head?'

'Yes.'

'Wiggins is no idiot,' Mac said. 'He knew how to take crime scene photos. That was only the first photo, Jonah. He took more pictures at the Devil's Backbone, useful photos, photos that didn't obscure the wound. Photos he could have been told to destroy.'

'Photos that would show an entry wound up from the base of her neck, in case she was ever exhumed?'

'Photos that would now prove the skulls were switched,' Mac said, 'but still I ask: why switch skulls in the first place?'

'For now, consider availability. Not just anyone can go to a local Skulls 'R Us?' Ridl laughed at his joke.

'A mortician or a doctor would know how to get one; Bud Wiley or Doc Farmont.'

'No help there. One's dead and one's taken off, likely never to be made to come back,' Ridl said.

'I've got to find a way to squeeze Horace Wiggins, the man who took the pictures that got destroyed.'

'How long will the wrong people in Grand Point let you play at this?' Ridl asked.

'They must be thinking my conviction will end things for good. Believe it or not, I'm still scheduled to introduce the town's honoree on the Fourth of July.' He managed a smile for Ridl. 'Clamp Reems is the honoree.'

Ridl managed his own small smile in return. 'And after the Fourth?'

'Even my lawyer says I'm going away.'

FIFTY-SEVEN

He called Reed Dean as he crossed into Illinois. 'What are they going to do with the skull?'

'My sister's head? I asked Jimmy after you went flying out of his office. He put on one of his phony smiles and mumbled some crap about them keeping it as evidence. I don't understand. They wrote their report; they've washed their hands. They're not going to do anything more.'

'We expected this whitewash, Reed.'

'I was also expecting more of a ruckus out of you. Instead, you took off like your pants were on fire.'

'I told you I had an appointment with my lawyer.'

'How'd it go?'

'I might be found guilty.'

'You can't be serious.'

'Have a lot of faith in the justice system lately?'

Reed took the point. 'Damn.'

'You'll have to take over.'

Reed hesitated. 'I don't know . . .'

'You ever hear anyone say your sister got shot through the nose?'

'Nobody until that report writer. He got Doctor Brown's notes wrong.'

'I think he got Brown's notes right.'

'Mac, you really think that's not her skull?'

'Yes.'

Reed paused for a moment, and said, 'Then how can the beginning of the report, where is says all the skeletal parts came from the same person, be correct?'

'That's the only mistake. Obviously they didn't check to see if all the bones matched the skull.'

'What do we do?'

'First thing tomorrow, make some phone calls. Start with Bales, but then call State's Attorney Powell and then Darrell Thompson, the author of that report. Say you won't rest until she's whole again. Tell them you have to put back all her bones.'

'What does that matter, if it's not her head?'

'Stay with me on this, Reed. They'll object. They'll say your sister's case is still an active murder investigation and they need to retain the skull, femur and those vertebrae. Be insistent; threaten to take the whole matter to court. They'll try to frighten you by highballing the cost of opening the grave yet again. Tell them none of that matters; you need to bury her intact, no matter what the cost. Say you're not going to give up until you get everything back. Tell them you'll call every reporter you can think of to say you're being deprived of your right to bury your sister decently.'

'What's up your sleeve?'

'I remember from a college anatomy class that each person's skull and vertebrae are unique. One person's skull can't fit someone else's vertebrae. We need to get the skull and vertebrae to show the skull doesn't belong to your sister.'

'Then what?'

'Then we unleash enough hell to force a proper investigation of your sister's murder.'

FIFTY-EIGHT

B y the time the first rays of Thursday morning touched his living-room windows, Mac had made a list of a half-dozen board certified forensic anthropologists. One of them ought to be willing to compare the skull to the vertebrae that had been cut from Betty Jo Dean.

He'd gotten the names from the Internet. Sleep had been out of the question, and Web surfing kept him from thinking about how the rest of the day was going to go to hell.

But now, at eight-thirty, it was time for a different horror. He put on his dark suit, a white shirt and a conservative blue tie. Then he went out to drive to a bench outside a courtroom, to wait while a judge, a state's attorney and his own lawyer argued about how long it should take to try his case and send him to prison.

The Linder County Courthouse had used to seem to Mac to be everything Peering County's was not. It was modern, built of sand-colored bricks, and seemed to have too many wide windows to harbor secrets. But that was before he was indicted.

Courtroom assignments for the day's cases were posted on computer sheets behind glass-fronted wall cabinets. People of Linder County v. M. R. Bassett, up for status review, was being heard in courtroom 208.

He walked up the broad, glossy beige stairs and sat on the bench outside the courtroom. He took the narrative he'd prepared for Rogenet out of the breast pocket of his suit jacket. He would make sure to give it to the lawyer, whether it would be of use or not. As though anything could be of use. Or not.

Ryerson Wainwright's glossy black wingtips came tapping down the hall at nine-fifty. His face was slightly upturned, like a feral animal smelling meat. 'A fine day, don't you think, Mac?'

'My emotions are always sharpened by seeing you, Ryerson.'

The bastard stepped inside without a further word.

Ten o'clock, and then ten-fifteen came without Rogenet having come down the hall. Mac supposed his lawyer had entered the courtroom through an interior door. Mac rolled and unrolled his narrative for perhaps the tenth time.

Three Latinos came out of a courtroom down the corridor. The two women were weeping, while the man clutched the brim of a stained felt cowboy hat so hard Mac could see the white in his knuckles. They went down the stairs, and the hall again went silent.

Ten more minutes passed.

At ten twenty-five, Mac's cell phone vibrated in his suit jacket.

'Mac? Reed. Bales says we can't have her parts. Active investigation, unsolved murder, all the baloney you predicted. He says giving us her parts will destroy the chain of custody of the evidence and they'll be of no use to anyone in law enforcement.'

The door to courtroom 208 opened and a uniformed officer stepped out. 'Mr Bassett?'

Mac stood up, the phone still pressed to his ear. 'Hold on, Reed.'

'You're wanted inside,' the officer said.

'Reed, I have to go. Call Powell, and anybody you can think of down in Springfield. Put them on notice: you're going public if you don't get your sister's remains back.'

'I'll bet Bales already got to them.'

'Mr Bassett,' the uniformed officer said more loudly.

'Do as I said, Reed. Tell everyone you're going to the newspapers and the Rockford television stations. Tell them you're going to let the world know that the State of Illinois and Peering County won't give a grieving brother back the remains of his—'

The officer reached for Mac's cell phone. 'Inside, now.'

'Gotta go,' Mac said, clicking off. Jamming the phone into his pocket, he felt the envelope he'd forgotten was still in there.

The judge sat up high on his bench. Wainwright sat at the prosecution's table.

Jim Rogenet was nowhere in sight.

'Mr Bassett?' the judge asked.

Mac nodded.

'Your attorney, Mr Rogenet, has suffered a heart attack.'

FIFTY-NINE

'How bad?' Mac asked.

'We don't know,' the judge said. 'His wife called the clerk's office a half-hour ago. The message I received says merely that he's been hospitalized. Right now, our issue is to determine the best way to proceed. When you leave here, Mr Bassett, you'll contact Mr Rogenet's office and ask them to assign another of their attorneys to this case.'

'We can then do status the middle of next week, Your Honor,' Wainwright said, standing up. 'This is a simple case. We can go to trial beginning the week after next.'

Mac remembered Rogenet's concern that Wainwright was lining up Grand Point people to testify against him. 'I don't believe we've even seen the prosecution's witness list yet, Your Honor,' he said.

'We'll have it to your new lawyer this afternoon,' Wainwright said.

'You're thinking the sooner I'm in maximum security, the safer the planet will be?'

'Mr Bassett!' The judge leaned forward. 'I understand your concerns, but we'll maintain civility here.'

'Mr Rogenet practices alone, Your Honor, as Mr Wainwright well knows,' Mac said. 'He shares an office only with an answering machine and a part-time secretary. It will take me some time to get a new lawyer.'

'The Linder County Bar Association can swiftly give you a referral,' Wainwright said. He turned to the judge. 'The people are best served if this matter is handled expeditiously.'

Mac forced a smile for the state's attorney. 'It isn't that I don't know any lawyers, Ryerson. It's that honest ones are hard to find.'

'Mr Bassett!'

'Sorry, Judge, but I'm being hustled by our fast-talking friend here, and that's denying me due process. I need time to consider all this, and to bring a new lawyer up to speed,' Mac said. 'Ninety days, I'm thinking.'

'Come on, Bassett. How much is there to consider?' Wainwright said. 'The facts are clear.'

'We'll check status in a week, Mr Bassett,' the judge said. 'Please secure representation by then.'

Mac held up the narrative he'd been clutching, fanning it to make it look thicker. 'There's a lot of detail in here, Your Honor. This recounts the board meetings I attended, my honest and open conversations with the chairman and other board personnel about my eventual relocation to Grand Point, and their request that I finish out my term as trustee. Most importantly, it recounts the couple dozen nights I estimate I was too fatigued to drive home to Linder County from my restaurant.'

'*Estimate*, Mr Bassett?' the judge asked.

'Well, yes. I estimated to avoid bogging down the court in minor details.'

'Two dozen is too many, Your Honor,' Wainwright said.

'I have filed a countersuit, Your Honor, that must also be studied by my new counsel,' Mac said.

'Totally frivolous,' Wainwright said. 'It's nothing but a pack of—'

'Gentlemen!' The judge glanced at the clock on the wall. 'Let's see if we can move this along, shall we? We'll take an early lunch, during which I'll look over Mr Bassett's material. We'll reconvene promptly at one o'clock, at which time I'll offer my assessment as to how much time Mr Bassett's new representative will need to prepare his defense.'

He reached for Mac's narrative and left the courtroom.

Mac passed the longest two hours of his life in the over-lit cafeteria in the basement of the courthouse. By the number of families, mostly poor, sitting at the shiny, Formica-topped tables, Mac guessed that

most of the cases before the courts that day were either domestic
disputes or involved small claims. Everyone in the cafeteria looked
tired rather than unduly frightened. None of them looked like they
were sweating jail time.

Mac sipped at his coffee, and tried not to hear the clock ticking
away free minutes on the wall.

At one o'clock, the officer assigned to courtroom 208 escorted Mac
through a side door and down a narrow carpeted hall to a small,
six-person conference room. The judge and Ryerson Wainwright
were already seated at the table.

The judge motioned for Mac to sit down and slid the narrative
across the table. 'I've read your summary, Mr Bassett. You've done
an admirable job of presenting your position. However, it's interpre-
tive, not definitive. There are very few hard facts supporting your
claim that while you were a board member you spent the overwhelming number of your nights in Linder County. Consequently,
your attorney must argue the merits of your case formally, in court,
with respect for the precise requirements of the law. Using your
summary, I believe any lawyer you choose can get up to speed
quickly. Therefore, I'm inclined to agree with the state's attorney
here and set status for next week, with the trial to follow two weeks
after that.'

Mac picked up the summary and slipped the sheaf into the side
pocket of his suit jacket. Again he touched the envelope Maggie
had left under his windshield wiper. Except now he felt outrageous
opportunity.

'What about these?' he asked, not daring to wonder what he was
doing. He pulled the envelope out of his pocket and upended its
contents onto the table.

A hundred gas receipts spilled out – every purchase Maggie must
have made before she moved out to Grand Point. Always frugal,
she shopped every station in Linder County for the cheapest gas.
And bought it two or three gallons at a time, for cash. Which meant
that she bought gas almost every day.

'All these purchases were made in Linder County,' he said, careful
to not lie by claiming he'd made them. 'They show an awful lot of
spending across a lot of days.' He pushed the loose pile of receipts
across to the judge.

'This has no bearing—' Wainwright said.

'Let's be indulgent, shall we?' the judge said, scooping the pile toward him.

He began examining the receipts. Several times he shook his head. 'Do you always buy your gasoline in such small amounts, Mr Bassett?'

'I'm not a wealthy man.' It was the truest thing he'd said in the past few minutes.

After ten minutes the judge rubbed his eyes, pushed the receipts back across to Mac and shifted to look at the state's attorney. 'Mr Bassett has offered credible evidence that he spent one heck of a lot of time in Linder County.'

'But Your Honor—'

'Credible evidence,' the judge repeated. 'This case is dismissed.'

Stunned, not believing, Mac grabbed the receipts in fistfuls, jammed them into his pockets and walked out like he was on springs, through the empty courtroom and into the hall.

It was justice of a sort, though even a month ago, Mac would have recoiled at such a notion.

A lot had happened since then.

He laughed at the fraud of it.

SIXTY

B reathing purer oxygen than he had in months, Mac called Rogenet's office first, from his truck. He intended to leave a message, but Rogenet's wife picked up.

'The doctor doesn't think there will be any lasting damage, Mr Bassett,' she said. 'He's bright-eyed and talking. And worried about your situation.'

'Tell him the case got kicked.'

'Seriously?'

'Case dismissed after the judge reviewed some receipts I found.'

'He'll be so pleased.'

'Tell him I'll take him out for pizza and beer when he gets out of the hospital.'

'The heck you will. Congratulations again, Mr Bassett.'

He called Maggie at home. 'Case tossed,' he said, 'thanks to you.'

'So we expected,' she said, without asking more.

'You and April?'

'Me and . . . Let's just say there are people who need you free.'

She might have been talking about Abigail Beech or perhaps she was talking about Betty Jo Dean. It was too fine a day to argue with such thinking.

April picked up her phone on the first ring.

'We're pouring free tonight at the Bird's Nest,' he said, and told her of the dismissal. 'Change the letters on the outdoor sign: "Case Dismissed. Celebrate With Us. Drinks On The House."'

She was ecstatic, of course, but still practical. 'Mac, do you really think we can afford—?'

'Number one, I'm feeling lighter than air. But number two? I don't think we can afford not to. I want everybody to know we're going to be around.'

'Around, as in keeping the Bird's Nest afloat? Or around so you can alienate more people about the death of Betty Jo Dean and—?'

'I'll see you back at the restaurant,' he said, and hung up before she could see any further into his head.

He didn't want to look too deeply into it himself.

April hadn't indulged his instructions fully. She'd lettered 'Case Dismissed' and 'Celebrate Tonight' on the outdoor sign, but no degree of euphoria would cause her to give away booze. The sign offered drinks at half-price.

It hadn't mattered. By seven o'clock that evening the Bird's Nest was packed.

'Can it really be because of the half-price booze?' Mac overheard April asking Maggie above the din.

'They came for Betty Jo Dean,' Maggie said.

Mac thought the truth was somewhere in between.

Reed Dean had been among the first to arrive. He'd been the fourth call Mac had made from his truck, but they'd had the most to discuss.

'They're still denying my request,' Reed said. 'Bales, I can understand; he might be covering for somebody local. But those state police people down in Springfield, and Powell, the state's attorney? What have they got to lose by giving me my sister's bones?'

'If we prove the skull was switched it will open up Peering County and perhaps the State of Illinois to a lawsuit. The county was the custodian of your sister's remains from the time she was discovered until she was put into a casket; the skull was switched on their watch. That alone implicates one or more county officials – a sheriff's officer or the coroner, along with the people at Wiley's acting as their agents – as being involved in a conspiracy to cover up the identity of your sister's killer. There might have been state police involvement back then somehow, too.'

'You're still sure more than one person was involved in covering up?'

'Then, like now, the people who ran this town stuck to one another.' Mac recited the list he'd gone over with Ridl: 'Bud Wiley, the undertaker. Luther, his nephew. Doc Farmont, if the switch happened during the autopsy. Randall White, because he's admitted knowing the head was removed. Clamp Reems, simply because he was in charge of the investigation, along with any number of his deputies. And last, but maybe most important, Horace Wiggins, because I believe he took more than one crime scene photo, and knows darn well your sister was shot from behind.'

'There are all kinds of maybes in there.'

'Tonight's our best opportunity to start narrowing our list.' Mac pointed to the people starting to fill the dining room. 'How many of them do you know?'

Reed took a minute, and said, 'Maybe half.'

'Excellent. Chat with as many as you can. Tell them how relieved you are that I'll be around.'

'Because of that other thing?' Reed was talking about the plan Mac had outlined earlier, on the phone, from his truck.

'That's the most crucial part. Tell everybody. Be excited.'

Jen Jessup came up to him as he stood in the back, watching Reed work the booths and the tables. Waitresses and busboys jostled each other, grinning as they bustled through the room. Even April smiled, the times she passed through. It was ten o'clock and people were still waiting to get tables.

'Looks like Reed Dean is running for office,' Jen said, watching Mac's eyes.

'From personal experience, I don't recommend it.'

'Here's what I know,' she said. 'You were set for a status hearing this morning. You showed up unaware your attorney just had a heart attack. The judge reviewed something you'd written, unimpressed. Then you dumped out an envelope full of nickel and dime gasoline receipts, proving you'd spent an awful lot of time buying gas in tiny amounts in Linder County. And proving as well you weren't sleeping here, most nights, because you'd been too busy buying little dribbles of gas in Linder County. The judge dismissed the charges against you, provided you dropped your countersuit. Am I right so far?'

Now it was his turn to study her. She really was beautiful. 'I hear you're really tight with Powell.'

'Maybe not as tight as you think. Know what else I did today?'

She was crafty, too. He shrugged.

'I visited every gas station within five miles of Grand Point.'

'Lotto tickets?' he managed, knowing well what was going to come next. 'I heard the jackpot's up to five million.'

'I did hit a big-enough jackpot, at the Shell Station just north of here. In the most casual way, I asked if you bought your gas there. The owner knows you, though he's not proud of that. He did say you've always filled your tank, even before you moved here.'

He kept his eyes on Reed, working the room. 'Sure, but I was driving a Corvette back in those days. They get lousy gas mileage, and I had to top off most mornings back in Linder County.'

'Want to know what I really don't understand?' she asked.

'I can't imagine,' he said.

'Why sometimes you're tenacious like a ferret, and other times you leave things alone.'

It surprised him enough to risk looking at her. 'What are you talking about?'

'A sister,' she said.

She wasn't talking about Reed and Betty Jo. He wasn't even sure she was talking about her own sister, Laurel. Jen Jessup was a digger; she might have discovered something new.

When he said nothing, she said, 'I respect tenacity,' and then she laughed, obviously enjoying the discomfort she saw on his face. She nodded slightly toward Reed, who was talking to two people sitting in a booth. 'Let's talk about a brother, instead. I've heard he's quiet and shy, not given to schmoozing. Yet all evening he's been moving from one table to the next, with the forced humor and persistence of a man selling raffle tickets.'

'He knows a lot of people,' Mac said, daring to relax, just a little.

'He's telling everybody a new crime scene photo of his sister has surfaced.'

'Really?'

'Cut the crap, Mac.' She stepped in front of him so he'd have to look directly at her. 'What's going on with Reed Dean?'

'He's excited that the new photo might interest the FBI.'

'Where's the photo?'

'Safe.'

'I heard you raised hell about the state's report on Betty Jo's remains.'

'Powell, again?' he asked. 'Or merely Powell, as always?'

'The report's false?' she asked, dodging the question.

'The report was sloppy, done in less than forty-eight hours.'

'Especially the part about her being shot through the nose,' she said.

'You know that from your own research.'

'Yes.'

'And from Laurel's.' It was time to venture the name.

'My parents never told me she'd co-authored a story for the *Sun-Times*. I lied to you, Mac, when I said I did my research locally. Not true. I went into Chicago to use their library for the twenty-fifth anniversary piece. I saw her byline on a microfilm.'

'No one in your family wondered about her death?'

'It was easier to think she'd fallen asleep behind the wheel.'

'You'll help, now?'

'You sticking around is in my best interest, if it leads to any sort of validation of what Laurel was attempting to do.'

'Reed needs the rest of his sister's remains back. Bales, the people at the lab downstate and Powell are all fighting him on that. It will be bad politics for Powell if news hits the paper that he's denying Reed's request for a proper burial.'

'You think Roy Powell is dumb enough to believe Reed Dean is interested solely in burying his sister intact?'

He shrugged.

She looked at him for a long minute. 'Roy Powell and I have been over for quite some time,' she said.

SIXTY-ONE

Reed eased gingerly into Mac's truck at eleven o'clock the next morning and groaned. 'I haven't had this kind of head since I turned twenty-one.'

'I didn't figure things would happen so fast, either,' Mac said, starting up.

Reed slumped down on the seat. 'People kept buying me drinks. I'd only take a sip or two and carry it with me to the next table, but your waitresses kept bringing fresh ones, bought by everybody in sight. All those sips added up.'

'You worked magic. People are excited about a new crime scene photo of Betty Jo.'

'Exactly as you predicted.' Reed managed a weak grin. 'You must have worked some magic yourself.'

'Jen Jessup called Powell. She was predisposed.'

'What are you talking about?'

'There were more than two bad deaths that summer.'

'You already said that besides my sister and Pribilski there was Sheriff Milner, if your suspicions about him being a suicide or worse are correct.'

'There was a bartender, Dougie Peterson. He shot off his mouth about seeing Pribilski, shot in the groin, over at Wiley's. He drowned a month later.'

Reed looked out the side window. 'Oh, Jeez.'

'There was a fifth death, Reed: a college girl who wanted to be a reporter. She found out some things. She got run off the road before she could tell anyone.'

'What the hell, Mac?'

'Laurel Jessup.'

Reed whistled softly. 'Kin?'

'Sister. Jen's had an agenda all along. She's on our side.'

'I was shocked when Roy Powell himself called this morning, saying he'd heard about my dilemma and that the rest of Betty Jo's remains – minus her femur, which he said they wanted to keep in case additional DNA testing was required – are waiting for me in Springfield.'

'I can't see Powell believing it was the moral thing to do. More likely, Jen convinced Powell it's bad politics to deprive you of those bones.'

'And Bales?'

'He'll think turning over the skull and vertebrae frees him from being accountable for them.'

'Because we're breaking the chain of custody, right, and now there can be no telling where those remains are from?'

Mac grinned and stepped down on the accelerator. 'We need to grab those bones.'

'You think Powell and Bales are in on the cover-up?'

'Powell, no; Bales, maybe.'

They drove for a time in silence. And then Reed turned on the seat. 'I almost did something real dumb last night. All those sips got me angry, thinking Horace Wiggins shot more pictures than he released. Leaving your place, I intended to drive straight home. But I didn't, Mac.'

Mac gripped the steering wheel tighter, fighting the need to look at Reed.

'I drove over to Wiggins's place,' Reed said. 'He lives west of town, about a half-mile.'

'Damn it, Reed.'

'Like I said, I had too many sips. I was furious thinking the bastard was hiding pictures that maybe could have helped the investigation back in 1982. I pulled up in front of the house next door, cut the lights and coasted forward.' He leaned back and shut his eyes. 'Wiggins was going crazy out in the garage, throwing things every which way. The rumor we'd started about us having another picture must have scared him, big time. Boxes were spread all over the floor, and he was pawing through big white envelopes, scattering them all to hell.'

'Looking for prints or negatives he feared he'd lost track of,' Mac said.

'The sight pleased me greatly.'

'Then you drove away, right? Please tell me you then drove away.'

'I was drunk enough to be angry, but not drunk enough to be stupid. I sat for five or ten minutes, watching Wiggins rummage through his boxes, frantic as a gnat. But then I did drive away. I figured we'd started enough agony for them for one night.'

'What do you mean, "them"?'

Reed sat up, his hangover forgotten. 'Somebody else was there, standing in the shadows of the garage.'

'Could you tell who it was?'

Reed sighed. 'I'm not even sure I did see a second person. Obviously, I didn't want to risk getting out for a better look.'

They drove on, silent again. Each wondering, Mac supposed, exactly what they'd set in motion.

SIXTY-TWO

Not surprisingly, Darrell Thompson, the man who'd written the shoddy Illinois State Police report, was not available when they arrived in Springfield. No matter; two cardboard boxes were, along with a release form, prepared in quadruplicate, stating that Reed Dean, the recipient of the contents of the two cartons labeled Betty Jo Dean One and Betty Jo Dean Two assumed all responsibility for the contents they contained. That, moreover, those aforesaid contents were being released to Reed Dean solely for the purpose of being interred with the rest of the remains of the aforementioned Ms Betty Jo Dean. Reed signed, and they each took a box out to the jump seat in Mac's truck.

They did not head north back toward Grand Point. They drove east, toward Champaign, breathing easier than they had at any moment coming down.

One hour and fifty-five minutes later, they carried the two boxes into an ornate old stone building on the quadrangle at the University of Illinois.

Dr Francine Wilhausen, Professor Emeritus of Anthropology and a Diplomate of the American Board of Forensic Anthropology, was waiting in her laboratory. She wore dark jeans, a loose tan pullover, and had enough lines on her face for Mac to guess her age to be around seventy. With her was Dr Robert Hargrave, a professor of anthropology. He was younger, and deferential toward Dr Wilhausen.

She motioned for them to set the boxes on a long, black stone-topped table.

'As we discussed on the phone,' Mac said, 'I'll be grateful for any impressions you might be able to offer.' He handed her an envelope. Inside was a check for three hundred and seventy-five dollars, money April thought was to be used to buy new seals for two of their freezers.

Dr Wilhausen frowned. 'I will give you no impressions. I will give you specific, defensible conclusions. It may take some time.'

And there it ended. The woman and her colleague wanted no

additional information, no background details beyond what little Mac had already provided on the phone.

Their footsteps echoed loudly on the wood floor in the hallway as they left Wilhausen's lab.

'She didn't even open the boxes,' Reed said.

'She wants to work without us hovering over her shoulder.'

'If she finds the skull doesn't match the vertebrae, that proves the sheriff's department botched the chain of custody before my sister was buried?'

'It's real leverage. You can threaten to sue the Peering County Sheriff's Department for mishandling their custody of your sister's remains. What we really want is to light a fire under someone, Fed, state or local, to reopen the investigation.'

'I still can't believe Bud Wiley or Luther would have switched her head.'

'Or Doc Farmont, or Randall White. Or your midnight buddy, Horace Wiggins, whose sleep you've probably forever ruined.'

Reed chuckled. 'All by spreading the word there's another picture.'

The campus was almost deserted. Summer classes were done for the day; few students lazed on the grass between the broad walks. They stretched their legs for a time, walking around the quadrangle, admiring the century-old architecture. And then they headed toward Campus Town, that strip of stores adjacent to the quadrangle that looked to sell toothpaste, T-shirts, and decals for those who had cars, to have dinner before heading up to Grand Point.

'They look so very, very young,' Reed said, of a pair of coeds passing them, heading in the opposite direction.

'Nothing like a college campus to make you feel old,' Mac said.

'Those girls are barely older than Betty Jo was.'

Or Laurel Jessup, who'd actually gone to this college. Mac thought then of Jen, wondering if she'd attended Illinois, like her sister.

'Did your parents ever mention what Betty Jo's plans might have been?' he asked as they crossed a street.

'People in our neighborhood didn't spend a lot of time talking about plans.'

'Pinktown?'

'Pinktown,' Reed said.

They went into a place that advertised itself as a microbrewery. The young waitress called each of them 'Sir,' took their orders for cheeseburgers and Cokes, then left.

'I don't think we fit in,' Mac said.

'Pinktown?' Reed asked, grinning for the first time that day.

'Nah, it's your redneck NASCAR cap.'

They both laughed and talked of other things as they drank their Cokes.

'It must have been someone I talked to at the Bird's Nest last night who called Wiggins to alert him that I'd gotten a new picture,' Reed said as the waitress set down their burgers.

'Or someone who called someone else who called Wiggins.'

Mac's cell phone rang.

It was Francine Wilhausen. 'Are you close enough to turn around, Mr Bassett?'

'We never left. We're having dinner.'

'You might want to come over.'

Mac left cash next to their untouched burgers and they bolted for the door.

SIXTY-THREE

The skull and seven small, irregularly-shaped, thick round pieces of bone – the vertebrae that descend from the base of the skull onto the larger vertebrae of the spinal column – lay on the black stone table, almost white in the harsh glare of powerful lights on adjustable arms.

Dr Wilhausen set a small digital voice recorder on the table and switched it on.

'For the record, I am Doctor Francine Wilhausen. I was asked by Mr Mac Bassett and Mr Reed Dean to analyze skeletonized head and neck remains that they provided, with special attention to age at death, sex, ancestry, cause of death indicators and compatibility of the skeletal elements. I am joined by Doctor Hargrave, professor of anatomy, path physiology and forensics at Parkland College in Champaign, Illinois. Any comments I now make are very preliminary in nature and subject to revision upon more detailed analysis.'

Dr Wilhausen then went through the markers she found in the skull that determined that it belonged to a Caucasian female greater in age than fourteen and probably younger than twenty-three.

'There are multiple and conflicting signs of trauma,' she continued. 'First, cervical vertebra C2 presents evidence of a crude decapitation. The skull and the vertebra C1 immediately at its base do not correlate this finding—'

'Meaning the skull does not belong to the vertebrae?' Mac said.

Dr Wilhausen frowned at the interruption and switched off the recorder. 'I'd prefer to finish my preliminary presentation, but yes, all indices are that there is no match. The C2 vertebra we have here, which fits the rest of the vertebrae, does not match the C1 which came with the skull.'

'The C2 here was chopped off from another C1, which – along with its skull – is not here?'

She sighed. 'Sawed off, and very roughly.'

'No chop marks on the C1 we brought?' Mac pressed, to be sure.

'The C1 you brought belongs to the skull you brought, but not to the rest of the vertebrae we have here. Now, may I continue?'

Without waiting for an answer, the anthropologist switched on the recorder. 'The skull offers evidence of a gunshot wound entering the left side of the nasal cavity, destroying the medial maxillary wall . . . and exiting through the posterior-inferior portion. In other words,' she said, looking directly now at Mac, 'the bullet entered the skull through the nose and exited at the base of the skull, in the back.'

'We now move on,' she continued. 'The seven cervical vertebrae, numbers two through seven, articulate well into a cervical column.'

Mac raised his hand like a confused school kid. 'Articulate?'

Dr Wilhausen smiled a teacher's indulgent smile and left the recorder running. 'They nest together like they were made for each other, which they were. Each of us has unique cervical vertebrae that nestle perfectly into one another. If they didn't nestle perfectly we would be unable to move our heads or upper bodies.'

She went on: 'As I've already indicated, the uppermost cervical vertebra, C1, does not articulate with C2, the next vertebra going down. There was a poor fit on all three articulation points.' She named the three places where the top vertebra – C1, immediately at the base of the skull – should have fit perfectly into C2, the next vertebra down.

'Yet, to repeat: C1 fits perfectly into the skull,' she said.

She raised her voice just enough to alert everyone in the room that what was to follow was her most crucial finding. 'There is only one obvious explanation for this. C1 and C2 do not belong to the same individual. In other words, C1 and the skull are from one individual, while C2 through C7 are from another individual of similar age.'

She switched off the recorder, stepped back from the table and looked at Mac, then Reed. 'But you knew that,' she said.

'We were told only that the skull was detached so that a bullet could be extracted.'

She frowned. 'There are two problems with that explanation.' She took a pencil from her pocket and pointed to the base of the skull at the back. 'See this beveled, slightly pushed-out matter around the hole?'

'Yes,' Mac said.

'That defines it as an exit hole. As I said earlier, the bullet came out. There was nothing to find inside this skull.'

'No bullet.'

'No bullet, and anyone with forensic experience would have seen that immediately. But there's a more obvious indication that this skull, so cleanly severed, would never require removal to get at a bullet.' She held the skull upright and lifted off the top.

'Do you see?' she asked. 'This is exactly like taking the lid off a jar. This skull has a calvarium cut. Its lid – the domelike, superior portion of the cranium, known as the calvarium – was cut completely around so that it could be removed to expose the inside of the skull. With this sort of cut, a head would never need to be severed from its cervical vertebrae to extract a bullet. One would merely lift off the top to probe around inside.'

'Then there was no need to remove flesh and soft tissue from this skull to get at a bullet?'

'You've been lied to, Mr Bassett. Your skull does not belong to your vertebrae. And this skull was opened from the top.'

Reed crossed the room to sit in a chair. Mac remained by the table to ask the question that had been forming for the last few minutes. 'It's unlikely that a doctor or a mortician was responsible for the cuts on the C2?'

'Only if the doctor or mortician had gone berserk. More likely, it was someone without surgical knowledge.'

'Anything else?'

'Given that the skull we have was removed so professionally, and recognizing the presence of the calvarium cut, I suggest this skull was used for teaching. They use them in medical schools. Most have the calvarium cut so students can see inside.'

'Anywhere else?'

'You used to see them in doctors' offices, too, stuck in a corner. They were cheap and entertaining. But that was years ago. You don't see them so much now.'

Dr Wilhausen walked over to Reed and asked if she could keep the skull and vertebrae to do a more formal analysis.

Reed nodded. They would need a thorough, undeniable report.

'Can you email a preliminary report to me tomorrow morning, stating that the skull does not match the vertebrae?' Mac asked.

'Yes,' she said. 'But I'll put cautions all over it, saying I want to double-check my findings.'

Outside, Reed stopped at the base of the worn cement stairs. 'Who cut her?'

'Doc Farmont would have done it cleaner.'

'What's that mean?'

'It could have been either of the Wileys, or Wiggins.'

'Or anyone else with a saw,' Reed said.

SIXTY-FOUR

'You want to what?' April's voice was incredulous above the whine of his truck's engine. He could hear the clattering of pots and dishes in her background. She was in the hot steam of the restaurant's kitchen, helping to clean up. It was ten o'clock at night.

'News conference,' Mac said again. 'At the Bird's Nest. Tomorrow afternoon at two o'clock.'

'You're sure the skull wasn't Betty Jo's?'

'We got a preliminary report. We just left Champaign. If you go online now you can get email addresses for the television and print newsrooms. Say a major update in the long-unsolved Pribilski-Dean murders is going to be announced.'

'Bales and Powell will come at you for this.'

'Legally, they're entitled. The remains were released only so they could be re-interred.'

'You need new frickin' legal troubles?'

'Just, please send out the emails.'

'She trusts you a lot, doesn't she?' Reed said when Mac clicked off.

'More than has been good for her. She was scared stiff I was going to prison. Plus, she'd have to pay off the restaurant's bills from what's left of her savings.'

Reed shifted in the darkness. 'A chief suspect, Bud Wiley, is dead. Doc Farmont is gone, maybe never to return.'

'Leaving Horace Wiggins feeling like he's hanging out all by his lonesome?'

'It was indeed a pleasure, rattling him last night.'

'We have to get him to testify he took more pictures, and identify who ordered their suppression.'

'If Wiggins doesn't budge?'

'Our news conference announcing that the skull doesn't match your sister's vertebrae will expose the Peering County Sheriff's Department as being a co-conspirator in your sister's murder. That will set reporters loose on the cops, along with Randall White, Luther Wiley and anybody else they think was involved. With luck, the reporters will shake something loose.'

Reed had turned to look out the side window. 'Why would anybody want her head, Mac?' he asked after a moment.

He had no idea, and for a few minutes they drove in silence, staring out the windshield at the interstate disappearing under the front of Mac's truck.

Reed pulled out his phone. 'I better call Bella, warn her about what's going on.' He thumbed in a number. 'Bella? Reed. Mac Bassett was right: it wasn't Betty Jo's head that was buried with her. There's going to be a news conference tomorrow to announce that. You best turn off your phone until I stop by and give the all clear.' Then: 'Well, sure: Doc Farmont and Randy White; Horace Wiggins from over at the paper; Bud Wiley and Luther; likely old Clamp Reems himself.' He listened for another minute, then clicked off. 'Bella said Luther Wiley was quite shook up when Bella got to Wiley's to identify Betty Jo. Almost irrational, Bella said.'

'Bella have an opinion about that?'

'She said Luther was saying him and Betty Jo were an item, freshman year. Bella had never heard a thing about that.' Reed slumped back in the seat. 'Thirty years on, this thing keeps getting thornier and thornier.'

They crossed into Peering County at one o'clock. A moment later, the cab of Mac's truck was lit red by the flashing lights of a police cruiser charging up from behind.

'What the hell?' Reed said, turning to look out the back window.

Mac pulled over and two deputies walked up, one on either side of the truck.

'Reed Dean?' the cop on the passenger's side asked.

'Of course,' Reed said, his voice up an octave.

'Please step out of the vehicle, sir,' the deputy said.

'What's this about?' Mac asked.

'Easy does it, Mr Mayor,' the deputy on Mac's side leaned on the door so Mac couldn't open it.

'Am I under arrest?' Reed said.

The cop just shrugged.

SIXTY-FIVE

Mac followed the sheriff's cruiser as it sped north. Several times Reed turned around to look back at Mac's truck. His face was white and frightened in Mac's headlamps.

Mac's first thought was that something had happened to Reed's wife or her two adopted children, but sheriff's deputies didn't wait along a dark highway to intercept for that. More likely, Jimmy Bales had finally realized that Reed's need for his sister's bones had less to do with proper interment and everything to do with proving the sheriff's department had been corrupt from the beginning. Bales was probably pulling out all the stops to get the bones back.

There were no lamps lit in the cabins along the river, no lights flickering from cars parked along Poor Farm Road. The Bird's Nest was dark as well, its parking lot empty. He wondered if April had sent off the emails to the news organizations. That had been important, two hours ago. It might be more important now, if Bales was determined to shut down Mac's investigation.

Two other cruisers drove into the sheriff's parking lot at the same time they pulled in. It was no coincidence. Those cars must have been posted to watch the other main roads leading into town. Jimmy Bales had been hell bent on making sure they were intercepted.

Bales was waiting just inside the door. 'You wait there,' he said to Mac, pointing to a bench against a wall.

'What's this about?'

Bales grabbed Reed's arm and steered him down the hall.

Reed came down the hallway two hours later, ashen-faced and shuffling with fatigue.

Mac went toward him. 'What the hell, Reed?'

'They tell me I need a lawyer.'

'What's going on?'

Bales had followed close behind. 'You,' he said, pointing to Mac. 'Follow me.' They went down the hall and into an interview room that smelled of sweat, coffee and cigar smoke.

'What's going on?' Mac asked, sitting on one of the scuffed green plastic chairs.

'You want a lawyer?'

'I want an answer.'

Bales switched on an old cassette recorder and slumped into another chair. His forehead was perspiring and his white shirt was sweat-stained around the neck.

'Record of interview,' he said to the recorder, 'I am Sheriff Jimmy Bales, conducting an informal interview with Mac Bassett, of Grand Point, Illinois. First off, Mr Bassett agrees he's here voluntarily, and understands that he is free to go at any time.'

'I've said no such things. What's this about?'

'If you want, you just get up and walk out. Is that clear, Mac?'

Mac nodded. He'd learn nothing if he left.

'Say that you understand, for the tape.'

'I understand what little you've told me.'

'Tell me about Thursday night,' Bales said.

'Thursday night?' Mac asked, confused.

'What did you do Thursday night?'

This wasn't push-back for grabbing Betty Jo's vertebrae and the skull. 'I was celebrating at the Bird's Nest.'

'You had an agenda.'

'It was a joyous time. The trumped-up case against me had been seen for the political sham it was. It was dismissed, after costing me a ruinous amount in legal fees that I'll have trouble paying off.

Still, I'll pay any amount to stop bullying by officers of the law.'
He tried his best to not blink, staring Bales in the eye.

'Goddamnit, Mac.'

'What the hell is this about?'

'You and Reed Dean were shooting off your mouths about finding
a new crime scene photo of Betty Jo Dean. Such a photo could only
have been taken by Horace Wiggins.'

'Ask Wiggins how many pictures he really took.'

'How, and when, did you and Mr Dean come into what should
be official sheriff's department evidence?'

Reed hadn't given in by telling Bales there was no photograph.

'This is incredible, Jimmy. You posted cruisers on every highway
into town, in the middle of the night, to drag us in about that?'

'Where did you get the damn picture?' Fresh sweat was growing
on Bales's forehead.

'Horace Wiggins knows more about Betty Jo Dean's murder than
he's ever said.'

'Thursday night, Reed Dean was pretty angry at Horace about
that photograph?'

'Everyone should get angry about concealed evidence.'

Bales shut off the tape recorder. 'I'll get you, too.'

Nothing was making sense. 'For what?'

'The murder of Horace Wiggins.'

Reed told the story as Mac drove him home.

'Horace Wiggins's garage went up in flames early Friday, just after
two in the morning. By the time the firemen arrived, the garage, a
seventy-year-old wood tinderbox crammed full with old newspapers
and photographs, had been totally destroyed. When efforts to rouse
Horace from inside his house failed, the fire chief remembered talk of
Horace being especially close to his assistant. He drove to her house.
She was alone. It was then that the fire chief realized the destroyed
garage might be a death scene. He called the sheriff's department.
Jimmy Bales arrived with two of his deputies. By then it was dawn.

'Scorched human remains were discovered in the smoldering
rubble. Because the fire had so totally ravaged the garage it was
not yet known whether they belonged to Horace Wiggins. The body
was sent to the hospital in Rochelle for examination.'

'I suppose a neighbor noticed one particular Mustang parked in
front of Wiggins's house?' Mac asked when Reed finished.

'The only thing I forgot was to honk my horn and turn on my emergency flashers.'

'This, after telling one and all you'd come into possession of a photo Horace had suppressed. What a beautiful idea I had. I set you up as a murder suspect.'

'You couldn't know what would happen. Whoever was in the shadows at Horace's garage saw me.'

'And saw an opportunity to be rid of Wiggins and get you blamed for it.'

'He waited until I left, killed Horace and torched the garage. Maybe he was hoping I'd been seen by a neighbor, idling out front, but it wasn't necessary. I'd been talking up my anger, all over your restaurant, about a picture Horace had kept hidden. That alone was enough to show I had motive.'

'Your sister's case keeps killing people.'

'Without us getting any closer to the killer's identity.'

SIXTY-SIX

Mac was on his way to the Bird's Nest the next morning when the realization of what he'd overlooked slapped him like an open palm. He slammed on his brakes at the courthouse and ran up the stairs.

'I'd like to look at a couple of death certificates,' he told the mouse-woman in the county clerk's office.

'Heard you're having a press conference this afternoon. Big news?'

'I don't want to leak anything beforehand.'

She frowned. 'Which certificates?'

'Paulus Pribilski and Betty Jo Dean.'

The frown deepened. 'Heard the report from Springfield said you dug her up for nothing.'

'It's an unsolved crime.'

'Only vultures pick at the dead.'

'May I see those certificates?'

She walked away, huffing.

Five minutes later she was back with the same big ringbinder that contained Sheriff Milner's death certificate. That made too much horrible sense; the deaths had occurred within days of one another.

She flipped to Betty Jo Dean's death certificate first. 'Both certificates were filed on July 8, 1982.'

Betty Jo's death certificate looked ordinary, a neat listing of the dates of the girl's birth and death. The cause of death was listed as homicidal: 'Death resulted from a bullet wound from a .38 caliber revolver fired from behind into the base of the skull. Shot was fired by person or persons unknown.'

'. . . *fired from behind into the base of the skull.*'

Such a simple phrase, so obviously overlooked, and so damning. Proof enough, on its own, that the skull exhumed had not belonged to Betty Jo Dean.

He turned the page to Pribilski's certificate. At first glance, it looked just as succinct – dates of birth and death, age at death, and so on. Oddly this time, the county clerk had editorialized: 'Death resulted from multiple bullet wounds inflicted by person or persons unknown. A .38 caliber handgun was used – bullet penetrated directly through the heart causing instant death. He was shot while with Betty Jo Dean on a lonely road parked in his car.'

Mac read it again: '. . . *while with Betty Jo Dean on a lonely road parked in his car.*' Somehow, the phrase seemed to infer that Pribilski had it coming because he was out with a slut, enjoying what sluts did so well.

Different words, but in their own way, just as damning as those on Betty Jo Dean's death certificate.

He glanced at the clerk's name typed in the last box on the form and got another jolt. He didn't recognize the first name, but the surname was a surprise.

He flipped forward a week, and another, to see the certificates prepared after the Pribilski and Dean murders. On none of them had she offered the sort of commentary she'd given Pribilski's death. In mid-August, the name of the clerk changed.

He called out that he wanted copies of the two death certificates. The woman took the book, made the copies and returned.

'That county clerk, back when the murders occurred?' Mac asked.

The woman didn't have to look at the form to know what he was asking. 'Clamp's first wife,' she said. 'She left town right after she filed for divorce. Bad summer all around, that year.'

That triggered a hunch. 'When did Bud Wiley die?'

'You want a copy of his death certificate, too?'

'No. I'd just like to see it.'

He expected her to trundle off to get another binder, but she merely flipped forward a few pages in the same book. Emerson. G. 'Bud' Wiley died on September 15, 1982 of acute alcohol poisoning. He drank himself to death that same summer.

Pauly Pribilski and Betty Jo Dean had been shot to death in late June. Laurel Jessup had been run off the road two days after Betty Jo Dean was discovered. Delbert Milner had died from a gunshot wound, self-inflicted or otherwise, the next morning. A cabin down by the river had burned in July. That same month Dougie Peterson had his head bashed in, drowning.

Clamp Reems' wife took off sometime in August, a short while before Bud Wiley drank himself to death.

Calling it a bad summer all around didn't begin to describe it.

SIXTY-SEVEN

April stood by the doors to the kitchen. She was not smiling. Thirty reporters and cameramen had crowded into the dining room of the Bird's Nest, pushing the tables and chairs into a jumble along the side wall. They'd come from as far away as Chicago, Madison and Des Moines because they'd been promised new news about sensational old killings – not to eat or drink or buy any damned thing at all.

Maggie Day, black shawl draped loosely around her shoulders, cowboy hat low on her head, was at her usual perch at the hostess station by the front door. She smiled at the news people as they came in and handed each a thin packet of photocopies. Every few seconds she looked out the window. She was waiting for the man who was to join Mac at the table at the far end of the room, a man who might now be facing a murder charge, thanks to circumstantial evidence, proximity and Mac Bassett's fevered brain. She was waiting for Reed Dean.

Mac looked out at the news faces. He remembered some of them from his mayoral campaign. He smiled at the television reporters for the Fox and NBC affiliates out of Rockford. TV would get the word out the fastest.

Maggie got up and stepped outside. She came back in a moment, caught Mac's eye and shook her head. No Reed, not yet.

It was ten past two. Mac pulled the microphones a little closer and cleared his throat. Bright camera lights switched on him.

'Everybody ready?' he asked.

Some nodded, some did not.

'I'd like to make a statement, and then I'll answer questions. My name is Mac Bassett. I am the mayor of Grand Point, Illinois. In that capacity, I was asked to look into what progress, if any, had ever been made in investigating the 1982 murders of Paulus Pribilski of Rockford and his companion, Betty Jo Dean, of here in Grand Point.'

He paused to look again at the door. No Reed.

He went on: 'The Peering County Sheriff's Department made no progress whatsoever. I hope you will leave here today determined to learn why that is.

'Today, I am saddened to report atrocious new developments in the case. At the request of the Dean family, Betty Jo's body was exhumed and the detached skull, her cervical vertebrae, her femur and various samplings of fingernail and other tissues were examined by the forensics department of the Illinois State Police. It took them less than forty-eight hours to issue the sketchy report you've been handed here today. It states that all the skeletal remains belong to the same individual, and that Betty Jo Dean was shot through the nose.'

Mac paused for a moment to make brief eye contact with several of the television reporters. 'The second and third documents in your packets are copies of the death certificates of the murdered couple. Pay particular attention to Betty Jo Dean's. It states that she was shot from behind, as was reported extensively in the press back in 1982. Yet the Illinois State Police forensics examiner, based upon his examination of the skull that was exhumed, found that the skull exhumed, loose, with Betty Jo Dean was shot through the nose.

'I agree with the state's examiner,' Mac said. 'That skull was shot through the nose.' He paused to let that sink in, then went on: 'Once the state's examination was completed, the exhumed skull and cervical vertebrae were submitted to two forensic anthropologists, Doctor Francine Wilhausen of the University of Illinois and Doctor Robert Hargrave of Parkland College. Their preliminary finding is detailed in the email copied in your packets. It states that the skull does not articulate with the cervical vertebrae. In other words, the loose skull exhumed with Betty Jo Dean was not hers.'

Several hands shot up, but in deference to the television cameras, no one called out.

Mac ignored them. 'Now I will address what I think will be some of your questions. The first, of course, is whether I know who killed Paulus Pribilski and Betty Jo Dean. Answer: no, I do not, though I believe several individuals might know.

'Question two must be why Betty Jo Dean's head was removed prior to burial. One person who may have assisted in the decapitation says there was a mad panic to retrieve the bullet lodged inside Betty Jo Dean's skull so that it could be compared with those recovered from Paulus Pribilski. Yet to go to such a barbaric extreme would have been unnecessary. The usual means of extracting a bullet involve a probe and, occasionally, the cutting away of a section of the skull. The whole head does not need to be removed. In this particular instance, the whole head removal theory is particularly laughable, since the exhumed skull has been cut all the way around, above the eye sockets, to make the top easily removable for study. This probably indicates that the skull exhumed was a teaching device, bought long ago from a medical supply house.

'There is an obvious, partial answer why Betty Jo Dean's head was switched: the killer was taking no chances. He wanted her head so others could not examine it. Why? Or, for what? I don't know. Neither does the Peering County Sheriff's Department, which has demonstrated little curiosity about any aspect of this case.

'The third question is obvious: who had access to the skull before her burial? I won't give you possible names, but you, as investigative reporters, can easily find out for yourselves who had such access.

'Finally, some of you have heard that our local newspaper publisher, Horace Wiggins, died in a fire of suspicious origin early yesterday morning. Mr Wiggins was responsible for taking photographs of Betty Jo when she was discovered. Interestingly, only one such photograph has ever been shown to the public, though it's suspected others were taken. In fact, it's rumored Wiggins' death was related to the rumored emergence of a second, more revealing photo. Perhaps he was killed because he possessed even more information about the murders of Pauly and Betty Jo Dean.

'That's it, ladies and gentlemen. Now I'll take your questions.'

'Why won't you tell us who you think took her head?'

'As I said, I can't be sure because I don't understand who would want to remove it in the first place. Most likely, the person who removed the head wanted the bullet, but what good would that do? Four or five were already extracted from Pauly Pribilski. You must start with the most basic question: who had access to Betty Jo Dean during the brief time between when she was discovered and when she was buried?'

'Well, for starters—' the NBC reporter yelled out.

'No,' Mac shouted back. 'Don't speculate. Investigate. Rip this case wide open. Find the truth. Begin by isolating who *could* have taken her head.'

'And that will reveal the identity of the killer?'

'It might reveal someone who conspired to conceal the murderer's identity. In the eyes of the law, those who conspired and still conspire to cover up these murders are just as guilty as the person who pulled the trigger.'

Maggie was waving her hat to get Mac's attention. Reed Dean was making his way through the throng of reporters.

He was holding something. And grinning. He came to the table and sat next to Mac.

'I'm Reed Dean, Betty Jo's brother.' He smiled like he'd won a lottery. 'I'm going to be charged with the murder of Horace Wiggins. I didn't do it, but I must confess I occasionally fantasize about killing every one of the bastards who covered up the identity of my sister's murderer.'

He held up a stack of computer discs. 'I just picked up copies of the X-rays taken of my sister's corpse at Rochelle Hospital.'

'Why is that important?' one of the newspaper reporters called out.

'I suspect you'll learn that as soon as our sheriff opens his mouth,' Reed Dean said.

SIXTY-EIGHT

'**N**obody said this was OK. I snuck up here on my own.' Jen Jessup, in tailored blue jeans and a white blouse, sat in the chair across from his desk.

Mac had spent the last hour fencing with the reporters who'd hung around after the press conference. They'd been looking for more. He didn't give it to them. They needed to reach the obvious conclusions on their own.

'Masterfully played,' she said. 'You raised explosive questions, answered some and so few of theirs, and brought in Reed Dean for a boffo ending.'

He crossed the room and sat behind his desk. 'Reed's still going strong down there, grateful that someone's paying attention at last.'

'Yes, I'd love a short one,' she said, nodding at the bottle of bourbon and two glasses he'd set out earlier for himself and Reed.

He poured an inch for her and one for himself.

She knocked hers back in one swallow. 'Bastards,' she said. 'Problem is you really don't know which is the one?'

'There are several possibilities.'

'Not Roy Powell, if that's your concern.' She held out her glass for another whiskey.

'Yeah, but you and Powell . . .?' The words had tumbled out before his brain had the sense to stop them.

'I already told you,' she said, giving him the sort of flattered smile that might have come from seeing too clearly into his head. 'It's been over for a long time.'

'The reporters will chase this?' he asked, pouring her another inch.

'Like hounds for the rest of today and maybe even tomorrow if there's no wreck out on the Interstate, or a store doesn't burn.'

'Reed is being set up for arson and murder.'

'Like you set up dear, departed Horace?'

After he didn't answer, she asked, 'Is there really another crime scene photo?'

'Confidentially, not to be repeated to anyone?'

A smile, anticipating, spread across her fine face. 'Fair enough.'

'Had to be.'

She laughed, loud – a bark. 'Ah, that's rich, meaning there once might have been, but you have no idea whether it still exists.'

'Reed saw Horace trashing his garage a few hours before he was killed.'

Her face turned serious. 'Worried he'd left a picture out there?'

'Apparently he was in a real panic.'

She took a small sip of the whiskey. 'That neighbor who was watching the goings on through his window said that, too.'

'The one who fingered Reed?'

'She told one of Jimmy's deputies that someone was in the

shadows, talking with Horace. She said she noticed the mystery man after she saw Reed drive away without getting out.'

Mac leaned back in his chair. 'Son of a bitch. Bales put Reed and me through the third degree, knowing Reed never got out of his car?'

'Jimmy's kicking up a dust screen.'

'Maybe on orders,' Mac said.

'Only one person could control Jimmy Bales like that.'

'Clamp Reems,' Mac said. His head had been dancing with the suspicion for some time.

'He killed Horace?'

'If he didn't, he knows who did.'

'And Betty Jo Dean?'

'If he didn't, he knows who did.'

'And Laurel,' she said, showing no surprise. 'It seems so futile.'

'Why would the killer need Betty Jo's head? Answer that, Jen, and I'll give you the killer.'

'It's why you called in the press?'

'I can't figure why anyone wanted the head.'

'It's bizarre enough to catch their interest,' she said. 'Maybe they'll come across something.'

'I tipped two of them they ought to start with Randy White. He knows more than he's said.'

'He checked into the Hotel Excelsior yesterday,' she said, 'a few hours after Horace was found.'

'He got nervous, living so far out in the sticks?'

'It's one of my questions, but he hasn't been in.' She stood up. 'I'm going to try again.'

He followed her down the stairs.

'I still don't get the significance of these,' she said, holding up one of the discs Reed Dean had handed out.

'The hospital X-rays? You will, as soon as Jimmy Bales starts to sputter. It will convince you just how dumb he is.'

'You know what else I still don't get, Mac Bassett?'

'I can't imagine.'

'Your motivation.'

'A constituent—'

'You were a man under indictment; a man running a restaurant into the ground; a man who, near as I can figure, is flat broke. Yet you drop everything to nose around a cold murder case, for a waitress who didn't live in town . . .?'

'I've got to find Reed, give him the good news about the nosy neighbor.'

'I'm good at looking into backgrounds.'

'I'm not the story,' he said.

'Perhaps. What else haven't you told me?'

'Jonah Ridl said Laurel had a source,' he said. 'What she learned probably got her killed.'

'I need to know who.'

'You might never know who ran her off the road.'

'I'm thinking hard about it."

'And if you find out?'

'Then I'll know who to kill.'

SIXTY-NINE

A reporter from the *Milwaukee Sentinel* called the Bird's Nest within an hour. 'I called your Sheriff Bales.'

'Yes?' said Mac.

'He said there can be no telling whose skull you're having examined in Champaign.'

'Yes?'

'Those discs of Betty Jo's X-rays Reed Dean handed out to all of us after your news conference?'

'Yes.'

'The Rochelle Hospital, where the state police took Betty Jo immediately after exhumation, will authenticate them as being authentic copies?'

'Yes.'

'Those X-ray discs can then be used to verify that the skull Doctor Wilhausen examined is the same one that came out of the ground?'

'Yes.'

'I told all that to Sheriff Bales. He said you were full of shit anyway.'

'Yes.'

The reporter hung up, laughing.

'Yes,' Mac said again, this time to no one at all.

*   *   *

Mac was in the bar, watching the first of the evening's news broadcasts, when a polite young man showed up. He was dressed in a suit and looked about twenty-five years old.

'Am I catching you at a bad time?' the young man asked.

'Reporters have been calling ever since the press conference. So long as you don't mind my catching the news, you're free to fire away. Be warned, though; I expect you to do your own investigating. You're more likely to be convinced that way.'

The young man made a small cough. 'I'm actually an assistant vice-president of the First Bank of Grand Point, sir. I stopped by to inquire whether you have any questions about our letter.'

'What letter?'

'The registered one that was signed for yesterday.'

'Wait here.' Mac went into the kitchen. April was opening a carton of catsup.

'Did we get a registered letter?'

'It's crap. I'll tell you about it tomorrow.'

He headed back into the bar. 'I assume you want me to resume paying on the mortgage?'

A tiny line of concern appeared on the kid's otherwise unmarked forehead.

'I've had some distractions,' Mac said. 'I'll begin paying soon.'

The picture on the screen changed to an establishing shot of the Bird's Nest. He pressed the remote to turn up the volume.

A young anchor appeared on the screen. She looked to be the same age as the boy banker. 'The mystery of two unsolved 1982 Grand Point murders took a bizarre turn this afternoon. The town's mayor, Mac Bassett, announced that he has proof that Betty Jo Dean, one of the victims, was decapitated and buried with someone else's skull.'

The screen flashed to a high-school photo of Betty Jo Dean. 'According to Bassett, a forensics expert at the University of Illinois is preparing a report that will prove that the skull buried with Ms Dean is not hers.

'Peering County Sheriff Bales, however, strongly disputed Mayor Bassett's assertion.'

Jimmy Bales appeared, red-faced, on the screen. 'Who knows what skull they're examining?' he blustered.

Reed appeared in the next shot, sitting at the table during the press conference. 'Anticipating such questions, Reed Dean, the dead girl's brother, distributed copies of the X-rays made at the Rochelle Hospital which, he claims, can be used to verify that the skull and vertebrae taken from the casket are those now being examined at the University of Illinois.'

The screen switched to a new story. Mac switched off the set.

'Your loan has been in technical default for quite some time,' the young man said.

'I'll work diligently to catch up on my payments.'

'I'm afraid it's gone beyond that.'

Anger at the sanctimonius young man prickled the top of Mac's scalp. 'Well, we can't have that. You must work at calming your fears.'

'Sir—'

'Do you really believe your being sent here, so late on a Saturday, is coincidental?'

'We sent you a registered letter—'

'Luther Wiley. Isn't he the chairman of your board of directors?'

'Yes, but—'

Mac hustled him to the door and the young man retreated across the street, to the parking lot. But he, or one of his fellow bankers, would be back. All the stops were being pulled out now.

Mac Bassett had to be driven from town.

SEVENTY

The rain was torrential on Sunday, hard enough to blur the shapes of the houses along Mac's street.

By one o'clock that afternoon Mac had heard from a total of twenty-two reporters. Some had called the day before at the Bird's Nest; some had called him that morning, at home. All had called for his reaction to Sheriff Jimmy Bales's assertion that Mac and Reed Dean had switched the skulls.

'Mr Dean handed out the X-rays from the hospital,' Mac told each of the twenty-two. 'They can be used to verify that the skeletal parts taken to Rochelle by the state police are the same ones examined at the University of Illinois.'

'Sheriff Bales says there are other ways to corrupt those findings,' most reporters shot back.

'I respect the sheriff's expertise on corrupting evidence, but on this he's wrong.'

'The sheriff also suggested that action may be taken against Mr Dean because the skull and vertebrae were released into his custody solely on condition that they be immediately interred with the rest of his sister's body,' most said, as well.

'You mean buried like the truth has been? Did Sheriff Bales mention harassing Mr Dean about Horace Wiggins's murder? Did Bales tell you he hauled Mr Dean into the sheriff's department in the middle of the night without cause?'

'Murder? Wiggins's death is being treated as a homicide?' every one of the twenty-two reporters asked.

'I'd watch Bales closely, to see if he ever comes up with a suspect, or if he's covering up again,' Mac said to each of the twenty-two.

But then came the twenty-third call. It was not from a reporter. It was from Darrell Thompson, the man who prepared the state's forensics report.

He'd called to whine. 'Reporters have been harassing me since yesterday afternoon.'

'I'm delighted. You prepared a sloppy, erroneous report.'

'I was told it was shot through the nose.'

'"Told?"'

'They say I misplaced Doctor Brown's file. I didn't. I just can't find it. There was pressure to release a report, so I got the information verbally.'

'From whom?'

'I called up there, talked to a sheriff named Bales. He said he was at the autopsy. He filled me in.'

'The skull didn't fit the vertebrae.'

'There have been cutbacks down here. Our pensions are under-funded by billions. I have no idea what things will be like when it comes time for me to retire.'

'Why didn't you verify the fit between the vertebrae and the head?'

'I'm not a forensic examiner; I'm in media relations. Look, I'm holding no hard feelings. I've written up another report, detailing what the reporters told me you said at your press conference. I'm putting it in the file along with my earlier report and the 1982 report.'

'There was a 1982 report?'

'We're not yokels, Mr Bassett. There's been a file ever since those stupid bullets were sent down for ballistic examination, like they wouldn't match, surprise, surprise.'

'Surprise, surprise?' Maybe the man wasn't just calling to whine. 'Are you telling me something?'

'I don't know; am I? Or am I not the only one who doesn't understand things?' He paused, his petulance sagging. 'People from Grand Point have been playing us for chumps since the beginning.'

'What's wrong with the bullets?'

'Nothing, and that's the problem. You fire a bullet into something, it almost always gets nicked. Even if you fire it into water, or cotton, it comes out marked from the gun barrel. In the case of these bullets, you'd expect at least one of them would have changed shape from hitting bone or even tissue. The bullets we got in 1982 for testing were pristine. No nicks, cuts, or scratches on the five from Mr Pribilski, or the one from Miss Dean.'

'Like they were never fired at all?'

'Someone sent us the wrong bullets.'

Mac breathed in slowly. The skull now made perfect sense.

'Does your file say who submitted the bullets?' he asked.

'No, sir, it does not. I'll add a brief summary of this conversation to the file, to show my impartial objectivity. And Mr Bassett?'

'Yes?'

'You're welcome.'

Pristine bullets.

He sat in his living room, drinking coffee. He needed to think, over and over, about what could only be true.

Pristine bullets.

Finally he called the sheriff's department. He left a message for Jimmy Bales. Bales returned the call from his home five minutes later.

'What's the bullshit, now?' the sheriff asked.

'Those suspects interviewed back in 1982. Do you think most of them lived on farms?'

'What the damned hell? You're talking Betty Jo Dean?'

'We're rural here, right, Jimmy? Most everyone either lives on a farm or is close to someone who does?'

'What the hell are you getting at, Bassett?'

'If a police officer wanted bullets from a particular suspect's gun for a ballistics comparison, and that suspect lived on a farm, the officer could simply go out to that suspect's property, find a fence post or a side of a barn that the suspect had used for target practice and dig out as many as he wanted, right?'

'This sounds nuts.'

'Don't you want to understand what I'm talking about, Sheriff?'

Bales swore and hung up. Mac wasn't surprised.

Mac dialed Bales's home number. It was busy. He wasn't surprised about that, either. Bales was calling someone who'd shot at fence posts and barn boards, back in the day.

He slipped on his yellow rain jacket and went out. He had a lot more to think through.

But at least now he knew why her killer wanted her head.

SEVENTY-ONE

The rain kept on. It shrouded the Bird's Nest in fog. April's car was already there. So was Maggie's. Ever purposeful, they were soldiering on, prepping for a new night.

The rain would keep people away. With the bank poised to seize everything he owned, he didn't think it much mattered anymore.

He drove on, through the intersection and up the overpass. He needed to see, even in the gloom. He needed to imagine.

Turning onto Poor Farm Road, he had the thought he should stop to say some words of understanding at the spot where the bullets had been blasted into Pauly Pribilisky – bullets that had been so carefully and totally retrieved and then likely thrown into the river, for they would never be allowed to be examined. But mumbling incantations to the dead, especially in a driving rain, was an Abigail Beech kind of thing, and he wasn't that nuts. Yet.

He continued on to the bend and followed the river. It was the cabins he needed to see – the place where Sheriff Milner had used a lie to send a squad of searchers. Milner had been the decent man in the investigation and he'd died for it, probably a suicide from guilt but perhaps a victim of murder. The difference didn't much matter.

The cabin that had been burned, the one they'd called the Country Club, had been the last one in the row. He parked, tugged his slicker tight and walked into the rain.

The river was high, already lapping at the top of the bank. The old dam, upriver, had always prevented that, but then the Army Corps of Engineers had added a second one, south of Grand Point. Now the river threatened to overflow, in the middle, each time there was a heavy rain.

Only a few scorched cinderblocks remained to show where the cabin had been. It must have been agony to wait even a couple of weeks to torch the cabin, fearing someone would link it to Betty Jo Dean. He wondered what it was that had to be burned. Blood, he supposed, but perhaps fingernail scratchings or maybe even words she'd managed to carve into the floor or a wall when she'd been left, tied, alone. Certainly there'd been no worry about finding fluids there. DNA testing wasn't an option back in 1982.

The Country Club. A place for bait, rods and reels, and coolers for beer. And for a camp cot, originally for naps, then for the rape of an underage girl, though surely the bastard wouldn't have called it that. Likely, he'd called it love.

He hunched further into his yellow slicker. The rain was pounding hard as daggers now, though no matter how fierce it had come the last thirty years, the ground on which he stood could never be cleansed. Likely she'd heard the searchers combing the woods outside; likely she'd tried to scream, through the rag in her mouth, over and over for one hellish day, and then another. Likely, she'd wept at not being able to hear herself.

The edge of the water frothed at the bases of the trees. To the north and to the south there were maples and oaks, spread irregularly apart, but only Chinese elms lined the bank of the old Country Club site, tight and neat in a perfectly straight row. Chinese elms grew much faster than maples and oaks. They might have been planted to keep the soil from eroding, perhaps replacing maples and oaks that had been destroyed when the cabin burned in 1982.

But they were weak trees, those elms, and one in the center of the row was tipping toward the river. Its leaves were brown and curled, a sign of death in early July. He walked up to look closer.

The ground near its base had heaved; the rush of the river was pulling away its soil.

'Odd day to be out, Mr Mayor.'

Mac spun around. A half-inch cigar stub smoldered comically in Clamp Reems's pipe, sending absurd little smoke signals up into the wide brim of his hat. He wore an olive drab slicker that blended into the color of the woods behind him. His hands were caked with dirt.

'Odd day for you, too, Deputy.' He pointed to the man's hands. 'Weeding?'

Clamp's face stayed blank as he came up to within two feet. It was technique; it was intimidation.

'I never did trust them Army Corps of Engineers,' Reems said. 'That new dam is holding our water too high, destroying our river-banks.' He'd been checking the soil around the trees.

'Horrible about Horace Wiggins,' Mac said. 'Any idea who knocked him out before torching his garage?'

'We're investigating.'

'Like Betty Jo Dean?' Mac had the thought that the deputy might be carrying a gun beneath his poncho, perhaps a .38. They were alone, in the rain, in the woods, just feet from a river that could clutch at anything and carry it away.

'I understand you're doing your own detecting, Mr Mayor, offering up all sorts of new theories.'

'More like throwing out the litter of old ones that never did fit.'

Clamp Reems took the pipe out of his mouth, licked his lips, and reinserted it. And smiled.

'Like that skull,' Mac said. 'That doesn't fit either.'

'Says you.'

'Says at least one of the other photographs Horace Wiggins took.'

It worked. Clamp Reems blinked. Not hard, not long. But the tough man blinked.

'I surely don't remember Horace taking more than one,' he said. 'And now that Horace's garage burned, well . . . Don't stay out in the rain too long, Mr Mayor.' Reems touched the tip of his forefinger to his hat in a mockery of a salute and headed toward his own cabin, a hundred yards upriver.

'I'll see you tomorrow, Clamp Reems,' Mac called after him. But of course, calling out from behind, there was no way of telling whether that had triggered another blink.

SEVENTY-TWO

'**B**een playing in the rain?' April asked, eying Mac's wet clothes as he came in the kitchen door.

'Looking at the river.'

'Everybody's worried how it's rising,' she said, no doubt deciding she didn't want to know what he'd really been up to. 'A man just called for you.'

'The banker? Tell him we might not get rich tonight.'

'No. This guy was so ancient I could barely hear him. He could have been calling from a bar. Had a bad cough.'

'Jonah Ridl?'

'He didn't leave a name, only a number.'

Mac went up to the office and dialed the number. April was right; a man in a bar answered. Ridl came on two minutes later. His voice was very weak.

'I got my car running and motored here to my favorite tap. I was nursing the first of the afternoon's delights when I looked up. And what did I see, right next to the eight-point head mounted above the antique Schlitz sign? A video of you on the TV, holding a press conference, unleashing the dogs of hell.'

'Now if they'll only dig.'

'Somebody switched the channel so I didn't see the whole thing. That skull has given your newshounds something to chase?'

'That, and Horace Wiggins.'

'I missed that part. What's your favorite crime scene photographer up to?'

'He's dead. I started a rumor there was a second crime scene photo. He beat it out to his garage to paw through old boxes. Someone was with him and incinerated Horace, the boxes and the garage.'

'To get rid of old photos and negatives?'

'And one old witness that knew too much.' He told Ridl about the pristine bullets.

A gurgling cough seized the old reporter for a full minute, before he said, in a voice barely above a whisper, 'Hell, man. I heard they found at least two bullets lying on the gravel, shots that went clear

through Pribilski. Those alone should have been nicked up all kinds
of ways.' He stopped to suck air. 'I remember Clamp making a big
deal about recovering every one of those bullets from Pribilski and
Betty Jo Dean. He said he was going to take them to the ballistics
lab himself.'

'He took unfired bullets instead.'

'The son of a bitch,' Ridl said. 'He controlled everything, didn't
he?'

'He had his thumbs on it all: the crime scene photograph, the
leads the other deputies chased, the bullets, everything.'

'Still—' Ridl coughed again. 'That doesn't explain cutting off
her head.'

'Yes, it does. Imagine Wiley's when Betty Jo was brought in.
The bullet was embedded deeply in her skull. Doc Farmont must
have announced it would take quite some time to get at it with a
probe. There was no time; Clamp was on fire – he needed that bullet
because he knew Sheriff Milner was on to him, inventing that false
rumor about a man fighting with a girl to send a team of searchers
down to the cabin. Milner might arrive at Wiley's at any time and
seize control of the room, telling Farmont to take all the time he
needed to extract that bullet. That bullet was everything; that bullet
was doom, because it could so easily be linked to him. So he did
what he needed to do to get the bullet. He threw everyone out of
the room and hacked off Betty Jo's head.'

'Why risk all that? Why not simply ditch the gun and throw it
in the river?'

'Clamp lives on a small horse farm. The bullet inside Betty Jo
didn't need to be matched to a gun, just to another bullet from the
same source. Like any cop with open land, he stayed proficient with
his .38 by firing hundreds, perhaps thousands, of bullets from that
same gun into his fence or one of his trees. Each one of those bullets
could be tied to one taken from Pribilski or Betty Jo.'

'So he cut off her head? Jesus.'

'Such was his power and impunity. He took the head and left,
leaving Doc, Bud Wiley, maybe Luther Wiley and perhaps even
Horace Wiggins to scramble to cover everything up. With Betty Jo's
sister on way to identify the body, they had to think fast. Most
likely, it was Doc who had the inspiration. He had a skull from his
med school days, or perhaps one of those skeletons physicians used
to keep in their offices. It would have to do. They kept a sheet over

Betty Jo, but if Bella insisted on seeing her, they could point to the skull and say the flesh had to be removed to extract the bullet. With the flesh off, no one could say whose skull it was.'

'And no else ever questioned a thing, since Clamp Reems himself was heading up the investigation,' Ridl said.

'The bullets went into the river, with her head and the gun, in a weighted sack.'

'Then how are you going to prove any of this?' Ridl asked.

'I can't, but tomorrow is the Fourth of July. I'm supposed to present a Chamber of Commerce Humanitarian Award to Clamp Reems in a public ceremony at the courthouse.'

'And that will require a speech?' Ridl asked, understanding.

'I intend to say that even without the head, bullets, or testimony from others, there's enough circumstantial evidence now to warrant a thorough investigation by the state police.'

'Will that get justice?' Ridl asked, after a time.

Mac couldn't give him the words he wanted to hear.

'He killed Laurel,' Ridl said.

'Be well, my friend,' was all Mac could think to say.

But of course, Mac doubted that Jonah Ridl would ever be well again.

'Happy days are here again,' Jen Jessup said when Mac came back downstairs. Alone at the empty bar, she waved a hand at the almost empty dining room beyond.

Their bartender had phoned in earlier, telling Maggie he'd found a job that offered some potential. Maggie told Mac she hadn't asked what their ex-bartender meant.

'Maybe everyone's inside, resting up for the Fourth,' Mac said, taking the stool next to her.

'Or it's the rain,' Jen said, eying Mac's still damp clothes. 'Word's out the bank is going to seize everything you own.'

'Is that why you're here?'

'In part.'

'Luther Wiley's on the board of the bank.'

'You're not outraged?'

'I'm tired.'

'Tired enough to resign as mayor?'

He shrugged.

'Tired enough to quit on Betty Jo?'

'All I can do now is goad others.'

'I just came from the Excelsior. Randall White is still checked in, but they haven't seen him in two days.'

'You checked his cottage?'

'He's not there either.'

'Leave a message at the hotel. He might call, if only to lie.'

'I did better than that. I bribed the desk clerk to let me into his room. His clothes, his shaving stuff, his cologne – God, his oily cologne – and his blood pressure medicine are all there.' She shivered. 'I'm thinking we'll never see Mr White again.'

'That leaves who?'

'Doc Farmont, wherever he might be, Luther Wiley . . . and Clamp Reems.'

'I saw Clamp Reems today,' he said.

'He was here?'

'Down by the river, watching the soil erode.'

'Did he say anything interesting?'

'He said he's investigating the death of Horace Wiggins.'

'Did you say anything interesting?'

'I told him I'd see him tomorrow.'

She studied his face. 'You're going to go through with it – be up on the dais to introduce the guest of honor, Clamp Reems?'

'It's the most important thing I'll ever do.'

SEVENTY-THREE

He left the office lights on – he'd be back up to struggle with bills – and went downstairs to make sure the doors had been locked.

It had been another disastrous night financially. It could have been the rain that kept the diners and the drinkers away. It could have been that tomorrow was the Fourth of July, a day of picnics and barbecues. He doubted it was either, but rather that folks were simply tired of being reminded of the drama he'd brought to Grand Point. He was tired of it, too.

He looked out through the new glass on the back door. The rain had stopped. The sky had cleared, the stars were bright.

He stepped outside. The cool, damp air felt good – liberating.

He stepped out of the shadow of the building and crossed Big Pine Road. The overpass offered the highest, best view of his spot in Grand Point. It might be the last look he'd have. Luther Wiley's bank could seize the Bird's Nest at any time now.

He walked up to the top of the overpass. To the south, a lone pair of brake lights beat erratically on Poor Farm Road, arrhythmic red signals being tapped out by the foot of an impatient young man parked with a girl. He wondered if Pauly Pribilski had sent out such unknowing, taunting red flashes on that long-ago June night, and whether they'd further enraged the man who was coming up on foot.

Jen's article had reported there'd been much talk about what got tough, tall, ex-Marine Pauly Pribilski out of his car. Most assumed it had been the prodding of a gun. Mac wondered now whether it had been the glint of a badge instead, just as it might have been a badge that kept Betty Jo Dean from trying to run. A man with a badge could compel anyone to get out of a car, just as a man with a badge could likely find a girl, no matter where she ran.

It was all so very circumstantial, and felt so very right.

Something moving beneath a street lamp in the west caught his eye. He knew the spot. It was where the Devil's Backbone dead-ended into Big Pine Road, the place where Betty Jo Dean had been found. A car, running without headlights, was pulling off onto the shoulder.

That late at night it could have been lovers looking for better privacy than Poor Farm Road. It could have been someone on a long night's journey, looking for a few moments' rest. All sorts of things could explain why a person would pull over there.

An interior light flashed and went dark. The driver had gotten out. Another light flashed for an instant, farther back. The driver had opened the trunk.

There didn't need to be anything ominous in what he was seeing. He stopped anyway, and waited.

A dark figure hurried into the light of the intersection below. His shoulders were dipped slightly forward from the weight of the two five-gallon gas cans he was carrying. He crossed into the shadows alongside the Bird's Nest.

The arsonist had come back. This time he'd brought ten gallons instead of one puny quart. He hadn't come to scorch part of an outside wall. He'd come to burn the place down.

For one long, insane moment, Mac thought to stay where he was and enjoy the view as the bastard lit the sky. Let the flames lick at the curtains and the old, dry paneling; let the oils explode in the kitchen; let the whiskey bottles crack and spill their alcohol until all the flames came together to send the whole place up in one grand finale of a million fiery cinders.

And then let Luther Wiley's people at the bank wrangle with the insurance company. Let everything be over.

Except Mac would be blamed. The fire would be seen as a desperate act to collect insurance to fund his future.

No.

No more indictments, no more shadows, no more stigmas.

The figure appeared at the back of the restaurant, a shadow black in pantomime against the light spilling from the open kitchen door. He'd stepped back, to look up at the lights coming from Mac's office upstairs, to be sure Mac was inside.

He wasn't just there to burn. He was there to kill.

He disappeared from the light. A second later, a creak came from the restaurant. The arsonist had opened the kitchen door and gone inside. He was going to torch the Bird's Nest from within, to make Mac's death look like a crazed suicide.

He felt for his cell phone. Only keys were in his pockets. He'd left his phone on his desk upstairs.

His truck sat alone in the parking lot, close to the building. The Shell station was just a few blocks away. They could call the cops and the fire department.

He came out of the weeds, running toward the truck.

He hadn't run since college. He pounded down the overpass and across Big Pine Road, wheezing, his heart thudding like a pump gone bad. There was no traffic, no cars to stop for help.

Focus on the truck; get to the Shell station.

He slammed against the south wall of the Bird's Nest, gasping. His heart was a jackhammer, his lungs teabags too weak to suck air. Just an instant's rest, a last sprint to the truck, and he could be gone. He tugged out his keys.

The siding rumbled against his back; brilliant orange shot out the back door, followed by the heat of a thousand Hells.

He ran toward the truck.

The fireball shot into the night sky behind him. Glass, glittering yellows and oranges and reds, rained down everywhere. He threw up his hands to protect the back of his head.

The fireball found him, ten yards from his truck.

BOOK IV: INDEPENDENCE

SEVENTY-FOUR

The Fourth of July

The rubble of the Bird's Nest still smoldered at eight o'clock in the morning, despite the rain that had come down steadily since before dawn. The wood and the dirt and the air still stank of the gasoline, though the fire had fed from it for almost an hour before they could extinguish the flames.

Ever-folksy Clamp Reems, puffing his fool's corncob pipe, faced the reporters gathered under a hastily erected square canvas shelter. Besides Jen, there were only six, including the television pair that had scrambled from Rockford when the news came over their scanner. A small diesel backhoe idled behind Clamp, waiting to resume its careful probing. Clamp had just allowed as to how no one knew anything yet, and he had time for only two or three questions.

Though the day was dark with rain, Jen wore enormous black sunglasses beneath her broad brimmed hat. She touched at her cheek. It was dry, for now.

She glanced again at Roy Powell, holding an umbrella that ludicrously matched the khaki plaid lining of his double-breasted Burberry raincoat. He'd called her at two in the morning to give her the news. She'd made him promise to not let the Peering County Sheriff's Department head the investigation. True to his word, he got two state troopers dispatched to the scene immediately and stood with them now, waiting for the state's crime scene team to arrive. He was a decent man. He knew about her sister, Laurel.

She'd gotten to the Bird's Nest at two-forty, when the flames were still high. At four-eighteen, she'd watched the body being taken away, and remained to watch the others watch – Clamp and the cops and the firemen and Roy Powell – as the backhoe continued to pluck gingerly at the debris for signs of more corpses. Only four hours later, when Clamp moved to stand beneath the makeshift shelter and profess amazement to the press, did she get out of her car.

'What are your feelings about the death of Mayor Bassett?' the grizzled veteran from the *Des Moines Register* asked. She'd seen him before, over the years. He was tenacious.

'I prefer to believe Mayor Bassett is alive and doing just fine.' Reems took a fast puff from his pipe, trying for his usual confident Colonel Cornpone, but his voice was higher than normal. Oddly, he kept glancing south, to the overpass, where there was nothing going on at all.

'Please don't fence with me, Deputy,' the reporter said. 'There was a body in the rubble. Bassett's truck was the only vehicle in the parking lot. It's Bassett.'

'Let's be patient and hope for the best.' There was no doubt: Reems's voice had a squeaky element of nervousness that she'd never heard before.

'Mayor Bassett was quite vocal about the way the Betty Jo Dean case was botched,' another reporter said. 'He inferred you were involved in the desecration of her corpse.'

Reems sent another puff of smoke up to the brim of his hat, where it hung for an instant, the only cloud in an otherwise guileless face. 'We get along fine. In fact, Mac is going to introduce me at today's festivities.'

Again, he spoke as though Mac were alive. The corncob, the present tense; it was the innocence of a clever man.

'If not Bassett, who was pulled dead from here this morning?'

Clamp lowered his pipe conspiratorially. 'Some might argue it was a hired man, an arsonist, but don't print that.'

'Insurance?' the television reporter asked.

'This is off the record,' he said, glancing at the overpass before looking directly at the television camera, 'but there are rumors poor Mac is having financial difficulties. Best we wait for the investigators to do their jobs.' He put the pipe to his mouth and sent up more smoke. 'Now, if you'll excuse me—'

Three decades of bile rose up fast in Jen's throat. 'Were you aware Bassett was going to announce big news at the courthouse today?' she asked. It was a stretch, but that didn't matter now.

'What?' The word came out dry, a rasp. Clamp tugged the pipe from his mouth.

'Bassett inferred that instead of introducing you, he was going to conduct his last press briefing.'

'About what?'

'Come on, Deputy. It could only have been about Betty Jo Dean.'

'That was a long time ago, Miss Jessup.'

'You had so many leads.'

'All of them were lousy. We ended up chasing our tails.'

'Yes, but now there's the news that the head is not hers.'

'If you'll excuse me—'

'A question on another topic?' she shouted.

'One more. That's all.'

'It's about my sister, Laurel.'

Reems put a confused, tentative smile on his face for the television camera. 'I don't believe I've met your sister.'

'Supposedly, you investigated her death the same week as the others back in 1982. She was run off the road. Then again, you might not remember. So many people were being murdered around here.'

'Now wait a—'

'No, you wait. Laurel was looking into the killings—'

Reems gave a jerky wave to the backhoe operator. The diesel fired up. The press briefing was over.

Reems hurried through the rain to his car. Spinning his wheels out of the lot, she expected him to head north, to the sanctuary of the sheriff's department or to his horse farm, farther still. But Reems swung his black Crown Victoria south, toward the overpass.

She ran to her own car and followed, staying well back when he turned east onto Poor Farm Road and disappeared around the bend. He was headed to the river. It was no surprise; Mac had seen him there, checking erosion, just yesterday. The tears started again. She wiped them away with the back of her hand. Not now. Now, she needed to see.

She slowed to a crawl, rounding the bend. He'd left his car across from the woods by the last cabin.

She parked and moved through the trees. The roaring river and the steadily beating rain covered the sound of her footfalls.

He was kneeling, checking the erosion at the partially uprooted base of a tree. The tree was dead, its leaves brown and curled, and had canted a few degrees toward the water, beginning a slow, perhaps months-long fall into the water. It seemed an odd thing to worry about when a man had just been killed in a fire.

She went back to her car to wait. Reems appeared ten minutes later. His hands and forearms were muddy. He'd been digging in the dirt.

She gunned her engine and sped forward.

He looked up slowly as she skidded to a stop on the wet gravel. His face was blank, confused. She powered down her window.

'The river,' he said slowly, almost as though he were in shock.

She stared at him for a moment, until she was sure he was barely aware she was there. And then she sped back toward the ruin of the Bird's Nest.

SEVENTY-FIVE

C lutching everything so she wouldn't have to risk another trip to her car in the rain, April eased inside Maggie's front door. Maggie quickly shut it behind her.

'I've been afraid to move the curtains,' Maggie said. 'Any reporters out there?'

'Not so far, and none at my place, either,' April said, 'but two were at Mac's house.'

'They say anything about those?'

April dropped the shoes on the carpet and draped the blue suit and white shirt across the back of an upholstered chair. 'Considering the condition of the body, they must have thought I was crazy, fetching casket clothes.'

'Did you go by the Bird's Nest again?'

'It's the same as when they first called me, a pile of black lumber, no more than six feet high, except it's freakier in the daylight. It's still smoking, even with the rain. A backhoe is picking through it, real slow.'

'You're sure the body's gone?'

'They scooped up what they could before they called me, Maggie.'

'Found him fast enough, they did.'

'Our cockroach of a fire chief knew what to look for.'

'When will they say for certain?'

'They said the body was bad. They've only got his frickin' teeth, if they weren't destroyed. You can bet those state people will take their time after the mess they made of Betty Jo's case.'

'Who else was down there?'

'Hard to tell, under all the umbrellas. Roy Powell is still there, with a couple of state troopers. Maybe state arson investigators and probably an insurance investigator hoping to find anything that proves Mac set the fire himself. There are a few news people, including one van with a little broadcast dish that was packing up. I think Clamp had a briefing earlier, but he's gone now.'

'Jen Jessup?'

April shook her head. 'Not to be seen.'

'Who from the sheriff's?'

'Just one deputy, looking bored.'

'Any strange car get towed into the sheriff's garage?'

'I didn't bother to go to the courthouse because I didn't know how to ask about a strange car. I heard the program this afternoon will be part memorial for Mac – our lost Mayor, and all that crap.'

'Clamp – he'll still be there?' Maggie asked.

'He's the honoree. The live one, at least.'

'And Luther Wiley?'

'He's a trustee,' April said. 'He'll be up on the stage, too, dabbing at imaginary tears like the rest of them, no doubt.'

'No matter that he's spent the last few days getting ready to seize the Bird's Nest, and the last few decades lying about Betty Jo Dean's murder. Him and that Randy White are the only two left who know anything, other than Doc Farmont.'

'Besides Clamp.'

'Clamp, most of all.'

'Luther's got to be nervous as hell, thinking about Horace,' April said.

'Worrying whether he's next.'

'Mercy that,' April said.

'Mercy that,' Maggie agreed.

They looked across the cramped little room.

'Mercy that,' Mac agreed, raising his coffee cup with bandaged hands to toast them both.

SEVENTY-SIX

'I apologize for interrupting you on this most chaotic of days, but I assure you, it couldn't wait,' Jen said. Strangely, she felt calm.

Luther Wiley, rouged as always but seeming even more red today, got up from his desk. His hands shook as he pressed his fingertips to the desktop.

She forced a grateful smile and sat down. 'It is a horrible day, is it not?'

'Indeed,' he managed, sitting down.

She noticed, then, the fine beads of sweat on his forehead. Perhaps Luther Wiley was delicate, incapable of a big sweat. She'd know, soon.

'They brought the body here, from the Bird's Nest?' she asked.

'We have the county contract.'

'Was Mac Bassett murdered?'

He looked away. 'The medical examiner will make that determination.'

She leaned forward. 'It's Mac, right? I mean, his truck is still there and no one's seen him since.'

'The medical examiner will have to say.'

She pressed on. 'I've been trying to find Randall White – slick, oily creature, prone to running off at the mouth? You and he go way back, from when he used to assist Doc Farmont.'

'I barely know him.'

'Not according to him. He's been telling everybody he was here, assisting the doctor and you and your drunken Uncle Bud with Betty Jo. Chopping away, were you, Luther?' They were wild charges, meant to break loose the truth.

Luther's rouge froze around a tentative smile. 'I was never near the body.'

'Dougie Peterson said otherwise. He said you invited him in for a peek.'

'Dougie was lying.'

'Dougie was drowned. That's why I'm so concerned about Randy White. I can't find him. Maybe he's dead, too, because of what he knows.'

'Disgusting rabbit of a man, really.' Luther took out a white silk handkerchief and dabbed at his mouth. The white silk came away pink.

'Think Randy White is bobbing like Dougie Peterson?'

'My God, Miss Jessup.' He reached for his handkerchief again.

He might have been sweating tiny beads, but they were coming fast. Encouraged, she went on: 'Things keep happening to people who know about Betty Jo Dean. As I was driving back to town, bummed about Mac Bassett, bummed about never getting a statement from Randy, I recalled something from long ago. Do you remember my sister, Laurel?'

'I've never had the pleasure.'

'Really? She was killed, run off the road right after they found Betty Jo. Laurel was a darling, quite beautiful. I was always so envious. I was in sixth grade when she went, just like that.' She snapped her fingers. 'Anyway, you know how younger sisters are? They're the nosiest creatures on earth. Always snooping. And . . . well, I'd blush if I wasn't so insane with a new thought . . .' She stared straight into his eyes.

He was looking past her. Ideally he was thinking about bolting for the door.

'Little sisters are always listening,' she whispered. 'Like little mice in the walls, mice with big ears?'

He managed a nod, but he was looking at the door.

'Now, we only had the one phone,' she prattled on, 'and it was in the kitchen, so it wasn't like I could pick up an extension to listen. But there was a spot in the dining room where, if I pressed my ear just right, I could hear through the wall.

'The night before she died, she was talking on the phone. She was speaking low, so I couldn't hear all of it. She must have assumed I'd overheard something, though, because when she came through the dining room and saw me standing there, she said, "My, my, another red-faced creature," making a joke of it, you see. "Everywhere I look, I see red-faced people."'

She raised what she hoped was a knowing eyebrow. 'Do you understand what I'm talking about, Luther?'

He shook his head, but that was to be expected.

'Your red powders, Luther, though I did not understand what Laurel was talking about at the time, me being so young. But here's something I have been sure of, all these years. That evening, in the dining room, Laurel was real excited, almost giddy, and she was carrying a little notebook, one of those narrow ones that reporters use. She hadn't been talking to just some boy there in the kitchen. She'd been talking to a source about something that required her to take notes, or at least refer to them, possibly for confirmation – something that had to do with Betty Jo Dean, since that was what she was working on. I'm thinking now that source developed second thoughts about what he'd passed on to Laurel and reported his indiscretion to someone else, a killer.

'A week after Laurel was buried, I snooped through her things, including her purse, crazy with grief. The only thing that was missing was that precious notebook. It was gone.'

Luther Wiley checked his watch. 'I'm sorry about your sister, but I've got to get going. I'm up on the dais at the courthouse this afternoon.'

'It's raining like crazy,' she said.

'I've still got to be there—'

'I've always wondered who that source was,' she interrupted. 'Randy White was young enough, back then, to be subject to the charms of a beautiful college girl. Jimmy Bales was a high-school kid, too young to know much about what was going on. But then I got to thinking about you, Luther. You were the right age and were in a position to have witnessed, even done, all sorts of hasty things that would have interested my sister.' She made a chopping motion with the edge of her hand.

He popped to his feet like he was on springs, a red-faced jack-in-the-box man.

She reached in her purse and came out with her own narrow reporter's notebook. 'See? Just like Laurel's,' she said.

'I must leave,' he said.

She took out her tiny voice recorder. 'To make sure I get things right.'

He started to move around the desk.

She took out a revolver. 'Sit the hell down, Luther.'

SEVENTY-SEVEN

'You should be putting on a hospital gown instead,' April said, holding up the short-sleeved white shirt so Mac could slip an arm in.

The backs of his hands had been burned the worst, thrown up reflexively the instant he'd felt the first blast of the fireball. The aloe April slathered on them took away some of the pain, but the thick gauze bandages she'd then wound on made his skin hurt every time he moved his fingers.

'I was healthy enough to have walked the mile here last night.' He winced as he eased in his arm.

'With burned-off pants,' Maggie said, laughing.

'And a cunning-enough brain to want people to think you're dead,' April said, holding up the other shirtsleeve.

'It's cowardice,' he said. 'I won't be safe until I speak at the courthouse.'

'Might be that nobody will come,' April said. 'The river's so swollen you can't get a boat under the bridge, and it's still raining. Hell, they might even cancel it.'

'Nonsense,' Maggie said. 'Hundreds will come to hear about their crazy mayor getting incinerated, even if they get soaked to the skin.' She turned to Mac. 'All you need is a few folks to spread the word. Sooner you say your piece, the sooner you'll be safe, so talk real fast.'

'I don't care how frickin' fast he talks,' April said, 'Clamp Reems will come at you again, no matter how big a crowd the happy news of your death summons.'

'I don't think Clamp was behind the fire,' Mac said.

April gave the front of the shirt an unnecessary tug.

'Damn it, April.'

'If not Clamp, then who? How many other murderous enemies have you got?' April asked, starting to button the shirt.

'Clamp's not stupid; he wouldn't risk another fire,' he said. 'I see him scorching the siding to warn me off Betty Jo Dean. And I see him torching Horace Wiggins's garage, to eliminate him and whatever pictures he might still have.'

'But killing you is difficult to figure, because you're so sweet?' April reached under his chin to do the last button.

'My dying in a fire, exactly like Horace, draws too much attention to Clamp because of the accusations I've been hinting at.'

'Unless Clamp has gone plum crazy,' Maggie said, 'and thought he had nothing to lose by setting fire to you.'

'Maybe someone wants it to look that way,' he said. 'April, you're sure there was no car left on that wide patch down Big Pine Road, west of the Bird's Nest?'

'For the tenth time: no car was left on either side of the road down there.' She reached for his necktie. 'Your fire-starting friend had an accomplice, either someone who waited in the car then drove away when things went wrong with the explosion, or someone who knew to come later, to fetch the car when the arsonist didn't return.' April looped the tie around his neck and quickly tied an expert knot.

Maggie's landline rang. She picked it up. 'Slow down!' she said, then asked, 'Miss Jessup?' She turned to look at Mac. 'Should I tell her?' she mouthed silently.

He shook his head.

Confusion took Maggie's face. 'You're laughing too hard, Miss Jessup. I can't understand—' There was more silence, then: 'What the hell do you mean? Didn't you hear about the fire?'

Thunder boomed outside, and a sudden sheet of rain slapped against the curtained window.

Maggie listened another minute. Then, not bothering to cover up the mouthpiece, she held out the phone to Mac. 'She's hysterical, talking gibberish, but she knows,' she said.

'Ah, hell.' Mac took the phone with both bandaged hands. 'Jen?'

'Mac? Oh, Mac. Here.'

'Mac?' A different voice, weaker, came on the line.

'Tell him, damn it,' Jen said in the background.

'Mac?' the weak voice said. 'Luther Wiley here. I hired someone to set your fire. I . . .' He paused.

'Say it all now, Luther,' Jen said.

'He never came back to his car,' Luther said.

'You got that?' Jen asked, coming on the line.

'What's going on?' Mac said.

'I'm interviewing Luther, of a fashion. I might be overstepping it. I have a gun.'

'Jen!'

'Luther overheard his uncle and Doc yelling at Clamp, telling him he couldn't do that, or take that.'

'Her head?'

'That's Luther's guess,' she said. 'Isn't that right, Luther?' Someone, presumably a petrified Luther, murmured a response in the background. 'Listen, Mac,' Jen went on, 'Clamp held a press briefing this morning, of sorts, down by your . . . land. He was entirely too vague about the burned corpse they found, so I think he's guessed you're still alive. But he's acting crazy. After his little talk, Clamp tore down to those cabins by the river. I followed him. He was kneeling by a tree on the riverbank. I think he's lost his mind. You need to stay away from the dais this afternoon.'

'Where was he by the river, exactly?'

'No place special, just at the base of some old dead tree.'

'The one that's tipping into the river?'

'Maybe . . . yes.'

It was the tree Mac had started to approach when Clamp materialized out of the trees.

'What was he doing exactly?'

'Digging at its roots, I think. He was all muddy. The tree's dead; it makes no sense.'

'Powell? Is he honest?'

'As the day is long,' she answered. 'He gets a bad rap.'

'Call him, Jen. Tell him to get down to that tree. Tell him if he doesn't hurry, it will all wash away.'

'Mac, what are you talking—?'

There was no time. He hung up.

SEVENTY-EIGHT

They sped south in Maggie's old Trans Am, Mac hunched down in the back, hoping to be unrecognizable under one of her tugged-down straw cowboy hats; April grim-faced, riding shotgun; Maggie driving, alternately shrieking and laughing at the craziness of it all. Only Maggie glanced at the state and insurance investigators and the one lone, indifferent Peering County deputy milling about as they sped past the ruin of the Bird's Nest.

Jen, Powell and two state troopers had beaten them to the river-bank. Gray sky showed through a new gap along the water. The dead elm had toppled into the Royal but its base was still anchored to the bank by a last few large roots and a thick nest of smaller tendrils. The tree bucked wildly from the waters buffeting it. The fallen tree had created a dam, channeling water up onto the bank and washing away the dirt surrounding the uprooted base. The hole was growing. Soon the last of the roots and the nest of tendrils would rip free, sending the tree tumbling downriver.

'There's no time!' Mac shouted above the rain. He dropped to his knees and began pawing into the hole the ripped out base had made.

'What the hell, Mac?' Jen asked, dropping to her knees beside him.

April, Maggie, Powell and the two state cops all came closer and bent down.

'Clamp planted these trees! It's why he's so worried!' Mac yelled, scooping mud backward like a dog gone berserk. His burned skin raged as his bandages clotted up with muck.

They all dropped down to claw the dirt from the hole, as the river raged up and swirled around their hands.

A fat root snapped, loud as a gunshot. The tree shuddered and swung out farther, bucking more wildly. Only two of the large roots now tethered the base of the elm to the bank.

They scooped and pulled at the sodden ground, all of them tight to each other. The base of the tree shuddered from the pounding water; the last of the roots were sure to snap soon.

The base of the tree lifted then, and the bigger of the last two roots rose up out of the water swirling around their hands. Maggie screamed and jerked back, pointing at something in the muddy water. It looked like the tiny top of a softball. And then the water surged, and it was gone.

Mac plunged both hands in after it. His bandages had loosened, entangling his fingers, numbing his feel. He clawed, desperate, to find the round top in the hole.

And then his fingers closed around something hard. He dug deeper, his fingers wide, straining for a better hold. It would not come free; it was entwined tight in the fibrous roots.

The last of the big roots snapped, and the great tree began sliding slowly into the river. The round, hard, slippery thing tore free from his hands, tugged away by the tendrils that still clung to the base of the tree. Mac stabbed after it, and found it again. Powell's hands joined Mac's. Together they clung to the small, round thing as the great tree slid away, dragging them onto their bellies and into the water as the tree finally freed itself from the bank. And then, incredibly, the thin fibrous roots tore away and gave it up. The tree pivoted, and with a huge last splash, bobbed downriver.

Both troopers had grabbed Mac and Powell by the ankles and tugged them back onto the bank. A trooper helped Mac to his feet. Powell, hugging the treasure to his chest, scrambled up on his own.

In that same instant, the rain stopped and the sun filtered down in ribbons from the tops of the trees.

'Wait!' Jen yelled, standing up. She grabbed her phone from her purse.

They all blinked up into the sudden brightness, and began laughing at the cheesy, B-movie symbolism of it. All but Maggie. She merely nodded, accepting. Jen snapped a cell phone picture, and another. It was a moment out of impossible fiction, a moment due a girl for more than thirty years.

Powell held the last of her tight to his ruined Burberry coat. She was caked with clay, her jaw hanging loose as though to scream. But she would not need to scream anymore. There could be no denying, not ever again.

'You'll be careful?' Mac asked Powell.

'Like I'm holding a bomb, which,' he said, a grin splitting his muddy face, 'I guess I am.' He took off toward the road, flanked by a state trooper on each side.

Mac pulled off his flapping, sodden bandages and knelt to rinse his burned hands in the shallow pool where the elm had been. 'What time is it?' he called up to the women standing around him.

'One forty-five,' Maggie said.

April, who knew him best, laughed. 'Your frickin' suit trousers are ripped. Your white shirt is ruined, your tie is drenched. You've got mud everywhere. And your hair – your hair is burned off.' She stopped, giggling too hard to say more.

Mac straightened up. Jen Jessup looked back and forth between him and April, not understanding. 'Surely you're not thinking . . .?' she asked Mac.

But, of course, he was.

SEVENTY-NINE

'I told you there'd be a crowd,' Maggie said, slowing in the traffic clogging at the courthouse.

Tugging the straw cowboy hat down another inch, Mac raised up just enough to see out the rear side window. Two hundred people already sat on lawn chairs, and more were streaming in across the sodden lawn.

'What's that old line?' April asked. '"Give the people what they want, and they'll come?"'

'Toasted mayor,' Maggie said.

'Damned right, toasted mayor,' April agreed.

'Check out Clamp and Jimmy Bales over by the sheriff's door,' Maggie said. 'Jimmy's pissed, and he's busting Clamp's chops. The mouse is roaring.'

'He thinks Clamp set the fire,' Mac said.

'You can read minds?' April asked.

'Mac's like Abigail Beech,' Maggie said. 'He sees things the rest of us can't.'

'Clamp's not paying attention,' April said. 'He's looking up at the sky, worrying it's going to rain again.'

'Or praying if it does it will wash away that leaning tree, and her head with it.' Jen said. She sat in the back, beside Mac.

'Too late for praying on that,' Maggie said.

'Luther's gone?' Mac asked Jen.

'If he's smart. I told him I was going to come back and shoot him. He tried telling me he had no choice but to hire that arsonist to get Clamp blamed and arrested. He said Clamp was going to kill him like he killed Horace Wiggins, since they were the only two left who knew about Clamp and Betty Jo Dean.'

'Actually, there are four left, counting Doc and Randy White.'

'I don't suppose Doc Farmont will ever come back and by the way Randy seems to have vanished, I'm guessing Luther no longer counts him among the living,' Jen said.

'So Luther rationalized torching Mac as justifiable if it saved his own skin?' April asked.

'That's the way thoughts get thunk sometimes, in Grand Point,' Jen said.

'Thunk is right,' Maggie said.

'Even pointing a gun, you couldn't get Luther to say anything about Laurel?' Mac asked.

'Not a peep,' Jen said. 'I think he loved her.'

'All sorts of folks must have loved her,' Mac said, thinking of Ridl.

Maggie stopped at the entrance to the sheriff's parking lot. 'I'm not liking this, Mac,' Jen said, looking around and seeing no television vans. 'I expected at least that TV crew from the Bird's Nest to keep Clamp from acting out.'

'We're safe without them. There are hundreds of townspeople here,' Mac said.

'I didn't like Clamp's faraway look, down by the river,' Jen said. 'It's like he wasn't engaged with reality.'

Mac held out his hand. He'd washed them both as best he could in the river, but the burns were red and raw and they throbbed.

Jen handed him her recorder. 'It's set to the proper position. Your fingers will work enough to turn it on?'

'This is frickin' nuts,' April said, getting out of the car. She pulled the seat forward so Jen could climb out the back.

'Why are you getting out?' Mac asked April.

'In case your burned hands need help with that frickin' switch,' she said. She handed him four Advil tablets. 'Remember what Maggie said: talk fast.' She grinned and walked off with Jen.

He looked across the lawn as he chewed the tablets. Almost all the trustees were up on the dais, along with the city engineer. There was one empty chair, presumably for Luther Wiley. Understandably, there was none for Mac.

Clamp had climbed the stairs to the dais and now sat to the right of the lectern, stiff in a white shirt, subdued tie and dark suit – and perhaps stiff from worry that everything he'd kept hidden was about to burst forth into the sunshine.

Mac looked again at the empty chair on the dais. He'd heard that honoring Clamp had been Luther Wiley's idea. The late newspaperman, Horace Wiggins, might have approved of the honor as well. Mac imagined that, given recent events, they'd both change their votes, if it were somehow possible.

Two minutes later, at precisely two o'clock, the high school's football coach – the grand marshal of the parade that would have taken place had it not rained – stepped up to the lectern. He welcomed everyone to yet another magnificent Fourth of July celebration in the finest town on the planet. Only a few people set down their beers and sodas to applaud.

'This is one of our saddest Independence Days,' the coach said. 'Our mayor, Mac Bassett, perished this morning in a fire at the Bird's Nest.'

'Oh, please,' Maggie said, from the front seat.

There were few gasps. Most had already heard. April and Maggie had been right; they'd come to hear more.

'The state fire marshal is investigating this tragic turn of events,' the coach went on, 'and will issue a report. The best thing we can do now is to keep Mac's memory in our hearts and get on with celebrating our freedom and good fortune to live in such a marvelous town.'

'Stupid bastard,' Maggie said.

The coach went on to make announcements about the day's festivities, most especially the fish fry over at the VFW and later, the fireworks after dusk, east of town along the river. He sat down to disappointed silence. People knew about the fried fish and the fireworks; they wanted to know how Mac Bassett had caught fire.

The county engineer spoke briefly about future road and sewer improvements before turning to bigger concerns over the new dam south on the Royal River. 'I know many of you are worried about the rising water,' he said. 'The Army Corps has assured me it's the result of the spring's abnormally high snow melt. They're watching it closely, and will open the south dam if needed to alleviate any risk of flooding.'

Mac looked below the dais. April stood next to Jen, in the middle of the line of reporters just below the lectern. Both were muddy from the river.

The city engineer cleared his throat, about to introduce the next speaker, who was supposed to have been Mac.

It was time. He clambered out of the back seat.

Maggie smiled up through the open car door. 'Whip off that straw hat and give 'em a Will Rogers cowboy wave, so everybody can see what burned-off hair on a dirty dead man looks like.'

He grinned, took off the straw hat and started waving it as he crossed the lawn. A murmur of shocked voices built into shouts as

he approached the dais. Most everyone was scrambling to stand up
– many were snapping cell phone pictures. It wasn't a welcome that
had gotten them all to their feet; they wanted good views of Mac
Bassett rising from the dead.

He climbed the stairs. Everyone on the dais looked wide-eyed,
save for Clamp Reems. He was looking south along Second Street,
thinking for sure about one particularly unstable tree down by the
rising river, and what it might lift up to reveal.

Mac took care to smile at the chief deputy. Clamp was trapped
by the eyes of hundreds of people; he couldn't leave.

Mac stepped up to the microphone and waved a raw, pink and
blackened hand.

EIGHTY

'**W**elcome, everyone!' His amplified voice reverberated
not quite simultaneously off the many brick fronts
facing the square, as though several Mac Bassetts had
returned to taunt those who'd felt relief at his death.

A few people thought to applaud. Most had simply gone silent,
anxious to hear directly from the mud-caked, burned man who was
supposed to be dead.

'And an especially big welcome to you, Clamp Reems,' Mac
said, half turning to face the chief deputy. 'I intend to make this
the second most important day of your life.'

The killer stared into the crowd, impassive.

No matter. Mac would soon enliven him. He turned back to face
the people on the lawn.

All stood frozen, waiting, except for one frail old man with a
.35mm camera dangling on a cord around his neck. He was laboring
forward through the crowd, stepping haltingly, apparently intent on
getting to the front to take a picture. In spite of the heat, he wore
a sweatshirt and a windbreaker two sizes too large. His sweat-stained
canvas hat was pulled down tight to shield his face from the sun.

'When I was elected just a few short months ago,' Mac said, 'I
looked forward to this day as my first chance to address you as
your mayor. I thought of the words I was going to say – words of

thanks, words of optimism, words of hope about the future of this town.'

People were turning, distracted by the old man's precarious progress. He'd paused for breath, teetering. The lower part of his face, clean-shaven, was sallow and unhealthy looking, as though it hadn't felt the sun for years. His shoulder looked barely wide enough to support the strap of the small camera bag bouncing against his side.

'I've decided . . .' Mac said softly, '. . . to say none of that.'

Everyone looked back at the lectern. They'd heard something going bad in the way Mac lowered his voice.

'Damn it, Bassett!' someone yelled. 'What the hell happened?'

'You mean to these?' he shouted, holding up his blistered hands. 'Or to Betty Jo Dean's head?'

A hundred people gasped. Mac smiled, faking a calm he didn't feel, and pressed on. 'Today we're here to focus on Clamp Reems.'

A few people, confused, began to applaud that. They quickly stopped when no one else joined in. The others had heard the tension in Mac's voice, and were straining to hear more.

Except for the old man. He'd started up again on his snail's journey toward the dais.

'Ah, but I can't do Clamp justice,' Mac said. 'Let me yield to Luther Wiley.' He held Jen's voice recorder a foot from the microphone and switched it on.

'Hell, yes, Clamp killed Betty Jo,' Luther's voice boomed from the speakers at the sides of the dais. 'There isn't a fool in this town doesn't know that, or at least suspect it. I witnessed nothing first-hand, mind you, but my uncle, and Doc and Horace, and even that numb-nutted Randy White, were all there at the funeral home when they brought her in. Doc was taking too much time with the probe, trying not to disfigure her—'

The old man had tottered to the front row and was reaching into his camera bag when he stopped like he'd been struck by lightning. He was staring at Jen Jessup like she was a ghost.

'—for viewing in an open casket,' Luther's voice went on. 'That business about bloating and decomposition? There was none. He loved her, see? He'd kept her alive—'

Back on the dais, a chair scraped loudly and fell over; Clamp might have been lurching up. Mac didn't turn; he was transfixed by the old man, now standing right below the dais. He'd pulled a revolver from his camera bag.

The beard was gone, but Mac knew the man. He stepped quickly from behind the lectern and threw up his arms. Someone yelled.

A gun fired once, and again.

He fell, wondering crazily if it had been him, shouting.

EIGHTY-ONE

They said four days passed.

Four days of blurred shapes and bright fluorescents and IV drips and deep drugged sleep interrupted by brusque doctors and nurses tugging him to consciousness to look at his back. And each time seeing April or Maggie or Jen Jessup, and not being able to tell whether it was night or day or whether that even mattered.

Other snatches, too, he remembered.

April smiling. 'The bullets were lodged so very close to your spine. They got them, Mac. No impairment.'

Then: 'I've had enough of your frickin' bullshit.'

Men in dark suits, hovering at the foot of the bed. Powell was among them, dressed flawlessly in faint pinstripes, asking Mac why he'd stepped out from behind the lectern.

Maggie furious as a hornet, raising her spare five feet under Powell's chin to tell him to get out.

Jim Rogenet sounding stronger that he'd been in months, saying, 'Oh, they'll pay,' squeezing Mac's shoulder and leaving.

Reed Dean shifting from one foot to the other, twisting a NASCAR cap into rope and mumbling, 'Thank you,' over and over.

Maggie talking to Jen Jessup like they were old friends, to which Mac said, 'This must be meds,' and both of them laughing hysterically.

Jen alone, crying at the side of his bed.

On the fifth day, he woke to pain and clarity.

April sat beside his bed, reading through a sheaf of papers.

'Was it the first or second bullet that got me?' It came out barely audible, a dry croak.

'Water?' She dropped the papers on the chair beside her.

'Sure.'

She poured a little into a plastic cup, bent a straw and brought it close to him. 'Don't lean forward.'

He leaned forward and gasped at the pain.

She laughed as he slumped back, moaning. 'Thank goodness your mulishness survived.'

'First, or second?' he asked again, when the pain had subsided.

'Both, actually. Even with Ridl raising a gun, Clamp Reems had the presence of mind to keep his priorities straight.'

'What does that mean?'

'Clamp shot you first . . . and second . . .' She looked at the door, as though to make sure no one was close by. 'There's confusion over who is responsible for that. Some think Clamp was aiming at Ridl in self-defense and you stumbled into his line of fire, waving your damned arms. Some say – though this is too incredible for most folks to believe, except those who know you well – you were trying to protect Clamp and deliberately stepped in front of him, to face Ridl. Of course, there's a third scenario that has Clamp aiming right at you, since he shot you twice, and in the back. Fortunately, that's the one Roy Powell likes. Clamp's been arrested. Powell's been here a half-dozen times, antsy to get your statement.'

He remembered seeing Powell, and Maggie throwing him out.

'Jonah Ridl?'

'Powell's real frustrated with Jen Jessup,' April said, ignoring his question. 'He thinks she took cell phone pictures of you on the dais. Jen says she didn't, and no one else has come forward with other photos, so there's no proof you're dumb enough to step in front of a gun.'

'Jonah Ridl is dead?'

'Jimmy Bales got him, though it took four shots, the first three of which struck the dais and the lectern. It was justifiable; Ridl was waving a gun. He just couldn't hold it steady enough to fire.'

Mac closed his eyes. 'Ridl asked me if there'd be justice.'

'He was full of cancer, Mac. He had a month, two at most.'

'What's Clamp saying?'

'You stepped into his line of fire, obviously.'

'I meant about the skull.'

'Nothing yet, but it's Betty Jo's, top and jaw, and it's screaming bloody hell. That professor from Champaign drove up the vertebrae. They fit the new skull perfectly.'

'Was there a bullet?'

'Incredibly, still wedged deep in her forehead. It's been removed at long last.'

'No wonder Clamp hacked at her head, just as Luther admitted in Jen's recording.'

'Unfortunately, Luther's statements are not admissible, since he made them under threat of a gun. Besides, they're hearsay; he's claiming he only overheard things.'

'Luther will slither out of everything?'

'They're saying they might never identify the arsonist, so badly was he burned.'

'So Luther skates.'

'Jen says no, but she's holding something back about that, like some think she's holding back about having cell phone pictures.'

'I suppose Luther's a small potato, anyway.'

'A Tater Tot for sure, if you can overlook the fact that he hired an arsonist to kill you.'

'What about linking Clamp to Betty Jo?'

'Now that he's got that bullet from Betty Jo, rumor is Powell is going to charge him. Another rumor has it that Powell is seeing a run at the governor's mansion from this, and is going to prosecute the case himself.' She held up his cup for another sip, then said, 'Want a laugh? Once the shooting was done, Jimmy Bales led a team of deputies up to Clamp's farm, saying he'd had a brilliant inspiration.'

Mac managed a smile. 'To extract a few slugs from Clamp's fence or barn, on the hunch they'll match the one from Betty Jo Dean?'

'Just like you told him.' Then: 'Powell is saying Clamp will do life for Betty Jo.'

'And Pauly?'

'No bullets from him still exist, so Clamp won't be prosecuted for that.'

'How about the other victims?'

'You want Clamp punished for killing Horace Wiggins?'

'I want him accountable for Delbert Milner and Laurel Jessup and Dougie Peterson.'

'Roy Powell is a smart politician. He'll only try cases he can win. Be happy for Betty Jo Dean.'

'Rogenet was here?' he asked, changing the subject to another blur.

She smiled broadly. 'To drop off those,' she said, pointing to the papers on the chair. 'Peering County is offering me three hundred thousand dollars for my half interest in the pile of charred wood once known as the Bird's Nest.'

'They're nervous because Luther's a county trustee, even though he won't be charged for the arson.'

'They want us to forget about suing them.'

'You'd still have a lot left over, after we pay off the note.'

She grinned. 'That three hundred thousand is net, same amount for each of us. Luther's bank will cancel the note if we also promise to not come after them. Everybody wants to make us rich, Mac.'

'What's Rogenet say?' he asked.

'He says we ought to take the deal on the arson, and you should sue Peering County in civil court for their chief deputy shooting you in the back while Powell tries him in criminal court for shooting Betty Jo Dean.'

'What about Reed?'

'Rogenet is representing him as well, and that's where the huge money is going to rain down. Peering County is going to pay big-time for their chief deputy murdering Betty Jo Dean. Reed and his sister Bella are destined to become two of the wealthiest people west of Chicago.'

He asked for another sip of water.

'There's other good news, Mac,' she said. 'Pam Canton, your waitress friend from the Willow Tree, saw us on the national news and called Maggie. She'd gotten a threatening call, no doubt from Clamp though she didn't recognize the voice, and decided she'd always wanted to work in California. She's fine, and relieved to be gone. And a kid from Dixon turned himself in for running down Farris Hobbs. It was a hit and run, not at all connected to your investigation of the Dean case.'

'Randy White?'

'Likely enough, Clamp weighted him well. No one expects he'll ever come out of the water.'

'I suppose . . .' He let his voice fade away and shut his eyes.

Suddenly, he didn't want to hear anything more.

EIGHTY-TWO

F ive weeks later, when it was not quite September, Mac had
stepped out his front door to throw the last of his duffel bags
into his truck, when Jen Jessup came up the front walk, carrying
a folded newspaper and a brown paper bag.

'April called me. She said you're heading north.'

'You've been avoiding me.' She'd returned none of the half-dozen
calls he'd made after he got out of the hospital. He held the door
open for her and they went inside.

'I figured I'd give you some time; I figured I'd give Laurel some
time. And,' she said, 'I figured I'd give me some time.'

'You know I submitted my resignation?'

She nodded.

'The city manager is capable, though he's going to have a long
rebuilding process, now that all the city trustees have quit and hired
their own lawyers.'

'You were going to slink out of town without saying goodbye?'
she asked.

'That gets back to you not returning my calls. Anyway, I'm
keeping my house. Grand Point is going to be a mud pit of lawsuits,
countersuits and criminal complaints for years. I'll be back for
depositions.'

'For your own suit against the county as well, though I hear you
still can't remember those last few seconds on the dais?' She fingered
a ragged bit of jewelry hanging on a slim chain around her neck.

'Peering County is talking a two million dollar settlement.'

'It will be fascinating to see what your sense of morality does with
two million dollars.' She handed him a copy of the *DeKalb Examiner*.
'Every fact is there, plus as much as the editor let me infer.'

Her story took over the entire front page. 'About Laurel?'

'Roy Powell tells me it's justice for Laurel if Clamp gets life
without parole for Betty Jo Dean. Roy says going after anything
more is greed,' she said.

'Anything more is more justice,' he said. 'I heard Clamp is
talking.'

'He wants to visit Betty Jo's grave, can you believe?'

'He loved her, according to what Luther Wiley said on your recording.'

'He said he promised he'd take her to California and marry her, even try to have another baby.'

'She was pregnant?'

'Only until Doc Farmont fixed it.' She shook her head. 'Clamp said he begged her for two days in that cabin, trying to convince her things could be fine, but she kept looking at the walls, at the floor – everywhere but at him. Roy says that even now, Clamp sounds more regretful than horrified, as though he and Betty Jo had had a spat, is all, and that it could have been mended, if only that damned Sheriff Milner hadn't started sending searchers down to the cabins and given him no choice other than to kill Betty Jo.'

'He cut off her head, for the bullet.'

'He said he had no choice about that either, but he couldn't bear to part with it afterward, and kept it so he could visit her regularly down by the river.'

'My God.'

She opened the brown paper bag and took out a pint of Scotch and two clear plastic cups. Her hand shook as she filled one and handed it to Mac. Then she filled another cup for herself and raised it in a toast. 'To Betty Jo Dean. She spat in his eye.'

For a moment they said nothing, then Mac asked, 'What's Powell doing about Luther?'

'Since they'll likely never identify the arsonist, prosecuting Luther for burning your place is on the back burner, if you'll forgive the metaphor. Luther thinks he's scot-free.'

'Damn that Luther,' he said.

'Page two,' she said.

He opened the paper. Her byline ran above a smaller story, about abuses at Maryton Cemetery.

'I was there when they exhumed Betty Jo Dean, remember?' she said. 'The digger exposed the side of an adjacent casket – a rotting casket. It was buried not two years ago, without a vault. Luther's going to do long, hard time for cutting corners at Maryton.

'April said she's leaving in a month for a teaching job downstate?' Jen's voice quivered slightly. Something more was on her mind.

'It's poor and rural, but she'll live like royalty with her half of what we got from the Bird's Nest.'

'Plus whatever you pass along from your two-million-dollar settlement?'

'She's more than earned it.'

'Maggie is already down in New Orleans?'

He grinned. 'Abigail Beech told her the spirits are friendly there, if she's interested.'

'And she's interested?'

'Apparently she saw things here – apparitions.'

'Betty Jo Dean's ghost?'

'I didn't ask.'

She nodded, her smile gone. 'I keep seeing the way Jonah Ridl stared at me when he paused with his gun. He was seeing a ghost, and that gave Jimmy Bales enough time to kill him.'

'He was seeing Laurel, and he wouldn't have wished for a finer last sight.'

'I saw your ghost, too, Mac.'

He groaned.

'Not you,' she said, 'but the ghost that haunts you.' She poured another inch into her cup and raised the bottle.

He shook his head. 'I'm driving.'

'And not commenting,' she said.

'I've got a cabin rented through Christmas.'

'Autumn in the piney woods? Sounds marvelous.' She looked away. No doubt something more was on her mind.

'As I said, I'll be back for depositions.'

She set her cup next to the bottle on the table. 'Remember I said I was good at rooting out old information, and that I might need to understand why a man would ignore an indictment and a failing restaurant to concentrate on a decades-old murder of a girl he hadn't even heard of until recently?'

He took the bottle and poured himself a shallow sip.

'Holly Anderson,' she said, 'was born two weeks and two days before Betty Jo Dean. Holly was a pretty girl, an excellent student and, according to the meager press accounts at the time, beloved by her friends and family. In 1982, Holly Anderson was abducted outside the drug store where she worked. She'd been waiting for her stepbrother to pick her up.'

Mac knocked back the drink. 'Her stepbrother was paying no attention to time that day. He was hanging out with a couple of pals three blocks down, being cool, being stupid.'

'Holly was found murdered three days later, but the cops never developed a single workable lead. The story disappeared from the papers right away.'

'Dead girl. Dead case.'

'Is she with you all the time?'

'Not all the time.'

'Want to know about something else I'm wondering about?'

'Sure. I mean, I guess.'

She lifted the small, odd-shaped piece of plastic hanging around her neck. 'I've taken to wearing this to remind myself of nobility.'

He looked closer, still not understanding.

'It's part of the micro SD card from my cell phone,' she said. 'If intact, it would store pictures.'

'Ah,' he said, understanding.

'I know only one person who would step in front of a son of a bitch to protect justice. That could only have been instinctual.'

When he said nothing, she nodded her head abruptly, as though making up her mind about something, got up and headed to the front door. He followed her out, puzzled.

She'd parked next to Mac's truck. She opened her car trunk, took out a large suitcase and threw it in the back of Mac's truck, alongside his duffel bags. And then she opened the passenger door and got in, to wait.

He locked the house and got in behind the wheel.

'Autumn in the piney woods?' he asked, starting the engine.

She smiled a smile that was going to brighten the darkest of any north wood's night.

'Instinctual,' she said.

CPSIA information can be obtained
at www.ICGtesting.com
Printed in the USA
LVOW12s1613251017
553729LV00001B/228/P